DATE DUE			
JAN 2 1998			

THE JUDGMENT

Also by William J. Coughlin
in Large Print:

In the Presence of Enemies
Shadow of a Doubt

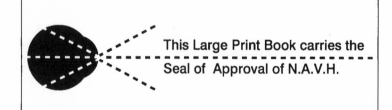

THE
JUDGMENT

William J. Coughlin

Thorndike Press • Thorndike, Maine

Published in 1997 by arrangement with St. Martin's Press, Inc.

Thorndike Large Print ® Cloak & Dagger Series.

The tree indicium is a trademark of Thorndike Press.

The text of this Large Print edition is unabridged.
Other aspects of the book may vary from the original edition.

Set in 16 pt. Plantin by Juanita Macdonald.

Printed in the United States on permanent paper.

Library of Congress Cataloging in Publication Data

Coughlin, William Jeremiah, 1929–
　　The judgment / William Coughlin.
　　　　p. (large print) cm.
　　　ISBN 0-7862-1243-8 (lg. print : hc : alk. paper)
　　　1. Large type books.　I. Title.
　　[PS3553.O78J83　1997b]
　　813´.54—dc21
　　　　　　　　　　　　　　　　　　　　　　　97-36861

THE JUDGMENT

1

The jury came in just after four o'clock. It was Halloween, and they wanted to get home before dark. There wasn't anyone in Detroit who didn't want to get home before dark.

It hadn't been much of a trial, just one day, although the charge of armed robbery was serious even in Detroit's Recorder's Court, where murder sometimes is considered small change. My man looked guilty, although there had been some question about identification. But the jury wasn't about to sit around and waste a whole lot of time arguing about it. They gave him the benefit of the doubt, under the circumstances, and acquitted him so they could leave early.

Everyone told me I had done a good job, but they knew it was the clock that had really swung things in my client's favor.

I walked to the nearly empty parking garage and retrieved my car. There was a chill in the damp air. My footsteps echoed in the concrete silence of the place, and even traffic sounds outside the garage seemed muted, as though the entire city were creeping on cats' feet.

It was an hour's drive back to Pickeral Point, the little city forty miles north of Detroit where

I have my home and office, my private sanctuary on the banks of the St. Clair River. Detroit had once been my home, but that was before my own troubles had nearly ended my legal career. Troubles that had forced a quiet exile to a quiet place.

In other American cities this was a special night, a magical one, a night for children and harmless mischief. Halloween. Armies of costumed kids carrying candy bags would assault lighted porches screeching the challenge, trick or treat.

But in Detroit, All Hallow's Eve had reverted to the Celtic horror that inspired the death masks and mystic rituals of the ancient Druids and now echoed in those kids' costumes. In the city, it had become a malevolent night for mindless burning. Porch lights were on, as well as back-alley lights. Detroiters waited, armed usually, behind curtains, watching for the silent figures who might emerge from the darkness and try to burn them out.

The situation had improved since the days when hundreds upon hundreds of houses went up in flames on Devil's Night and Halloween, when television crews from all over the world came to film the blazing phenomenon. Still, it had been dry all day, so the shadowy figures would come, they always did. Fires, both large and small, would be set.

Everyone wanted to get home early. Hoses

and guns would be at the ready. Here, trick or treat carried a more ominous meaning.

I was glad to get on the expressway headed north.

A fender bender plugged up traffic and it gradually became dark as all of us waited to move. Eventually, cars slowly rolled forward, locked together like prisoners on an endless march.

Finally, at the city limit, things began to loosen up, and by the time I reached Mt. Clemens, just twenty miles out of the city, we were all traveling at well over the speed limit, and I was filled with a sense of release and escape.

The freeway after Mt. Clemens cuts mostly through farmland. Empty fields in autumn. A few spectral trees outlined against the dark clouds lent a real Halloween aura to the chilly night.

I was listening to Detroit's classical music station, which was playing appropriately macabre music.

It first began as a light mist. I flipped on the windshield wipers, hoping that Detroit would catch some of the developing rain. It would help keep down the fires.

I was almost to the Pickeral Point turnoff when the flakes started. In lower Michigan, the rule of thumb is snow flurries approximately by Halloween and real snow by Thanksgiving.

It was the first snow of the season. Just a few wet flakes initially and then a quick and fierce whiteout. I slowed, adjusting to the new road conditions, and drove through.

The streaky pattern of the swirling white snow reminded me of skeleton hands, hands with long and bony fingers clawing at the windshield as if to seize the soul within.

Halloween thoughts. I was beginning to spook myself big time. I switched the radio to a jazz station, but it didn't help much. Those ghostly snow fingers still relentlessly slapped against the windshield like a silent warning. I reminded myself that it was only snow.

Mrs. Fenton, my secretary, came quickly into my office midmorning next day. She, who generally was almost expressionless, looked liked her eyes were about to pop. Dear Mrs. Fenton, efficient and organized and about as humorless as a dead mackerel. Plain and simple, her appearance was completely unremarkable. You could set your clock by Mildred, the name I never dared call her. She's always on time and leaves each night at five. It's a never-varying routine, but sometimes we cling to routine because it offers small comfort in a chaotic world. You don't get to chat a lot with Mrs. Fenton because she disapproves of small talk. Sometimes I think she disapproves of me, too, but I don't dwell on it too much.

"There's a bishop on the phone, a real bishop," she now said, "and he wants to talk to you."

Titles meant so much to her. I don't know why, but they did. I hoped for the sake of her health that the pope or the president would never have occasion to call the office, since I found the prospect of maybe having to administer CPR to Mrs. Fenton distasteful.

"Does this bishop have a name?" I asked.

"Bishop Solar," she said. "He's a Catholic bishop." Her tone implied she would have preferred a Protestant denomination, but a bishop was still a bishop.

"I'll take the call," I said. I waited until she left the office. I wondered what was up. It was still very early in the morning, even for a bishop.

"Charles Sloan," I said, thinking I would be talking to one of his assistants.

"Formal, aren't we?" It was the bishop himself.

"Always. How are you, Joe?"

"Fine, Charley. This is a Holy Day of Obligation, All Saints' Day. I trust you were able to get to Mass?"

"Would it make you feel better if I lied and said yes?"

He laughed. "Not really. Just testing. We're going to get you back one of these days."

"Anything's possible, but I wouldn't bet your retirement fund on it," I said. "Now, besides my immortal soul, what else do you want?"

I could talk like that to him. We both be-

11

longed to the same organization. Even bishops could become alcoholics. Joe Solar, like me, was a member of AA. We had first become acquainted at a meeting, and a kind of loose friendship followed. He was a compact man, fiftyish, who had the hard look of a corporate executive, even when in his full bishop's regalia.

I did a little legal work for him and the church once in a while. He ran a newly formed diocese that comprised most of Michigan's Thumb area. It was a comedown from his former position as a big-city bishop marked for better things. Like myself, the booze hadn't exactly enhanced his career. He had been on his way to a cardinal's red hat. But now that would never be. Still, if he regretted it, it didn't show.

"I have a priest who's in a spot of trouble and I think he could use some legal advice," the bishop said.

"What kind of trouble?"

"A young man has accused him of molesting him."

"Has the priest been charged?"

"I'm informed there will be no charges."

"Are they giving licenses to the clergy now for that sort of thing?"

He laughed for the sake of politeness, but the tone reflected a flat lack of amusement. "The lad who made the charge withdrew it, then changed his mind. He has a history of

12

mental problems. Also, the priest isn't the first person he's made this kind of charge against."

"From the sound of it, then, your man doesn't have much to worry about."

"Not as far as the police are concerned. But the parents have called and threatened civil suit. I wonder if you might look into it, Charley. I think he could use some help."

"And who do I look to for my fee, the Holy Ghost?"

"If you had true faith, you would. However, the diocese will pay reasonable legal fees. This sort of thing can rip up a parish, just the hint of it, not to mention the reputation of the priest involved. And the Church. If you could get the matter quietly taken care of, I would be most grateful."

"I'm not big on child-molester cases."

"This isn't one of those things, Charley. As far as I know, the priest is quite innocent. Frankly, he's a bit of an eccentric, but he's a good priest. The people love him. You'd be doing an act of Christian charity if you undertook helping him out."

"I'll do what I can. What's his name?"

"Father Charles Albertus. Everyone calls him Father Chuck. That's the name he goes by unless he's writing checks. Maybe even then, as far as I know."

In my mind I formed a picture of a rail-thin priest in a sackcloth shirt, with long hair and

13

a wispy beard, smoking a cigarette held in the European fashion. And sandals, Roman style.

"Does he know you're contacting me?"

"I told him I would. He'll be expecting your call. He serves as pastor of a small parish in Hub City, and also he's the priest for a half dozen rural missions, small churches spread out all over the Thumb. We used to have priests for all those places, but there's a shortage, as you probably know."

"Give me the number," I said, with a slight touch of annoyance and resignation in my voice.

I sighed to myself. No longer was I a churchgoing Catholic, but there was still a strong pull, an echo, I suppose, of boyhood loyalty and a nod to how I was brought up. Confession every Saturday; early Mass on Sunday morning and Holy Communion; the almost reverential respect my parents taught me to have for our parish priest.

Perhaps because of all that, I never charged Bishop Solar my full fee. Sometimes I didn't charge him at all.

Which is probably one of the main reasons the good bishop thought of me in the first place.

I was about to dial the priest, but before I had a chance, Mrs. Fenton popped in again.

"Do you know a Mark Conroy? He says he's a police chief."

14

I nodded. "He's Detroit's deputy chief. Why?"

She raised a disapproving eyebrow. In Mrs. Fenton's mind you were either what you said you were or you were a rank pretender. By her expression, I knew that she did not approve of deputy chiefs running around claiming they were the big cheeses.

"In Detroit, the deputy chief is called chief. Like a lieutenant colonel is called colonel in the army. Besides, Conroy is the real chief. He runs the Detroit Police Department," I said. "The other chief you read about is a political front man for the mayor. I know Conroy. Why do you ask?"

Her deepening frown indicated she wasn't completely satisfied despite my explanation. "He's on the phone. He wants to speak to you."

It wouldn't be like hearing from an old friend. I dislike very few people, but Mark Conroy years ago made it to my short list. The feeling, as far as I knew, was mutual.

"He's on line two," she said as she left.

I picked up the phone and punched the button.

"Sloan here. What do you want?"

"It's a personal matter." The voice was as I remembered it, smooth but with an underlying hint of authority, perhaps even menace.

"Legal?"

There was a pause. "Yes."

15

"Look, Conroy, you and I have never really been friends. I think you'd be better off seeing another attorney."

"Are you afraid to talk to me?"

"Of course not."

"It's urgent."

"I'm busy this afternoon. Tomorrow I can see you at three o'clock. All right?"

"How about right now?"

"It's an hour's drive up here. I have an appointment in an hour."

I didn't, but I didn't want to admit it, not to Conroy. I wanted him to think I was so successful, I didn't have a free minute in the day.

"I'm in your parking lot," he said, a humorless chuckle in his voice. "All I need is an hour of your time, probably less."

"Car phone?"

"What else?"

"All right, if you insist. Come up."

"Up that outside stairway I see?"

"It's the only way up. It may not look it, but it's safe enough."

The top cops of the Detroit department wear uniforms that a South American dictator might envy. Their hats have enough gold braid to supply the British navy. And medals! I never knew what they were for, but each top cop has row after colorful row on his uniform chest. The official police badge, set above the ribbons, looks almost dowdy by comparison.

16

They like white gloves, and anything leather on their bodies is always polished to mirror quality.

Mark Conroy came dressed in civilian clothes. It was almost a disappointment.

He was a handsome man, the product of a multitude of bloodlines. Thick chested, wide shoulders, and an inch shy of six feet. Officially, he was black, but he could have been anything — Italian, Greek, South American — with a slightly tanned skin, by genes rather than by sun and strong features topped by black, close-cut, curly hair.

It was his olive-black eyes everyone always remembered. Hard eyes, knowing. Eyes that seemed to search other faces like two probing lasers. Friendly one minute, frightening the next.

I didn't get up. He took a chair across from me and looked around at my office.

"Who's your decorator, Charles Dickens?"

A half smile, an expression closer to a sneer, played on his full lips.

"You don't like it?" I asked.

The sneering smile broadened. "I love it. It looks like something out of the last century. Cracked leather and musty books. It has its own special atmosphere, but then so does a morgue. Where the hell did you get this stuff?"

"Most of it was here when I moved in a few years ago. It belonged to a very old lawyer who died."

17

"You should have buried all this with him."

I studied him for a moment. His slate gray suit didn't look like it came off the rack. His shoes appeared handmade, as did the monogrammed shirt and silk tie. Conroy was forty-five but looked younger. He had made his reputation as a gutsy cop who worked undercover and feared nothing. Combining brains with nerve, he rocketed through the ranks to chief of detectives before the age of forty, a first in the department's history. The mayor appointed him as deputy chief when he appointed the new chief. The new chief was smart politically, but had proved himself a stupid cop. Conroy got the second top job to keep the department running and out of trouble. "You still hate me because of the Mickleberg case, don't you?" he asked, those black eyes fixed on mine.

"You lied on the stand and you sent an innocent man to prison for life for a crime he didn't commit."

"Innocent?" This time the sneer was definitely a sneer. "The problem with lawyers is you people treat crime like a game of tennis, little rules for everything. Clay court or law court, it's the same thing to you. You have to stand in a certain place, do certain things, and you can't step over certain lines. Justice for you people is just a game for gentlemen."

"Nice speech. Give it often?"

Those eyes hardened even more. "Harry

18

Mickleberg was going up and down Gratiot Avenue, killing and robbing the owners of small stores. He was good at it. That's how he got your fee, by the way, from one of those robberies. We knew it was him who was doing the killing, from informers and other information, but none of it good enough to make a case, at least under your rules. Mickleberg grew up in reform school and spent more time in prison than he did out. He had nice hobbies like sodomizing his sister. Did you know that? If you were making a list of undesirables, you'd have to put Harry pretty high up there."

Those damn eyes of his had an almost hypnotic effect. He continued in his command voice. Crisp, professional, no nonsense.

"We caught him with a gun that had been used in a murder. It wasn't his gun, and he hadn't done the killing, but we took the bastard down anyway. I took him down. I was the homicide detective in charge, as you recall. I told a few small white lies on the stand, as we both know. Even you couldn't shake me, which is the real reason why you don't like me. I beat you. But from my point of view, I took that prick off the streets for life and saved a few lives in the process. I didn't play by your neat little rules, but justice got done anyway."

I could feel anger rising and I knew my face was reddening.

He looked past me at my view of the river. "I don't need you to like me, Sloan. But I do need a good lawyer. An honest one."

"I don't want the case."

"You don't even know what it is. Don't your rules call for some measure of fairness?"

"Yes, unlike yours. Mine are called professional ethics."

"You still off the stuff?" he asked.

"Booze, you mean?"

He nodded.

My problem had often been headlined in the newspapers, and not so long ago. It was all a matter of public record, though I resented the question. But I answered him, to show, I think, that it didn't bother me.

"I'm what is termed a recovering alcoholic. What that means, as a practical matter, is that I don't drink today. Sobriety is a day-to-day thing. So far, I've been successful for quite some time."

He nodded slowly. "You're something of an enigma to me, Sloan. You were once one of Detroit's courtroom big shooters, then the booze got you and you got disbarred. You seem to have licked your problem but you're still tucked away up here. Why?"

"I wasn't disbarred. They suspended me from practice for a year. To lawyers, there's a big difference between disbarment and suspension. Disbarment marks you for life. I escaped that."

His chuckle was devoid of humor. "Tennis rules, like I said."

20

"If that's how you look at it. In any event, after the year's suspension, I came up here to live a quiet life and to stay out of trouble."

"You've had some big cases since then," he said. "And you won them."

"I'm good at what I do. I'm a trial lawyer, and experienced. That's all I have to offer as my stock-in-trade. And, when I want to, I pick my cases."

He smiled, exhibiting perfect white teeth. "Years ago they whispered you were crooked, that you weren't above pulling a few dishonest tricks to win. You know, a little bribe here, a little bribe there."

That was the media. It made a better story. And, frankly, at that time, it was good for business. "Everybody wants a lawyer who can put the fix in. I didn't then, and I don't now."

"I know that." Those eyes of his seemed to almost glitter. "I'd know if you were crooked, believe me. You're honest. And that's what I need, an honest lawyer."

"There are a lot of them around. I told you, I don't want your case."

"But you haven't heard what it is yet. At least give me that courtesy."

"You'd only be wasting your time" — I paused — "and money," I added, to remind him that this was business and I didn't have to sit there and listen to him for free.

He nodded. "It's my time." He smiled. "And my money."

21

"If that's what you want to do, go on."

He shifted slightly to make himself more comfortable in the old chair.

"The mayor appointed me as deputy chief in an off moment just to make sure the department wasn't run into the ground or sold to France."

"I know the situation."

He paused. "Am I protected here, the lawyer-client thing?"

I nodded. "For this visit only, you are my client. I will charge you for my time. What you say here is privileged and can go no further."

He blinked, then continued. "I knew what I was getting into when I took the deputy chief job. The department has been my life. I watched it go from a spit-and-polish outfit to a Turkish bazaar. Half the cops have something going on the side. It's like being the chief operating officer of a mall. Everybody is doing a little business."

"If you knew that, why did you take the job?"

"It was important to me. I thought, over time, I might be able to make things better."

"Sure."

He smiled. "I mean it, whether you believe me or not. Anyway, I think in the past couple of years I've done some good. We don't have the money or the people to do a proper job, but I like to think we have come a long way."

"How about crooked cops?"

He raised his hands as if in surrender. "There are a lot fewer than when I took over. There's a lot of money out there on the street. Sometimes, especially for a young cop, temptation overcomes common sense. Anyway, I cleaned up Internal Affairs, put my own people in there, and we've been weeding out as many bad cops as we can, as a practical matter."

"A practical matter that can cover a lot of territory. Or very little, depending on your point of view."

"I'll get down to specifics," he said. "My boss, on paper anyway, is too stupid to steal. That's done for him by others."

"Oh?"

"Our mayor is a multimillionaire. He had to borrow car fare when he was elected. Does that tell you anything?"

"The feds have tried to nail him, and each time they failed. He's either honest or smart as hell."

"Smart. He has the mind of a twelfth-century Italian merchant. And he has his hand in almost everything that goes on in this town."

"So arrest him."

"I can't."

"Why not?"

He smiled, but it slid into another sneer. "Because of lawyer rules, mostly. We know who his bagmen are. Who his drug contacts are. We have everything, except a willing witness, or something to convince a jury of a payoff."

"Did you actually start an investigation?"

He nodded. "With my own selected people, or so I thought, called the Untouchables. We have more spies at headquarters than the CIA ever did in Russia. Some report to the drug dealers, some to me, some to the mayor."

"What's all this got to do with your problem?"

"If you had a bloodhound on your trail, what would you do?" He paused only for effect. "You'd shoot the dog, right?"

"Maybe."

"Well, this is the mayor's version of shooting the dog. He can't fire me. That would raise too many questions, and it would be embarrassing if I told what I know. That leaves murder, which is messy, especially if you don't need to resort to it."

"Are you saying the mayor is trying to frame you?"

"God, you're quick, Sloan."

"And just how does the mayor propose to do this?"

For the first time he looked nervous. Those eyes seemed to have lost some of their intensity. "They say I stole from a police department fund, a fund founded with confiscated drug money."

"Aren't those things audited?"

"Not this one. It's all cash. We use it to pay

informers. The city has been after us for years to have their auditors take a look."

"And you resisted, obviously."

"Sure I did. That would open a whole list of informers for the mayor's inspection." He smiled. "Hell, the first thing he'd do is sell that list to the highest bidder. We'd have bodies all over the street and no one would ever give us the time of day again."

"You must have some procedure for keeping track?"

"I did. My own auditor. The Mouse. Remember him?"

It would be hard to forget the Mouse. He was a policeman but looked like a mountain. Six and a half feet and three hundred pounds. He had played one year for the Green Bay Packers but injured his knee, probably in someone's throat, an injury that cut short his football career. He had become a Detroit cop and had attached himself to Conroy and had become his very large shadow, his aide, and possibly Conroy's only friend.

"The Mouse any good at keeping track of money?"

He chuckled softly. "He may look stupid, but he isn't. He kept books, in code, but every dime is accounted for."

"Well, if that's the case, you don't have anything to worry about." I paused. "If you're honest."

He nodded. "I'm told the Mouse is going to

be the chief prosecution witness against me."

I whistled. "That puts a different color on the horse."

"I'm also told the mayor is arranging everything, like the producer of a Broadway play. He'll select the judge, the prosecutor, everything except the color of the courtroom walls." He paused. "He'd like to select the defense attorney, too, if he could. Short of that, he'll try to get to whoever defends me. This is one case he doesn't want lost. Pick a good man, and the mayor won't touch him."

"Wally Figer is one of the best. He wouldn't be able to get to Figer."

Conroy's eyes began to glitter once more. "That shows how out of touch you've been. Wally is the mayor's personal attorney."

"Really?"

"Anybody who's any good has some connection with His Honor. Power and money pulls you in like a magnet. I want to be able to go to trial without wondering if this is the day my own lawyer makes a small but intentional mistake that will send me to prison. Like I said, I need an honest man."

"Someone unlike yourself?"

He raised an eyebrow.

I continued. "How much did that suit cost? Or the shoes? You must have several thousand dollars on your body. That's not the kind of clothing one associates with an honest, hard-working cop."

26

He chuckled, plucking at his suit. "So you think this is drug money?"

"It's a short jump to that conclusion."

He shrugged. "Do you know how much the city pays me in salary?"

"No."

"Ninety thousand a year. On top of that, I teach as an assistant professor in criminal justice. Part-time. That brings in another twenty thousand. My wife is a commercial artist, a good one. Pick up any fashion magazine and you'll see her work. She brings in another hundred thousand plus. We have no children, Sloan. I can afford the clothes, plus a Mercedes, if I wanted one. I spend on clothes, and that's about all."

"Have you ever dipped into the fund?"

He shrugged. "Once or twice. But it always went back the next day. And the Mouse always knew about it. He handled the money, physically. I left all that to him."

"How about his books?"

"He explained the code to me. Every so often we'd go over how much we had. Informers don't come cheap anymore. Other than that, I had no connection with the money or with the books."

"Just the Mouse."

"Yeah."

"If you're on the level, the Mouse must have been stealing."

"I doubt it."

"You do? Even if he's going to testify against you?"

He looked past me again. "That's the part that's screwy. The Mouse controlled the books and the code. Even if he was looting the damn fund, no one would know, not even me, and certainly no one could prove it. Why he's testifying I don't know."

"The case will be a circus, you realize that?"

He nodded. "Yeah."

"Frankly, I don't want the case. I've had enough of these courtroom circuses to last a lifetime."

He shrugged. "I can't blame you, I suppose."

"Have you talked to the Mouse?"

"No. He's disappeared. I put some of my best people out on the job of finding him. He doesn't want to be found. Like I said, he may look like a dumb mountain, but he's smart, street-smart."

"Obviously, you know the game plan. When are you supposed to be arrested?"

"Tomorrow morning, at Police Headquarters. I'm supposed to surrender there with a lawyer. They'll take me to Recorder's Court and set bond."

"Who told you all this?"

"The prosecutor. I don't think he's in on any of this, but it's his office that's bringing the charge. Like he said to me, he's just doing his job." Conroy sighed. "I'm to be released on personal bond. I will be given a leave of absence without pay until a jury makes the final decision."

"It sounds like they have a pretty good case."

"You think I'm guilty?"

"What I think doesn't matter, does it? It's up to the jury."

"You have any suggestions about who I can get to be my lawyer?"

"Are you interested in making a deal?"

"I told you, they won't go for anything. Nor will I, for that matter."

"I don't mean with the court, I mean between you and me."

"What kind of deal?"

"If I take the case, I can drop it anytime if I think I want out."

His eyes bore into mine, and he paused before replying. Finally, he nodded. "Okay."

"My services won't come cheap."

"I know that."

"I'll need a ten-thousand-dollar retainer."

He took a checkbook from his inside pocket and quickly scribbled out a check and then handed it to me.

"You still don't like me, do you, Sloan?"

"If you want love and affection, you're at the wrong store."

He laughed. "I got the right store. Can you be at my office at eight in the morning?"

"Sure," I said. "Oh, one more thing. Wear

your dress uniform and don't say anything. From here on in, I'll do the talking."

He got up and walked to the door, then turned. "I feel better already," he said. "Thanks."

Then he was gone.

I looked at the check and wondered why I had taken the case. I didn't like him, and the case sounded like a loser, a big, public loser.

Still, defending people was what I did for a living. I stuck the check in my wallet.

Our only real problem was my line of work. Cops work hard to take felons out of society. Sue had reservations about someone who worked equally hard, in her view, to put them back in business. Her idea was that I should run for county prosecutor. Fat chance.

Other than that, we were especially at ease with each other.

Tonight was my night for dinner. I could cook it or take her out. Since frozen dinners were my level of expertise, we always went out when it was my turn.

I picked her up after work and we drove to Port Huron, the "big city" in these parts, and only ten minutes away. Port Huron wasn't exactly the Left Bank, but it had more restaurants than Pickeral Point. We had come to favor an Italian place near the Blue Water Bridge, the big bridge over the St. Clair River to Canada.

The food was Italian although the owner and cook was Hungarian. The place was decorated like a Hungarian's idea of a Lake Como villa.

We ordered our favorites, Sue favoring the veal and I, the spaghetti. The cook made spaghetti like my mother used to do, sloppy and spiced to the eyeballs.

Sue ordered wine and I had my usual Diet Coke.

"How was your day?" she asked. It was her standard opening when she really wanted to

2

Maybe Conroy was right. Perhaps my office did look like it should be lighted by gas lamps. But I felt comfortable in it, and most of my clients didn't care if I practiced out of the back of a truck. They had far too much trouble in their lives to even notice what kind of furniture their lawyer owned.

But my office, decrepit and a bit musty, had a feature that compensated for any shortcomings. You couldn't beat the view. The office had been built, almost as an afterthought, on top of a squat marine insurance agency building located on the river, hence the outside wooden stairway was the only way up.

My window looks out on the magnificent St. Clair River, the connector between Lake Huron and Lake St. Clair, part of the Great Lakes waterway chain. On the other side of the river is Canada, but not the pretty part. It is a Canada of chemical factories, miles of them, looking like a set for a science fiction movie. I tend to ignore that far shore — it is the river itself that I enjoy, nearly half a mile wide, providing a waterway for everything from canoes to ocean-going freighters.

I swung around in my slightly tilted office

chair and looked out upon my private view.

I tried to think of how I might defend Conroy, but I was distracted by a large ore carrier as it approached, tossing a white plume in front of its huge prow. It was coming from Lake Huron and I was surprised to see that part of its superstructure was covered with ice. Soon the Great Lakes shipping season would come to a halt. It was the beginning of November, that month when ships would be in the greatest danger from winter storms on the lakes. Things could get very deadly when, as the song goes, the witch of November went riding. It seemed that the huge ship would be immune from any force of nature, but it only looked that way. Nature, like fate, unpredictable, played according to its own laws.

Reluctantly, I turned from the window. I had things to do. One of which was to call Sue Gillis and find out what time I should pick her up.

I'm not married, not at the moment, anyway. If the institution of marriage paid veteran's benefits, I would have done all right, having been married three times. All to beautiful drunks who managed to sober up long enough to take me for everything I had at the time. Then it didn't matter, the money just kept rolling in, so I waved good-bye to each wife and fortune, knowing a new wife and fortune would be just around the corner. But eventually alcoholism and near ruin had been

waiting around that corner.

My first marriage produced my dau Lisa, raised until recently by her mother. a drunk like dear old Dad, is also a me of the double-A club now. I was proud o Having taken honors at the Universi Pennsylvania, she is a student at Colu Law School. Lisa was living with a fellov dent, a boy whom I had yet to meet. A marriage, I guess you'd call it. I never a She was an adult. It was her business.

I wonder at my own reluctance about rying again. Sue Gillis, a cop, had her apartment. So did I. Most nights we together, either at her place or mine. She in charge of sex crimes for the Kerry Co Sheriff's Department. Looking much you than her forty-plus years, she had the pe a blond and bouncy cheerleader and was as cute. Almost. Once, she had blown brains out of a robber and that had earned within the department the kind of respec awe the people of Dodge City used to sh Wyatt Earp.

We had talked of marriage. Those ta seemed to be increasing in frequency lately was the one balking, although I wonder why. She had become a very important p of my life. We liked the same things and enjoyed each other. Disagreements were ra My resolve, I knew, was slowly crumbling. think she sensed that, too.

unload about what had happened to her.

"Not bad," I said right on cue, "and yours?"

She had been the arresting officer of a retarded young man who had raped his grandmother. It was a sordid case involving a sordid family. She described them as she might in court, formally and factually, but what came out was a story about animals. And definitely not the cuddly kind. Grandma had been badly hurt and if she didn't make it, the charge would escalate to murder.

Sue had another glass of wine when the food was served, and she seemed calmer, as if she had managed to purge herself of the sights and sounds of the day.

"That was my day," she said, sipping the wine. "Can you match it, Charley?"

"I wouldn't even try. I did, however, pick up a couple of clients. One of whom you'll read about tomorrow."

"Who?"

"Mark Conroy, Detroit's deputy chief of police. He's surrendering himself, in my company, for arrest on the charge he stole from a special police fund."

Her eyebrows raised in surprise. "I know Conroy, or at least I've heard him speak. He's all cop. I doubt if he'd do such a thing."

"From what he tells me, they seem to have a pretty good case. It looks like it might be a tough one to win, maybe impossible."

"Any possibility of a plea?"

"He says he's being framed. He says he's innocent and a plea is out of the question. This one will go to the jury."

"You like that, anyway."

"Maybe. The other client is someone who plays in your ballpark."

Her eyes widened in horror. "Not the retarded kid!"

I smiled. "No." I paused to slurp up some of my sloppy spaghetti. It was not a pretty sight. By meal's end I would have destroyed a multitude of napkins and the composure of any diners nearby.

I wiped away the evidence and took a swallow of my Diet Coke.

"My other client is a priest. He was accused of fondling a boy who later withdrew the charge. Now his parents are threatening civil suit."

"The Evans kid?"

"I don't even know the name yet. I haven't talked to the priest."

"Father Chuck," she said.

"Bingo. Father Charles Albertus, alias Father Chuck. You know the case?"

"Sure. It was my case, if you could even call it that."

"Can you tell me about it, Sue? You know, ethically?"

"No reason not to. It's closed. I'm surprised his parents have the balls to even think about

36

suing Father Chuck."

"Why?"

"Charley, I view these clergymen as being guilty until proven innocent. I shouldn't, I know, but there is so much of it, or so it seems. Altar boys, choir girls, kids of both sexes, adults of both sexes. Once these guys start going wrong, there's no limit. Look around you. It's become almost a national epidemic. Priest, minister, rabbi, it really makes no difference. So when they get to me, they already have two strikes against them. I know that isn't fair, but that's how I see it."

"Did you feel that way about Father Chuck?"

"At first. I knew him because he's very active in youth groups throughout the county. That alone was almost strike three. Anyway, the Evans kid, his name is Sam, said he attended a youth meeting at Our Lady of Sorrows in Hub City. The kid isn't Catholic, but at age nineteen in that part of the county there aren't many places a boy or girl can go to socialize with other kids. Anyway, he claimed that after the social, Father Chuck lured him into the rectory and groped him. His actual words were that the priest had grabbed his thing.

"Sam Evans is, I found out later, borderline retarded, and looks it. Tall, gawky, and strange, sort of staring all the time. His story didn't sound right. He could never get beyond the groping, and he couldn't describe how he got lured into the rectory by the priest.

"Then I checked and this wasn't the first complaint the kid had made. He said a store owner in Hub City had grabbed his thing, too. The store owner had witnesses for the time the kid claimed it happened. Nobody touched him.

"Sam Evans was a Boy Scout for about a month. He said the scout leader got him off in a room and grabbed his thing. Later he admitted he lied. He was jealous that the scout leader was showing more attention to the other boys. Obviously, that case also was closed."

Sue ordered another glass of wine, unusual for her. "I talked to the Evans kid about Father Chuck. Nicely, understand. He still couldn't come up with any answers to key questions. Finally, he admitted he lied again. By the time he finished, he was trying to save himself by claiming the priest had made an indecent proposal. His parents were in my office and heard everything. They are as strange as their son. It turned out Sam is being treated for a severe personality disorder. They knew he was lying. I'm surprised they're even talking about a lawsuit."

"If I talk to them, can I use what you've told me?"

"Sure. Sam's not a juvenile, except in intellect, so it's not protected."

"You sound like you like this Father Chuck."

She grinned. "Jealous? Father Chuck is a great guy. It's like he was born to be charming.

If he wasn't a priest, and if I weren't entangled with a crooked lawyer, I could find myself strongly attracted."

"Young guy?"

"Are you sure he's your client?"

"I haven't talked to him yet. I know nothing about him."

"I remember his age exactly. It's part of the interrogation form we fill out. Father Chuck is fifty-eight but he looks fifteen years younger. He's about six feet. I would guess about two hundred pounds, sort of a rugged, outdoors type."

"So you were mad for his chaste body?"

She shook her head. "Not the body. But I wouldn't trust me around that smile of his. The man is all teeth. When he smiles it's like seeing the lights on Broadway."

"So I have a rival, do I?"

"If that will keep you on your toes, think what you will. By the way, I checked him out, just to be sure I wasn't dazzled by the smile. I interviewed some of the townspeople and parishioners. No one had a bad word to say about him."

"Do I hear a slight note of discord in your tone? A reservation perhaps about this paragon of virtue?"

"Part of the standard interrogation is to ask if a suspect has ever had psychiatric treatment."

"Did he?"

"He said he has been hospitalized twice, both times for depression, but nothing in the past ten years." She laughed. "He says he is now your standard garden-variety neurotic, nothing more. He makes a joke of it."

"He doesn't sound too outdoorsy to me."

"Don't be jealous."

"Did you find out anything else about him?"

"Not a whole lot, really. His parishioners apparently think very highly of him. He's a decent guy who obviously cares about people. But I'm told that sometimes he's somewhat at odds with the Church authorities."

"A liberal?"

"Actually, the opposite. He'd prefer to say Mass in Latin — the old way, as he calls it. Vatican II didn't please him much, I guess. He says he misses the pomp and circumstance and the rituals of the Latin Mass. It sounded to me like he was much more of a conservative, really, rather than a liberal."

"But you liked him?"

"Absolutely. You will, too. You know how it is when you meet some people for the first time? He's just hard not to like."

We had finished the meal. My side of the table was a disaster of spilled tomato sauce. I was anxious to escape the scene of this particular crime.

"I have a splendid idea," I said.

"What's that?"

"We return to my place. We can play bad

priest and naughty nun."

"Which one will I be?"

"Sue, you really ought to think of getting another job. You're beginning to sound a lot like your customers."

The arrest and arraignment of Deputy Chief Mark Conroy turned out to be a cross between a Roman circus and a military rally. We walked from police headquarters to the court between files of silent uniformed policemen who stood at attention, each face a mask of grim outrage. In South America it would have marked the beginning of a coup. But here in Detroit, nothing followed the silent demonstration of support for Conroy.

The circus began at the press conference following the quick arraignment in court.

There were enough television lights to illuminate a night baseball game. The reporters had come out in platoons. Whether because of the early-morning hour or not, they seemed especially unpleasant.

I wouldn't allow Conroy to respond to any of the questions, most of which were insulting. He stood there, at the position of parade rest, his stern expression fixed as if sculpted.

Most of the questions didn't merit an answer. They were shouted in unison, so I could pick and choose those I wanted to respond to. Then I made a quick statement that the chief was innocent, just a good cop doing his duty,

41

nothing more, nothing less, and that all this would be shown at trial.

Then it was over. It was like the relief after getting a tooth pulled. I took a few minutes to instruct Conroy on how he should conduct himself, then I left the court building, got my car, and headed back to Pickeral Point and peace.

What did Patrick Henry say, 'Gentlemen may cry peace, peace, but there is no peace'? He was right.

When I got back to my office, Mrs. Fenton gave me a fistful of messages from various members of the Kalt family. Each begged me to come to the Anderson Funeral Home and as quickly as possible.

I remembered the Kalts. I had done the old man's will, and his six grown children had attended the signing as though it were a major treaty between nations. I had arranged the old man's estate — he was then well over eighty — so that probate could be avoided. He didn't have much, so it had been no challenge. Everyone had been very nice and the old man seemed genuinely glad to be the center of attention.

"Did old man Kalt die?" I asked Mrs. Fenton.

"Yesterday," she said. She knew almost everyone in Pickeral Point. "Heart attack. I sent the usual flowers. He's laid out at Anderson's." I always sent flowers when clients died.

I drove to Anderson's, the only funeral parlor in town. Lawyers become accustomed to funeral parlors. Often, they can be great sources of business.

I parked and walked in. The late Jeremiah Kalt, according to the board, was laid out in one of the prominent front rooms. In the viewing room Kalt was in a burnished coffin, surrounded by a lot of floral displays. He looked content.

There was no one there except his children. The rows of chairs were empty. His children, with assorted spouses, were standing in three separate clusters, looking like warring islands.

They came at me like sharks going for chum. I was suddenly in the middle of outraged middle-aged faces, and mouths that were snarling in anger. Everyone was talking at once.

I held up a hand. "One at a time," I said. "What seems to be the problem?"

"You made him executor of the will," one of the daughters snapped. "And that's the problem. He's hogging everything for himself." She pointed at her brother Amos Kalt, who glared back at her.

"I merely kept the picture for myself," he said, his voice dignified but angry. "Everything else was divided without objection. I wanted the picture. I'm the oldest, and I'm entitled."

"You're a pig, Amos," another daughter barked.

"Whoa," I said. "Amos was made executor. As I recall, you all agreed. More important, your late father agreed. The will provides that the executor has absolute say in what happens to the personal property." I didn't remember the will, but all the wills I draw usually have that provision. It sounded to them as if I remembered every word. I could see some were definitely impressed.

"What about this picture? What are we talking about?"

"It's in my father's living room," Amos said. "It was his favorite. It's just a scene with water and boats. My father said it reminded him of his native village back in the old country."

"My father said I could have the picture," one of the daughters said, her voice shaking with hostility.

"Me," another protested. "He promised it to me."

Others chimed in. Apparently the old man had promised the picture to every one of them.

"What is it, this picture, an oil painting?" I asked.

For a moment there was silence, then Amos spoke. "No, it's a photograph. Big, though, like a painting."

I looked at each of them. "And that's what this is all about, the picture, nothing else?"

"I was promised," one daughter whined.

"I'm the oldest. I'm entitled to something," Amos whined. The others grumbled about their rights.

"Look, this is nonsense. You are a happy family and you're fighting over something symbolic. I'm sure your father would be mortified if he knew what was happening."

They didn't look any less hostile, or any more reasonable.

"If it's a photograph," I said, "why don't you just take it to a place and have five identical copies made? There's a place in Port Huron that does that. That way each of you has the picture."

"What about the frame?" the daughter said.

"Get five frames that are close to the original."

For a minute everything was silent again.

"I suppose that would be all right," one of the sons said grudgingly. "That would be okay with me."

They all turned and looked at the daughter who had protested the most. "I should have the original," she insisted stubbornly.

Amos shrugged. "If it's all right with the others, it's all right with me."

Several nodded.

"Is it agreed then?" I asked.

"I suppose so," Amos said.

"Anybody object?" I asked.

They looked at each other, but no one spoke.

45

"Anything else I can help you with?" I asked.

"I guess not," Amos said. "Thanks for coming over."

The others, still grim faced, nodded and turned toward the guest of honor. I wondered if the Kalts would ever be one happy family again.

I started to leave. Amos followed me out to my car.

"I guess you must think we're all pretty silly," he said.

"Families are very touchy at times like this," I said.

"What do we owe you?"

I shook my head. "Nothing. I was glad to help out."

He took out his wallet and held it so I couldn't see what was in it, then he extracted a bill and shoved it into my pocket.

"Thanks," he said, then returned to the funeral home.

I started the car, then fished out the money. Five bucks.

Apparently, the wisdom of Solomon was going pretty cheap lately. Well, I reasoned philosophically, it was five dollars more than I had when I got up that morning.

I made an appointment to see Father Chuck. On the phone he had sounded friendly, almost too friendly, like a salesman who wants to sell you some aluminum siding. But maybe I was biased because Sue seemed to like him so much.

I drove out to Hub City. Like a number of rural Michigan cities, it was a place that time and progress had passed by. Once the center of a thriving farming and manufacturing center, the small town had seen prosperous times. Then the manufacturing left for various reasons, leaving small deserted factories behind as monuments, like grave markers. The town itself looked neglected. Storefronts, those that were still open, needed painting. It wasn't much of a place, but the supermarket was open, as was a large gas station. There was a drugstore and several other businesses still operating. Most of the retail stores were closed and boarded up. Those that could had moved to a large mall south of the town.

The redbrick Catholic church was the centerpiece of Hub City, built at the turn of the century by the rich German families who had come to the place and prospered. It was big, large enough to seat hundreds. Next door, built at the same time, was a three-story brick rectory. There had been a school, but it had been razed, leaving acres of open land behind the church and rectory.

There was a Lutheran church at the other end of town, but it was not nearly as grand as its rival. I parked in the church lot, which needed an infusion of gravel. There were many bare spots. The woodwork on the church and rectory badly needed paint. I walked up the steps to the front door of the rectory and rang the bell, listening to it ring inside.

As I waited, I noticed the wind had picked up and it was becoming quite chilly. Low clouds scuttled across the sky. It had the look and feel of snow. I hoped it would hold off until I got back to Pickeral Point. At last the large wooden door opened and I was face-to-face with Ernest Hemingway, or at least his twin brother, or so it seemed.

"Father Albertus?"

The smile Sue had warned me about lit up his bearded face.

"Father Chuck," he corrected me. "Mr. Sloan, I presume? Please come in."

He was as Sue had described him. Six feet or nearly, thick through the chest and shoulders, with large hands, one of which he extended to me. He had a strong and reassuring grip.

"Let's pick a place where we can be comfortable." I followed him as he walked through the old rectory. It brought back memories of my youth. The place had a permanent aroma of old wax, and the woodwork inside gleamed from a century of care. The furniture was all dark leather and heavy wood. The rooms we passed had the look of little cells, places where parishioners could come and unburden themselves of whatever troubles they had without distraction.

We went to the back of the house. The large rear room had probably been a meeting room for the priests, a recreation room. But it had been converted to look like a kind of lodge, with the furniture looking like something taken from a north-woods cabin, comfortable but masculine. Guns and tackle lined the pine-paneled walls. There were several mounted deer heads with polished antlers. A large muskie and several bass had been preserved on the walls as trophies.

"This is my room," he said. "Of course, it makes no difference. They're all my rooms since I'm alone here. I have a housekeeper who comes in twice a week to straighten up, but that's it. This place used to have a pastor and four associate priests, plus a permanent house-keeper and cook. But no more. I'm the only one living in this mausoleum now. Would you like a drink?"

"No, thanks," I responded. He had no way of knowing that I was a member of the club, and it didn't seem to me that he needed to know. Besides, it's one of the things we learn early on. You don't have to blurt it out any-time anyone offers you a drink.

"Do you mind if I do?" he asked.

"Not at all," I said, thinking back to when I was a kid and my friends who were altar boys would always make jokes about some of the priests who really got into knocking back the wine during Mass. I wondered if they, like me, had ended up in AA, too. Father Chuck, though, didn't look like a boozer to me. He was so robust and appeared to be in terrific physical shape. He walked to a polished mahogany cabinet and opened it to reveal a number of decanters and ornate glasses. After filling his glass, he gestured for me to sit down and took a chair across from me. Again, the dazzling smile helped to light up the room, and I noticed that his brilliant green eyes were filled with a keen intelligence.

"I understand that my dear friend and colleague Bishop Solar has told you about my difficulty," he said. Straightforward. To the point. No nonsense.

"He did, but I'd like to get your version."

"Sure. There's not a lot to tell. We don't have a school anymore, so there isn't much we can offer Catholic kids in the way of social life. I have a teen club that meets here once a month. It's not just for Catholics. Everyone is welcome."

He sipped the drink. "Anyway, Sam Evans came by and asked if he could attend. I said we'd be delighted to have him. It's not much of a crowd, maybe eight to ten kids on a good night. Anyway, Sam showed up, stayed awhile, and then left."

"Did he talk to anyone when he was here?"

"Not that I saw. He's a strange kid, painfully shy, or so I thought."

"Did you talk to him, or were you alone with him anytime during the night?"

"No. Oh, I said hello and introduced him to the others, but other than that, nothing."

"Go on."

"The next thing I know, I get a visit from a policewoman."

"That would have been Sue Gillis."

The smile broadened. "Yes. Quite a gal, frankly. We take a vow of chastity, but we still look, if you take my meaning."

I did, and I didn't like it.

"She told me that the Evans kid accused me of 'fondling him,' of grabbing his penis. Frankly, when I heard that, I was shocked. But all I could do was tell her essentially what I'm telling you. That nothing happened. I don't know whether she believed me or not. Her professional manner is fairly inscrutable. But she continued her investigation, talked to Sam's parents, his former teachers, and so forth. Then the kid admitted he had been lying."

"I'd think you'd have been downgraded to a maker of illicit proposals."

"Well, I didn't do that, either," Father Chuck said rather defensively. "As I told her, and have told you already, I wasn't alone with him at all. So nothing could've been said without all the others hearing."

"Cool your jets, Father. I'm here to help. I understand you've heard from the Evans family about this recently."

"Yes." He sounded quite glum. "Just last week Sam's father telephoned me and said they were considering suing me for sexually abusing Sam. But he hinted that they might forget everything for the right sum."

"And how did you respond?"

He chuckled. "If I weren't a priest, I would have told him to go fuck himself." He laughed like a bad little boy who had said something shocking. "Didn't expect to hear that from a priest, did you? Listen, we hear more salty language in the confessional than a drug dealer does out in the street. Sometimes I'm tempted to let loose with it, but don't worry, I didn't say anything like that to Evans. I just told him I'd have to contact my bishop, and that the bishop's office would get in touch. I've heard nothing since, Mr. Sloan."

"Call me Charley. Please. Everyone does."

"Sure, Charley."

"I'll talk to the parents," I said. "I doubt you'll have any trouble from them."

"A tough lawyer, are you?"

"No. But I think I can be persuasive."

He laughed. "I'll bet you can. Tell me, Charley, are you Catholic?"

"Lapsed," I said.

He nodded. "So many are nowadays. Ever think about coming back?"

This time I laughed. "Not seriously, no."

"Don't be alarmed," he said, grinning. "The

subject is closed. If you ever change your mind, let me know."

"I appreciate it," I said. And I really did, because I thought he was a true believer and not a holier-than-thou type at all. Over time, a number of well-intentioned people have tried to lure me back into the fold, even one of my ex-wives, but I never thought of her as being exactly well intentioned. All she wanted was to be married at St. Lucy's in a high-class, High Mass ceremony, replete with all the mumbo jumbo.

"Are you a hunter, or a fisherman?" asked Father Chuck, changing the subject and sensing accurately that I would be more comfortable if he did.

"Not recently, but I can see that you are," I said, pointing to the antlers, the deer heads, the guns, and the tackle on the walls.

"I used to enjoy fishing and hunting a great deal as a hobby, but these days there isn't much time for it. This is a needy parish, filled with needy people, and I try to give them almost all of my time. It's part of the job description, you know," he said with a laugh. "Sometimes, not very often, I do a little skeet shooting out back, but I don't think the Big Guy upstairs would like it too much if I paid less attention to my parishioners because I was skeet shooting or fishing."

"I understand." I nodded. "But aren't you afraid of having these guns around when there are teenagers in the place?"

"Not at all, Charley. You have to understand that this is my haven, my *sanctum sanctorum*, if you will. And this room is always securely locked when I'm not here or if I'm expecting visitors. When you're a priest, you learn how to be cautious. You have to be because you've been given the charge of taking care of people and looking after them."

"What do your neighbors think about the skeet shooting?"

He laughed. "I have no neighbors, Charley. When you go back out through town, you'll see the closest thing to me is a store, and that's a block away. Nobody complains. They know it's just my hobby. The parishioners use it, too. The men's club has an annual trap shoot here to raise money. We all get along here, Charley. It's a very amicable place."

"How long have you been pastor here?"

"Not long. Maybe five years. Rural posts like this aren't exactly sought after. I suppose that's why they made me pastor. I like the solitude." He sighed. "Actually, I have five other churches that I serve as priest. We call them missions now. Maybe that's what I am, a missionary."

"Tell me," I said. "Have you ever had any other complaints like this one by Sam Evans? Things they could dig up from the past?"

He shook his head. "No, never. I'm a priest cut from the old cloth, Charley, or at least I

54

like to think I am." He grinned. "Look, I'm a normal man, not some pansy hiding behind a Roman collar. Does that answer the question?"

"Yeah, it'll do."

He drained the glass and put it on a table. "Besides, I don't have much time for being wicked. This is a rural parish but we have all the problems of the big city. Drugs, crime, you name it; we have it. Maybe not in big-city numbers, but there is just as much evil here as anywhere on earth. I do what I can and it really keeps me hopping. I used to be able to get away for a little hunting and fishing, but I haven't even managed that the last couple of years."

He saw me looking at the empty glass. "Oh, I drink a little, Charley, but not to excess. I play a little poker, too, mostly with other priests or members of the parish men's club." He chuckled. "Most of the priests are card sharks. I make up my losses off the locals. Anything else you want to know?"

"I understand you've had some psychiatric treatment?"

There was no smile, only an expression of sadness. "That's true. I was hospitalized twice for depression. After all the changes in the Church, a lot of men like myself began to doubt their purpose in life, perhaps even their faith. I did. Some fell into a bottle or took a walk. I just withdrew into myself. I feel fine

55

now, by the way."

He studied me for a moment. "You certainly do your homework."

"I try. If I know what's coming, I can usually get prepared."

"That's wise."

"Thanks for your time. It was a pleasure."

He grinned and slapped me on the back like a politician running for office. "Hey, maybe next summer I can get away for a little fishing. You could come along. You look like you could use a little serious recreation. I keep a small boat on the river. I guarantee more walleyes than you've ever seen before."

"Sounds good."

He walked me to the front door. "Will you need me next week?" he asked.

"I doubt it."

"Good. I'm going off tomorrow on a retreat. The Dominicans are going to sock it to a bunch of us mission priests, tell us how to do our jobs better."

"If I need you, a week won't make that much difference."

We shook hands, and again I noticed how firm and sincere his handshake was.

"You're a good guy, Charley," he called after me as I headed toward my car. "I can't begin to tell you how glad I am that you're in my corner."

I looked back at him as he stood in front of the rectory. He seemed both solid and at ease.

56

As I drove away, my mind was filled with memories of the priests I had known as a boy, those seemingly selfless men who embodied goodness and God. Father Charles Albertus was a lot like them — hearty, cheerful, and often intuitive. And, as I look back on it now, comforting. I admired them then and I suppose, to a certain extent, I still did. But I also had to acknowledge that their narrowness and their certain rigidity had gone a long way to help in driving me out of the Church. And as I grew older and began to seriously question the existence of God, I also began to question the validity of the priesthood.

Almost in spite of myself, I found I liked Father Chuck.

3

The sky remained ominous, but rather than hurry home, I decided to try to make the trip pay doubly. The Evans family lived only a mile or two out of Hub City.

It was rude not to call first, but sometimes rudeness can provide a tactical advantage. They wouldn't be ready for me.

The Evans house wasn't much, just a small frame bungalow with some deserted outbuildings. Someone had once raised chickens there but the effort had been long abandoned and the coops and wire fences were neglected and falling down.

I pulled in behind a pickup truck and parked.

I waited for a minute in case they had a dog, but there was no barking, so I walked up to the front door and knocked.

The house badly needed painting. From what I could see, everything in and around Hub City needed painting.

I glimpsed someone peering out from a front window, then the door opened and a woman's face appeared. She reminded me of those Dust Bowl photos from the thirties.

"What do you want?" she asked, her tone

half hostile, half fearful.

"My name is Sloan," I said. "I'm a lawyer representing the local Catholic diocese and Father Charles Albertus. I'd like a moment of your time."

The door closed and I could hear muted conversation inside. Finally, it opened again, this time wider.

"Come on in," the woman said.

Inside, the furniture looked as worn as the woman. An old television set flickered in one corner of the small living room. A bald-headed man lying on the sofa clad only in trousers and a ragged T-shirt glared up at me but made no effort to get up.

"Mr. Evans," I said, "my name is Sloan —"

"I heard," he snapped. "It's about time someone showed up. I'm about to have my lawyers bring suit."

"If you decide to do that, Mr. Evans, you'll be arrested for extortion."

"What are you talking about?"

"There's no use in beating around the bush. Let me give you the facts hard and fast. You have no case and you know it. You were there when your son told the police he had lied. He has a history of doing exactly this kind of thing, as you know. You even whisper *lawsuit* and I'll have your ass behind bars so fast your head will spin. Are you getting this?"

For a minute his mouth gaped open in shock. Finally he spoke, trying to summon up

59

outrage. "You have no right to come into my house and —"

"I'm saving you a trip to jail, pal. You should thank me."

"I told you we were going to get in trouble," his wife whined.

"Goddamn Catholics got a shithouse full of money," he snarled. "I don't see why they can't give us some."

"That's not the point, is it?" I said. "You're causing trouble, Mr. Evans. And there are ways for taking care of people who do that. That's what the law's there for, to protect citizens against people like you."

"Get out," he said, but he didn't sound nearly as sure of himself as before.

"I'm going," I said, "but I hope you won't think this an idle threat. I've talked to the police already. One word, one peep, and you've had it."

He looked away. This time his voice was just above a whisper. "All right," he said, "just get out."

I turned and walked to the door.

"I'm sorry," the woman said quietly. "I told him we'd get in trouble."

"You aren't yet. But you could be. Big trouble."

I walked back to my car and wondered where the son and heir might be. I hoped he wasn't up in his bedroom targeting my head with a .22 rifle.

Snowflakes were starting to drift down. I backed out of the drive and headed home toward Pickeral Point. I didn't feel very proud of myself. I did what had to be done, of course. But still, bullying people always left a bad taste in my mouth, even if they deserved it.

It would have been nice to stop for a quick drink. But I didn't.

I reported what had happened to the bishop and Father Chuck. Both seemed as genuinely delighted as if I had just saved Rome from advancing Vandals. I sent the bishop a bill for a hundred dollars, which was probably well below the going rate for stopping advancing Vandals. Common sense told me to charge a regular fee; that way, I wouldn't be called upon to handle the nickel-and-dime matters confronting the bishop from time to time. But I didn't do that.

Mark Conroy's examination was coming up, and during the week the deputy chief had driven up to my office several times so we could go over the case the prosecution might present. I felt instinctively that he was holding back. Not lying, but not telling me everything he knew. I wondered if I felt that because I didn't like him, or whether my instincts were correct. We would find out at the examination.

Conroy was again in my office when I returned.

In Michigan, the prosecution must either

present a case to the Grand Jury or present it to a judge in open court, called a preliminary examination. The defense doesn't offer proofs. The only thing that needs to be shown is that a crime was committed and there is reasonable cause to believe the defendant committed it. Either procedure keeps the prosecutor from bringing frivolous cases that he knows he can't win.

The prosecutor had decided to go the preliminary examination route with Chief Conroy. It was a highly public case and the Grand Jury method was secret. The preliminary examination would allow the prosecution the chance to try the case in the newspapers and on television. Wonderful new careers could be carved out from such a juicy case.

I liked preliminary examinations. It gave me a chance to look at the opposition's cards. Also it gave me some idea of how their witnesses would do on the stand in the main event.

Although Conroy denied it, I knew he had an army of policemen loyal to him combing the streets trying to locate the Mouse, the cop who was going to be the chief witness against him. I tried, too, but they had the Mouse tucked nicely away.

The prosecutor provided me with a list of witnesses, which I went over with Conroy.

Mostly, they were city officials whose only role was to say that the confiscated cash had been handled by Chief Conroy in a way forbidden by regulations. The Mouse would say that Conroy stole the money, or so I assumed.

A Mary Margaret Tucker was listed as a witness.

"Do you know her?" I asked Conroy.

"She was a civilian employee in the department," he said. "She worked as my secretary."

"Why would they call her as a witness?"

Conroy didn't answer at once, but paused, then spoke. "This is somewhat embarrassing."

"Girlfriend?"

He nodded. "It happens, Sloan."

"How long did the affair go on?"

"A year or so."

"When did it end?"

"It didn't, or at least I didn't think it had. She stopped seeing me just before they dropped the net. I suppose, now that I look back, she was trying to break the thing off for some time."

"She must have some connection with the missing money, or the prosecutor wouldn't call her. I can keep her off the stand if his only intention is to embarrass you."

"She didn't have anything to do with the witness fund. In fact, she hasn't worked for the department for the past month."

"Where does she work now?"

"She doesn't," he said, dropping his voice.

"Were you taking care of her? Giving her money?"

He paused. "More or less."

"It's either one way or the other."

"She's living in a building I own. She's a senior in college. As soon as she graduates, she's going on to law school. I was, well, sort of financing her education."

"How much a month?"

"Depends. Usually about a thousand, give or take."

I looked at him. "Did your wife know?"

He shook his head. "No. She's very busy. Works all the time. I don't think she even suspects."

"This is going to give you some problems at home."

He sighed. "What's to be is to be."

"Did you give her money, or did the Mouse?"

"I did." He hesitated. "Once in a while I'd give money to the Mouse to give to her. It depended on how busy I was."

"You've got problems, Chief."

"I know."

"Everyone will think the money came from the secret fund."

"Do you?" he asked.

"As I told you in the beginning, it doesn't make any difference what I believe. Can you show the money came out of your personal accounts?"

He shrugged. "Maybe. I had to do some bookkeeping magic so my wife wouldn't suspect. I opened a special account. It got complicated."

"Complicated or not, you had better start thinking of proving the money came out of your own pocket."

"I'll go to work on it," he said, but without enthusiasm.

"When was the last time you talked to Mary Margaret?"

He thought for a moment. "A week or two back before all this went down. Later, when she didn't answer the phone, I went over to the house. Some of her things are still there, but not her clothes. It looks like she's skipped, too."

"Like the Mouse?"

He nodded. "Like the Mouse."

"Do you believe in prayer?"

"That bad?"

"I think so. We'll find out more at the examination."

He left the office. If he was worried, he didn't show it.

But I was worried.

Now the snow was really coming down. "Be careful driving back to the city," I said.

I had two more clients before the day ended. An elderly couple wanted a will. They had one child, a son. The purpose of the will wasn't to see that the son got everything, quite the opposite. They wanted to ensure that he never got a cent. They were angry over a family matter. I tried to persuade them to wait, to cool off before making that kind of decision, but they wouldn't hear of it.

I took down the facts I needed and told them the will would be ready in a few days. I hoped by that time they would reconsider. It didn't take much to split a family forever.

The other client was a man who wanted to incorporate a small business he owned. He operated a pizza restaurant and was about to start a delivery service. Someone told him incorporation might limit his personal liability if his drivers hit someone. They were right. As I'd done with the couple before him, I took down the information I needed and told him it would take a couple of days.

My secretary had left, so I escorted him to the door. The snow was slowing now, but a few inches covered the ground. It looked pretty, pure white against the dark river.

I went back inside and dialed Sue Gillis at her office. It was her night for dinner. Sometimes she cooked; sometimes we went out. I liked her cooking best, if the choice was mine alone.

I called the familiar number, then swung around and watched the dark river.

"Gillis."

"It's me," I said. "I'm starved."

"Bad news, Charley. I'm going to be working late tonight."

"How come?"

"We've just been given a murder. A kid. They found the body up on Clarion Road. I'm going over to the medical examiner's now."

"Sex crime?"

"They don't know yet. But I've been asked to work along with Homicide, just in case."

"Shall I wait for you? You have to eat at some point."

"Don't wait. This may be an all-nighter. I'll grab a sandwich someplace."

"Would you like me to bring you one? I know where the medical examiner's office is."

"That's sweet, Charley, but no. I'll call you tomorrow."

"You're not off the hook, Sue. It's still your turn tomorrow."

"So much for chivalry," she said as she hung up.

I turned out the office lights and continued to watch the river. The snow had stopped so that the lights of Canada were visible again. It was a good feeling, just watching, not thinking about anything.

Then my stomach reminded me that I was hungry.

I didn't want to go to a restaurant solo. Sue had spoiled me. Dining alone, even at a hamburger joint, seemed just too lonely.

I decided that I would go to my apartment, pop in a frozen dinner, and watch some television. The road was now covered and slippery, so I drove very slowly.

The fried chicken dinner, complete with mashed potatoes and corn, came out of the microwave looking like the illustration on the package and tasting like the cardboard. I ate about half and tossed the rest away.

I fell asleep in front of the television until I was awakened by the insistent ringing of the telephone.

I don't know what kind of dream I was having but I remember being grateful at being jarred back to consciousness. I glanced at my watch. It was just a few minutes after one o'clock.

I presumed it would be some husband or wife in the midst of a domestic dispute. Reluctantly, I picked up the phone.

"Yes?"

"Charley, it's Sue. Can I come over?"

"Are you in trouble?"

"No. Nothing like that. I just need to talk. I know it's late."

"Never too late to see you. Come on over."

"I'm really sorry to be a nuisance." Her voice had a sad, keening tone, the kind of sound she got after a few drinks.

"I can pick you up," I said.

"No. I'm a block away, calling from a pay phone. I'll be right there."

I put on some coffee while I waited.

When she arrived, we kissed. I could smell the gin, but she wasn't drunk. She held me in a long embrace before letting go. I thought

I felt her tremble.

She took the coffee I poured and sat down. "I feel like a fool, Charley, barging in at this hour."

"You're not. Bad case, eh?"

"In a way yes, but in a way no."

"Do you want to talk about it?"

She sipped the coffee and smiled weakly. "I suppose that's apparent, isn't it?"

"Tell me about it."

"A little boy," she said slowly. "There was identification on him. His name was Lee Higgins, a kid from Hub City. Eight years old. He didn't come home from school. His parents had called the Hub City police and they had taken a report, but that sort of thing happens often — kids stay at friends' and forget the time, so no one except the parents really got excited."

"How was he killed?"

"Asphyxiation. The medical examiner thinks he may have been suffocated with a pillow. There were no marks or bruises. The blood work won't be back until tomorrow, but the doctor thinks he may have been sedated. There was no sign of a struggle. Just a dead boy, a beautiful boy. He looked like a sleeping angel."

"Raped?"

"Apparently not. There were no signs of sexual abuse. He was a small little boy. No anal penetration. Nothing to suggest oral contact, although it's possible."

"No murder is gentle, but this one sounds relatively shock free. How come it shook you up so?"

She shook her head. "I don't know, honestly. I think it was that he was so beautiful and so young. The parents, of course, were in shock, but they described him as a perfect little kid."

"How did they find him? I would have thought the snow would have covered him up?"

"A motorist saw him on the side of the road. Whoever dumped him must have done so just minutes before. The motorist stopped and walked all around the body. Other people stopped to see what happened. Tire tracks, footprints, everything is pretty much screwed up, although we'll get some."

"There are a lot of crazies out there, Sue."

She nodded. "This one especially."

"Why do you say that?"

"The medical examiner says whoever murdered the boy washed the body and the clothes afterwards, then redressed the dead child. He was wrapped in plastic wrap, the kind you buy at any grocery store."

"I suppose the killer was counting on the snow to cover up what he had done."

"Not really. The body was set out there on the roadside as if the killer wanted him found."

"Well, don't worry, Sue. The sick ones usually are the first caught."

"Sometimes." The word was just a whisper.

"You'll get this guy, whoever he is."

She stood up. "Hold me, Charley?"

"Sure."

We ended up in bed, but not for sex. She fell asleep almost instantly, her arms wrapped tightly about me. Her breathing, at first troubled, became even.

It was the first time since I'd known her that a case had affected her so deeply. I wondered if she was upset because her cop instinct told her this was the beginning of something, and not the end.

She had given me something to think about, too. The name Higgins and Hub City had clicked in my memory. A couple of years ago I'd handled a routine matter for a couple in Hub City named Higgins. Frank Higgins and his wife, Betty. Lying in bed, I remembered it had been a real estate closing; they were buying a big old place right in Hub City. They had kids, of course, enough to make the purchase of an eight-room house reasonably practical. I suspected, and feared, that one of those kids was named Lee.

In the morning Sue went back to her own place to shower and dress. I selected my clothing with more care than usual. I'm of average height and build, but there is something about my body that seems to make my clothes look instantly rumpled. I try to dress to stop this process, but it never really works. Juries, in the main, like well-dressed lawyers. And I had a jury case.

I drove to the courthouse and took the stairs to the second floor, the floor housing our three circuit judges. It wasn't a famous case, so the courtroom was nearly deserted. Just a few policemen, the prosecutor, myself, and my client.

The facts were simple. My client, Ernie Barker, had a small roofing company, consisting chiefly of himself and his cousin. They specialized in tarring flat roofs, usually commercial buildings.

Ernie was coming back from a job in Detroit. It had been hot, gooey work and he needed a shower and a few quick beers. So he was in a hurry and drove that way. A Kerry County sheriff's deputy clocked him at seventy in a fifty-five-mile-an-hour zone and pulled him over. The policeman asked to see Ernie's truck registration and when Ernie opened the glove compartment to get the document, a .38-caliber pistol fell out.

The policeman asked if the gun belonged to Ernie. Ernie said no, he was just holding it for a friend named George. He didn't know George's last name.

Ernie got the speeding ticket and was arrested for carrying a concealed weapon. This weapon, loaded, had its serial number filed off and the presumption was that it was stolen or had been used in a felony. There were several possible charges. The police were content with bringing the felony charge of carrying a concealed weapon.

Ernie confessed to me that he had bought the gun in Detroit on the street for fifty bucks and that he only stuck the pistol in the truck when he had to drive in the dark and dangerous streets of Detroit. He had no record except for an old conviction for driving under the influence. The prosecutor would not agree to a plea. Guns had become a political issue in Pickeral Point, so no pleas were being accepted, except in rare circumstances.

Which brought all of us to the courthouse on a sunny morning, so sunny that the snow of the night before had already begun to melt.

Jury selection went quickly. The prosecutor excused a man who was a longtime member of the National Rifle Association, and I kicked off a lady who said she hated guns and anyone who owned one. Otherwise, the jury was run-of-the-mill, all Pickeral Point people who lived and worked in our small community. Both sides said they were satisfied.

Ernie Barker, a man in his late thirties, looked uncomfortable in what I suspected was his only suit. Ernie's world was not populated by people in suits. He associated with men like himself, people who worked hard and asked very little of life except a friendly bar, beer, and hamburgers.

The idea of prison frightened Ernie, and sitting next to me at the counsel table, he looked ready to faint. He kept sneaking glances at the jury, the twelve people who would decide if he was to return to tar roofs, or something much more confining.

The deputy who arrested Ernie spoke in a quiet but firm voice. He was experienced, and it showed. I pretended that I didn't believe the gun fell out of the glove compartment, but he ignored me and answered in a way that denied me the opportunity to raise the question of illegal search. I sensed the jury believed him, too, so I let the matter drop. Ernie had told me that the gun, indeed, had fallen out, just as the policeman said.

The policeman was the prosecutor's case. The gun was introduced into evidence, and the prosecutor tried to make Ernie appear like the progeny of Al Capone by commenting on the missing serial number.

Then it was my turn. He would make a nervous witness, but he had no major record, so I put Ernie on the stand. I led him through the preliminary questions, quickly establishing who he was and what he did for a living.

"You told the police you got the gun from a man named George," I said. "Is that true?"

He sadly shook his head. "Not exactly, no."

"Where did you get the gun?"

"I bought it from a colored guy in Detroit. I think his name was George, but it was the only time I saw him. I was working on a job when this guy comes up and asks me if I wanted to buy a gun. He showed it to me and said it would cost fifty bucks. Bullets included."

"And what did you do, if anything?"

He hesitated, glanced over at the jury and then back at me. "I do a lot of work in Detroit. It's a dangerous place. I myself have seen two gunfights, honest to God. Anyway, this guy said everyone in Detroit carried one and that I should, too, just to even up my chances of survival. Like I say, it's a dangerous place, so I bought it."

"Did you always carry it in the truck?"

He shook his head. "No. Just when I had to go into Detroit."

"Ever fire it?"

"No."

"Did you ever tell anyone you had it?"

"Show it off, you mean?"

"Whatever."

"No. Even my wife didn't know I had the damn thing."

"That's all I have," I said to the court.

The prosecutor tried to make a lot about the filed-off numbers. Ernie told him he didn't know about that. He didn't know much about guns, period. It was a good answer and it shut up the prosecutor. Then we argued. The prosecutor, who has the burden of proving guilt beyond reasonable doubt, went first. He made a standard argument. If the jury didn't convict Ernie, he said, it would send a signal to the street and soon Pickeral Point would be alive with gunfights and gunfighters. His summation was more political than legal, although he did mention they had proved every essential point needed for conviction.

Of course, they had, which made things a bit difficult for me. I abandoned the facts and argued that anyone who worked in the dangerous streets of Detroit needed to be armed.

The prosecutor tried Ernie Barker.

I tried the city of Detroit.

Frankly, I thought I did a better job.

The jury must have thought so, too. They came in with a compromise verdict, finding Ernie guilty of possessing an unregistered gun, misdemeanor.

The judge sternly lectured Ernie about the evils of pistols, which was a little hypocritical since I happened to know the judge carried a small chrome automatic at all times.

He gave Ernie six months' probation and a three-hundred-dollar fine and ordered the gun confiscated.

I thought Ernie was going to lick my hand.

I hurried back to my office.

The jury trial had been a good way to warm up for the Conroy examination. While just a handful had been present to witness Ernie Barker's case, it seemed that scores of the curious and the press of the entire western world had turned up for a look at Deputy Chief Conroy. The local contingent was out in strength, but also in attendance were camera and press crews from the New York tabloids and even a writer for one of the big British newspapers. Big-city graft, big-city cops — it was a strong brew. Dope money taken and stolen. It was the kind of thing where the headlines practically wrote themselves.

Conroy, again pursuant to my instructions, was decked out in his dress uniform. He looked calm but grim. His wife was with him, a nice woman, a bit stout, but attractive. She was very quiet.

"Does she know about Mary Margaret Tucker?" I whispered to Conroy.

"I told her," he said. "She said she'd stick with me through the trial, but then she's going to get a divorce."

"Can you blame her?"

"No. I guess I can't."

I didn't know the judge, James Horner, a young black man who had just been appointed to the 36th District Court, the one that had jurisdiction over examination in Detroit felonies. He seemed to know what he was doing, although his manner was just a bit too crisp and a bit too authoritative. He would have to run for election, and the publicity resulting from the case was like a political donation, a big one. He wasn't about to risk such advantage. This would be all business.

We started on time. The courtroom was jammed.

It was a big case, too, for the assistant prosecutor assigned. He had been picked to try the case on the recommendation of the mayor. Benjamin Timothy, the assistant prosecutor, was just thirty and a graduate of Yale. Despite his Ivy League background, he apparently enjoyed rolling around the dirty floors of criminal courts and had earned a fierce reputation. He had his eye on high office, and the Conroy case was going to be his ladder up.

Timothy was rail thin and wore his hair close clipped. He had a quick smile, but it seemed more mechanical than genuine. He was all business, too, as he led a procession of city officials to the stand, one after another, all testifying to the regulations regarding city funds, audits, and procedure.

It was all as dull as toenail clippings, but the kid prosecutor was doing a good job building the technical side of his case. I looked around for Conroy's erstwhile pal, Ralph "the Mouse" Smerka.

"He's not in the courtroom," Conroy whispered, as if reading my mind. "They have him parked in an office upstairs."

The officials finally completed the testimony. I had asked few questions. I didn't want to swim in the murky accountant-filled waters, at least not yet.

It was time for the main witness.

Conroy remained at the counsel table, but I gave a brief interview to the man from *The New York Times*. He was looking for color. I gave him as much as I could, at least some color that would help our side of the case.

The judge rapped for order, and we all resumed our places.

The Mouse came in through a side door. It was like the entry of a human mountain. He was a courtroom veteran and he looked out with complete self-assurance at the assembled people; it was as if he had called them there himself.

Like Conroy, his face was calm and stern. Veteran cops had veteran faces.

He took the oath, then squeezed himself into the witness chair. It creaked in protest.

"What is your name, please?" the prosecutor asked.

"Ralph Smerka."

"Are you employed?"

"Yes. I'm a Detroit police officer."

"And your rank?"

"Detective Sergeant."

"Sergeant Smerka, what was your last assignment?"

The Mouse sat quietly. His face was the kind that gives small children nightmares. Whether acquired on the football field or by genetics, his features looked as if each had been broken several times. Hollywood would have cast him as a gangster, a very mean, very tough gangster.

He paused, then spoke. "I was a member of the chiefs' squad, assigned to Deputy Chief Mark Conroy."

"How long were you assigned?"

"Three years. I came to the squad when Conroy was made deputy chief."

"You served as his assistant before that, did you not?"

"Yes."

"As a member of the chiefs' squad, were you assigned to handle a special fund?"

I stood up. "Objection," I said. "The question is leading."

"Sustained," the judge snapped.

The prosecutor looked unruffled. "What duties were you assigned as a member of the chiefs' squad?"

"A number of duties, whatever Chief Conroy wanted me to do. I handled the W-91 Fund."

"Please tell the court what that fund was for."

The Mouse looked relaxed, as if this was just another day in a routine job. "When narcotics or a precinct confiscated cash money as part of a raid, we took that cash and applied it to the W-91 Fund."

"What does that mean, W-91?"

"The *W* stands for witness. *91* was the year

we started. It sounds mysterious, but it isn't."

"The cash was brought into you by the arresting officers?"

"Usually, yes."

"Did they get a receipt?"

"Always."

"What was the purpose of the fund?"

"We bought information."

"What kind of information?"

"The names of drug dealers, how drug networks worked, that sort of thing."

"How much money was collected, if you know?"

"Total?"

"Yes."

"A million and a half, roughly."

"All cash?"

"Yes."

"How much is left?"

"Nothing."

"Nothing?"

"That's right."

"Did you keep the money in a bank?"

"No. In a safe in Chief Conroy's office."

"Who had access to that safe?"

"The combination was known to the chief and myself, no one else."

"Did you make any payouts yourself?"

"Under the direction of the chief."

"Did you keep books?"

"No. It was a secret fund. Books would have showed who got the money. We wanted to protect our informers. No books were kept."

"Did you take any of the money for yourself?"

"No."

"Did the chief?"

There was a pause. The courtroom was absolutely quiet.

"The chief took money, yes."

"In cash?"

"Always."

"What happened to the money that the chief took?"

"Objection," I said, sitting up. "He's calling for conjecture at best. He's laid no foundation for the question."

"Sustained," the judge said.

I sat down. "Tennis rules," Conroy whispered in my ear.

"Did the chief, Conroy, ever tell you what he took the money for?"

"Sometimes."

"And what did he say, if anything?"

The Mouse was expressionless. "He said sometimes the money was going to informants he was running himself."

"Did you believe him?"

"Objection," I snapped.

"Sustained. Stick to facts, not belief," the judge said. "Continue."

"What were some of the other uses he said he found for the money?"

"He gave money to Mary Margaret

Tucker." For just a moment, the Mouse seemed uncomfortable, but then the mask slid back in place.

"Who is Mary Margaret Tucker?"

"His girlfriend, or she was."

"Objection," I said. "I see no foundation laid for this testimony. It's not relevant."

"Overruled," the judge said. "I presume you're going to tie this all up, Mr. Timothy?"

"I will, Your Honor."

"Go on, then."

Timothy did a good job, extracting from Smerka the beginning details of the romance, and detailing the financial arrangement between Conroy and the girl.

I glanced back at Mrs. Conroy. Her face was just as calm and grim as her husband's.

Finally, Timothy quit the Tucker girl and had Mouse testify to other payments — cars, vacations, and other luxury items — all paid for by Conroy, according to the Mouse, with the confiscated public money.

On cross-examination I tried to dent the Mouse a little, but he didn't budge. I tried to get him to admit that he, too, had tapped the special fund, but he denied it. There was no jury, so there was no need for a show. It went quickly, too quickly.

We didn't waste much time arguing. There was no need to. The judge bound Conroy over on the main charges, and continued his personal bond.

I made certain that Conroy was escorted away so that he wouldn't have to face the press.

But I didn't have that luxury.

I was the point man. It was my duty to try to spin-control what had come from the stand. I did my best, talking into a battery of microphones, and later to individuals.

I pointed out that the only case the prosecutor had came from the lips of Det. Sgt. Ralph Smerka.

I said we would show Smerka was lying.

They didn't believe it.

Nor did I, but it was at least something to say.

4

When I got back to the office, I had a message from Sue. I reached her at her office.

"Dinner tonight?" she asked.

"No more late-nighters?"

"Not tonight, although I've been paying for it all day. I feel exhausted."

"Nerves can do that to you. You lost that professional detachment for a minute; that's all. A nice meal, a good sleep, and you'll be the same tough, noncaring cop you've always been."

"You certainly know how to cheer a girl up. Would you mind if we went out? I'm not up to cooking tonight."

"I'll pick you up at your place. Six okay?"

"Perfect."

"Anything more on that kid? I'm not prying, just curious."

"The blood work shows the Higgins boy had been given a large dose of Valium, just as the medical examiner thought. He thinks it was stuck into ice cream, judging from the stomach contents. The boy will be buried next Friday."

"That'll be a sad day."

"Tell me about it. As a matter of fact, Father

Chuck is going to say the funeral Mass. The boy and his family are members of Father Chuck's congregation. I plan on going," she said.

"Why? I should think you'd want to distance yourself from anything personal."

"This is work. I'm checking on all sexual deviates in Kerry County. I just might see someone I recognize at the Mass. Anyway, it's worth a try."

"This business is weird enough. You don't mean you think the killer would have the balls to show up at the funeral?"

"We're dealing with someone strange, very strange. There's no telling what he might do."

"Or she."

"Yes, that's always a possibility. Men don't have a lock on psychosis. There are plenty of sick women out there."

"Maybe I can get away and go with you."

"You don't have to, Charley."

"It would make me feel better. I handled something routine for the family some while ago. Father's name Frank?"

"That's right, Francis. He took it pretty hard; so did the mother, of course."

"I'll pick you up at six tonight," I said, cutting it short, hanging up.

I was just about to pack it in for the evening at the office, leaving me with enough time to

86

grab a shower before picking up Sue. Then the phone rang.

Mrs. Fenton had gone for the day, so I picked it up on the second ring.

"Sloan," I said.

"Sloan, this is Mark Conroy."

"What's up?"

"Nothing much. I just received some information I thought you might like to have."

"Like what?"

"Where they're keeping the Mouse."

"No kidding."

"They have him stashed at the Whitehall."

"That's a retirement place."

He laughed. "Good selection, when you think about it. All you have to watch out for are young people. Everybody else has white hair and walks with a cane. A gunman would stick out, unless they come up with a very old one. They have an apartment there for him, but they have enough guards to hold off an army."

"Is he registered?"

"Not under his own name. He's listed as Philip Marlowe. I suppose that was some cop's idea of humor. Anyway, I thought you might want to drop by and pay him a social visit."

"Why do I get the idea that he doesn't want to talk to me? Maybe the guards, eh? How did you come by this little piece of information?"

"Friends," he said, his tone indicating that was as much as he wanted me to know.

"Why do they have him covered like they do?"

There was a pause. "I suppose they're worried that someone might just drop by and knock him off."

"Someone like you."

"Yeah. No Mouse, no case. But remember, the Mouse knows a great deal about who does what kind of drug business in this city. The dealers might be getting a little antsy on how much he is spilling in that retirement home."

"They won't let me see him."

"Probably not, but it's bound to have a profound effect."

"Why?"

"The Mouse will see that you know where he is. Other people, too, maybe? That might just stop his mouth."

"I'll drop by, but I don't deal in terror."

"Look, Sloan, I know you don't believe me, but I am telling the truth. If that money's gone, the one who would have stolen it is the Mouse. He's got to be getting nervous, no matter what. He's got a million parked away somewhere and someone might just stumble on it."

"I'll try to see him, maybe put it to him just like that."

"Let me know, one way or the other."

As soon as I hung up, the phone rang again.

"Mr. Charles Sloan," a brisk young woman asked, her tone pleasant but not familiar.

"This is Charley Sloan," I said.

"Just a moment for John Rivers."

I waited. Rivers was about my age and a senior partner in one of the big Detroit firms. We had tried some cases against each other when we were younger. I hadn't seen him for years.

"Charley, how are you?" he said, his voice as oily as a snake.

"I'm fine, Jack. And yourself?"

"Just fine, Charley. Couldn't be better if I tried. I've been reading about you. You've become famous."

"Working at it. What can I do for you, Jack?"

"How about lunch tomorrow, Charley? I think I have a proposition that might interest you. I can drive out there, if you like."

"I plan to be in the city tomorrow anyway," I said, and I did. I planned on dropping in on the Mouse. "Name the time and the place."

"How about the Rattlesnake Club. One o'clock?"

"Suits me."

"Good. I really look forward to seeing you."

I hung up. I wondered what he wanted. His firm was a law factory and highly political. Maybe he was going to offer me a job, or was looking for one. Whatever it was would have to wait until tomorrow.

★ ★ ★

Sue spent the night at my place. Our love-making had become less frantic, more comfortable, like an old married couple who understood the needs and desires of the other.

In the morning, she went home to change, and I fixed myself some toast and coffee.

I read the newspaper and took my time. I wasn't enthusiastic about seeing the Mouse, and doubted if I could get to him. Still, he was the key witness in the Conroy case and I had to make the attempt at least.

The morning was cold and brisk, with clouds driven by a fresh wind scudding across the sky. Thanksgiving was just around the corner. Sue wanted me to go with her to her parents' for dinner that day. I had gone along last year. They were nice enough, but they made a point of bringing up marriage with every other sentence. I remember being uneasy, so this time I begged off.

I drove into Detroit just after the rush hour, so the traffic was no problem.

The Whitehall had been a posh residential apartment house, then a hotel, and had flourished during the Twenties and Thirties in Detroit. Built on the Detroit River, just across from Belle Isle, the city's island park, it had been a fashionable place, with a huge, tiled indoor pool.

Like the rest of the city, the Whitehall had slipped slowly economically and would have

90

closed if it hadn't been rescued by the religious group that established it as their retirement facility. It offered private apartments where meals would be provided if needed, and other levels of care right down to a skilled nursing staff.

When you checked into the Whitehall, you knew it was for the last time.

Except if you were Det. Sgt. Ralph Smerka, alias the Mouse. And, given the circumstances, that thought might have crossed the Mouse's mind as he entered the Whitehall for the first time.

I found a parking space near the entrance and walked through the doors into the lobby. The lobby had been maintained with much of the splendor as when the place had enjoyed better days. The furniture looked a bit worn and old people, very old people, were sprinkled around the place. Some reading, some playing cards, and some just wandering about, pushing their walkers before them.

I half hoped the Mouse wouldn't agree to see me. The place made me feel uncomfortable.

The Whitehall still had a hotel-style desk, but no one was there. I rang a bell and waited.

"Don't move." The voice came from behind me. Expert hands ran up and down my body, searching for a weapon.

"Okay," the voice said, "you can move now."

I turned and faced a young man dressed in running togs. He looked as out of place among the white-headed residents as a preacher in a house of ill fame. But that didn't seem to bother him.

"Charles Sloan," I said. "I've come to talk to Smerka."

"I'm Patrolman Jenkins. I saw you in court. How did you find out we were here?"

"Friends," I said, echoing Conroy's explanation.

"Pretty sharp friends. Do you have a court order, or something from the prosecutor?"

"No."

"Then you can't see him. Orders," he added, smiling.

"You can check with the prosecutor," I said.

He paused. "Well, even if I got his okay, maybe the Mouse might have some objections."

"Check with him, too."

He thought that over. "Okay, I'll do both. Have a seat over there. I'll be back."

I sat in a high-backed chair, the kind all hotels used to have in their lobbies.

An old man, wearing two sweaters, limped up. He had an aluminum cane.

He must have been close to ninety.

"This is a nice place," he said.

"Looks that way."

"Food's not bad. Most of these places load

you up with cheese and potatoes, but this place is pretty liberal with meat and chicken. It makes a difference."

"I suppose it does."

"The women, too." He cackled. "Lots of 'em, mostly widows and lonely, if you get my drift."

I couldn't help smiling.

"It's a little chilly, that's my only complaint."

"I take it you'd recommend it?" I presumed he thought I was looking the place over for a parent or some other relative.

"Sure would." He winked at me and leered. "You'll love it here."

Jenkins returned before I got into any other conversations.

He was smiling. He seemed to be smiling all the time.

"The prosecutor says you can have five minutes, but one of us has to be present."

"Fine by me."

"The Mouse didn't want to talk with you, but finally he said he would. I don't think he likes you much."

"I run into that a lot."

Jenkins laughed. "I bet you do."

They had the Mouse in a suite. I was surprised that the Whitehall still provided such elegant residences.

He was sitting at a table playing solitaire.

Jenkins stayed, although two other young policemen left.

"You got five minutes," Jenkins said. "Not a second more."

"What do you want, Sloan?" the Mouse growled.

"I want to know why you're testifying against Conroy. You've been lifelong friends."

"Because he's a prick," he said, placing a card down on one of the stacks. "A crooked prick. He was setting me up. He's a user, that one. Be careful, Sloan. He'll use you, too."

"Maybe. But why the sudden change after all these years? If he's a prick and a thief, it sure took you a long time to find that out."

"He's clever," he said.

"Do you think he was making you the fall guy for the W-91 Fund?"

"Sure. If anything went wrong, he'd point at me and say I was the only one handling the money."

"When did you realize all this?"

"Not long ago. I'm a cop, too, and a good one. One morning I woke up and realized what was happening. I was probably the closest friend he ever had, yet here he was putting a noose around my neck if he ever needed it to save his own. He uses people, then throws them away."

He laid down another card. "But not this time."

"You realize that without you there's no case."

He nodded.

"Did you go to the prosecutor, or did they come to you?"

He raised an eyebrow. "I'm not even supposed to be talking to you. But I went to the prosecutor. Actually, I went to the Mayor's Squad."

"Why the Mayor's Squad?"

"The mayor's the source of all power in this city. I figured I'd be safer if he was on my side."

"I take it I can't change your mind about testifying?"

"Not unless you want to take a fall for obstruction of justice." He laid down another card.

Jenkins coughed. "Your five minutes are about up." He smiled again. "Orders, you know."

"Do you have any message for Conroy?" I asked.

"Sure," the Mouse said. "Tell him this is one time he won't get away with it. Tell him he's abused one too many people. Tell him . . . oh, fuck it, what's the use?"

"That's it, Mr. Sloan. Time's up," Jenkins said.

"Okay. Thanks for seeing me."

The Mouse merely nodded and went back to his cards.

Jenkins walked me out of the room and into the hall.

"Not much of a conversationalist, is he?" I said.

Jenkins shrugged. "This is the most he's said since I've been around him."

"Why is that? Why the heavy guard? Nobody wants to hurt the Mouse, at least not that I know of."

"That's just it. Nobody knows. We're playing it safe."

"Are you a member of the Mayor's Squad?"

He nodded.

"Like it?"

He laughed. "Like I said, your time is up, Mr. Sloan."

In the old days I knew how to kill time. It was simple then, just park on a bar stool and put the mind on autopilot.

But I couldn't do that anymore.

I had a couple of hours to kill. I hung around the shops in the Ren Cen, shopping, or at least giving that appearance. I visited a bookstore and browsed until they began getting suspicious.

Finally, and gratefully, it was time to go. I retrieved my car and drove to the Rattlesnake Club, one of Detroit's finest restaurants. It wasn't a club and was open to the public. And there hadn't been a rattlesnake in downtown Detroit since 1692 — if there were any then.

The owner just liked the name.

I liked the Rattlesnake, all brass and cherrywood and shiny with good food and good service.

I handed over my coat and saw Jack Rivers seated at the table in the far corner of the room, next to a brace of large windows. The Rattlesnake's view of Detroit's river was nice, but it wasn't better than mine.

Jack Rivers had lost most of his hair since I'd last seen him. And he was stockier. But his expensive clothes and assured manner proclaimed a man who had arrived.

He gripped my hand. "Damn, it's good to see you, Charley."

"You, too."

I took a seat and ordered a Diet Coke.

Jack had a martini before him and he sipped at it from time to time. He ordered another with his lunch. They seemed to serve as ammunition for the heavy barrage he laid upon me across the table.

Jack wanted to talk about the cases we had had together — at length. I wasn't particularly interested. I had won both of them, but that didn't seem to bother him; he sang my praises in the key of C. I wondered what this was all about.

It wasn't until late in the meal that he got down to business.

"Charley, as you probably know, our firm represents the mayor."

"I didn't know."

"Well, we do, at least in major matters. The mayor is upset that the city's law department seems to be losing so many cases. Millions are literally walking out the door. They can't seem to win over there."

"I've read something about that."

"It could be a scandal unless something is done. The mayor proposes farming out the larger cases to experienced lawyers who know how to win."

"So?"

He sipped his drink. "We, that is, the mayor, would like you to represent some of those cases. He's willing to pay top dollar to get good people."

"I've never done much negligence defense work. As you know, I take plaintiffs' cases but my main practice is criminal law."

"You're a trial man, Charley, and a good one. That's what we need. The mayor is willing to go as high as three hundred dollars per hour, with an annual guarantee that you'd earn at least two hundred thousand."

"There is an army of defense men out there. How come you're bringing this to me?"

"Because you're good, and that's what we need. How about it?"

"It's tempting, Jack, but it might interfere with my regular practice."

"Take it, Charley. It's like money in the street. Just pick it up."

"Any restrictions?"

"One or two. You couldn't handle anything that might appear to be a conflict of interest." He paused, drained the martini, then signaled for another. Then he made his message plain. "For instance, you'd have to back off of Mark Conroy's case."

"Why?"

"He's a crooked policeman. We couldn't have you representing the city in civil matters, but defending someone who's been caught with his hand in the city's cookie jar. It wouldn't be ethical."

"So all I have to do is walk on Conroy and the money's mine? Is that what you're saying?"

"More or less."

I had almost finished my lunch, and I was glad I had.

"Jack, what are you? The mayor's dog robber, or what?"

He tried to smile. "Just a messenger boy."

"Go back and tell His Honor that it's no deal."

"Think about it, Charley. Give it a day or two. You're kicking away a great deal of money. The mayor is powerful. You'd have a powerful friend. You might be surprised how much good he can do you."

"Why does he want Conroy so bad?"

"The man's a thief. He had a public trust and he violated it. The mayor is outraged."

"Half of the mayor's appointees have gone

to jail at one time or another. He holds welcome-back parties for them. What makes Conroy so different?"

"Charley, I hate to even say this, but while the mayor can be a powerful friend, he can be a more powerful enemy. Take the money, Charley. What do you care?"

"Maybe I care a lot." I stood up. "I'm sorry to see you've come to this, Jack. I'll pray for you."

I'm not a praying man, so I'm not really sure why I told him I'd pray for him. Maybe it was a knee-jerk reaction because I'd grown up hearing that phrase bandied about almost every day of my life. Maybe it was because I'd been bribed before in a major case I was involved in. I didn't like it then any more than I liked it now. I felt sullied, dirty. I felt, oddly enough, like I should go to confession for just being in the presence of this sleazebag. And, yes, maybe I even felt that I could say a prayer against this kind of lousy corruption.

Jack Rivers's mask of friendliness immediately dropped away, revealing him to be the mean, hard-eyed man he was.

"If you go against His Honor," he said through clenched teeth, "you're the one who's going to be needing the prayers."

The drive back to Pickeral Point seemed longer somehow. Of course, maybe it was the two hundred thousand. I don't ordinarily walk away from fees like that, no matter what the source. But they weren't buying legal services. I tried to keep that foremost in my thoughts.

Conroy must have come very close to making a case on the mayor. The mayor didn't fork over two hundred thousand for nothing, either. Even if it wasn't his money. Also, the blatant attempt to bribe me gave some credibility to Conroy. Maybe he didn't steal the money after all.

When I got back, I worked on some files and returned some phone calls. Attorneys were forever being suspended or disbarred for not returning calls from clients. Usually, it was more of a symptom than the main disease. But I had come close to losing my law license once and I was determined that it would never happen again. So I cheerfully made the calls.

It was my night to provide dinner, which meant we either went out or I tried to master frozen dinners once again. I didn't feel like accepting the challenge. I called Sue and she seemed relieved that I had chosen the restaurant route. As before, I arranged to pick her up at her apartment at six.

The skies had become more ominous and the clouds seemed to skim the top of the water. There was very little river traffic now, just an occasional ice-covered ocean boat or little fishing craft piloted by fanatics getting the last of the season in. As I watched the water, snow began to fall. I switched on my radio and picked up the weathercast. The forecast hedged, a smart thing to do in Michigan, but heavy snow of four or more inches was predicted. The weatherman made some weak joke about a white Thanksgiving. I sat back and soon the lights of Canada on the other side of the river vanished. It was a peaceful scene, the kind you see on greeting cards.

I almost fell asleep but recovered myself in time to pick up Sue.

Driving was a mess. The snow was approaching blizzard conditions and the windshield wipers were almost useless. Everyone moved along at a crawl.

Sue was dressed to the nines when I arrived. She usually dressed up like that when she had something important to discuss. Eventually, she would bring it up, so I didn't inquire. But I raised my defensive shields just a bit. She took off her high heels and slipped on snow boots, more or less ruining the effect she wanted. We settled on a restaurant in town, a burger and fries place, rather than risk the drive to Port Huron or St. Clair. Sue seemed a trifle nervous and rattled on about police gossip and other inconsequential things. I merely nodded. It was a one-way conversation.

Finally, she got down to business. "I would really like it if you came with me to my folks' for Thanksgiving. I think they'll be offended if you don't show up."

"I'd rather not," I said. "You know the reason."

"Charley, they're my parents. They care about me. It's only natural they would want to see me happily married. They mean no harm. They just try too hard."

"True. But they make me feel as if I was actively despoiling their little girl. Your father, I think, would like to punch me in the eye."

She giggled. "They're from a different generation, that's all."

"Or horsewhip me, maybe. Perhaps that would satisfy him. Just take me out back and give me the beating I so justly deserve."

"I can tell them to knock off the marriage business. They like you, no matter what you may think. That's just a guilty conscience talking."

"About sex. It takes two, dear. I don't recall having to beg."

"Maybe that would help things along."

"Begging?"

"Maybe. Although in all the handbooks it says to save that up until after the knot is tied." Her little joke. She smiled and reached across the table, taking my hand. "I'm not rushing you, Charley, really I'm not."

"I know that, and I appreciate it."

"Would you reconsider Thanksgiving?"

I sighed.

"For me?"

"Okay, I'll think it over."

"Thanks, Charley," she said. She toyed with her food. "Do you ever think about it much?"

"What?"

"Marriage."

"Sue!"

She laughed. "Okay, I'll leave you alone, but I might reconsider the begging question."

"Who knows? You might like it."

Sue called from the restaurant to check the messages on her machine. That was a big mistake.

"Charley, drive me to my place. I have to get my car. There's been another one."

"Another what?"

"A child, just like the Higgins boy. There was a body left on Clarion Road not far from where the Higgins boy was left."

Outside, the snow had just about stopped, although the roads were still covered and slippery. "I'll drive you out there," I told her.

She hesitated. "Okay, just don't mix in. Working cops get nervous when a lawyer is hanging around a murder scene."

I drove slowly. Clarion Road was a two-lane highway that passed through farm country.

"Another boy?" I asked.

"No. A little girl this time. Just like before, all neatly wrapped in plastic and left at the side of the road."

It took a while, but we could see all the lights as we approached on Clarion. A uniformed officer approached us. Sue rolled down her window.

"The road is closed, Miss."

"I'm a policeman," Sue said, flashing her badge.

"Oh, hello, Sue. I didn't recognize you." He flashed the light on me. "Hey, Charley," he said. His face was familiar.

"Go on up. Park in back of the police cars. We're trying to keep the scene clean."

As we drew near to the gathering of vehicles, I saw a truck with overhead lights. It lit up the area like a night baseball game. Yellow tape had been raised to protect what lay at the side of the road. We got out and walked up. She nodded to several officers. Some knew me and looked puzzled that I was there.

One of the pathologists from Port Huron stood on a cardboard walkway, looking down, past the tape.

We followed his gaze.

She looked more like a doll than a human being. There was a little snow on the plastic. Her small hands had been crossed at her chest and she wore a school uniform, the kind worn by Catholic girls, a kind of muted plaid skirt and a white blouse. Beautiful was the only way to describe her. One tiny hand clutched a little purse.

Suddenly my stomach churned and I bolted back the way we had come, finding a space behind a scout car before I threw up. I breathed deeply and waited until I was sure the spasm had passed. I sensed someone was looking at me.

I straightened up and wiped my lips.

"Hello, Charley." I recognized the voice before I made out the face in the twirling lights. "Got to you a bit, huh?"

"Yeah."

He was Stash Olesky, the assistant prosecutor who handled all the county's homicides. As the prosecutor's best trial man, he was paid accordingly, which is to say Stash was doing okay but he wasn't raking it in and leading a life of luxury. He could leave the prosecutor's office anytime he felt like it and triple his income, but Stash loved what he was doing. Years ago when I was defending Becky Harris on a murder charge, Olesky had taken a good run at me. He was smart and fair. Not a lot of that going around these days. I liked him enormously, and now, under these circumstances, I felt we were kindred spirits, thrown together in what anyone would call a tragic situation.

He had dark blond hair and a broad Polish face, with high cheekbones and eyes set well back in his head. They called him the "Cossack" and he looked like one.

"If it makes you feel any better," he said, "I did the same thing. I see bodies ripped apart and it doesn't bother me. But there's something about this one that is so, well, obscene, it just blew me away."

"You got a make on the kid?" I asked.

"Not for sure. A little girl, answering her description, was called in as missing earlier. The ID is probably in that purse she's holding. The medical examiner didn't want anything touched until he got her in for the autopsy."

I looked back. Technicians were working away, measuring, taking photographs. Policemen watched them silently.

I had been at a number of crime scenes, but this one was different. Usually, cops laugh a lot. It's a kind of black mordant humor that helps ease the horrors they see from day to day. But there was no laughter here. People did their jobs or just stood around silently.

"How come you're here, Charley?"

"I was having dinner with Sue Gillis. I'm her driver for tonight."

The medical examiner directed the police as they removed the body to a waiting ambulance.

Everyone watched, again in silence. The ambulance drove away, followed by two police cars. They didn't use their lights and it was a slow-moving procession.

Sue came up and nodded to Olesky. "Are you in charge?" she asked.

He nodded. "Yeah. I've got the parents of the missing girl at the medical examiner's office. They can identify her if she's their child.

I hate to handle that sort of thing, Sue. Could you?"

"Do you think anyone in their right mind would like it?"

"No, but women always seem to do these things so much better."

"We make great coffee and we can type, too."

He shrugged. "Maybe while you're there, you could whip up some coffee."

"Fuck you, Olesky."

He looked at her and pretended to be puzzled.

"Come on, Sue," I said, "I'll drive you."

"It's going to be a long night, Charley. I'll drive Sue there and make sure she has a ride home when we're done. She'll be a lot safer with us than with you."

"Go on home, Charley," Sue said. "This is going to take a while."

"Whatever," I said.

"I'd feel better if you weren't underfoot. Go home and get some sleep."

"You, too," I said.

"Did you see her?" she asked softly.

"Yeah."

"Like an angel," she said, just above a whisper. "How could anyone . . ." Her voice trailed off. I got in my car and drove home. The snowplows hadn't gotten out yet, and the roads were becoming even more treacherous. I went into a skid several times, but somehow managed to regain control of the car. The memory of that sweet little face burned into my consciousness, as Sue's question kept echoing in my mind.

How could anyone?

5

Sitting there alone in my kitchen, a cup of coffee in front of me, all I could do was try to put my mind on something else. I'd tried TV already. Once I'd unlocked the door and struggled out of my galoshes, I'd gone straight to the set in my living room and turned it on. I stood there a couple of minutes and stared at the screen as I switched from channel to channel with the remote. Then it struck me that this was pretty dumb. Did I really think an old movie or some inane sitcom could wipe out the picture of what I'd seen out there in the snow? I went into the kitchen and put on the water for another coffee. Did I want a drink? Yes.

I knew where I should have gone. There was a regular AA meeting that night in the basement of St. Jude's Church. But that was clear on the other side of Pickeral Point, and by the time I got close to home, I figured it would be just about over.

No telling how long it would take to get there now in the snow. But I'd only been in the house about ten minutes at most, and I certainly needed to talk to somebody. Maybe, just maybe, Bob Williams would still be around. It was worth a try. I grabbed my coat from the kitchen chair where I'd tossed it and headed for the door.

I was lucky. By the time I got back on the road, the snowplow had been through. With the wind whipping the falling snow, visibility was bad. But there wasn't much traffic, and my tires held the road at a steady twenty-five all the way to the church parking lot.

There were just two other cars when I turned in. The meeting was over, or maybe on a night like this had never begun. But one of those two cars belonged to the man I wanted to see.

He was just leaving the building with somebody else — the two-man cleanup crew. He banged the church door shut, made sure it was locked, then parted company with his companion and headed for his car. I'd pulled up beside it, motor idling, headlights on. He knew it was me.

"In case you haven't figured it out, you're a bit late," he said. Through my open car window I saw that snowflakes were already caking on his eyebrows.

"Anybody show up?"

"Some, even on a night like this. Maybe especially on a night like this."

"I need to talk."

"Well?"

"I noticed on the way over that Benny's Diner's open. Come on, I'll help you clean off your car."

So not much more than five minutes later, Bob Williams and I were settled in a booth at Benny's with cups of coffee in front of us. There were a few other refugees from the storm in the place. Most of them were along the counter. One couple had claimed a booth at the other end of the line. The waitress padded back and forth, coffeepot in hand, keeping cups filled, an angel of mercy, with a sour face.

I'd have to say that Bob Williams is my best friend. Tall, big, and broad as the bow of a ship, he wore his hair in a brush cut, à la the marines. At any given moment, you half expected him to start talking about the march on Parris Island.

Robert J. Williams, M.D., a board-certified psychiatrist with a private practice in Pickeral Point, was also my AA sponsor. His heart was about the size of Texas and there wasn't a time I could remember that he had let me down. Like a beacon on a dark and starless night, Bob was always there.

Now he listened intently while I recounted what I'd seen under the glare of the police lights at Clarion Road. The plaid uniform, the clean white blouse, the little purse, all perfectly wrapped in plastic.

I told him about the girl's face, too. Angelic, beautiful, innocent. And dead, very dead. It was an image I found impossible to shake.

"Well, it's understandable," Bob said, looking at me with concern.

"What do you mean?"

"Innocence, Charley. Cops, lawyers like you and Olesky, you don't get to see much of it in your daily rounds. Not guilty you get to see, but very little innocence. There's a difference, you know."

"Oh, yeah," I said. "I know. I *certainly* do."

He made a quick, little apologetic smile. "Sorry if that sounded patronizing. But look, when you see innocence in that state, defiled and destroyed, then something seems really, really wrong."

"Yeah, that's what bothers me." I took a sip of coffee. He waited until I'd collected my thoughts and could go on. "You know, the twelve-step program, that's all about the Higher Power. It depends on it. You're sort of one-on-one with the Higher Power."

"That's right."

"A lot of people want to get into the program, but they can't accept anything to do with the Higher Power. Everything else, but not that. So they go out and try to make it on their own."

"And mostly they fail."

"That's not the point."

"What *is* the point?"

"Maybe they're right. Maybe there is no Higher Power."

"Charley, it's a question as old as religion itself — any kind of religion. You know. How can a just God allow the suffering, the destruction, of innocents?"

"All right, how can He? Sure, you can pose it as a philosophical question. You can read about all kinds of horror in the newspapers. But believe me, Bob, it's a lot different when you see it."

We'd been talking in a loud whisper. I don't think anyone there at Benny's could actually hear what we were saying. But I looked up and found the waitress and one of the men at the counter looking our way. It must have been my intensity they noticed. Maybe something wild in my eyes. Anyway, when I calmed down, they turned away.

"Charley, I'm probably not the one to talk to about stuff like this," Bob said. "I have my problems with it all, too. Maybe what you should do is drive back to St. Jude's, and if there are any lights on in the rectory, just bang on the door and ask for a priest. Father Phil Leclerc is okay. Better than okay."

"Come on, Bob. You can do better than that."

"No, I can't."

"Well, it helped just getting it out."

"I'm glad of that."

"Your usual rates?"

"Yeah. You pay for the coffee."

Maybe it really was getting those things said to Bob Williams. Or maybe I was just plain exhausted after all that snow driving. Anyway,

I fell into bed as soon as I got back home and slept right through to morning. No nightmares. No dreams of any kind, as I remember.

The sun woke me up. That's the way the Michigan fall goes — a day of winter, followed by a week of Indian summer, then back to winter again.

By the time I got to my office, the snow was starting to melt. At the end of the day, the town would be swimming in slush. It's not often I beat Mrs. Fenton in, but this was one of those times. Keeps her a bit off balance. I like that.

There I was in my office when I heard the outer door open. Then there were the sounds of stomping and grumbling — grunts and what might have been words. She was taking off her boots. The outer door shut. The next thing I heard was the clicking of her heels on the hardwood floor. I coughed discreetly to announce my presence.

She appeared at the door to my office. "This is a surprise," she said.

"Life's full of them, Mrs. Fenton."

"Have you turned over a new leaf?"

"Same old leaf, I'm afraid. Coffee's ready," I said, holding up my steaming office mug, half full. It's one of the few things I've kept from my former life — black ceramic, with a legend in gold: *"Cui bono?"* The lawyer's favorite question. "I make pretty good coffee," I said to her. "Have some. It's a little stronger

115

than yours, though." Hers was like colored water.

"No thanks," she said primly. "I prefer to keep the enamel on my teeth." Then she disappeared from the doorway.

"Wait till I get my second cup before you pour the pot out," I called after her with all the stern authority I could muster.

More grumbling. Indecipherable.

Cui bono? is Latin for *To whom the good?* In other words, *Who gains? Who profits?* You can cut through a lot of bullshit by asking that. And as I sat at my desk, going through the Mark Conroy file, that was what I was trying to do.

According to the Mouse, he had gained by fingering Conroy because he was sure that he was being set up by Conroy to take the fall for the missing funds.

Reasonable, from his point of view. But how long had these suspicions taken to develop? And when had he first decided that Conroy was helping himself to the funds? How long had the Mouse waited before blowing the whistle?

But that lunch I'd had with Jack Rivers opened up a whole area of possibilities that now had to be seriously considered. First and foremost among them was that Chief Conroy was on the level. That anything he'd taken from the W-91 Fund he'd paid back. That the Mouse had all the transactions down in coded books, just as Conroy said.

The big question, though, was the mayor's interest in all this. What did he gain by sending Conroy off to Jackson for ten to twelve? Revenge? Could it be as personal as all that? Conroy had looked to be pretty cozy with His Honor at one time. He certainly couldn't have made it to deputy chief without at least an okay from the top man. Could the two of them have had a falling-out? Or something more than that? Had the mayor been so offended by him that he was reaching out to destroy him? He was known as a man you didn't cross, and that was a burden I had to carry now — Jack Rivers had made that pretty plain.

No, more likely it was silence, or the next thing to it, that the mayor hoped to gain. It seemed to me that Conroy must have something on him. If he spoke up now, under indictment, nobody would listen. If he was convicted, then he was silenced forever.

Quite a situation.

By that time, I had worked my way through the Conroy file. But I stopped and looked again at one of the last items in it, a list of the witnesses to be called at the preliminary examination. One of them hadn't been called. It seemed important now to know why.

I reached for the telephone, flipped over the file, and dialed the number on the cover. A woman answered. Mrs. Conroy, of course.

"Hello? Yes?" With just those two words,

you could detect a certain level of tension.

"I'd like to speak to Chief Conroy, please."

"He's not —" She hesitated. "Who is this, please?"

"Just tell him it's the guy who plays by tennis rules."

"Tennis rules?" She repeated it with a frown in her voice.

"That's right."

She sighed. "Just a minute."

In fact, it was more than a minute. More like three or four before Conroy came to the telephone. It seemed I could hear a brief, distant row between them as I waited. Not words exactly, just those jagged tones I remembered from my own past marriages. I was glad to be spared the details. At last he was there at the other end of the line. He answered with a curt "Yeah?"

"You recognize my voice?"

"Sure. Of course."

"Then call me from a pay phone."

"You really think that's necessary?"

"Just to be on the safe side."

"It'll take a little while," he said. "I just got up."

"I'll be waiting." I hung up the receiver.

Deputy Chief Mark Conroy had a pretty good deal for a condemned man. Although he was on suspension, he was drawing full pay. I looked at my watch. It was after nine. Since I didn't think he was taking his suspension as so much vacation time, it seemed pretty likely that if he was sleeping in, then he'd been out late the night before. Who with? Those friends of his who let him know where the Mouse was stashed? I wanted to know more about that. I wanted a lot more information from Conroy.

And was this cloak-and-dagger drill with the telephone really necessary? Maybe not. But the Conroys lived in Detroit, and since the long arm of the mayor reached everywhere in the city, it was probably only practical to take such precautions.

I'd finished my cup of coffee. I went out to refill my mug and got involved in a brief wrangle with Mrs. Fenton on the hours to be billed Ernie on the concealed weapon case we'd just won. I told her the retainer he paid would cover it. Mrs. Fenton, being Mrs. Fenton, wanted it exact.

"I don't keep good logs on stuff like that. You know that."

"Well, you should. It's time you started."

The telephone rang. She answered it the way she always did. "The law offices of Charles Sloan." She listened a moment. "One moment, please." Then, pushing the hold button, she said, "It's that *deputy* chief." Put him in his place, didn't she?

"I'll take it in there."

As I settled down into my chair, I managed to spill coffee on the desktop. Not the first time. "Yeah," I said into the phone. "Sloan here."

"This is Conroy," he said. "What was it you wanted?"

"I was prepared for a wait. You're not calling from home, are you?"

"No. Two blocks away."

"All right, look, I'd like you to come out here so we can have a talk."

"Did you see the Mouse?"

"Yes. That's part of it, but we've got a lot to go over."

"When do you want me there?"

"As soon as you can make it."

"An hour and a half?"

"If you say so. But hold on. There's something else."

"Okay," he said, "what is it?" Was he sounding annoyed? He'd better not be.

"This may be important. Those friends of yours who found the Mouse — do they know where Mary Margaret Tucker is?"

There was a noticeable silence at his end. Finally, he said, "It's possible. I doubt it."

"Ask them. Tell them to look. I want to talk to her."

Another silence. "All right," he said, "I'll see what I can do."

"Be here in an hour and a half, then."

He said he would and hung up.

I was left holding the receiver, trying to figure the ups-and-downs, the ins-and-outs of this cop's cop. Anybody who could inspire the turnout he did at his arrest and arraignment had lots of support on the force. But for the first time I considered the possibility that he was getting help from some other source. There were too many unanswered questions, too many questions unasked. I was sure now that he was holding out on me in some way.

As I was going through Conroy's file once more, a man and woman came in without an appointment. They looked familiar. If I hadn't had my mind so firmly fixed on other matters, I would have recognized them right away.

It was that elderly couple who had come in a few days before to make out a will that excluded their son completely. Now they wanted to change everything. Had the will been prepared? I said it had. They said things were different now. Could I perhaps do another one so that their son would get everything? I said that could be arranged. Then I said something to the effect of I-told-you-so. That was when the wife explained that their son had decided not to marry "that woman" after all. The husband looked embarrassed. The wife looked smug.

Once again I took down the facts and got rid of the couple as quickly as possible. I decided to keep their original will on file for their next visit. When would parents stop using money as a weapon against their children? Maybe never.

Once they'd left, I dialed Sue at her office. "Gillis."

"It's me, Sue. How did it go last night?"

"Oh, Charley." It came out in a sigh. She sounded exhausted. "By the time I finished up at the medical examiner's, it was nearly two. When I got home and went to bed, I couldn't sleep. Kept seeing that little girl on the slab."

"The parents identify her?"

"Yes. Her name was Catherine Quigley. She was an only child."

"Jesus, those poor people."

"I sent them home in a patrol car and stuck around to get some details from the medical examiner."

"What does it look like for cause of death?" I asked.

"Well, it's all preliminary, of course — the autopsy won't be until this afternoon — but it looks like asphyxiation, the same as the boy. No marks on the body. Again, probably a pillow was used."

"Any sexual evidence?"

"No, nothing detected. But I don't care what the physical evidence says, Charley, this was a sex crime. By whatever sick, screwed-up logic, that's what it was."

She sounded overwrought, strung out, on the verge of tears.

"I understand, Sue." And I did, too. It was this sense of desecration that had her going, the same reaction that had sent me out into the night, screaming to Bob Williams for help.

"She was so clean!" Sue went on. "Bathed! Her underpants had even been washed. Oh, this guy is sick, really sick."

She had that right. What kind of geek was doing this?

"We're going out around noon to take another look at the area where the body was found now that the snow's melting," Sue said. "Maybe we'll find something we didn't see last night."

"I hope so."

"Later then, Charley. Thanks for the call."

I swung around in my chair and took a look out the window. The sun shone down brilliantly on the river and what was left of last night's snow. Already the streets were clear and so were the sidewalks. There were dark patches all around where the snow had melted to reveal the bare ground. And slush, a lot of slush.

I felt vaguely guilty because I'd slept so well last night. Did that mean I was callous and indifferent where Sue was sensitive and responsive? No, I remembered just how frantic I'd been. I decided the difference between us was that I'd gone to confession and she had not.

Mark Conroy arrived a little earlier than he'd promised, and he seemed willing to talk. One thing he asked was that we conduct our interview away from my office.

"What's the matter?" I asked. "You afraid Mrs. Fenton will listen in? You think I'll tape-record you on the sly?"

He gave me one of those ironic smiles that seemed a specialty with him. "No," he said. "I'm starving. I was hoping we could go someplace where I could get something to eat. If it's not too crowded, we can talk."

So we wound up together back at Benny's Diner. It was between the breakfast rush and the noon rush, and the place was just about as empty as it had been the night before. We sat in that same back booth that Bob and I had been in. There was no question of being overheard, not even by the waitress. After rudely slamming down Conroy's order of ham and eggs and my coffee, she seemed to make it her business to ignore us. I think she disapproved of his two-thousand-dollar suit. I wasn't too keen on it myself.

I told him about my visit to the Mouse. The main thing was that the Mouse had claimed that Conroy was setting him up to take the fall for the missing funds. That was his justification for his sudden fit of righteousness.

I put it to Conroy directly. "Was there anything to that?" I asked. "Did he have reason to think you'd tag him with the blame?"

"Look," said Conroy, "the safe was in my office. Only he and I had the combination. There was over a million in it, give or take.

The money went missing all at once. Maybe the Mouse saw it was gone before I did, and if he did, he'd think I took it. And if he thought that, then who else was there for me to blame but him? Since we were at least theoretically the only two who had the combination."

This was confusing. It was a little like one of those puzzles, or whatever they were, that consist of boxes inside of boxes inside of boxes. "Now, wait a minute," I said. "In spite of all this, you don't think the Mouse took the money? I remember you said that earlier. It bothered me then."

"No, I don't think he took the money."

"Why not?"

"We've been together too long. You get to know somebody. Frankly, I'm disappointed that he felt he had to cover his ass and didn't come to me to talk about it."

"So what do you think is the answer? If he didn't take the money, and if you didn't take it, who did?"

"Somebody else must have had the combination to the safe, somebody we don't know about." As he said that, I looked at him, studied him. For the first time since we'd started talking, I had the feeling that he wasn't telling me the truth, or the whole truth. I knew he was reading me, too. He was perceptive. But Conroy added nothing, said nothing more.

Finally, I said, "What about those account books that the Mouse kept, the ones in code?"

"What about them?"

"Where are they? I understand that if he's fingering you, the Mouse isn't going to say, 'Oh, by the way, I was bookkeeping the entire operation.' He's going to say what he did at the preliminary hearing. That you were entirely in charge of disbursements, that he was only your gofer."

"So?"

"The books exist, don't they?"

"What're you saying?"

"That he might have destroyed them, or . . ."

"Or what?"

"Or passed them on to interested parties."

Conroy was getting elusive. Obviously, at this point, I felt that I wasn't getting everything from him he had to give. But I couldn't for the life of me figure out why he should be holding out when it was in his interest to tell me what he knew, or suspected.

Rather than lecture him, I decided to take a new tack. "All right," I said, "let's talk about one of those interested parties."

And then I told Conroy about my troubling lunch with Jack Rivers. I omitted Rivers's name, just called him "a prominent Detroit attorney." But the rest I summarized just about as it had happened, the bait and then the threat.

Conroy listened, expressionless, until the very end. Then he gave me another one of those smiles that seemed more like a sneer. "You should have taken the two hundred thou," he said.

"You think so? Well, maybe I should have. But that session at the Rattlesnake Club told me a couple of things. Number one, it told me why you'd come all the way out to Pickeral Point to hire me as your lawyer. There are bigger lawyers with better records in Detroit. So why me? Because I'm so far out of the loop that I wouldn't know you're too hot to handle. Nobody in town would take you on. Am I right?"

I waited for a response, returning the stare from those laser-beam eyes of his.

At last he shrugged and said, "Something like that."

"Okay," I said. "Another thing I found out at the Rattlesnake Club — and this really surprised me — it was that you might, just might, be telling the truth, at least about being framed for the theft of the W-91 Fund."

That smile again. "Well, it's nice to know my own lawyer might possibly believe me."

"I'll tell you, frankly," I said, "I was prepared to conduct your whole defense by tennis rules. Lawyers do that all the time. It's called making the prosecution prove its case. You cops hate us for that. The guilty sometimes go free."

He cast a look around the diner, like he really wasn't very interested in what I was

127

saying. "Just doing your job, I suppose."

"That's right, doing my job. And that's the kind of job you would have gotten from me, still might get from me, unless you give me some answers." I stopped then, smiled unhappily, and shook my head. "Answers? I don't even know the questions to ask."

"All right, listen, Sloan. Even if you knew the right questions, I might not be able to answer them. All I can say is, I haven't lied to you yet."

"That's something, at least. But what are you holding back? What, for instance, have you got on the mayor?"

"Me?" he said, all innocence. "I don't have anything on the mayor."

"Then why is he trying to get you put away?"

"Ask him."

This guy was blocking me at every turn. It seemed almost useless to go on. But I'd gone into this meeting with a three-point agenda. I'd covered two, more or less. I might as well get on to the third.

"Mary Margaret Tucker," I said.

"What about her?"

"Did you mention her to your friends?"

"No. Not yet. I will."

"She wasn't called at the preliminary hearing," I said. "Got any idea why not?"

"Well," Conroy said coolly, "maybe they couldn't find her, either. Or just maybe they decided she didn't have any connection to all this. Which is what I've been trying to tell you."

"The first is a possibility, I suppose. But as for the second, just introducing her and establishing your relationship the way the Mouse did discredited you further. And that's really what this is all about, isn't it?"

"Yes. It looks like it."

"I need some details on her. You said she was a senior in college. Which college?"

"Wayne State. She's in the prelaw program."

"Wants to be a lawyer, huh? What did you think of that?"

"I never tried to talk her out of it. I never tried to talk her into or out of anything."

This was a guy who would lie on the witness stand. But here and now, in Benny's Diner at eleven-thirty in the morning, with those dark eyes fixed on me, it seemed impossible to doubt what he said.

"You said she was living in a building you owned until she disappeared. I'd like the address of that building she was in and the key to her apartment."

He looked at me. This was a challenge, an intrusion. He thought it over for a moment, then he took a ballpoint pen and wrote an address on a paper napkin. He took out his keys, selected one, and pulled it off the ring. Then he laid it on top of the napkin.

"This is a residence that you have maintained with Mary Margaret Tucker. Is that correct?"

"What is this? More tennis rules? Yes, that's correct."

"And I have your permission to enter it?"

He sighed. "Yes."

"Just one more thing," I said. "Do you have a picture of her?"

His mask of self-control slipped for just an instant. I had a glimpse of the sense of loss he felt. "No," he said, his voice close to a whisper, "I never needed one."

The address Conroy had given me was on Parker in Indian Village, a part of Detroit that dated back to just after the turn of the century. It was a neighborhood filled with oversized mansions and stately old apartment buildings. Maybe this was where the moguls of the auto industry first decided to build. But whoever they were, these first residents were sure out to prove something. The houses were relics of conspicuous consumption in the grand old manner.

The name given to the area had to do only with the streets that ran through it. They all carried the names of Indian tribes — Iroquois, and so on. All except Parker.

I turned off Jefferson right at UAW headquarters and started up the street, driving slowly, checking the addresses as I went along.

The building I was looking for was right on the corner. A three-story apartment house that must have gone up about the time America entered World War I, it had two big Greek columns supporting a fancy roof over the entrance, which was now laden with melting snow.

I checked the mailboxes and buzzers in the hall, found the name Tucker, and went up to the second floor. The key fit. I let the door swing wide and hesitated a moment before stepping over the threshold. Well, it wasn't breaking and entering, anyway. I went inside and shut the door behind me.

There's something weird about being alone, uninvited in a place that's not your own. No matter how certain you may be otherwise, there's always a lurking fear that you'll be discovered. I've heard burglars get a thrill from this. Not me. As I started to walk through the apartment, room by room, my stomach began jumping, and I noticed I had started to sweat. Even so, I kept my gloves on.

It was a big apartment. A couple of the rooms in it stood empty. The rest were furnished in basic Salvation Army style — typical student stuff but not quite what you'd expect for a deputy chief.

The exception was what might be called the master bedroom. It was large by any measure, maybe fifteen by fifteen, living-room size. In addition to an obviously new bedroom set — matching dressers, full-length mirror, king-sized bed — there was what the catalogs call a home entertainment center — television/radio/CD player — on shelves that took up most of one whole wall. Conroy had put his money where it counted. The master bedroom was clearly where they had spent most of their time. This was the place to look.

I began opening drawers — and finding most of them empty. This was more or less as Conroy had described it. There were a few items of his clothing in one of the dressers — socks and underwear, a couple of shirts, and a pair of jeans, all laundered and ready to wear.

The most interesting thing about the other dresser was the picture I found in the top drawer. It was a photograph, standard print size, of Mark Conroy and a young woman who looked to be in her twenties. They were both smiling — no trace of a sneer from him this time. She had a lot of red hair and looked sweet, if not exactly innocent. She seemed capable and intelligent, but not innocent. The picture wasn't exactly hidden, more like buried beneath a pile of feminine odds and ends — torn pantyhose, an old lipstick, a bent barrette, and a half-empty card of hairpins — exactly the kinds of things that would be left behind when packing in a hurry. The other drawers were all empty.

I tucked the picture into my pocket and went in to check the bathroom. Nothing surprising in the medicine cabinet — quite empty, really, except for aspirin, a packet of cold tablets, and a man's shaving paraphernalia. There was a pricey silk robe hanging on the back of the door. Conroy's, I was sure. A lot of empty hangers. None of Conroy's two-thousand-dollar suits were to be seen, just an old leather jacket that he might have worn on stakeout a dozen years ago.

But Mary Margaret Tucker was a student. Where did she do her studying? I hadn't seen anything like a desk or a work area in any of the rooms I'd been in so far. So I kept going farther back into the apartment and found what I was searching for in the kitchen.

It was the big, old-fashioned sort with a good-sized table right in the center. She had taken over half of the kitchen table. There was a coffee can full of pencils and ballpoint pens, a couple of new, legal-sized yellow tablets, and a beat-up copy of *Merriam-Webster's Collegiate Dictionary*. All quite neat and orderly, just waiting for her to sit down and get to work. But over to one side, behind the table, was something that caught my attention.

It was a big brown grocery bag overflowing with discarded wads of yellow paper from the tablets on the table. I plunged into it, not paying much attention to what was written in a small, neat hand on the crumpled sheets of paper. No, what I was looking for was something different, though I didn't know quite what it was. There were Xeroxed assignment sheets. These I looked at more carefully, noting the class and teacher, putting them aside. Finally, toward the bottom of the bag, I found exactly what I wanted.

It was her schedule of classes for the semester. She must have thrown it away when it became routine. I had to think for a moment about the day of the week. Then I checked my watch. Yes, Political Theory, Professor Novak. The class had just begun. I had a little less than an hour to get down there.

6

If Detroit had a subway, then Wayne State would be its subway college. Located only blocks away from downtown along the notorious Cass Corridor, it's one of those big-city universities with big-city policies and big-city problems. But you can get a good education there if you choose the right courses and get the right teachers. And if that sounds sort of lukewarm, maybe it's because I went to the University of Detroit. Jesuit. Back in the Dark Ages when I was a Catholic.

I hoped to find Mary Margaret Tucker there at Wayne State's Social Sciences Building, Room 117. That was where I was waiting, anyway, just outside the door of the classroom.

It seemed to me that Miss Tucker would be a lot less likely to give up her education than the apartment she had shared intermittently with Mark Conroy. She'd dropped out to work full-time at the police department. That was where the two of them had met. If she'd gone back, it was because she was determined to finish. And if she had her eye on law school, then she was *very* determined.

Conroy's pride would have kept him from searching her out here. But if she was on the prosecutor's list of witnesses for the preliminary examination, why hadn't he sent someone out to subpoena her in class? It seemed odd, inconsistent.

So here I was, picture in hand, trying to fix that face of hers in my mind so that when she emerged from the classroom, I'd recognize her immediately. I looked from the photograph to my wristwatch, which told me she'd have to be coming out soon.

Just then, down the hall, the door to another classroom opened, and students began pouring out, then another, and another one after that. I pocketed the picture and waited. Professor Novak must have had a few words to get in before the end of his class. But then, at last the door opened, and mostly young, serious-looking males, white and black, began to emerge from Political Theory.

I might have missed her entirely. There were, along with the men, three young women who came through the door. Miss Tucker was the second. But her red hair was so well hidden beneath a shapeless hat, and her eyes concealed behind big sunglasses, that I let her walk right on by me. She didn't even glance my way. I had to take a look at the third to be absolutely sure she'd already passed.

Perhaps that was just as well. I still had her in sight. I took off after her, telling myself that it would be better to talk to her outside. If there was to be confrontation — and maybe there would be — it would be better to have it without an audience.

We crossed Cass more or less together. I may have been about a step behind. Anyway, when we came to the slush and pool of water at the far curb, I muttered a courtly "Allow me," and gave her a lift at the elbow. She leaped the mess gracefully. I didn't do quite so well.

She stopped and turned to me with a curious smile on her face. "Thanks," she said. "You've been following me, haven't you?"

So much for Charley Sloan, private eye.

"Which one are you?" she asked. "Are you Timmerman?"

What did that mean? Who was Timmerman? I was tempted to play along and find out, and in my former, more adventurous legal life, I might have done just that. But these days, I played it strictly by the book.

"My name is Charles Sloan," I said. "I'm the attorney representing Mark Conroy. I was hoping we could talk."

The smile faded fast. "I don't think so," she said. "They said I shouldn't talk to you unless I had to."

"Who's 'they'?"

"If you don't know, then I shouldn't tell you."

"Look," I said, "how about a cup of coffee? Just one. That's how long we'll talk. Frankly, my client hasn't been very forthcoming. It's pretty hard to help him, knowing as little as I do."

A frown wrinkled her forehead just above her sunglasses. "No. I have to go to a class."

"No, you don't. You're through for the day."

"You seem to know a lot about me. How'd you know where to find me? And hey, how did you know what I looked like?"

"Well, in answer to your second question, I had this." I took the photograph out of my pocket and showed it to her. "And maybe it answers the first question, too."

"That's mine. Where did you get it? Did Mark have it?"

"No," I said, "he didn't have it. I found it under a pile of odds and ends in one of the dressers in that place on Parker."

"You were nosing around my apartment!"

"May I remind you, Miss Tucker, you moved out. It's no longer your apartment. It belongs to Conroy, along with the rest of the building. He gave me the key."

She reached for the photo. I moved it away, just out of her grasp. "It's still my picture."

"Like to trade it for a cup of coffee? A little information?"

"Keep it. I don't care." She broke away from me and started walking purposefully up the side street that led to Woodward.

I stuck the picture back in my pocket and caught up with her. "All right," I said, "look, you're going to your car, right?"

"Right."

"I'll just accompany you there. We can talk along the way."

"Go ahead." She shrugged. "Talk."

"You were on the list of witnesses at Conroy's preliminary examination, but you weren't called. In fact, you were the only one who wasn't. Were you subpoenaed?"

"I wasn't served."

"Do you know why?"

"I've got a fairly good idea, but I'm not about to tell you."

"Why not? Wouldn't *'they'* like it?"

"No, *they* wouldn't, and I'm playing it just the way they say." With that, she stopped, turned, and faced me. "This is as far as we go," she said, and pointed at an old gray, rusted VW Beetle that had been squeezed between a full-sized Ford and a Jeep.

"Is this your car?" I was disappointed. I thought I'd have at least five minutes with her.

"I'm afraid so."

"You're only half a block from school." The way I said it, it must have sounded like an accusation.

"Guess I just got lucky."

"But I've got some more questions." I didn't really. I was just trying to get her to loosen up and give me something, anything.

"Too bad. Maybe next time."

"Where can I reach you?"

"You found me once. I guess you can just look me up on the class schedule." She pulled off her sunglasses and gave me a fierce look with her blue eyes. "Aren't you ashamed?" she said. "Going through people's garbage?"

And you know, when she put it like that, I really felt just a little ashamed. She started past me to the car. Then I had a thought. I put out my hand and detained her.

"Tell me something," I said. "If I gave you this picture of you and Conroy, what would you do with it?"

She looked me straight in the eye. "What would I do with it? I'd destroy it."

I pulled out my cigar lighter and handed it to her. Then, gripping it tightly with my thumb and forefinger, I brought out the photo and held it between us.

"Go ahead," I said. "Burn it."

The look she gave me was more than skeptical. She seemed to be asking herself if I was sane. At last she asked, "Are you serious?"

"Go ahead."

With another dubious look, she struck the lighter, got a flame, and put it to the picture. The photo-print paper took a moment to catch. Once it had, it burned steadily. I looked around, suddenly aware that we'd attracted a little crowd of three — two boys and a girl. They watched, fascinated, not so much curious as enjoying the spectacle.

I felt the heat on my fingers, watched the

flame consume Mary Margaret and then begin eating away at Mark Conroy. It was getting harder to hold on. I shifted my grip, took it as long as I could, and with less than an inch patch left to burn, I let the photo drop to the sidewalk. My thumb and forefinger hurt like hell.

The little crowd applauded. "Way to go, man!" one of them shouted. Then, the show over, they drifted away.

"You're crazy," said Mary Margaret Tucker.

"No, I'm not."

"Well, have it your way. I'm getting out of here." She put the lighter back in my sore hand and pushed past me to the Volkswagen.

I followed her into the street, watched her fumble with her keys to unlock the car.

"What about the negative?"

"What about it?" She almost screamed it at me.

"Have you got it?"

"No!" She'd gotten the car door unlocked at last. She threw it open. I jumped out of the way. "He took that roll of film and burned it, said he didn't want pictures of us together. That was our first fight. But I had two prints of that picture — one for me he never knew about. That was the one we just burned."

She jumped into the car and slammed the door shut. I stepped back and watched her bang into the Ford behind her and narrowly

141

miss the Jeep ahead as she pulled out into the street and drove away. Before she left, though, I had my notebook out, and I wrote down her license plate number and the name Timmerman.

"Well," said Mrs. Fenton, "where've *you* been?"

I thumped in, worn out from the drive to Pickeral Point. The roads were now deep in water and slush. My car had been splattered and smeared by every eighteen-wheeler in southeastern Michigan. I was in no mood for Mrs. Fenton's unvoiced complaints.

"Working on a case," I said as I walked past her and headed for my office. "I take it there have been phone calls."

"Not many," she called after me. "Nothing I couldn't handle. There are a couple of please-call-backs on your desk."

I stopped, turned, and frowned at her. "Then why the third degree?"

"I only asked you where you'd been."

"Why should it matter?"

"Well, you were gone a long time, most of the afternoon. What if I'd had to reach you? What if there'd been an emergency?"

Through force of will, I fixed a benign and gentle smile on my face. "Mrs. Fenton," I said, "the places I was, you couldn't have reached me by telephone, or even by carrier pigeon. And besides, I have the utmost confidence in your ability to handle any and all problems that might arise."

That stopped her. She sat there, blinked once or twice, then at last said, "Well, thank you."

"You're more than welcome."

I went into my office and shut the door gently behind me. Maybe I'd discovered how to deal with her at last. A little flattery can go a long way.

One of the please-call-backs was from Jack Rivers. What would it be this time, the carrot or the stick? I wadded the note and threw it in the wastebasket.

The other one was from Ernie Barker. He hadn't received the bill yet. I wouldn't expect any difficulty from him on that count, anyway. He was probably still celebrating beating that gun charge. Who knows? Maybe he just wanted to thank me some more.

I picked up the phone and punched out the number on the note.

"Yah, hello, this is Ernie."

"Charley Sloan here. You called."

"Oh, hey, Mr. Sloan, thanks for calling me back. I, uh . . . well, there was something I been thinking about, I just wanted to ask your advice."

"Okay, shoot."

"You know, I hate to say it," he began, "but all the time I was carrying that .38 around in my glove compartment, I felt really safe. You know? I could go anyplace — down onto John R, or there around Gratiot — it didn't matter, just as long as I had that gun along."

I sighed. "I can understand that, I suppose. What's your point?"

"Well, Detroit's a pretty dangerous place. You said so yourself, right there in court. So I was just wondering, do you think maybe since they took that one I had away from me, I ought to get another one?"

"What?" He couldn't be serious.

"Oh, I'd do it all real legal this time." He was talking fast, trying to sound reassuring. "You know, I'd get a license and buy it at a regular gun shop, get a better one this time, maybe one of those big magnums that the cops all carry. Man, they'd scatter when they saw that!"

"Ernie, let me remind you of something. You've been put on probation for six months. Have you seen your probation officer yet?"

"Got a date next week. Next Tuesday."

"Talk it over with him then."

"With her. It's a her. Ms. Wodziak."

"All right, her. Talk it over with her."

"So that's your advice, huh?" He sounded disappointed, cheated.

"No, Ernie, my advice is a lot more simple: Don't even consider doing anything without talking it over with her first. She'll tell you the terms of your probation, and when she does, you pay attention and you do it just the way she says or you could still find yourself in the slam. I hope you understand that."

"Uh, yeah, I guess so."

"I predict your probation officer will tell you to forget about getting another gun ever again, legally or otherwise. If it's not in the terms of your probation, then it should be. Have I made myself clear?"

I realized then that I'd been practically shouting into the telephone. I took a deep breath to get myself under control.

"Uh, yeah. I mean, yes, Mr. Sloan."

"All right then." That came out in a fairly normal tone. I thought I was doing pretty well. "You'll be getting my bill in the mail tomorrow or the next day. If you keep thinking the way you have been, Ernie, then the next time I see you, you'll be up for manslaughter or murder. And I charge a lot more for them."

After I hung up, I sat brooding at my desk for a long minute or two, angry at Ernie Barker, angry at the city of Detroit and all its problems, angry at the kind of idiocy that said that guns and more guns offered an answer to them.

Without quite thinking about it, I swiveled my desk chair around and took a look out the window — at the river, the all-but-disappeared snow, and the fading afternoon light. That was when I remembered I'd promised to call Sue later in the day. I swung back to the telephone and punched out the number for her direct line at the police station.

Two rings, and then: "Gillis."

"Sloan."

"Oh, Charley, you did call back. Thanks. I was about to call you."

"Why? What's the matter?"

"Well, nothing really, except that it looks like it won't be easy for us to get together tonight. If that's what you had in mind."

"Something come in on the little girl last night?"

"Yes and no," she said. Sue sounded better than she had earlier. There was life in her voice again. "Yes, there might be something on the Quigley case. We went out there this afternoon and may have turned up, well, something."

"I'm glad to hear it."

"But no, that's not the problem. The thing is, there's a retirement party tonight — Dominic Benda, thirty-five years with the force. You know him, don't you?"

I thought about that for a moment. "Yeah," I said, "I guess we've had some contact." What came to mind was a burly guy, a joker, who once got in trouble on a false arrest suit. Not my case.

"I forgot about it completely," Sue continued. "And I really have to go. You know, being the senior female officer and all."

"Yeah, I understand. But listen, Sue, you shouldn't push yourself too hard. You didn't get much sleep last night."

"Oh, I know. I won't. But I've gotten kind of a second wind. I feel better. Really, I do."

"But watch it. Where's the party? Maybe I'll come over later on, if that's okay with you."

"Would you? That'd be great. Maybe you could get me out of there early."

"I could try."

"It's at the Glisten Inn. Do you know it?"

I laughed. "Sure," I said, "the go-go joint."

"Oh, Charley, come on!" She was embarrassed. "That's only on weekends."

"Okay, maybe I'll show up."

"Try. See you then."

I sat there, smiling, shaking my head. Wasn't it just like a bunch of cops to pick a moderately disreputable place like the Glisten Inn for a retirement party? I'd gotten the owner, Papa Klezek, out of trouble a couple of times. He probably thought he was buying insurance, hosting the cops for their big bash. Come to think of it, maybe he was. Old papa didn't just fall off the back of a turnip truck.

There was a knock at the door.

"Come on in, Mrs. Fenton."

Glancing needlessly at my watch, I saw that it was five on the button. She always left at the stroke of the hour. Unless I said otherwise — and I hadn't said so yet.

She came in bearing a sheaf of letters and documents she'd typed up that day on the computer. Handing them to me across the desk, she said, "Here are some things for you to look over and sign."

"Is the Barker bill in this bunch?"

"Yes?" Definitely an interrogative. She was curious.

"Let's hold that until tomorrow," I said. "I think I'm going to find about a thousand bucks' worth of extra time and expenses on that one. Don't worry, I'll justify it all."

"If that's all then, I'll be going." She always said that, just like she was really offering to stay. A little game we played.

"Have a good evening, Mrs. Fenton. Just leave my door open."

She was gone in the minute or so it took her to pull on her coat and struggle into her boots.

That left me alone to think for a while. There was something that had been playing at the back of my mind, a possibility I wanted to explore.

I pulled the notebook that I carried out of my pocket and paged through it until I came to what I had written down that very afternoon. There was the license number of Mary Margaret Tucker's Volkswagen, and below it that name I hadn't quite been able to remember. Timmerman.

Then, going through my Rolodex, I found a number, reached for the phone, and punched in the number. I waited as it rang.

Anthony Mercante had been, until recently, with the FBI right in the Detroit office. For years he had nursed a grudge against the Bureau. He was a good agent with a law degree and an exemplary record. But he was certain that he'd hit a glass ceiling because of his Italian name and because a distant relative he'd never met was connected in business dealings with someone who might be connected with the wiseguys. Back in my drinking days, I'd sat beside him at a bar and listened to him expound this theory. "Charley," he had told me, "that's all it takes. They can murder you with 'might's.'"

Eventually — and it was only a couple of months ago — Tony Mercante had found a solution to his problem, perhaps not the one he would have preferred but certainly an acceptable one. He'd resigned from the Bureau and taken a high-paying, grand-titled position in the security division of one of the Big Three automakers. It was about time I called Tony and asked him how he liked his new situation.

So when he answered the phone, that's how the conversation went for the first five minutes or so. He loved the new job, and he wondered why he had waited so long to leave the Bureau. He'd already moved his family out to a nice place in Birmingham to be nearer corporate headquarters, of course. Of course.

"But you, Charley," he said, "you seem to be doing pretty well yourself. You made a great comeback. I have to say I admire you for that."

149

"Thanks, Tony. I guess I found out a few things. About myself, mostly."

"I see in the papers you've got this Mark Conroy thing."

"Yeah, it's a tough one, too."

"For what it's worth, I always thought he was — is — a good cop. He may have cut some corners, but I think he's essentially honest. And he's committed to enforcement, too, which is more than you can say for his boss and fifty percent of the men in the department."

"It's good to hear you say that," I said. It was, too. A guy with Tony's years in the FBI's Detroit office had a special perspective on the local police. If he said Conroy was essentially a good cop, then you could take that to the bank. "There's something that's come up on that case I'd like to ask you about, Tony."

He hesitated. "Hey, Charley, you know I can't tell you anything about a case that is, or even might have been, under investigation."

"Absolutely. No, this is something that's probably public record, or the next thing to it. I just thought I might be able to find out from you a little quicker. It's a personal matter."

"Personal? Okay, try me."

"Is there anybody, any agent, working in the Bureau's Detroit office named Timmerman?"

Tony didn't take long to answer, just a moment or two. "No," he said with convincing certainty, "and there's nobody who's come in since I've left. I haven't been replaced. Government cutbacks, Charley. The Detroit office is in the process of downsizing."

"Well," I said with a sigh, "okay, just a thought. I appreciate it, Tony."

"But Charley," he said, "I don't know what has you thinking the Federal government might be involved in this Conroy thing. It *is* the Conroy thing, isn't it?"

"Yeah, it is."

"To my knowledge, not a chance of Bureau involvement. I've been out of the Detroit office almost two months, but I know the kind of operations that were in planning when I left, and there was absolutely nothing like this even contemplated. The Bureau's been out of the dirty-tricks business for years."

I'd evidently stepped on his pride as an *ex*–FBI man. "Sorry, Tony," I said, sounding contrite, "just a thought."

"And besides," he went on, "if, just if, something ever was planned in Detroit, Mark Conroy would be the last one anyone would think of targeting. I told you I thought he was a good cop. Well, I think I can safely say that opinion is shared by every Fed operating in and around southeastern Michigan."

"Okay, okay, I'm sorry I asked."

"You ought to look a little closer to home, Charley."

"How's that?" He'd taken me off guard. "What do you mean?"

"I mean there's a Timmerman on the Mayor's Squad. He's the number-two man, a sergeant, got an office right there in Manoogian Mansion, next to the mayor's kitchen."

There was a long pause at my end. I was wondering, among other things, why Tony hadn't told me this in the first place. He had his ways, I suppose. "What is it, exactly, that the Mayor's Squad does, anyway? I take it that they do more than guard the mayor in his mansion."

"It's a private police force answerable only to His Honor. There's the Detroit Police Department and the Mayor's Squad, separate entities. Ask your client. He'll tell you how things really work."

"I will, and thanks, Tony. Sometimes I have to be led by the hand."

"Sometimes we all do. And by the way, we're still getting settled in the new place, but we're planning an open house around Christmas, one of those all-day, stop-in things. I hope you can make it."

"Just let me know the date and the new address. I'll be there."

"Okay, I'll see you around Christmas."

"You bet."

Hanging up, I took a moment to reflect on Conroy's situation. It was evidently as bad as he'd said. Or worse. Someone, and it looked like it had to be the mayor, was doing everything possible to get him.

Just inside the Glisten Inn, I met a naked woman. At least I assumed she was naked behind that bundle of clothes she held tightly to her body. As she passed, there was no eye contact between us. She was probably on her way to the ladies' room to dress. Gentleman that I am, I didn't turn around to check.

This meant that the Strip-O-Gram, a predictable event in the evening, had come and gone. Off-duty cops showed no more class than a gang of construction workers. Kerry County's finest were no finer than any of the rest.

I paused at the entrance to the main room and surveyed the chaos. In the words of the immortal Fats Waller, the joint was jumpin'.

They were two-deep at the bar. Most of the crowd was male. There were a few policewomen and some female office help mixed. Off to the side, sitting at the tables, was a scattering of wives and good-sport girlfriends, talking among themselves, apparently wishing they were somewhere else.

With all this, the noise level was at a high screech. A jukebox blared. But the shouted conversation and idiot laughter was competing with the crashing sound of heavy metal. One way or another, it all seemed to blend together in a single, sustained roar.

Someone yelled my name nearby. I felt a

tug at my sleeve. It was the host himself, Papa Klezek.

"Hey, my lawyer man! You come, enjoy the party. That's good."

Klezek was almost eighty, not too tall but thick enough and obviously strong enough to give pause to any potential troublemaker. Up until three years ago, he had served as his own bouncer. That was when I got him off on an assault charge occasioned by a rowdy customer who kept grabbing at the girls one Saturday night. Since then, on my advice, he'd left the rough stuff to his fifty-year-old son.

"Quite a turnout," I said into his ear. "Not many cops on the road tonight."

"It's all right," he shouted. "They're good boys, they all have fun. You see the strip girl? No? Too bad. Nice, if you like skinny."

I thought back to the woman I'd met in the hall. "Skinny's okay."

"She sit on Benda's lap. Give him a kiss. Very funny." He gave me a pat on the arm. "You go. Have a drink on me. Just the first one, though. You tell my nephew behind the bar."

I laughed at that, gave him a wave, and plunged into the crowd. Pushing in at the end of the bar, I managed to attract the attention of one of the two bartenders as he whirled by and ordered a ginger ale. As he slammed it down in front of me, he said, "That's the first one of those tonight!" I held out a couple of singles. He shook his head. "Forget it. You're the designated driver for this whole mob. You can have all the ginger ale you want." I left a dollar on the bar.

No, they weren't drinking ginger ale, or Pepsi or Diet Coke or any of the usual substitutes. You could tell that just surveying the bar. One thing I've found out as a recovering alcoholic: You never feel quite so sober as when you find yourself in a roomful of drunks. Everybody else seems to be acting weird. They talk louder, laugh at things that aren't funny, and flail their arms in big, grand gestures. Was I like that once? Sometimes I was. When I was up, I'm sure I must have behaved just as they did — loud, laughing, and flailing. But when I was down, I was really down. It was those down days that drove me to AA.

I started up the bar, looking for Sue. Somewhere along the way, I felt a strong hand on my shoulder. It belonged to Bud Billings, a detective on the homicide squad. He looked bad, like me at my worst a few years ago. Somehow, in this milling crowd, he was all alone, perched on a stool and sipping at a whiskey. He seemed oblivious to everything around him. Except me.

"Charley." It sounded a little like a plea for help.

"Hello, Bud."

He pulled me close, so he wouldn't have to

shout. "I saw you there last night on Clarion Road."

There was no point in denying it. "Yeah, I drove Sue Gillis out. I was only there for a little while. Have you seen Sue here, by the way?"

Billings ignored my question. "What did you think of that — you know, the little girl?" Actually, he was pretty drunk and was slurring his words badly, but I understood him.

I hesitated, realizing I couldn't put him off. I had to tell him the truth. Leaning over, I said into his ear, "I threw up, I vomited, tossed my cookies."

"Good man, Charley. It's the only fucking thing you *can* do when you see something like that."

Was he waiting for a response from me? If so, I didn't have one.

But no. After collecting his thoughts, he went on. "I got a daughter, Caitlin. We live just outside Hub City, so she goes to school there, big yellow school bus, every day."

"Okay, Bud."

"Okay." Another pause. "She was in the same class as this Catherine Quigley, the one, you know, out there on Clarion Road. In plastic. Jesus! They were friends! *Jesus!*" There were tears in his eyes. "Caitlin and Catherine — same name, see? Basically, the same name."

"I understand, Bud."

"Anyway, the kids in the class, my daughter's class, hear that Catherine is absent today because she's dead. That's what the teacher tells them. What the fuck's wrong with that teacher? How coldhearted can she be? Can you beat that, Charley?"

Now there was something in my eyes, too. Suddenly I felt almost as bad as I had the night before with Bob Williams. All I could do was shake my head and tell him no, I couldn't beat that.

That must have been all Billings needed, because then he went on: "I don't think that's right, Charley. I don't think that's fucking right at all. You don't say that to seven-year-old kids and then tell them to open up their arithmetic books, which is what she did. She should've taken the whole morning to, I don't know, explain it to them."

"Well, maybe the teacher couldn't explain it. I can't explain it to myself."

"I know what you're saying, Charley, but it's a pretty rough way to treat those kids."

I nodded. "Right." And then I suggested that maybe it was time for him to go home.

"I ought to. I wasn't even going to come here tonight. Then I went out to the crime scene this afternoon, and it hit me again just as hard. I just wanted to go out and get smashed." He sighed. "Didn't help."

"It never does. Listen, you mind leaving your car here? I'm going to pick up Sue Gillis. We'll give you a ride home."

"Sue Gillis," he repeated.

"That's right."

"She's a great little detective. When we went back to Clarion Road, she found something."

Sue had mentioned that on the telephone. "What was it, Bud?"

"Footprints. In the mud before the snow covered everything. One good one right where the body was."

"Well, let's talk about it later. Stay here. I'll get Sue."

He thought it over a moment, then nodded.

I looked back at him once as I moved on. He sat like a crumpled tissue on the barstool, staring down blankly at the glass in his hand. He'd keep.

When at last I found Sue, I got a big surprise. She was as far gone as anyone else in the room. Talking loud and shouting, but not laughing. No, she was lecturing the guest of honor and a bunch of his fellow officers, really telling them off. I got that from her body language before I heard a word she spoke. Hands on hips, stamping her foot, shaking her finger.

By the time I got there, they were shouting her down, telling her to forget about it, she was way off base, this was all that feminist bullshit.

"It's not bullshit," she screamed at them. "It's insulting!"

"Aw, she wasn't insulted," said Dominic Benda. "She sat on my lap, didn't she? She gave me a kiss. I wasn't insulted."

"She got paid pretty good for that little number," one of his buddies said.

"You guys just don't get it, do you? What if they sent a male stripper instead? That'd be insulting to you, right?"

"A fag show for Dominic? Come on, Sue, you got the wrong boy for that."

One of them spotted me. "Get her out of here, Charley. She's ruining the party."

Sue turned toward me but had a little trouble focusing. "Oh, hi, Charley," she said at last. "I am not ruining the party. *You* guys ruined it when you brought that stripper in. Who's insulted? I'll tell you who's insulted, I'm insulted."

She was shaky on her feet. For no good reason she began to lean to the left. But she managed to catch herself before I could put out a hand to steady her.

"Sue," I said, "I think maybe we should go."

"Not before I get these guys to understand." She took a tentative step toward Benda. Again, equilibrium was a slight problem. "Listen, Dominic, your wife's here, right?"

"Sure," he said, "Peggy's sittin' at that table right over there. I could see her laughin'."

"I don't care if she was laughing, that woman —" And at that point Sue made a broad, theatrical gesture in the general direction of Mrs. Benda's table. It was a big mistake. Not only did she slosh what was left of her drink onto me and the floor, she also lost her balance completely. She threw out her arms and made circles with her hands like she was trying to fly. Yet she kept right on trying to talk. "Was. Insult." It was gibberish.

She threw me a wild, helpless look.

I was there to catch her when she passed out in my arms.

7

I haven't needed an alarm clock for years. Ever since I went off the sauce, all it takes is a few direct rays of the sun to get me stirring in the morning. And on cloudy days, of which we have our share here in southeastern Michigan, it doesn't even take the sun. I'm up and about, doing what needs to be done. Now, even on my worst mornings, I feel better than I did on the best ones during my drinking days. I guess you could call that sort of an unexpected side benefit.

Take that morning after Dominic Benda's retirement party. I woke up with the sun in my eyes, squinted at my watch, and saw that it was just a few minutes before seven. The sound of snoring from beside me in the bed reminded me that although it would probably come as a big surprise to her, Sue Gillis had spent the night with me.

It's a myth that women don't snore. As I eased out of bed and into my robe, she shifted her position, turning away from the light and, in the process, downgraded to heavy breathing. I went into the kitchen to begin preparations for Operation Wake-Up.

If ever I had reason for a bad morning, this

would have been it. As I set up the coffee maker, I reran the last hour or so of the evening in my mind. There had been a lot of driving. With the questionable help of Bud Billings, I had managed to get Sue out of the Glisten Inn, half dragging and half walking her to my car. Even when she collapsed across the backseat with all the grace of a hundred-pound sack of potatoes, she didn't regain consciousness.

I had given Bud a look then and told him to get into my car. He had started to make the kind of objections drunks usually do about being able to get home on his own, then broke off in midsentence. "Who'm I tryin' to kid?" he said sheepishly. "I'm in no condition." And with that, he had climbed onto the front seat beside me, shut the door behind him, and was asleep by the time we were five minutes out of the parking lot.

Since Bud Billings lived just outside Hub City, there was no way to get him home except to take the route I most wanted to avoid — Clarion Road, where Catherine Quigley's body had been found just the night before. Even though it had been dark for quite a while, the moon was out, still pretty full, and shining down upon the empty fields. There was no missing the crime scene. Yards of yellow tape marked it. Rather than slow down and look, I sped up, reached over and gave Bud a shake. "Wake up," I said. "We're getting close. I'll need some directions."

He gave them, and when we got there, he somehow made it into his house under his own power. On the drive back to Pickeral Point, I briefly considered putting Sue to bed in her own apartment but rejected the idea because she'd need a ride out to the Glisten Inn to pick up her car in the morning, anyway. So into my bed she went, and out of my bed she must now come. The coffee was ready. I'd mixed a batch of my old sure-cure hangover remedy — tomato juice, with Worcestershire sauce, a lot of Tabasco, and lemon juice — basically, if I'd remembered right, a very strong Virgin Mary. Preparations were complete. The big moment had arrived. I took a deep breath, headed for the bedroom, and bumped into her as I made the turn through the door.

"Oh, God," she moaned.

"Are you all right?"

It wasn't one of my smartest questions.

"I don't think so."

I took her arm and led her slowly back into the kitchen. I had to be careful because she refused to open her eyes. Positioning her at the table, I pushed down gently on her shoulders, and she sank into the waiting chair.

I poured a tumbler full of my concoction. "Here," I said, thumping it down in front of her. "Drink this."

She opened one eye and stared suspiciously

at the dark mixture. "What is it?"

"Just drink it. It's good for what ails you — Dr. Sloan's own remedy, proven in the past and certain to please. Take a deep, long drink of it."

Both eyes open now, she grasped the glass firmly, and did as I directed. She drank deep, all right, but had a little difficulty getting it down. She coughed, her gullet rebelling. At last she managed to swallow.

"Good Lord, Charley, what *is* that stuff?"

"It's my hangover cure. I hope I got the recipe right. It's been a few years since I brewed up a batch."

"Is that what this is? A hangover? I thought it was an abscess of my entire cranial cavity, requiring immediate amputation of the head."

"Ah yes, I recall that feeling. I remember it well."

"So smug," she sniffed. "Seriously, Charley, this is my first, really. You know how much I drink — or how little. I thought a hangover meant feeling slightly sluggish the next day. Not this. Do I have to drink your magic potion?"

"It'll help, I guarantee it. I'll get you a cup of coffee, too."

As I poured one for each of us, she sipped tentatively from the tumbler. I settled down across from her and waited. Somehow she'd managed to grope around and find my shirt by the side of the bed. She was, as my mother might have said, "decent," though unbuttoned. Although they fluttered shut from time to time, her eyes were now open. She seemed to like my coffee a lot better than my hangover potion.

"Why did I drink so much?" She asked it like she really wanted to know.

"Stress, exhaustion," I suggested, "exactly the reasons you shouldn't have been drinking at all. And I'll bet your fellow officers kept putting drinks in your hand."

She frowned, trying to remember. "You're right," she said. "They just sort of appeared by magic."

"A lot of men think it's great fun to get a woman drunk. They sure laughed hard when you passed out. I thought old Dominic Benda would fall off his barstool."

"Is that what I did? Pass out?"

"Right into my arms."

"Thank God you were there."

"Bud Billings helped me get you into my car. Then I took him home. He was in no shape to drive, either."

"All the way to Hub City?"

"There and back. You never let out a peep."

She seemed in better shape than she had only minutes before. Color had crept back into her cheeks. Her eyes held steady. All of which was good because in just a few minutes I'd have to drive her back to the Glisten Inn to

165

pick up her car. Thinking about that reminded me of something else.

"Bud Billings said you'd found something out there on Clarion Road. A footprint?"

"Bud talks too much." She was immediately professional, her guard up.

"Well, on the phone you said yourself you'd turned up something."

"Maybe I talk too much, too."

Cops — they always get tight-mouthed when something looks hot; at least the ambitious ones do, like Sue Gillis. Maybe they'd put someone inside that shoe. "It sounds to me like you're ready to make a move." I meant that as a way of congratulating her.

But that's not how she took it: "Charley, I refuse to talk about a case that's under investigation. There're a lot of people who think it's crazy for a cop and a lawyer to get together. I've been warned about it. If we're going to continue and, you know, move ahead, then we've just got to keep our professional lives separate. Can you understand that?"

I nodded, managed a smile, and said, "Suits me."

"Have you got any aspirin?"

"As I recall, Alka-Seltzer works better. I'll get you some. But you'd better get dressed, Sue. You don't want to be late. It wouldn't be professional."

On the drive back to her car, I pointed out that Lee Higgins and Catherine Quigley were the same age and must have been in the same class in school. Did they know each other? What else did they have in common? I suggested this might bear looking into. Although Sue didn't say anything, she must have heard. It was her silence that told me this case was getting to her.

I got to the office that morning with just enough time before Mrs. Fenton came in to have one of those call-me-from-a-pay-phone conversations with Mark Conroy. I dialed his home number to put the process in motion, and just as before, his wife answered. Without identifying myself, I asked to speak to her husband.

"Is this Sloan?" she asked. "Charles Sloan, his lawyer?"

There was no point in lying. There was no reason why she shouldn't know.

There was a pause of a minute or two, and then Conroy came on the line. "Mark Conroy here." It was his professional voice.

"You know who this is. Give me a call."

He sighed. "Okay. Same routine?"

"Same routine."

Without another word, he hung up. I replaced the receiver and got ready to wait.

Theoretically, the sort of small-town, full-service law office I run offers something known as estate planning. I write a lot of wills, and I'm supposed to know enough tax law to help people protect their bequests. No problem there. I subscribe to a service out of Skokie, Illinois, that keeps me up to date on that stuff — Federal and state. I read it as it comes through, then file it away for future reference in the looseleaf binders they provide. But estate planning also presumes my ability to give a certain amount of financial advice. Having blazed through three small fortunes in the course of three large divorces, I have reason to doubt my own competence in this area. I'm frank to my clients about my limitations and usually send them across town to Milt Hoffman, C.P.A., but you'd be surprised at the number of people who'd just as soon have me tell them what to do. I feel a certain responsibility toward them, and so lately I've been doing what I can to learn more. There are journals I take and a couple of basic texts recommended by Milt that I've read. I go through the *Wall Street Journal* every day. In other words, I try to keep up.

All of which will go to explain how, when I reached over and picked up the latest copy of *Financial Planning* to thumb its contents during the few minutes that it would take Mark Conroy to get to a pay phone, I wound up spending half an hour with it. I read an article on the current situation in municipal bonds — not good, it seems. I started another article, this one on the decline of the once-good-as-gold blue-chip stocks. About three quarters of the way through it, I heard the telephone on Mrs. Fenton's desk ring, and a moment later, I got her buzz on the intercom.

"It's the *assistant* chief," she said. "He didn't say, but I recognized his voice."

"Put him through, Mrs. Fenton."

There was a click as she made the switch. "This is Sloan," I said. Although I checked my watch as I spoke just to see how long he'd kept me waiting, there was no edge in my voice. Just good old matter-of-fact Charley.

"Mark Conroy. You . . ." He hesitated. "You wanted me to call. Is this going to take another trip out to Pickeral Point?"

"I don't really think so. I just wanted to give you a report on yesterday."

"What kind of a report?"

"On Mary Margaret Tucker."

"What about her?" He sounded suspicious, more than suspicious — almost hostile.

"I found her."

"Oh?"

"It didn't take much effort," I said. "I don't know where she's staying, but she's going to classes every day. Something tells me that you could have found her, or the prosecutor could have, or your friends. But since I'm talking to you, let me ask you, why didn't you look?"

"Maybe I didn't care. Maybe I figured it was her business if she wanted to go off and hide someplace."

"She might be able to do you some good."

"Or she might be able to hurt me."

"Well, either way, you or anyone else can reach her. I've got her schedule. All you have to do is wait outside the door until class lets out. That's what I did. If you want, I'll drop it in the mail."

"Keep it," he said. "Hold on to it. Maybe sometime down the line . . ."

"I got something from her," I said.

"What do you mean? You got what?"

"A name. She mistook me for somebody else."

There was a long pause at the other end of the phone. "All right," said Conroy, "what's the name?"

"Timmerman," I said. "Mean anything to you?"

If that last pause seemed long, this one was endless. I got the feeling that I'd given him the verbal equivalent of a deep right into the midsection. I waited him out. "Maybe it does," he said at last. "I know somebody by that name. I'll have to consider the possibility of a relationship of some kind between them."

"Do that," I said. "And let me know what you come up with."

I meant that to wind things up, but Mark Conroy had something more in mind. "I've got a question for *you*," he said.

"What's that?"

"Earlier, when you called, my wife answered."

"That's right."

"She knew it was you. What did you two talk about?"

"Nothing. I just asked for you, and eventually you came on the line."

"You haven't had any conversations with her when I wasn't around?"

"None whatsoever. What's this all about, Conroy?"

Again he was silent for what seemed like a long time but was probably only about half a minute. He seemed to be making up his mind about something. Was he rational? Most men, under the same strain, would have shown signs of unsteadiness by this time. How long could he maintain this facade of cold composure indefinitely?

"She and I had a discussion just after you called about plea bargaining. She argued strongly for it, and I wondered if she'd gotten some encouragement in that direction from you. I made it clear to her and I'll make it clear to you, Sloan, that any sort of plea bargain is out, repeat *out!* I'm not copping a plea for something I didn't do. Get it?"

"Okay, all right, but I want it understood, too, that I haven't had any discussions with your wife, and I haven't encouraged her to talk about plea bargaining or anything else with you. Is that understood?"

171

"I guess so," he said sullenly.

As I hung up, I couldn't help wondering what, exactly, Mark Conroy could possibly be thinking.

All the way to Hub City I debated whether I was doing the right thing. I was sure about the pretext of my visit. Since I'd known the Higgins family and done work for them, it seemed no more than proper that I offer to help out now. From the way Sue had described their state, it seemed likely that they were too stunned by their son's murder to even consider the legal and financial aspects surrounding it. My only fear was that I might be intruding. But when I called ahead, Frank Higgins assured me I'd be welcome.

What worried me a little and played at my conscience was that once I got there, I meant to ask Frank and Betty a few questions. Nothing harsh or hostile, nothing they could object to. They were just the questions I'd tried to interest Sue Gillis in earlier that same morning. It seemed significant to me that Lee Higgins and Catherine Quigley were about the same age, that they might have been in the same class in school, that they might have known each other. Why Sue had been indifferent to all this I couldn't say, though it was probably because of that footprint she'd found at the crime scene.

They were good, reasonable questions, but

I had no real need to know the answers. I am a firm believer in leaving the police work to the police and the detecting to the detectives. Lawyers must often, by necessity, deal with the facts of a crime but not until they're invited in. I hadn't been invited, but it was more than curiosity that drove me on. It was that awful image of the child in the snow. Wrapped head to foot in plastic, like a life-sized doll or an undersized mannequin left by the side of the road. The Higgins boy must have looked just like that, too.

The house Frank and Betty Higgins had bought two years ago was on a street of large houses. I pulled up at the right address and as I got out of my car, it occurred to me I'd never been inside the place before, or even seen it. The closing had been held in my office in Pickeral Point. It was an odd-shaped barn of a place, a two-story frame house in the grand old style. As I climbed the steps to the porch, the front door opened, and Frank stood there in the entrance. It was the face I had put together with the voice on the phone. But the life had been squeezed right out of it. He offered his hand, and I shook it. Hard and rough, it was a carpenter's hand.

"It was good of you to come, Mr. Sloan." His voice was hollow.

"Charley," I said. "Please call me Charley. This is no time for formality."

"Come on in."

He turned away, leaving me to shut the door, and led the way into an old-fashioned parlor just off the hall. He gestured to a chair and sat on a two-cushioned sofa nearby.

"Frank," I began, "as I said on the telephone, I'm sure there's paperwork of one kind and another connected with your son's death. If you'd like me to handle it for you — pro bono, at no cost — I will. I suppose there's an insurance policy?"

"Not on Lee, just on me."

"But your dependent children are probably covered for modest benefits, too. In most life policies they are. Do you have it on hand?"

"Betty's looking for it now. To tell you the truth, we hadn't given any thought to it at all. It's all been just too much."

"I'm sure it has. It's a terrible thing, Frank, the worst trouble people can have."

I listened to the words I'd just said to Frank and realized how insignificant they sounded. My God, what could be worse than the death of a child? Parents were not supposed to bury their children. It was against the natural order of things.

I remembered my friends Larry and Laura Rayburn and how they almost went crazy after their twelve-year-old daughter was killed by a drunk driver. Who could blame them? And now here were poor Frank and Betty Higgins confronting not only the death of their little boy Lee but also having to confront the perverse and inexplicable manner in which he was murdered.

"Yeah," he said bleakly, as though he had run out of words. "There's some other stuff, a form that the cops wanted us to fill out. I don't know, Betty may find —" He broke off. "Can I ask you a question? Why're you doing this?"

"It beats a sympathy card."

"It sure does. I'll never tell another lawyer joke as long as I live."

Just then there were steps on the stairs, and a moment later Betty Higgins entered the room. Her eyes were vacant and in her hand were two or three envelopes. I rose to meet her. Frank straightened up and made room for her on the couch. She preferred to stand, obviously in a state of shock.

"Now this," she said, dispensing with any sort of greeting or small talk, "is the insurance policy on Frank. It didn't occur to me to look for anything on the kids in it. You don't expect . . ."

"Of course not. I understand."

She looked at me severely as she handed it over. "Well, I should have thought to check. This funeral is setting us back some. God knows we can use anything we're entitled to."

"I'm sure you can."

Determined to soldier on, she offered me another envelope. "This one is the Victim Report that the county police asked for. They

175

just want details on Lee, I suppose. I don't know why. It's not like he was a missing person or a runaway. Now this one, I don't know what it is, but it looks official, and, well, that's it. That's all we have to give you, I guess." It was as though she couldn't stop herself from rattling on.

That last envelope was from the attorney general's Office of the State of Michigan; I noted that it hadn't been opened. Maybe they kept Victim Reports, too. What good does it do, all this paperwork? They had to get their statistics someplace, I supposed.

Betty Higgins looked like she wanted me out of there. I didn't blame her for that. But still, I hoped to ask those questions. Maybe I could ease them into it.

"I wonder if I could have some basic information on Lee," I said. "It might save a phone call later on."

Frank patted the seat next to him on the sofa, and his wife marched over and sat down, rigidly erect, her hands clasped tightly on her knees.

"What was Lee's full name?"

"Lee Thomas Higgins."

"Thomas was my father's name," Frank volunteered.

"Date of birth?"

He was seven years and two months old.

I took them through all the routine details — place of birth, height, weight, number of

176

siblings, and so on — and I wrote it all down in my pocket notebook in a businesslike way, a question following each answer, taking it as far as I could. Then I looked up at them, frowning, and asked, "Lee was just seven?"

"Just seven," said Betty. Frank nodded.

"The little girl who was murdered, Catherine Quigley, she was just seven, too. They must have been in the same grade in school. Did he ever mention her? Were they friends?"

Mother and father looked at each other, both puzzled. Then they shook their heads in unison.

"Did they have the same teacher?"

"I don't know," said Betty, "you'd have to check. Lee's teacher was Miss Dieberman. He liked her."

"But he never mentioned Catherine Quigley?"

"No."

"And you don't know the family?"

"Nope," Frank answered. "They live clear on the other side of town. And they've only been here about a year."

"Have you been in touch with them?"

"Not at all. We figure they've got enough on their hands just holding it together without listening to us."

"Is all this important?" Betty Higgins had that same severe expression on her face again. It was time to go. I flipped the notebook shut, pocketed it, and stood up.

"I guess not," I said. "It's just that it seems to me there has to be some logical connection between the two."

"What's logical about killing seven-year-old kids?" she asked as she rose from the couch; he followed. We headed for the door.

"Of course you're right. I guess I'm just searching for something."

"Well, thanks for the trouble. We really appreciate it, don't we, Betty?"

His wife nodded her head. She was like a robot operating on automatic pilot. He swung the door wide, and I stepped out onto the porch.

"There may be a letter for you to sign, another visit. Anyway, I'll call you first."

"Anytime. Except tomorrow morning, of course. The funeral's tomorrow morning."

I headed down the steps for my car, hearing the door close after me. I wanted to ask if they would find out from Lee's three brothers and his sister if he'd ever mentioned Catherine Quigley, but that would have been pushing it. I had the feeling I'd worn out my welcome at the Higginses' house. They'd already been asked too many questions, probably, and mine made little sense to them. After all, what difference did it make whether Lee knew Catherine? Or if the boy's parents had met the girl's? Hub City was a small town, smaller than Pickeral Point. Circles of acquaintance overlapped, but that didn't necessarily mean that everyone knew everyone else.

I jumped into my car and drove away, almost regretting the questions I'd put to them, yet still convinced that there was some link connecting the two killings. There was the school, of course, and very likely Lee and Catherine were classmates. Maybe Sue Gillis had talked with the teacher, or could be persuaded to. Perhaps this Miss Dieberman would have some ideas on all this. I wondered if she was the teacher whose insensitive and inappropriate announcement of Catherine Quigley's death had angered Bud Billings so. Was she as unfeeling as all that? I'd like to meet her myself.

On my way out of town, I caught sight of the spire of Our Lady of Sorrows Catholic Church not far ahead. Father Chuck's church. Just on an impulse I turned down the little side street that led to the rectory where we'd met and talked not much over a week ago. He probably knew this town about as well as anyone. It seemed to me he might have some ideas about this link I was trying to establish. At least it would help to discuss the murders with someone else in town, especially someone as intuitive and smart as he was. I pulled up at the rectory, got out of the car, and stood for a moment, listening to the sound of a flock of geese honking their way south. I rang the bell and waited. There was some sort of activity inside, noise of a distinctive kind, the whine of a vacuum cleaner. So I rang the bell again, harder and longer this time, and ended with a final flourish of dots and dashes that would surely have penetrated any wall of noise Hoover or Electro-Lux could have thrown up.

That did it. The whine ceased. There was a flurry of steps in the hall on the other side of the door. But when the door opened, it was not Ernest Hemingway's smiling face I beheld but rather a sour one much more like Margaret Hamilton's. The cleaning woman, of course.

"What do you want?" she asked in a voice filled with suspicion and grit.

"I was looking for Father Chuck. Is he around?"

"*Around?* He hasn't been around all week. He's at some retreat way up around the Sault someplace."

I'd forgotten about that, of course. He had told me he would be away on that retreat with the Dominicans all this week. But what about Lee Higgins' funeral?

"He'll be back tonight?"

"Late tonight. It's a long drive."

"But he's saying the funeral Mass for Lee Higgins tomorrow, isn't he? He knows about that?"

"He knows because I told him. Everyone was runnin' around, sayin', 'Oh, where's Father Chuck? We just got to get in touch with him so he can say Mass for that poor little boy.' Turned out I was the only one in the whole darned town knew where he was and how to get hold of him. He never goes anyplace but he leaves a number with me."

"Well, you sort of saved the day, didn't you?" I said, pandering to her silly self-congratulation. I couldn't get out of there fast enough.

I felt like I'd wasted the morning when I got back to the office. There was sturdy Mrs. Fenton behind her desk, back from lunch and looking disapprovingly at me as she always seemed to do. Yet subtly she shifted her eyes to the right, putting me on notice that the couch that served as my only piece of waiting room furniture was now occupied.

I turned and looked, and there were two people, middle-aged and not very distinguished looking. The man wore a suit, old but well preserved, and a shirt that was buttoned up to the top yet without a tie. The woman had on a Jackie Kennedy–style dress from the early Sixties, probably an antique of its kind. She held a purse tight in her lap, twisting its strap with such nervous energy that it looked for all the world as if she meant to break it off.

The two of them looked familiar. It seemed to me that I had met them recently, but where it was I couldn't quite say.

"Mr. and Mrs. Evans have been waiting to see you for a while," said Mrs. Fenton. "Nearly an hour."

And then it hit me who they were. They were the parents of the kid who had falsely accused Father Chuck of molesting him out in Hub City.

I was a little ashamed of the way I'd treated them, even though I got the result I'd aimed for. I was afraid this might be awkward. "Please come into my office," I said. They followed me inside. I left the door open and settled down behind the desk. "What can I do for you?" I asked.

Mrs. Evans leaned forward tensely in her chair. "It's our son. He's been arrested."

"No!" said her husband emphatically. "No, he hasn't, Marge. They just took him in for questioning. Now, there's a big difference there, ain't that so, sir?"

"Yes, there is," I said, "a world of difference. What was the matter they wanted to talk to him about?"

"Aw, it was those kids gettin' killed around the county," he said. "He don't know nothin' about that. It's just the last one was found out on Clarion, not too far from our place. And that woman cop, she's got it in for him because of that other business with that Catholic priest. That's all over. That got settled. I don't know why she won't leave him alone."

Just what I was afraid of. Sam Evans was Sue's big break in the case. The kid needed a lawyer, all right, and needed one right away. But if I were to take this on, it could do serious damage to our relationship. That much seemed pretty sure.

"When did they take him in?" I asked.

"What time was it they actually left, Marge?"

"I don't know, around eleven, I guess it was. They showed up earlier with this search warrant they waved under my nose. Poor Sam was out in the garage working on the snowblower, trying to fix it. She got him alone in there and started talking to him. The other cop, the one who had the search warrant, he started digging around the house. He just didn't have any respect at all! Me, I got on the phone to get Delbert here home to deal with this."

"I'm kind of a handyman," he put in. "I do little jobs for folks all over the county. Ain't too many want to do fix-it work anymore. We get by."

"So they took your son in about eleven?" I looked at my watch. It was almost two. There was no telling what the kid had said in three hours of intensive interrogation. He was suggestible and wasn't the brightest bulb I'd ever met. "And what did they remove from the house?"

"Wasn't much," said Mrs. Evans. "Just a pair of Sam's old shoes and some magazines. You know, the dirty kind. I didn't know he had them."

"Yessir, Mr. Sloan, we know he's entitled to a lawyer, and we'd like you to go over there, and kinda look after his interest. We know you're the best lawyer in the county, we've read about you, and then there was that visit you paid us that time — you were real tough. If you'd be just as tough to the cops, that'd suit us just fine."

I sighed. This wasn't going to be easy. "Look, Mr. and Mrs. Evans, you're right. Your son does need an attorney immediately. For reasons I'd rather not go into, I'm a little too close to the case to take it on. I recommend you go right over to John Dibble, across from the courthouse, and get him on it."

"What's the matter," said Mr. Evans, his indignation rising. "Our money ain't good enough?"

"It's not that at all."

"We can pay," said his wife, and then she started to cry.

"Look," I said, "I've got a potential conflict of interest here. I just don't think I'm the one to help. If you want to, I'll put in a call to Dibble, let you talk to him from here. He's a good lawyer. I've seen him work. But I think it's absolutely essential to get somebody over there right away to make sure your son's rights are being respected. You do understand what I mean, don't you?"

"What I understand is a lawyer like you is in with the cops and the Catholic Church and all the rich people. You're real cozy with 'em all, and you don't want to mess things up."

"Mr. Evans, you couldn't be more wrong."

He looked me straight in the eye, clenched his jaw, and had just two words for me. "Prove it," he said.

8

Even though they may have been used to seeing me around at Kerry County Police Headquarters, there was nevertheless a general murmur that ran through the front office when I announced that I was Samuel Evans's attorney, and that I wished to see my client.

"Who would that be again, Charley?" the desk sergeant asked as he shuffled through the forms on his desk. "Got no booking papers for him here."

"As far as I know, he hasn't been booked," I said. "Sue Gillis and another officer brought him in for questioning, probably around eleven-thirty today."

"Oh, well, questioning, I don't know." He shook his head, as if to indicate that this was completely beyond his range of responsibility. He was trying to play dumb, which for him was pretty easy.

"Tony," I said — his name was Tony Makarides, and his brother was the Benny of Benny's Diner — "you look in your logbook for today around eleven-thirty, maybe a little earlier, and I'm sure you'll find the right entry. Evans? Gillis? And just where I might be likely to find my client."

186

"Yeah, here it is. Interrogation Room Three. Would you like to take a seat, and I'll send in your request?"

"If I didn't know you better, Tony, I'd swear you were stalling."

"It's a big case, Charley. They like to have as much time as they can with the guy without a lawyer around."

"They've had plenty," I said, "almost three hours already."

"Sue's really gonna be surprised, Charley. I thought you and she were . . ."

"I'll handle that. Just get me back there, Tony. I'm in a hurry."

I meant that to sound a bit threatening. I had raised my voice a little, and so Tony waved over one of the civilian office girls and instructed her to take me to Interrogation Room Three and stay with me until I'd made contact with the officers inside. She may not have been terrifically bright herself, but she knew enough to do that. And she managed that long walk down the hall to our destination without once mentioning Sue Gillis to me. So maybe she was smarter than Tony, or at least more tactful.

Behind the door I could hear a voice raised, female. The words were garbled, but the tone was unmistakable — tough, stern, hectoring. There really was a cop voice, wasn't there? I just never before heard it in soprano. I knocked hard on the door and waited.

The door was thrown wide, and Sue stood there, looking angry and clearly annoyed at the interruption.

The expression on her face went from annoyance to confusion, then back to annoyance. "Charley," she said sharply, "what are you doing here?"

Careful to remove any trace of a smile from my face, I solemnly repeated the formula to her: "Officer Gillis, I have been engaged as Samuel Evans's attorney, and I wish to see my client." Then I added, "Alone."

"You . . . why . . . what?" She was speechless.

Then I heard a familiar voice behind her. "Let him in, Sue." It was Stash Olesky, the assistant prosecutor I had talked to out on Clarion Road the night before last.

She stepped back, exposing a room I'd been in a few times before. Interrogation Room Three was not much different from One or Two. But it was a little bigger than the others, accommodating a good-sized table and four chairs. The chief addition, however, was a large mirror set into one wall, which of course provided a view from a small closet-sized room on the other side of all that happened inside Interrogation Room Three. It would also be wired for sound, so that anything that was said would be piped into the little closet.

At the head of the table sat Sam Evans, the guest of honor. The kid seemed to be in pretty poor shape. His head hung low. As I walked inside the room and saw his face, it looked to me like he'd been crying. I doubted that he'd been mistreated physically, but three hours of intensive questioning, three hours of sustained antagonism, would be enough to penetrate any defenses most of us might put up. For a kid like Sam Evans, who would never make it as a rocket scientist, and whose recent history indicated some deep-seated personal problems, an ordeal such as the one he'd just endured could have a crushing effect. Looking at Sam, I wondered if I'd be able to get through to him when we sat down to talk.

In another chair, pulled back from the table, sat Stash. Our eyes met. What I read in them was something close to embarrassment, which seemed a little strange. I'd like to get him aside out in the hall to confer about this, lawyer to lawyer.

Finally, leaning against the wall, looking tired and hung over, was Bud Billings. His jacket was off, his tie was down, and his collar was open. He looked like he was ready to quit, even if Sue wasn't.

She certainly wasn't. The initial shock of finding me at the door in my official capacity was now gone. She may have looked disheveled and exhausted, but she pulled me over to one side and whispered, "Charley, you've got to give me more time with him. I've got him right to the point where he's about to break.

Can't you just go away and come back in an hour?"

"Then there's been no confession?"

"Not yet, but he's already changed his story once."

"Sue, you've had him three hours. It would be unethical for me to do what you're asking. He needs counsel. Don't blow your case by infringing his rights."

"He's right, Sue," said Olesky. "Let's get out of here and leave the two of them alone." He was already on his feet, heading for the door.

"Not in here, Stash, if it's all the same to you," I said, pointing at the big mirror on the wall. "Any private office will do for us."

He nodded his assent. Sue looked from him to me, suspicion and betrayal in her eyes.

"What're you going to do, tell him to plead the Fifth?"

"I always advise my clients to tell the truth."

If looks could kill, I'd be a dead man. She turned on her heel and clicked sharply out of the room. Bud Billings left, shaking his head. Stash paused, frowning. "I think Sue's gotten awfully close to this, maybe too close. It's put us all through the ringer. You, too, Charley, if I remember right."

"Me, too," I agreed.

"Well, you can use that office across the hall. Nobody'll be around there for a while."

"We'll only need about ten minutes."

"That's okay. We can all use a break." He nodded back at Sam Evans. "Your boy's in pretty bad shape."

I waited until Stash had cleared the door and turned down the hall, then I turned back to the sorry figure seated at the table and said, "Okay, Sam, let's take a trip across the hall."

All I got in response was a sniffle or two, but he heaved himself up out of the chair and started for the door. Mission accomplished. His eyes appeared to be open but only as narrow slits. I wondered if he might not be exaggerating his condition a little for my benefit. Playing along, I took him under the elbow and led him across the hall to the office we had been promised. Glad to find the door unlocked, I put him inside and let him find his way to a chair. He collapsed in it, perhaps a bit too dramatically.

I took a chair opposite him, pulled it close, but before speaking, I looked him over and tried to get some sense of just who I would be talking to. He was an ordinary sort of kid, skinny, badly in need of a haircut. He had a face inherited from his father — a prominent nose and a receding chin — the kind that might be called rat faced and probably was by the kids he grew up with. In any case, he seemed younger than his age. At nineteen, he was an adult in the eyes of the law, yet to me he seemed to be a child, probably because he was slow. Could he have murdered Catherine Quigley? I really had no idea. He hadn't shown me his eyes yet. Could he have laundered her clothes, dressed her up, and wrapped her in transparent plastic like a little doll to be found at the side of the road? Anything was possible. I looked at his hands. Although they were thin, and his fingers were long and slender, there was no grace or control in them. They seemed to coil and twitch as he began folding and unfolding his fingers nervously in his lap. Not a good sign. He was far too twitchy, his hands reflecting his instability.

"What have you told them?" I asked him.

"Not much." His voice was thin and cracked, like a twelve- or thirteen-year-old kid. "That's 'cause there ain't much to tell."

"You'd better let me be the judge of that."

He was still sniffling. I pulled out my handkerchief and handed it to him. He blew hard then and opened his eyes wide for the first time. He wiped them and blinked a couple of times. He may have gotten his features from his father, but his eyes were his mother's — a light blue, liquid, almost milky, the kind to which tears come easily. They seemed to be the eyes of a victim, rather than a victimizer, but maybe that was too hasty, a bit too easy.

"The first thing I told them," he began, "I said I wasn't even out there at all. I didn't know nothin' about it."

"But that wasn't the truth, was it?"

"Naw, but that's what I kept tellin' them because I didn't want to talk about what I seen out there. But they were real tough with me, especially that woman. She was real mean, said they had someone saw me out there on Clarion, had my footprint out there in the mud near where . . . well, you know."

"You didn't want to talk about that?"

"Nope."

"Why not?"

"Too weird, man. Give you bad dreams."

"Yes," I said, "it might. I was out there. I know what you mean."

"You get bad dreams from it?"

"Not yet. But dreams are funny. They sneak up on you."

"They sure do!" He said it so emphatically that it made me wonder what he had locked up in his unconscious. And given what a creep his father was, I also thought about what kind of repressed rage this Sam Evans was carrying around.

"But eventually you admitted that you had been out there on Clarion Road, and you told them what you'd seen. Is that correct?"

"Yeah, I told them."

"Tell me now."

And he did. In a halting way, prompted from time to time by questions from me, Sam Evans told his story. He said he had been out on Clarion Road coming back from a cleanup job for Mrs. Belder, a widow, who lives alone in a farmhouse about ten miles outside Hub City. It was a chicken coop he'd knocked down to haul away in the old Datsun pickup truck that his father let him use for such odd jobs. His father drove the family's big Ford pickup. It was pretty old, too, but in much better shape than the Datsun. The Datsun was badly in need of a clutch and had been giving them trouble for a long time. Finally, with the heavy load Sam was hauling away from Mrs. Belder's place, the little pickup broke down completely. He had managed to get it over to the side of the road, but that was as far as it would go. He was five miles from home, it was well after dark, and snow had begun to fall, but he had no choice but to go the rest of the way on foot.

As Sam had tramped along the road, he had noticed that traffic was thick and mostly in his direction. He'd stuck out his thumb a couple of times when cars passed going his way, but none had stopped. So when one coming from the direction of Hub City did a U-turn and stopped by the side of the road about a quarter-mile ahead, Sam thought that if he hurried, he might be able to catch the driver and talk him or her into giving him a ride home. He began to jog along, but as he got closer and saw the driver get out of the car, go to the rear, and open up the trunk, something persuaded him to slow down, proceed quietly, and try not to be noticed. He ducked down into the ditch that ran beside the road.

Quite some distance separated him from the car and its driver when Sam came to a complete halt and decided that this was close enough. He squatted down and stared. The darkness and the light snow made it difficult to see, but he thought he saw the driver pull something, a big package was what it looked like, out of the trunk. Whatever it was, it was difficult to carry, yet the driver managed it. Got it across the ditch, and just into the field next to the road. Then the driver hurried back to the car and tore off in the direction of Hub City.

Sam thought he had the place fairly well spotted, and when he set off to find it, he discovered it easily because of the fresh tire tracks in the new-fallen snow. There were footprints, too. He followed them down one side of the ditch and up the other, and there he found the plastic-wrapped package. He couldn't tell exactly what it was at first, because some snow had gathered over it, but it looked like a big doll, which struck him as a funny thing to leave beside the road. But when he wiped the snow off with his gloved hand, he saw the face of a little girl, unmistakably real and unmistakably dead.

"What did you do then?" I asked him.

"I ran! I ran real hard. Only thing was, when I scrambled out of the ditch, a car come along right behind me and saw me take off running.

He pulled over then, and I guess he wanted to see what I was running from. So at first I just kept on running, but then it come to me that he'd prob'ly think I put that there. He could come after me and catch me real easy in his car, and so I went off the road and just took off across the field. Nobody saw me there, I guess, but I like almost froze my feet because the snow was getting lots thicker then and I was just in my sneakers and they got real wet."

"Did you tell your parents what happened, what you'd seen?"

"You think I'm crazy? I was in enough trouble the way it was."

"Why?" I asked. "Why were you in trouble?"

"Well, I was real late home, and I had to tell Pa I left the pickup out there on Clarion Road because of the clutch. I thought he'd give me a whack because of that, but he didn't. He knew the clutch was gonna go, I guess, so I didn't get no whack. We went out, the two of us, in the Ford, hooked up the Datsun, and towed it back. There was cops all over the place by that time. They wasn't gonna let us through on the way back, but I guess Pa talked our way outta there. I don't know what he said because I was in back in the Datsun. But while we was waitin', I got a look at everybody crawling around where I'd been. I just wanted to get away from there. I was afraid they'd pull me out and start askin' me questions."

"Is this the story you told them in that room across the hall?"

"That's what I been tellin' them over and over," he said. "Only they say I'm lyin' because it ain't what I said at first."

"But you're not lying now? This is the truth?"

"It's the truth. Yeah." He said nothing more for a moment, then he looked at me questioningly. "You believe me, huh?"

I considered his question for a minute, trying to sort out any reservations I had. This guy had a big-time history of lying. Not only had he unjustly accused poor Father Chuck, he'd made other allegations about sexual abuse that turned out to be outright lies, purporting that people everywhere were trying to "grab his thing." Jesus, according to him, you'd think that his "thing" was about as sought after as the Holy Grail.

True, that ghastly, greedy father of his had probably trained him well in the ways of extortion, if either of them could even understand what the word meant, so maybe money was what was behind all those false accusations. This slow, goofy Sam Evans didn't seem like the most stable dude to come down the pike. It would be interesting to know his psychiatric history. Was he capable of committing this bizarre and heinous crime? And what, except madness, would be his motive?

I decided I really didn't know if he was

telling the truth. But as a lawyer, I knew one thing for sure: Sam Evans had been brought in for questioning as a witness. He hadn't been charged, and yet here he was being treated by everyone like a suspect. Even if I did have any reservations about whether or not he was telling the truth, I had too much respect for the law not to kick some ass around here and tell Sue and Olesky and Bud Billings that I wasn't going to let them continue on with their little game.

"We'll talk about that later, but I do have a question. Did you or your father ever do any work for the Higginses or the Quigleys?"

He looked at me blankly. "Who're they?" He really didn't seem to know.

"Never mind."

"Are you some kind of special cop or something? You're real different from the other ones."

At first I didn't understand his question. Then I wondered if he would understand my answer: "I'm your lawyer. I'm on your side. Your father hired me to represent your interests."

"Can you get me outta here?"

"I can sure try."

I took Sam Evans across the hall back to Interrogation Room Three. I glanced at my watch as we went back inside and saw that we had gone over by about five minutes. Our little conference had lasted fifteen minutes, no more, no less. Stash and Bud Billings were there waiting. I looked from one to the other, then pointed down the hall to where Sue had disappeared. Stash shrugged. I put Sam Evans in a chair and pulled one over so that I would be seated beside him. I gave him a pat on the shoulder and took my place. Nothing was said. We simply waited.

A couple of minutes later, we heard the steady click-click-click of her heels on the tile floor. When she made her appearance, it was obvious she had freshened up a bit, hair combed, makeup applied. She would have looked just fine, except that her full lips were set in a tight line. She went over to the wall, leaned against it, and folded her arms.

Billings sat down on a chair across the table from us. "Now, Mr. Evans," he said, "I'd like you to go through your story again. Give us all the details you can. Details are important. If you leave anything out, I'll be there to help you with a question or two. Go ahead." Typical good-cop approach — low-key, business-like, professional.

Sam looked at me. I nodded and gave him another pat on the shoulder. He began talking and covered exactly the same ground he had with me. Actually, this recital was an improvement over the one he had given just minutes before. The questions I'd asked him along the way seemed to have helped him put it all together. His telling was as detailed and orderly as anyone could expect from a kid with his obvious mental deficiencies. In the course of it, Billings questioned him on only three or four points.

One exchange gave Sam pause. He had come to the point in his story at which the driver had dropped off the mysterious package in the field, gotten back into the car, and driven off.

Billings stopped him there. "Did you recognize the person?"

"Well, I was pretty far away," said Sam.

"You were so far away I'm surprised you could see anything, Mr. Evans. Snow, a dark night like that. Your eyesight must be pretty good."

"I don't need no glasses!"

"But not good enough so that you could recognize the person or give us a description?"

Sam held back then, not for long, just for a moment, but long enough to make me momentarily curious. "Naw, I guess not."

"You guess?"

In response, Sam shook his head vigorously. "Naw, I couldn't see that good."

"And you can't tell us what kind of car it was?"

"Naw."

"And you didn't get the license number?"

"Naw."

"How far were you from that car? That driver?"

"I don't know. Pretty far."

"How far?"

"I don't know," he said, evidently trying to reckon the distance in some measure they might agree on. "Maybe it was, like, about as far as a football field is. Maybe more, maybe less."

"So a hundred yards, give or take?"

This was getting silly. "Look, Detective Billings," I said. "My client has made an effort to be accurate in his own way. I think his analogy to a football field is clear enough."

"He wasn't specific earlier about the time," said Billings, "just 'after dark' was all he said. I'm just trying to get him to be specific where he can. I'm sure you want that, too, Counselor."

I nodded, so did Billings, and Sam picked up his story where he had left off.

Stash had remained silent through all this, as had Sue. They seemed impatient, as if they wanted to get this over with as quickly as possible. So did I.

When Sam finished, having described his discomfort and fear at the police roadblock, I put my hand on his, indicating that he was to stop. He had told them all he had told me, and that was enough.

"Well, I give you credit, Charley," said Stash. "You sure know how to polish a witness. You got all that down in fifteen minutes."

That was meant to annoy me. It did. "What are you talking about, Stash? He just told the same story he told me. And it's the same story he was telling you just before I came in, isn't it, Detective Gillis?"

She held back. "More or less," she said, studiously avoiding my eyes.

"Then," I said, rising to my feet, "I think we've concluded our business here. Come on, Sam." I gave him a tug, and he stood up uncertainly, looking left and right and then back at me.

"Wait a minute," said Stash. "I think we ought to have a talk out in the hall, Charley."

"Wait a minute yourself. Sam Evans was brought in as a witness, and he's given you his testimony. I understand that he was a little less than forthcoming in the beginning. That's only natural considering his youth and inexperience. He was frightened. But he's told you now what he knows and what he saw. He has nothing to add. It's up to you now to have his story checked out."

"Do *what?*" Sue yelled, suddenly exploding as she sprang forward from the wall. "There's nothing to check! There is no story! He made it up!"

"Far be it for me to tell you your job, Detective Gillis, but I think a visit to Mrs. Belder would be in order. I assume that hasn't yet been done. She might have a better idea of the time my client left her place than he seems to.

That would ease your mind a little on specifics, wouldn't it, Detective Billings?"

He sighed. "Yeah, sure."

"And Sam," I said, "has that clutch in the Datsun been fixed yet?"

"Huh? No, you can't drive it nowheres."

"I'd confirm that, if I were you, Detective Gillis. It would tend to support his story, wouldn't it? What about drivers who were out that night on Clarion Road? Did they see a deserted pickup along the shoulder? That might bear checking out. No, I really think you've got your work cut out for you. But it's work you can do without our further assistance. Let's go, Sam."

Stash was on his feet, beckoning. "Charley, come on. Outside. Leave your guy here."

I'd made my power play. I had no choice but to hear what he had to say. Signaling to Sam to sit down and wait, I followed Assistant Prosecutor Stanislaus Olesky out of the room.

Once out in the hall, he shut the door after us, thrust his hands in his pockets, and walked us a little distance down the hall. He seemed almost reluctant to speak, his deep-set eyes reflecting confusion.

This act of concern on his part was getting on my nerves. "All right, Stash," I said, "let's hear it."

"Charley," he said, "we want to keep him."

"Keep him? How can you? You know you don't have enough to book him."

"Okay, Charley, on the level, straight up, here's what we've got on him. Number one, we've got the footprint which puts him right at the scene. His sneakers match the print exactly — off brand, distinctive tread."

"He admits he was there."

"Right. He has to, because, number two, when he was out on the road and tried to hitch a ride, he was recognized by somebody who knew him and drove right by. This person said your boy Sam was a bad kid, and he didn't want anything to do with him."

"I'd like the name of whoever that was."

"All in due time. It's called the discovery process. Number three, he fled the scene. He was not recognized by that motorist. But he was observed to be acting very suspiciously, and that was why the guy stopped. He was the one who reported the body in the field. He also told us he'd seen someone running from the scene. We kept that from the reporters, because it was the only lead we had until Sue found the footprint in the mud. Only one clear one, but that was enough, and then the other motorist came forward, the one who'd recognized Sam Evans out on Clarion Road. So they had him identified, and that was enough to bring him in."

"Okay, so they brought him in, and they questioned him, and —"

"One more thing." He interrupted me. "Sam Evans did not volunteer information.

He did not make a separate report of finding the body that night. He did not come forward the next day. And for the first hour of interrogation, he denied even being out on Clarion Road that night. This is not the sort of behavior you might expect from an innocent witness, Charley. You know that and I know that."

"But it's not the kind of behavior that gets someone booked on a murder charge, either," I said. "You know what we're dealing with. He's not very bright. You probably wouldn't have to dig very deep to find evidence of physical abuse by his father. Evans didn't even understand that I was his lawyer, what my function was. He's got no idea of the legal process. He was scared shitless, Stash. That's why he ran. That's why he shut up about what he'd found. That's why he denied everything."

"Yeah, well, we're not psychologists."

"That's for sure," I said. "But listen, there's a big hole in the facts just as you presented them. It's obvious he wasn't the one who dropped the body off in the field."

"Why?"

"He was on foot. The truck broke down, and he was hiking along trying to get a ride when he was spotted. Did the person who identified him say he was carrying anything?"

"I didn't say there weren't some inconsistencies. Granted, the body had to be moved to the scene in a vehicle. I say it all becomes a question of where the truck broke down, *if* the truck broke down. And as you so helpfully pointed out, there are a few points in his story that ought to be checked."

Stash gave me a sly look and waggled a finger at me. "It's not nice to tell cops how to do their job, Charley, especially when one of them's your girlfriend."

"Let's keep it professional, shall we?"

"That's what I'm trying to do. That's why I called you out here to talk this over. Now, the case is at a point where further investigation is required. I admit that. For good and sufficient reason, we intend to detain Sam Evans while that investigation proceeds."

"What's this good and sufficient reason? You don't have enough to book him and take him to the Grand Jury, and you know it. What I've heard from you simply doesn't constitute a case against him. You think he'll run away on you? He won't. He's too scared to try, and too dumb to get far, even if he does."

"All right, Charley, I said I'd give it to you straight, so here it is. You'll find out soon enough, anyway. The prosecutor let it out that there'd been a break in the case. He wants it to happen, and so he decided this was it."

I sighed. Leave it to his boss, the very famous Mark Evola, Kerry County's posturing prosecutor, a handsome hot dog who thought he was on a par with Vincent Bugliosi in his heyday. I was Evola's least ardent fan and he was my biggest adversary. We'd gone up against each other and I'd beaten him in the Angel Harwell murder trial, but then the superambitious Evola had jumped at the chance for appointment as a circuit judge. He loved life on the bench and cherished the robes, but when it came time for reelection, Evola tanked. Now he was back to being Kerry County prosecutor, Stash's boss and my nemesis.

"To whom did our esteemed prosecutor communicate this bit of wishful thinking? He wasn't stupid enough to call a press conference, was he? Should I get the thrill of my life and check *Eyewitness News* tonight?"

"Here's what happened. That guy Evan Magarshak who's been covering it for the *Free Press* had him on the phone and asked him if there'd been any new developments. Strictly routine. He'd just heard that Sam Evans had been brought in for questioning. Maybe Sue built it up a little. He was all pumped up about it, so he said there'd been a break and that we expected to have an announcement soon, tomorrow at the latest."

"Great. He didn't give Sam Evans's name, did he?"

"No." He shook his head reassuringly. Somehow I wasn't reassured. "But he did decide that he shouldn't play favorites, so he had the same information passed on to the *News*, the *Times-Herald*, and the three network stations. And that was when he sent me over to sit in on the interrogation."

"Oh, Jesus."

"You might want to slip out the back door. I understand they're already starting to gather out in front."

"All right, now look, Stash, you know you're not going to book him on homicide, so you must have some kind of holding charge in mind."

"Yeah, I do."

"What could you possibly come up with that could be made to fit?" I really wanted to know. I was more than curious.

"Misprision of a felony?"

I laughed at that, not very long or hard, and partly for effect, but I did laugh. "Now I know you're bluffing," I said. "Nobody uses that, Stash. If failure to report a crime were a legitimate charge in the State of Michigan, half of Detroit would be behind bars. It's a Federal charge. We both know that."

"Just thought I'd try it out on you," he said. "No, what I had in mind might make you laugh just as hard, but I really think I can make it stick for the day or two we need."

"Let's have it. What is it?"

"Leaving the scene of an accident."

"But that's a traffic law — hit-and-run. That's crazy. This wasn't an accident, it was homicide, and it didn't even take place on Clarion Road."

"We don't know that for sure. And as far as it being homicide, the medical examiner's report isn't in yet, so that's not official, either."

"Sam was on foot."

"He entered Clarion Road in a pickup truck, didn't he? If he fled the scene on foot, that changes nothing. I've looked at the law, Charley. Nowhere does it specify the means of departure."

"You'll never make it stick, Stash."

He made it stick.

Stash Olesky knew something I didn't. I took his advice and slipped out the back door. But circling the building, I saw them hanging out in front of Kerry County Police Headquarters, and still arriving. The Channel 7 news van pulled up as I all but tiptoed past. Nobody paid any attention to me. I went unrecognized even by the little crowd of locals that had gathered. They were probably there out of curiosity regarding the presence of the media, rather than having any real interest in what might be announced from the steps of the building. I hoped the reporters would be disappointed. So far Sam Evans's name hadn't been mentioned. I didn't see how Stash would dare bring it up in connection with that phony holding charge. But you could never tell just what his boss might do or say.

I cut across the parking lot behind them, jumped into my car, and headed straight back to the office. I was relieved to find that Mr. and Mrs. Evans had gone, maybe over to Police Headquarters to get a report from me. Well, let them wait. I had nothing good to tell them. I stood over Mrs. Fenton while she whipped out a *Habeas Corpus* form. She was always fast and efficient when it mattered most. She printed it out and handed it over. If she had been twenty years younger and not such a sourpuss, I might have given her a kiss on the cheek. As it was, she had to settle for a hasty thank-you as I hurried out the door for the Kerry County Courthouse.

Normally I don't get quite so urgently involved in this kind of legwork, so why was I doing this for Sam Evans? I wasn't even sure he was telling the truth. Maybe a part of me wanted to believe he was being straight, but frankly the whole Evans family gave me the creeps. You just never know where evil lurks.

And I sure wasn't doing it for that father of his who had backed me up against a wall with his peculiar brand of moral blackmail so that I'd take on his strange son as a client. So why was I doing this?

The closest I could figure was that it was pride. Stash had out-and-out offended me with the ludicrous traffic charge. I took it personally. I hadn't spent my whole life in the law — bad times and good — to fall for such blatant chicanery. I was out to show Stash that he just couldn't get away with it.

But he knew something I didn't. Maybe I should have been aware that a notice had been posted in the courthouse for a week or more. But I hadn't been inside since the day I got Ernie Barker off on that gun charge, and to tell you the whole truth, I am not an inveterate reader of bulletin boards. If I hadn't been in such a hurry and had paid better attention to that miscellaneous collection of county communications, I might have seen a neatly typed announcement to the effect that all proceedings of the Kerry County Court would be suspended at 1 P.M. on that day only "due to the Annual Conference of Southeastern Michigan County Judges to be held at the Hyatt Hotel, Southfield, Michigan."

I noticed it only on my way out. By that time, I had pounded on the doors of the judges' chambers and found them locked, looked into the courtrooms and found them as empty as the halls and offices. It looked like the last scene in *On the Beach*. Everybody had gone home early. They may as well have locked up the building. I couldn't figure it out. It was only then, the *Habeas Corpus* still flapping in my hand, that I stopped and surveyed the bulletin board, looking for some explanation. That's when I got the message.

I was annoyed, more than annoyed. I was angry. The law is a no-holds-barred competition played by overweight men in suits and ties. I had a pretty good reputation for rough-

211

and-tumble myself, good enough so that I knew when I'd been put down good and proper. There was no point in even considering a trip to Southfield. Out of their robes and pressing the flesh, they'd be on their second round of drinks by the time I got there. These annual conferences served better as occasions for meeting and greeting than for deep discussions of the penal code. The boys from Kerry County wouldn't take kindly to an interruption. I would have to wait until morning, and so would Sam Evans. I had no choice but to go back and tell him that.

Feeling frustrated and defeated, I came back from my visit with Sam and my confrontation with his father and told Mrs. Fenton I would be leaving early. She saw the papers in my hand but said nothing. I tossed them on my desk, deposited with her the envelopes I'd collected from Frank and Betty Higgins, and took off for home.

Home. Two bedrooms, a living room, and a kitchen. Even so, it was about one more room than I needed. I kept the extra bedroom for my daughter when she came back to visit from Columbia Law. I was glad to have her there and offer her a room of her own, so it was worth it to me. But as I rattled around the apartment, the usual Diet Coke in my hand, that spare, bare room, with its neatly made bed and chest of drawers, made me feel lonely just looking at it. Maybe I should hang a picture or two. Put in a desk. Something, anything, to make it look like somebody might live there. I made a mental note of it.

Just a few years before, if I'd felt the way I felt at that moment, I would have bellied up to the bar at Jacoby's and begun to drink my troubles away. I was good at that then. Old patterns die hard. Something in me said that what worked for me once would work for me again. That was the something that always seemed to be telling me I needed a drink, no matter what the circumstance. The desire never leaves you.

It was too early for television. That press conference on the steps of Police Headquarters probably wouldn't air until eleven, might not air at all if they hadn't come away with much. I'd have to watch Mort Crim to find out. Ordinarily, Sue and I might be checking it out together, sitting on the couch in her living room, holding hands, snuggling, engaging in that sort of pleasantly foolish behavior I should probably have outgrown after my last divorce. After what had passed between us in Interrogation Room Three, there probably wouldn't be any more of that, though I wondered why I'd allowed that old bastard Evans to con me into taking on his son. I was right to turn him down the first time. He had hooked me with that mean little speech about lawyers being servants of the establishment, only for the rich. There was in general just

213

enough truth in that for me to feel called upon to prove him wrong. I didn't like him. I had contempt for him and what he'd put his son up to with Father Chuck. But he wasn't my client. His son was.

When the telephone rang, I went into the living room and picked it up, then sank into a chair when I recognized Sue's voice at the other end of the line. She sounded cold and distant, which I would have expected, but also determined to have her say.

"I tried to get you at your office, Charley, but Mrs. Fenton said you'd gone for the day."

"That's right, I —"

"There's something I wanted you to know."

"Sue, listen —"

"You'll hear about it eventually, anyway."

I was just as determined as she was to speak my piece. We started talking simultaneously, but this time I won.

"You were right," I said. "You said yourself we have to keep our professional lives separate. Considering the number of lawyers in this county and the number of cops, it was inevitable that sometime we'd find ourselves on the opposite sides of the fence. Neither of us knew it would come so quickly, but it has. So why don't we just back off until this thing has run its course? Then we can get together and compare notes, like a couple of professionals. That'd be the mature way to handle it, wouldn't it?"

There was stony silence at the other end.

"Are you through?"

It was plain she had ignored what I'd said. I wondered if she'd even been listening.

I sighed. "Yes, I'm through."

"Thank you. I just thought you'd be interested in knowing that Bud and I visited Mrs. Belder, and yes, just the way you said she'd be, she was a lot more helpful on the question of time than your client was. She put it at six o'clock, no later than six-fifteen, that he'd left. But she also told us something else that was very interesting."

"Oh? And what was that?"

"She told us he had something under a tarpaulin. Sam Evans came with it, and he left with it."

"Okay, Sue, why is that such a big deal?"

"Because, Charley, Mrs. Belder said that whatever was under that tarp was something dead. She's eighty-seven years old, and she admits she doesn't see very well, but her sense of smell is just fine. And she's willing to swear that whatever was hidden under that tarp smelled dead."

"Have you talked this over with Sam yet?"

"No," she said, "I haven't. But Stash Olesky tells me there'll be plenty of time to do that in the morning. I'm going to go home a little early myself. I figure I've put in a good day's work. But I just thought you'd like to know. Good-bye, Charley."

And then she hung up on me. Just like that.

I looked at the receiver, shrugged, and replaced it in its cradle. She had meant to put me in my place and who knows? Maybe she had. Maybe Sam Evans had murdered Catherine Quigley, and maybe he'd murdered poor little Lee Higgins first. Anything is possible.

But one thing kept playing at the back of my mind: Would someone like Sam have prepared the bodies in the condition they were found — bathed, clothes laundered, hair neatly combed and laid out in the snow in clear plastic like they might have been in a mortuary? Would Sam — a total slob, unkempt with dirt under his fingernails and clothes that reeked from filth and body odor — take more care of a corpse than he would of himself? Maybe, maybe not. Had Sue even thought about that?

One fact was for sure, though. Right now Sam wasn't looking too good. He'd been at the scene, someone saw him. His footprint was there. And despite his mewling protestations about telling the truth, there wasn't another suspect, and the cops thought he was looking pretty good for it.

I looked out the window and saw that it was almost dark. I was getting tired of thinking. My watch said it was just a little after five. If I couldn't go out for a drink, then I would take myself out to dinner. Why not?

Glad to have something to do, I went into

the bathroom, showered and shaved, and then got my second-best suit from the closet. If I was going to do it, I might as well do it right. I even went so far as to call the Pickeral Inn and reserve a table. When the girl who took the reservations asked how many there would be in the party, she seemed a little disappointed when I said just one.

9

As I opened the door to my office and paused to knock the snow from my shoes, I got a look from Mrs. Fenton that was a little hard to read, something between a frown of disapproval and caution. There was a slight, quick movement of her head to her right, my left, in the direction of the office sofa.

It was old man Evans, combative as ever. He was on his feet by the time I stepped inside and pulled the door shut behind me. He was in his work clothes, unshaven, no longer making any pretense that he belonged here in town. He was who he was. I gave him a curt nod, then turned my back on him as I went over to Mrs. Fenton's desk.

"Anything special on the agenda?"

She consulted her calendar. "Today's the day you were going to file the papers on the Kelman divorce."

"Has he moved out yet?" I could hear Evans stirring behind me.

"I've no idea, Mr. Sloan. Better call and find out." The filing date had already been postponed once while they talked reconciliation. They needed a marriage counselor, not a lawyer. I was about to tell Mrs. Fenton to make the call for me when I happened to think what a pleasure it would be to walk into my little inner office and shut the door on my visitor.

"Okay, Mrs. Fenton, I'll just do that."

I turned around and almost bumped into Evans. He was blocking my way.

"If you'll pardon me." Always the gentleman.

"You mean you want to get by?"

"That's just what I mean."

He was about my height, lean and raw-boned. The fact that for a moment I considered pushing him aside should give some idea of the irritation he caused me just being there. I took a step to one side, and he moved with me. All the while he was giving me a look he meant to be threatening.

"Not until you tell me you're going to get my boy out of jail today," he said.

"We went through this yesterday afternoon," I said.

"It's what I'm payin' you for, ain't it?"

I sighed. "Mr. Evans, if you'll remember, I recommended John Dibble to you when you and your wife came in. He's a good attorney. He can do anything and everything I can do. I'd be happy to turn it all over to him."

He took a step back, slightly put off by my suggestion. He thought it over.

"Well, that ain't what I meant, exactly."

"I'll even return your retainer."

"Naw," he said, "don't do that. Just give

me some results. That's all I want."

"Results are what I want, too. It's just a matter of getting the matter before a judge."

"You need money to pay him off?"

"Mr. Evans" — I raised my voice — "get out of here. No payoff is needed. No payoff will be asked for. All I need to do, as I explained on the telephone last night, is get some paperwork processed. Now if you'll pardon me?"

He moved back, stepping out of my path. "Sure, okay. Sorry." Thoroughly intimidated now, he made his way for the door. It had been easier to get rid of him than I expected. I watched him go, barely managing to suppress a smile. But then I thought of something I wanted to ask and called after him. He turned back, looking almost suspicious, as if he were afraid I'd changed my mind.

"Mr. Evans," I said, "did Sam say anything to you about recognizing the person he saw out on Clarion Road?"

"No, no, he didn't say nothin' about that. He didn't say anythin' about what he seen out there."

"All right, thank you." And I let him go.

Why did I sense that he and his son were lying about this? Sam had been stopped cold by Bud Billings on that point, and the old man had been just a little too vehement in his denial. It made me wonder.

"I detest that man," Mrs. Fenton allowed.

I grinned back at her. "I'm not too fond of him myself."

"I can't for the life of me imagine why you took on his dim-witted son as a client."

"You know the family?"

"They're notorious all over the county — sneaky, mean, just thoroughly untrustworthy people."

"Why, Mrs. Fenton, how you talk! It seems to me you've been listening to gossip."

"It's more than gossip. I remember one or two years before you came here, Delbert Evans — the one who was just here — got into a lot of trouble when a child of his — that would have been the boy's sister — when she died, and he just buried her. No doctor, no death certificate. There was naturally some suspicion about that, so they dug her up and did an autopsy on her, but they found out she died of natural causes. Pneumonia, or something. But they didn't have a doctor in to take care of her, so the poor thing just died. They're just like animals, those Evanses. They seem to live so poor, but they come up with money when they need it. Like this time with that boy of theirs, Sam."

I stood for a moment, thinking about what I had just heard. "How old was the girl?" I asked at last.

"Oh, I don't know, seven or eight, something like that."

"Interesting." That was all I could say, but

perhaps it was more than that. "Mrs. Fenton, I'm going to go out to look for a sympathetic judge."

Judge Brown was sympathetic, all right, but he was a little too amused by Stash Olesky's stratagem to be truly helpful. I caught him in his chambers just before he opened up the shop for the day. He took *Habeas Corpus*, glanced at it, then tossed it aside. But he gave more careful attention to the booking sheet as I explained with all the gravity I could muster that the traffic charge was trumped up as a holding device and that my client had been on foot out there on Clarion Road after his truck broke down.

I knew that it looked bad for the home team when, after considering the matter for a moment or two, Judge Brown burst into laughter.

"They didn't have enough to book him on the homicide charge, Judge, so they took the easy way out."

"Easy way?" He kept right on chuckling. "No, Charley, I'd say it was the tricky way."

"He's just a boy, Your Honor — nineteen years old."

"I know, I know." He wasn't impressed. "Who came up with this, anyway?"

"Stash Olesky."

"I give him credit. This is the fanciest bit of flummery I've seen in quite some time."

"But you can't let him get away with this, Judge."

"This is a big case, Charley. They evidently feel an arrest is imminent, or they wouldn't go out on a limb like this."

"Mark Evola held one of his famous off-the-cuff press conferences and promised there'd be an arrest today. But it's wishful thinking. There're too many holes in their case. They wouldn't dare take it before a Grand Jury, much less hold a preliminary hearing."

"We'll just have to see about that, won't we?" He sighed. "All right, look, here's what we'll do. We'll wait for the medical examiner's report. We both know it will confirm homicide, so it'll be up to the prosecutor and the cops to fish or cut bait then on this one. You come back here during the recess, say, one o'clock, and I'll give you your *Habeas Corpus*. Then they'll have to book him properly or let him go." He gave me what he must have intended to be an encouraging smile. "Deal?"

I had no choice. "Deal."

I gathered up the paperwork I'd presented and left him as he began pulling on his robe. He waved and nodded sagaciously as I ducked out the door. He seemed to feel he'd acted, well, judiciously.

There was really nothing to do but go back to Kerry County Police Headquarters, where Sam Evans had been kept overnight in one of the basement holding cells, and explain the situation to him. Just how much of it he would understand was anybody's guess. And when they took him into Interrogation Room Three again, I ought to be there with him.

It was such a short drive over there that I was tempted to leave the car and walk. But the light snow that had fallen the night before — less than an inch — had barely begun to melt, and I'd neglected to wear my galoshes. It was a cold, clammy morning, with no sun in sight. All this, admittedly not much, was enough to quell my momentary impulse to exercise. No wonder I was getting so soft around the middle.

I jumped into the car and moved it from one parking lot to another about a block and a half away. I looked forward to seeing Sue with some degree of dread. Tramping over to the department entrance and up the steps, I thought about her and what we had, almost in the past tense. It seemed to me there was very little chance of putting things back together again. What I had said to her the night before had been right. It was certain we would eventually find ourselves in opposition, so perhaps it was better that it happened sooner than later. Nevertheless, I should have fought clear of this one. Stash himself said she'd gotten too close to it.

I wasn't quite prepared for what awaited me inside the door. There a small crowd around Tony Makarides's desk. Stash Olesky was there and Bud Billings, as well as a fellow in his twenties I recognized as a reporter for the Port Huron *Times-Herald*. But old man Evans was there, too, angry and loud, in that rasping voice of his. A uniform cop was on his way over to quiet him down. But the real surprise was that right there, in the middle of it all, looking befuddled by all the fuss, was young Sam Evans.

Stash grabbed me the moment I stepped inside and pulled me away from the door. "Get rid of this guy, will you, Charley?" Meaning the immensely convivial Delbert Evans, of course. "The kid from the *Times-Herald* is taking all this down." And it was true enough: The reporter had his notebook out and his ballpoint going as he looked up and down from the pad to the man who was doing all the talking.

"What is it? What's happened?"

"They found another body, a boy this time, been out all night on Beulah Road." Stash's face was fixed in a painful grimace.

"Around Hub City?"

"More or less. Sue's gone out there. Report didn't come in until about fifteen minutes ago. For some reason everyone drove right on by this time." He was agitated and miserable. "Where were you? I called your office as soon as I heard."

"I was trying to get a *Habeas Corpus* past Judge Brown."

"You won't need one now. Your boy's been checked out of here. Musta been some old

225

beer cans and a bunch of pizza crusts underneath that tarp in his car. Now, if we could just get him and that father of his to leave."

The cop had Delbert by the elbow and was pushing him toward the door, and the reporter was trailing along. So was Sam. It was going pretty well until old man Evans happened to turn and see me. He jerked away from the cop and came at me like a pit bull.

"And you!" he sneered. "You were useless, worse than useless. You and the cops cooked up that phony deal keepin' Sam in jail, didn'tcha? Didn'tcha?" He had his finger in my face, jabbing it toward me. I thought for a moment he might poke it up my nose.

"Mr. Evans," I said, "that doesn't deserve an answer."

"Listen to him, so high and mighty!" He was talking to the reporter. Then back at me: "I'll tell you what, Mr. High-and-Mighty, you're fired! Just try and get another nickel out of me. I'll get back the money I gave you already, some way or other I will, I swear."

The cop, who had kept the door open, managed to pull him through it. Sam and the reporter followed. A collective sigh passed through the room.

"Jesus!" Tony Makarides groaned. "What a dirtbag."

"He was carrying on like that for about five minutes before you got here," Stash said to me. "He showed up just about the moment we brought his son up for release. Said he wanted to talk to him, and all of a sudden there he was."

"Charges dropped."

"Of course."

It was good for Sam, naturally, that the charges were dropped, and I must say I had a small twinge of guilt that at no point did I honestly believe in his innocence. Nor did I fully believe in his guilt, for that matter. I'd been going back and forth on it, but at certain points I had to admit that he really did look good for it.

But now that a third victim had been discovered, it was getting even more horrific. Three small children murdered. It was baffling, and with Sam Evans clearly out of the picture, the horror was growing. If he wasn't the lunatic responsible for these grisly crimes, who was?

As I thought about that, I almost forgot that Stash was standing right next to me, and I couldn't help but put it to him.

I gave him a close look. "Were those eggs you had for breakfast scrambled or once over easy? You seem to have a little left on your face."

"Don't rub it in. Remember who I work for."

"For what it's worth, Judge Brown called your little ploy the fanciest bit of flummery he'd seen for a while — and I'm quoting him."

I took a step or two toward the door when someone called my name.

It was Bud Billings, beckoning me over. I gave a nod and followed as he led me through the front office and down the hall to the detectives' room. What did he have in mind? He wasn't telling.

He sat down and nodded at an empty chair. There was no one else there. They were all probably out on Beulah Road. Bud had been left to pick up the pieces after the mess that had been made by Sam Evans's arrest and release.

"This is all off the record, okay, Charley?"

"Okay with me."

"I don't know how close you looked at that booking sheet, but I'm down there as arresting officer."

"All right, so what?"

"Am I looking at a false arrest suit?"

"I don't think you've got too many worries there, Bud."

"I mean, it was all Stash's idea. He cooked it up, and I went along with it."

"It was a holding charge. Personally, I think it was a little too tricky, but it's not like the kid was booked for homicide. I watched the *Mark Evola Show* on the eleven o'clock news, and he didn't mention Sam Evans by name. If he had, you'd all be in real trouble."

He nodded, concerned but somewhat relieved. "You're not going to put any ideas in the old man's head, are you?"

"Are you serious? You must have heard what he said to me. He fired me. Not that there'd be any more business between us. Not that I'd take him on again. I wouldn't. Put any ideas into his head? Come on, Bud, what kind of ambulance chaser do you think I am, anyway?"

"Sorry, Charley." He really looked contrite.

"Now, I don't guarantee that he won't come up with the idea on his own. And there are other lawyers in Kerry County, one of whom might be foolish enough to take him on, but not me. I will tell you this, though, before I came over here, I stopped in at the courthouse and tried to get Judge Brown to sign off on a *Habeas Corpus,* and he wouldn't do it, not until the medical examiner's report was in, specifying homicide. He thought enough of the hold charge to let it stand." I paused to let that sink in, then added, "No, Bud, I really don't think you've got much to worry about."

He nodded. "Okay," he said, "thanks."

I stood up, ready to go. "Don't mention it," I said.

"Just one more thing, Charley." He leaned back and fixed me with a stare. "Did old man Evans have anything to say to you about the murders? I mean, either the Quigley girl or the one before it?"

Cops. They know the rules, but they like to push you. "You know the answer to that, Bud.

229

Even if he did fire me, that still comes under the heading of privileged information and client confidentiality."

"Yeah, well, the kid did see somebody out there that night. I'm sure of that, and I'm pretty sure he recognized whoever he saw. It could have been his father. There was a case a couple of years back that —"

"I've heard about it. All right, if this is really off the record, I'll tell you this. Delbert Evans didn't have a damned thing to say about those kids out in the snow. He just wanted his son back."

When I got back to the office, Mrs. Fenton was on the phone. Her manner was distant, professional, almost cold. I certainly wouldn't have wanted to be on the other end of the line.

"No, let me assure you, sir, it is *not* out of line, as you put it. Strict records were kept. We conduct things in a completely professional manner here."

She raised her eyes to me and gave them a roll.

"You may complain to them, if you like," she said. "Let me advise you, though, to put it in writing. A telephone call will not do. You have the address? Good. Please be more respectful to the Bar Association than you have been to me."

And with that, she slammed down the receiver.

"Ernie Barker got his bill," she announced.

I laughed. I probably shouldn't have. She was in no mood for a joke. "So Two-Gun Ernie finally appreciates the seriousness of his offense. Good. Some people you can only impress by biting them in the wallet."

"You wouldn't laugh if you'd heard what I had to listen to the last few minutes."

"I'm sorry, Mrs. Fenton. Really I am."

Apparently, she was willing to be mollified. She pursed her lips expressively and handed over a small stack of telephone messages — only about three or four.

"Mrs. Kelman in this bunch?" I asked.

"I talked to her. She's coming in at eleven-thirty."

"Did she say she wanted to go ahead and file?"

"Nothing at all. Just that she was coming in. She was kind of short with me on the phone."

"Better print out five copies of her papers with today's date. If she was going to stall again, she wouldn't have made an appointment, I suppose."

I started into my inner office, the phone slips in my hand but my mind on the scene down at County Police Headquarters. That reminded me. I turned back at the door.

"Oh, Mrs. Fenton, I think you'll be glad to know that I was just fired by Delbert Evans."

"He fired you? You should have fired him."

"You're probably right."

I eased the door shut behind me and sat down at my desk. I had a notion to send her over to the library to dig out the newspaper accounts of the Evans family's difficulties with the law a few years back. It probably wouldn't have made the Detroit papers, but the Port Huron *Times-Herald* would have covered it. It could wait, it was just curiosity on my part. An ugly business, though. If I'd known about it, I would certainly have gotten rid of him the moment I found him in my office.

There were two surprises waiting for me among my messages. The first was from Sue asking me to call her as soon as I came in. She'd called just before I arrived, and what seemed most odd, the number she had left was the one at her apartment. I grabbed the phone and punched in the digits I knew by heart.

When she answered, I could tell she had been crying.

"What is it, Sue? This message you left seems sort of urgent."

"Yeah," she said bleakly, "well, I guess it was. I feel sort of desperate."

"Why? Tell me."

"Oh, Charley, there's been another child murdered. The body was found out on Beulah Road. Same condition, same —"

"I heard about it," I said.

"Oh, sure, you must have been at the station this morning." She took a deep breath. "Sam

Evans was released."

"I know. But tell me about you."

"I just lost it out there completely. I got hysterical. I couldn't stop crying, then I — I guess I started screaming. I really don't remember that part so well, though. When they got me quieted down, the captain said I was impeding the investigation and sent me home. Told me I should take a couple of days off. I tried to argue with him — you know, assured him I'd be all right, all that — but he said it was an order. So here I am."

"I'm sorry it happened, but I'm certainly not surprised, kiddo. The last one was too much for me. I told you about that."

"Yeah, but I'm supposed to be tougher than you are. I'm a cop."

"Cops have their breaking points, too. Or so I've heard."

"Yeah, I suppose. But . . ."

"But what, Sue?"

"Uh, I was going to lie down for a while."

"Best idea I've heard for a while."

"I was wondering, could we have dinner together tonight?" Then she added, "My treat." That meant at her house.

"Sure, of course. When do you want me to come by?"

"Any time after seven. Say seven-thirty?"

"That'll be fine. I'm looking forward to it."

"Okay, good-bye — oh, and Charley?"

"Yes, Sue?"

"Thanks for calling me kiddo."

I translated the conversation I'd just had with Sue into emotional language that a dunce like me could understand and respond to. Let's see, what she seemed to be saying was something like this: Charley, I'm in deep shit with this case, in over my head. I may even have hurt my career out there on Beulah Road. I'd like your help in this, or if you haven't much of that to give, any advice you have to offer, but certainly your comfort — I could certainly use some of the old Charley Sloan magic.

Yes, something like that. How could I refuse her invitation?

The next couple of calls were strictly routine: a request for an appointment to draw up a will, a real-estate closing. But the last message gave me an even bigger jolt than the one from Sue. It was a call from Mark Conroy that had come in about an hour ago. I didn't recognize the number he had left, but I punched it in on the receiver and waited it out through three rings. Conroy picked up with a simple "Hello?"

"You called?" I didn't identify myself.

There was a pause. Maybe he was gathering strength to say something he wasn't sure he wanted to say. Maybe he was just looking for the right words. When he came out with it at last, what he said was quite simple: "I'd like us to talk."

"Seems like a good idea," I said, "if you've really got something to say."

"Let's talk." Emphatic.

"All right. My afternoon's pretty empty."

He considered that for a moment. "No, I don't think so. I've still got somebody else to check with, some things to get straight."

"You know best."

"What about tonight? We could meet someplace."

Under ordinary circumstances, I could have rearranged with Sue. Not tonight. "I'm afraid that's out," I said.

"Tomorrow then, early."

"Suits me."

"What about out at your place, you know, where you live?"

I thought about it. What was he afraid of? "Let's do it in my office," I said. "That's where I like to conduct business."

"Okay, but no wires, and I don't want your secretary listening in."

"Be here at eight o'clock. She doesn't come in until nine."

Pause. "Okay. Eight o'clock then."

"I never use a tape recorder. Don't even own one."

"Is that supposed to reassure me?" he asked, his voice heavy with sarcasm.

The remainder of the day held a few more surprises.

Clare Kelman came in at eleven-thirty sharp

wearing sunglasses. She didn't remove them. I asked her if she wanted to file her divorce papers, and she said she certainly did. We went into my office, and as Mrs. Fenton was putting them together and stapling them, I tried to make some small talk. Mrs. Kelman wasn't having any. Once they were laid out on my desk for her to sign, I understood a little better. She was forced to exchange her sunglasses for a pair of bifocals, and I saw that her left eye was bruised and swollen nearly shut. She signed quickly and replaced the sunglasses without comment. Physical abuse was not mentioned in the divorce suit. It didn't have to be. The State of Michigan has no-fault divorce and a fifty-fifty division of property.

"Will these be filed today?" she asked.

"I'll bring them over to the courthouse right after lunch."

"Good."

She turned and started to leave.

"Mrs. Kelman? I take it Jerry's moved out?"

"No, I have."

"I can get him out of there, if you want me to. All I have to do is file a separate motion with the court."

"I'm enjoying being away from the house. Too many bad memories there," she said, "ten years of them. He'll have to sell it soon enough anyway, won't he?"

"It looks like it. Tell me something, though. What made you put off filing earlier?"

"Oh, the usual. He promised it would never happen again, but it did."

"Okay, Mrs. Kelman. See you in court. I'll let you know the date. Give Mrs. Fenton your new address and phone number."

So I was wrong. She didn't need a marriage counselor, after all. She needed a lawyer.

I went over to Benny's Diner, just managing to beat the noon crowd by a few minutes. As I gobbled a cheeseburger, I read quickly through the pertinent parts of the two Detroit papers, relieved to find nothing in them on Mark Conroy. The Port Huron paper could wait. I had to have something to help me pass the rest of the afternoon. When I finished there, I kept my word and delivered the Kelman filing to the Kerry County clerk's office in the basement of the courthouse. Gladys Monk, the lady in charge, said we'd know about our court date in a week's time, or not much longer, but that they were already running well into next year. Too bad about that. Clare Kelman would have to remain married a little longer than she might like.

Back at my office, I spent a good part of the afternoon working on the Higginses' insurance claim. The way I read their policy, there was five thousand dollars coming to them on their son's death. I drafted a letter to that effect for Frank to sign, as well as a cover letter from me as their attorney to give support to their claim. Then I spent some time staring out at the St. Clair River, counting the ore boats and freighters and thinking about the Conroy matter. The Victim Report could wait.

About four o'clock the office phones went dead.

Or who knows when it was exactly? There had been no calls for over an hour before that, which was fairly unusual, but it wasn't until four, when Mrs. Fenton tried to phone out in order to let Frank and Betty Higgins know the insurance letter was coming, that she found the line dead. No dial tone, no white noise to let us know we were still plugged into the local exchange, nothing at all. Strange.

Mrs. Fenton asked me to try my phone. Same thing. The trouble was out there someplace.

"No wind, no thunderstorm, no lines down," I said.

"I wonder what's wrong."

"Why don't you go over to that insurance office downstairs and see if they've got the same problem?"

I looked out the big window, down on the street, and saw a Michigan Bell van parked nearby, which was more or less reassuring. Right on the job.

When Mrs. Fenton returned, she was waving her hands dramatically, slamming the door behind her.

"It's a madhouse in there," she said.

"The insurance office?" Whenever I peered

inside, they all looked like mummies at their desks — no visible movement at all.

"There's a crew from Michigan Bell just tearing the place apart. They say there was an irregular outage all through this grid area, something to do with the snow last night. Can you imagine? They're not quite sure why, so they say all this is partly diagnostic. Such a noisy bunch, really. They've just taken over downstairs."

Irregular outage? Grid area? Diagnostic? I could tell she'd picked up a few new words. They didn't quite fit well in her vocabulary yet, but she used then gamely.

"Well, maybe I'd better —"

I never got a chance to finish that sentence. I was interrupted by three hard knocks on the door. Before Mrs. Fenton could fly over to get it, it popped open, and in walked a big Michigan Bell hardhat, complete with tool belt and a dangling receiver.

"You folks having trouble with your telephones?" Then he spotted Mrs. Fenton. "Oh, yeah, you were downstairs, right? Said yours had gone out completely. How many lines you get in here?"

"Just one."

"Frank! Joe! Come on in here. This one's out, too."

Frank and Joe tramped in, one of them carrying a length of telephone wire and the other a box of equipment.

"How many telephones?"

"Two," said Mrs. Fenton, growing more flustered with each question. "The other one's in Mr. Sloan's office."

He gave me a glance, no more, and a quick shrug. "Joe, go in there and try it."

Joe went into my office, while the nameless boss went over to the phone on Mrs. Fenton's desk, picked it up, and listened for a moment.

"You get anything, Joe?" he shouted.

"Not a damned thing," Joe shouted back.

"Better take it apart." He turned to Frank. "Toss the wire out, okay?"

Frank went over to the window and began tugging away.

"Lady, how does this open, anyway?"

"Not *that* way. Here, let me show you." She bustled over to demonstrate how it was done.

"Al! *Al!*" It was Frank yelling down at another member of the crew through the open window. "Here, catch this." He threw a length of telephone wire out the window.

"Joe, how ya doin' in there?"

"I don't know. Can't tell yet."

These guys were driving me crazy. I turned to the guy in charge. "Look, how long is this going to take?"

"No idea, mister." He was attaching the other end of the line Frank had brought over to Mrs. Fenton's receiver. "See, this is the diagnostic part. We still don't have a good fix on what really went wrong. Can you beat that?

But we're putting them back on line. Just takes a while is all."

I grabbed my topcoat and asked Mrs. Fenton to hold the fort and lock up when she left. She seemed none too pleased about it, but she nodded and let me go without an argument. Occasions like this defined the distance between employee and employer.

I practically ran out of there and down the stairs. I caught a glimpse of Al running the line he'd caught back to the Michigan Bell van. Then I jumped into my car and drove to the library. I decided I could look up that material on Delbert Evans as well as Mrs. Fenton could. Maybe the Evans family was crazier than they seemed.

The reference librarian was helpful. She knew the year and was pretty certain of the season, if not the month. The Port Huron paper was on microfilm. A careful scanning brought me to the facts of the case. They were more or less as Mrs. Fenton had summarized them.

Annie Louise Evans, age seven, had been absent for over a week from school when the truant officer went to the Evans home to make inquiries. He was told abruptly by Delbert Evans that she had died from "a cold." Thinking this highly unlikely and quite irregular, he reported it to the Kerry County Police. Evans was visited by an officer, none other than Dominic Benda, who asked to see the death certificate. When it turned out that no doctor had been in attendance either before or after the girl's death and that she was buried in the backyard, Benda did the sensible thing and brought Delbert Evans in for questioning.

The story ran off and on for more than a month. The body was exhumed. The autopsy, which was held in Port Huron, proved the cause of death was pneumonia. There was a good deal of public indignation expressed. But Delbert Evans simply insisted he knew how to take care of his own. He was sorry Annie Louise died, but those things happened. They had done what they could for her. What Mrs. Evans had to say on the matter was never mentioned. It rated an editorial in the *Times-Herald* on criminal child neglect, and in the end that was the charge against Mr. and Mrs. Evans, both of them. They were brought to trial a month later and represented by a Hub City lawyer named Krantz, whom I'd never met. Delbert Evans must have shown more regret in court than he'd shown earlier, and Mrs. Evans was said to have cried copious tears. In any case, though they were found guilty, they were put on probation for two years and placed under the supervision of a social worker. The fact that they had a son, Samuel, played a part both in the granting of probation and in the decision to have a social worker keep close tabs on them.

It was an ugly story, something that might have been common a hundred years ago but today seemed primitive, if not downright eerie. Could it have anything to do with those little bodies in the snow? If anything, old man Evans had shown nothing but indifference throughout all three tragedies, and Mrs. Evans seemed nothing more than a cipher and a sidekick to her appalling husband. But could he have washed their clothing and groomed them? Would she have done it for him? Certainly they appeared to have known how to clothe and bury their own dead daughter right in their backyard, didn't they?

I spun the microfilm back to the first report on Annie Louise Evans's burial, noting the newspaper's date and calculating the probable date of her death. What I came up with was more or less the same month and date that Lee Higgins, the first victim, was found a few days ago.

Maybe it was just a coincidence, but if it was, it was still unnerving. There was no question that Delbert Evans was a loose cannon on the deck, capable of unleashing tremendous rage, an unstable man furious at the world. Maybe he wouldn't give a good goddamn about bathing and grooming the little children and then wrapping them in plastic, but surely Mrs. Evans was his accomplice in all things and would do whatever he ordered her to do.

I wondered if Bud Billings had noticed the coincidence and if it had been he who questioned Evans about his daughter's death and had worked the case from first to last. I wondered if maybe he was thinking the same thing I was thinking. Maybe Bud and I should have a talk.

Like a lot of men, I don't buy roses often, probably not often enough, so when I showed up at Sue's door, freshly showered and shaved, and thrust the bouquet at her, she seemed quite overcome.

She made a big production of it, leading me into her kitchen, selecting the right-sized vase, filling it, cutting the bottoms of the stems, instructing me as she went in what ought to be done and why.

"Now," she said, "where'll we put them?"

She led me into her living room, or actually the part of it that served as a dining area. The dozen roses in their vase were a little too big for the small dining room table, since we had to eat on it, too, so she chose a place on her bookcase.

"They'll get some light here," she said, "and open up all the way." Then she threw her arms around me and gave me a big hug, burying her head in my chest. "Oh, Charley, thanks. They're just what I needed."

Supplied with my usual Diet Coke, I stood in the kitchen doorway and talked about some of the events of the day. Some of them: I steered clear of my session with Judge Brown and my encounter with Delbert Evans at Kerry County Police Headquarters. I'd let her bring up the Evans business when and if she wanted to.

For somebody named Gillis, Sue makes pretty good spaghetti. As she stirred the sauce and dropped the pasta into boiling water, I got around to telling her how our phones had gone dead and how the crew from Michigan Bell tore things apart. Keeping things light, I made a real routine of it. In my drinking days, I was known as a pretty good barroom storyteller, and I thought I was doing a good job of it this time, mimicking Joe and Frank and the boss, throwing my arms around to demonstrate the chaos they created. But I noticed about half-way through that she got a kind of funny look on her face. She was frowning but curious, nodding for me to continue. I ended the story kind of lamely, put off my pace by her response. She said nothing, just busied herself with her cooking, dipping a fork into the boiling water to pull up a ribbon of spaghetti to give it the chew test.

Then she threw me another puzzled look. "You say the phones just went out all of a sudden?"

"We didn't notice until around four, but Mrs. Fenton pointed out that we hadn't gotten any calls for at least an hour."

"And these guys were right on the spot to fix it?"

"That's right."

"And they couldn't tell you what had gone wrong?"

"No, the guy in charge kept saying all this activity was 'diagnostic.' "

"And you left before they were through?"

"Yeah, they more or less drove me out of there."

"Charley, I wouldn't tell you this except that I'm absolutely sure it wasn't us, but I'd say those guys put a wiretap on your phone."

"Oh, come on, Sue, they were from Michigan Bell. I saw their van. They had it on their hardhats. Michigan Bell wouldn't do that."

She shrugged, tried the spaghetti again, and pulled the pot off the stove. She headed for the sink with it, and dumped the whole of its contents into a strainer. Then she looked me in the eye. "Did you ask to see their ID?" She shrugged. "That could've been faked, too."

"But they'd been downstairs at the insurance office. They fixed their phones. You're not saying they put a wiretap on them, too?"

"No, they wouldn't have any reason to do that, would they? But whatever was done to your phone would've been done to the nearest office to yours just to make the whole scam seem real. Think about it, Charley. Have you got a case that might interest somebody else that much?"

"I might have."

"You know, for a hotshot lawyer, in some ways you're pretty naive, you know that?"

"It's always a pleasure to be complimented."

"Now get out of here, and sit down at the table. I'll be serving everything in two minutes flat."

Maybe it was three. Not a moment longer, though. She came at me with salad and spaghetti, a plate in each hand, banged them down before me, and then she set a glass and filled it with a red liquid from a decanter that looked suspiciously like light Chianti.

"You can drink it," she said, "and so can I."

"What is it?"

"Cranberry juice. Try it. I think it sort of tastes like wine."

Whether it did or whether it didn't, the dinner was a grand success. As she herself sat down, she apologized for the modesty of the meal. "Been asleep all day," she said. "I had to hustle this up from what I had on hand." I assured her she was a great little hustler, and she gave me one of her raised-eyebrow looks.

She told me that because of the body out on Beulah Road, she'd missed the Higgins funeral. Maybe it was just as well. But then we just goofed around verbally, discussing personalities and situations. I told her one of the few Mark Evola stories she hadn't heard from me. She countered with the latest on Dominic Benda: He was using some of his retirement money to buy his old patrol car from the county because he said he was more comfortable in it than he was in his living room. Stuff like that. We knew we were skirting around the real issues, but that was all right. There'd be time for that later. Meanwhile, the spaghetti was fine. The meatballs may have tasted a bit more Swedish than Calabrese, the salad dressing may have come out of a Paul Newman bottle, and the cranberry juice — well, maybe only a *little* like wine — but the total effect was just right.

I think Sue's confidence had been restored by our exchange in the kitchen. Although I wasn't quite prepared to admit she was right about my visitors from Michigan Bell, she had made a good case, and she knew it. And she had shaken me up in the process. Score one for her.

What with dessert — ice cream from the freezer — and my after-dinner cigar, it was after nine before we got to the dishes and general washing up around the kitchen. I always take part. It was part of the bargain between us.

Somehow it wasn't long afterward that we found our way to her bed. And Dr. Charley Sloan performed another miracle of sexual healing. Miracle? That may be an exaggeration. Let's call it a successful operation. The important thing is that it got her talking afterward about the things that had moved her to invite me over in the first place. We lay together, the covers up around us, my arm around her, and we talked.

She admitted that they were probably right to send her home, that she was too emotionally involved in this case, and maybe too much in her work every day.

"I feel all this pressure to succeed," she said. "I got a late start, Charley. I feel like I have to show them."

"Them?"

"All right, the men. They're who I work with. I admit there's a definite gender thing involved here."

We talked about that a little, nothing new there. Our attitudes were as much generational as anything else. A number of years separated us, important years, important experiences.

I, in turn, admitted that I was wrong to have taken on Sam Evans as a client. I explained to her how his father had more or less trapped me into it. Then I told her about the scene with him when his son was released.

"He's a terrible man," she said. "Four years ago he let his little girl die, no doctor or anything. Then he just buried her like some dead animal or something."

"Yeah, I heard about that afterward. I looked up the newspaper accounts." I hesitated, then asked, "Tell me something, was Bud Billings involved in that case?"

"From first to last."

"He got a conviction on criminal neglect."

"Should have been manslaughter, from what I hear," she said. "Anyway, Evans got off on probation."

"*They* got off. Mrs. Evans was charged, too."

"She's so much under his thumb, though."

We were quiet for a little while.

"Charley?"

"Yeah?"

"You were so right about what you said on the telephone. You know, about it being inevitable that sometime or other we'd be in a situation like this Evans thing. It'll probably happen again."

"Probably."

"When it does, let's be careful. We've got a lot to protect here, don't you think?"

In answer, I gathered her up and kissed her as tenderly as I knew how.

"Want to stay the night? I'd like you to."

"I've got to get out pretty early. I've got an eight o'clock meeting tomorrow."

"I'll set the alarm if you want."

"I never need an alarm clock."

"Well, if you're as sure as all that, then there's no problem, is there?"

"None that I can see."

"Maybe just one."

"What's that?"

"All that sleep I got today. I need something to tire me out a little, to put me to sleep."

She giggled. Sue Gillis does not often giggle. "A little exercise?"

"That might do it."

She giggled again, and without really consulting on the matter, we came up on the idea of exercising together. We had a great time. I was proud of myself.

It had the desired effect on Sue, too. The last I saw of her she was curled up in a ball beside me, breathing deeply, in the last stages of wakefulness. She did manage to mumble one more thing.

"Charley," she said — I wondered if she was talking in her sleep — "will you go with me to my parents' on Thanksgiving?"

Without thinking much about it, I patted her on her naked shoulder and said, "Sure."

10

At about five minutes to eight, I pulled into the parking lot outside my office, switched off the engine, and waited right where I sat. I was all alone, as I might have expected, but there was a steady stream of traffic, most of it headed north to Port Huron. As I hunched over the wheel and burrowed down into my coat against the cold November morning, I surveyed both sides of the street in search of anything out of the ordinary. Turning a little, I spotted a van parked across the street. Not Michigan Bell, but brown and unmarked, completely anonymous. It was the only vehicle parked on the block at this early hour.

I had lain awake some time after Sue fell asleep the night before thinking about what she had said about our visitors from Michigan Bell. I'd decided that maybe she was right. The mayor's boys must really be worried enough to try something like that. All the time I'd been in Detroit, all the big cases I'd tried, I'd never had anything like it pulled on me — or not to my knowledge, anyway. How can you really be sure about a wiretap? But then, I had to admit that none of those big cases of mine were essentially political. This one involving Mark Conroy most certainly was.

Thinking about all this, I didn't notice his big Cadillac until it turned into the parking lot. He brought it to a stop near mine. I was surprised to see that there were two people in the front seat of the car. In the passenger seat, beside Conroy, was a middle-aged black man, very dark, very serious, very capable looking. Our eyes met. He didn't smile, but he gave me a sober nod. Conroy jumped out of the car and headed over to me.

"What is it? Anything the matter?"

"I think we may have trouble."

He listened as I explained as briefly as I could what had happened yesterday afternoon. He asked just about the same questions that Sue had, but somehow he managed not to tell me how naive I was. Instead, he gave me one of those ironic looks of his and said, "Friend, you've been wired. I wouldn't be surprised if they're not listening to us right now."

"Out *here?*"

"You notice anything out of the ordinary right now?"

"Yeah, there's a brown van parked right over —"

He grabbed my arm. *"Don't point!"*

Without giving it a direct look, he casually noted the van's location and turned us away from it.

"Okay," I said, "what I think is, we ought

to go back to your original idea and go over to my apartment to have this talk you wanted to have."

"How do we know it's not wired?"

"Got any other suggestions?"

He sighed. "No, but I may come up with some ideas once we get there."

I wasn't quite sure what he meant by that, but I told him to follow me over there. Then, as an afterthought, I gave my address just in case we should get separated in traffic.

No need to worry. Conroy stuck to my rear bumper like a tick on a dog. As we moved swiftly into traffic, I looked in the side mirror and saw the brown van start up and try desperately to make a U-turn to follow. The guys on their way to work in Port Huron weren't giving an inch. The van was marooned, probably for a minute or so. That gave me a chance to hang a left onto a side street with Conroy close behind — then a right and another left, and so on, until I was fairly sure we'd lost the brown van. Then I drove the four or five blocks to my place in a direct route and at a reasonable speed.

When we got to my street, the brown van was there waiting for us. Or — who knows? — it may have been that one exactly like the one near the office had been there all the time. I didn't see it at first, might not have noticed it at all, because it was parked in a row of cars opposite my building. As I drove past on the way to the parking lot entrance beyond, I turned for a look inside it, but there was nothing to see, no one at all in the front — as I should have expected.

I led Conroy into the lot. He pulled his car into the space beside mine. Conroy and his companion hopped out. Exchanging looks, the two seemed not so much agitated or angry as annoyed.

We stood between the two cars for a moment or two, saying nothing, looking tensely toward the street we'd come from.

"You saw it, of course," I said.

"Sure I saw it," said Conroy.

"How'd they get here so fast?"

"They know your address. They must have a whole file on you by now. Or maybe they got it when you gave it to me in front of your office. They've got directional receivers, pick up anything."

"It's a power move," said the big black man. "They just harassin' our ass now."

I began wondering specifically who "they" were.

"Well, what do you want to do?" I asked. "I could take you over to that diner where we talked before."

"Too many people there this time of day."

"Lot of noise, cover up our conversation."

"Too many ears, too. No, let's do it here. We'll see what we can do to mess things up for them."

My apartment is in one of two identical buildings that share a single parking lot. It's sort of project housing for the middle class. The same builders did a complex just like it on the other side of town, and that's where Sue lives. They keep the elevators running, the toilets operational, even liven up the halls a little with the kind of prints and posters found in frame stores. I keep the place fairly clean, but I don't have much furniture, and what I've got is strictly utilitarian. No pictures on the wall, no framed personal photos or mementos of any kind scattered around. Some of that stuff is in boxes in the closet and up against the walls. All in all, even though I've been there nearly three years, the place looks like I had just moved in, or was about to move out.

When I unlocked the door and swung it open, I caught the look of sudden consternation on Conroy's face as he stepped past me and got a view of the interior. He seldom held anything back except the facts. "Just look at this," he said. "And I thought all lawyers were rich!"

"Now you know the truth."

He grabbed the big man and pulled him over.

"You haven't met LeMoyne yet." The way Conroy said it, he made it sound like it was my fault.

The man's name was LeMoyne Tolliver. He gave me a strong handshake, murmured something friendly, but withheld anything like a smile.

"I trust him," said Conroy. "You can, too."

Then without asking permission, or explaining what he was up to, he embarked on a tour of the place. I followed him.

"Is that your only phone in the living room there?" he whispered from the bedroom.

I nodded and followed him into the living room and watched, astonished, as he tore the telephone apart. He looked it over and tossed it aside.

He continued on his way, looking into the spare bedroom, and then he went on to the bathroom. It took only a moment to turn on the shower full blast and both faucets in the sink. Returning to the living room, he switched on the TV set and turned up the volume — the last half hour of the *Today* show. And, beckoning to both of us, he led the way into the kitchen.

"You got a radio in here?"

"Sure."

"Turn it on." He looked around. "What about the dishwasher?"

"What about it?"

"If it works, turn it on."

"But it's not full."

"Turn it on."

So I got down the detergent, shook it into the little chamber, did the settings, and threw the switch.

"Now, LeMoyne," he said, "if you'll just turn on the water there in the sink, we can sit right down at the kitchen table and get this meeting under way."

While Tolliver was occupied at the kitchen sink, I stole a look out the back window as Conroy had done a moment before. I saw that the brown van had moved to the rear of the parking lot, and that it now had mounted on top a small dish antenna that was pointed straight up at us. The van was idling, great wisps of exhaust smoke bubbling out the rear, probably to keep them warm inside; or maybe they needed the motor running to power all the electrical equipment — what did I know? But what with the *Today* show coming in from the living room, WDET's morning program blasting in over the radio, and all that sound of running water coming in from the bathroom and kitchen, I decided they would have a hard time hearing anything that was said.

Conroy beckoned me over to the kitchen table; I took my place. With all three of us seated, the conference began.

"Now, Sloan," he began quietly, "I'm going to go back to the beginning on this. Some of it you'll have heard before, but some of the details might interest you."

"Details are what I'm after."

"I'll do what I can." He frowned, looked up at a spot in the kitchen where the wall met the ceiling, and began to tell his story in little more than a whisper. I had to strain forward to hear.

"When I was appointed Deputy Chief of Police, nobody was more surprised than I was. Oh, I was in line for it. I had the best record of the other possible candidates, but I wasn't political, wasn't in the mayor's pocket the way the other two were. On the other hand, I'd never been in on any investigation that targeted the mayor. Of course I hadn't. Things like that weren't even thought of four years ago. What I didn't realize when I got the nod was just how bad things had gotten under the chief and his old deputy. Four years ago you could hardly say that Detroit had a police department at all. It seemed like everyone was on the take. Internal Affairs was as corrupt as any other squad. I guess things were so bad that even the mayor knew that someone had to do something. He decided I was that someone. No doubt about it. I was his choice.

"What I hadn't realized was the extent that all crime in the city was drug related. Sixty, maybe seventy-five percent of the burglaries and stickups were addicts raising money to feed their crack habit. Something like half the murders were drug burns or territorial disputes. It seemed to me that if we could put a lid on the drug trade, we'd have everything else under control. That's when I brought the Mouse into the picture. I created a drug task force and made him commander, reporting

259

directly to me. We'd worked together since our days on the TAC Squad, and I trusted him — then. And if our own little war on drugs didn't get off to a great start, we didn't blame each other. We blamed the system. We were undercut, undermanned, but most important of all, we were underfinanced."

Conroy went on to explain that nothing much could be done about the situation until the Mouse came up with a satchel containing a hundred thousand dollars from the evidence room. A dealer, not much more than a kid, had been successfully prosecuted at Frank Murphy Hall of Justice. The cash taken at the time of his arrest was presented in evidence, along with the bags of cocaine the undercover cop had sold him, a small transaction by local standards — the dealer was a newcomer in the trade. The Mouse had his eye on that bag of money. He hovered over it as protectively as a vulture over a dying man. He kept it within sight as it was walked back to 1300 Beaubien under guard. And the moment it was returned to the evidence room, before it could be made to disappear, he presented the requisition that Mark Conroy had written out, and walked upstairs with the booty.

That was the beginning of what became known as the W-91 Fund. From it, they paid informers. Informers, as Conroy had told me once before, came high — but they proved productive. Arrests were made. Dealers were brought to trial and convicted. More buy-money was added to the fund. But just about all those who were taken down were beginners or small-time operators, those out of the loop, with no big daddies to protect them. Nevertheless, each new conviction yielded more money for the W-91 Fund. It wasn't long before it started to add up. To paraphrase the late Senator Everett Dirksen, a hundred thousand here and a couple of hundred thousand there, and pretty soon you're into some real money.

At this point, I interrupted Mark Conroy. He'd promised details, but I hadn't gotten enough of them. One, in particular, interested me.

"Wait a minute," I said. "I've got a question."

"All right, what is it?"

"That safe where you kept the money — where did you get it?"

"That's an interesting point," said Conroy. "The Mouse and I needed one in a hurry when we grabbed that first hundred thousand, so we got it from the property room. They had three of them down there. I took the one that looked like it was the strongest."

"Did you change the combination?"

"That was beyond me — and beyond the Mouse at the time. But as we added money to that first grab, it occurred to me that if we got that from the property room, they probably had the combination on file down there someplace."

"Good thinking," I said dryly.

"I'm not as dumb as I look. Anyway, I had a salesman come around, and I bought a good, strong, new Mosler safe. But the funny thing was, that was when the powers-that-be got interested in our little project. The chief came around making inquiries. I told him that the Mouse was keeping records of payouts and pay-ins in code. He seemed satisfied and gave me a slap on the back and told me to keep up the good work. Then one of the bright young attorneys from the mayor's office dropped by and asked to be briefed on the W-91 Fund. So I did. Then the attorney wondered if a little publicity might not help things along. He wanted to send someone from the public information office over — maybe a reporter or two. I told him that was the last thing in the world I would want. By the way, Sloan, you might be interested to know that the young attorney left the mayor's office not long afterward and became an assistant prosecutor. Benjamin Timothy is his name."

"Uh-huh — the guy who's now trying the case against you."

"That's the one."

"When was this?"

"Maybe two years ago," said Conroy, "maybe a little more. By that time, it had become pretty apparent that the reason we weren't making any real dent in the drug traffic was because the big guys, the major traffickers who bought direct from the cartels in Latin America, had the protection of the mayor. They paid for it. He got a generous cut. He was a working partner in the entire enterprise."

"Just how did it become apparent?" I was offering him a challenge. He'd never really been specific about any of this. "There've been rumors about the mayor for years but no prosecutions. Even the Federal government has kept hands off."

"Okay, I can give you a very specific instance of the mayor's protection of one of the major players. We had an airtight case against Big Boy Duckett. You remember? About a year and a half ago?"

"I remember the case from the newspapers, but not the details."

"All right, this is how it went. Duckett was trying something new — bringing it in from Canada. The word was out in Toronto that we were paying big bucks for hard information. And some Lebanese who was probably a small trafficker himself gave us the word that there was a metric ton of cocaine coming down the St. Lawrence Seaway on a Panamanian freighter — a metric ton! — final destination, Detroit. Maybe he was jealous none of it was coming to him. He had all the right stuff — where it was docking and when, and how the contraband was disguised, everything. We worked very closely with the Royal Canadian Mounted Police on this. We had to. And if you think it was easy getting the Mounties to cooperate, well, it wasn't. But in the end, they not only monitored the off-loading of the contraband in Toronto, they trailed the truck that hauled it west all the way to their side of the Detroit–Windsor Bridge. We picked it up on our side and followed it to a warehouse on the near East Side, down by the river, only about a mile from Manoogian Mansion, by the way. We were there waiting for it. As soon as the truck pulled in, we went after it. There was a small army waiting for us. They resisted. Shots were exchanged, maybe a few hundred rounds, total. Probably the biggest firefight in the history of the Detroit Police Department. We lost one man killed and two wounded, one bad enough he left the department on disability. But we got Big Boy's pistol in hand, and a metric ton of evidence against him.

"Airtight case, right? Not when it came to trial. It wasn't that Duckett had such a sharp defense lawyer. The prosecution was just completely inept — purposely, by intention. They were told to lose the case, and they did. The mayor looked after his boy."

"Something about the search warrant, as I recall," I put in. "Or that's how I remember it."

"Tennis rules! The guy who signed off on the paper was the guy who tried the case. You know who that was? Benjamin Timothy, just six months off the mayor's staff."

"Maybe he just isn't a good trial lawyer. Lots of prosecutors lose cases." That sounded pretty weak to me, even as I said it.

"He looked pretty good up there in the preliminary hearing. I think you'll find him plenty tough."

I sighed. "You're probably right. I hope it never comes to trial."

"How can that be arranged?"

I laughed in spite of myself. "It can't," I said. "Look, I'm hoping for a miracle or something close to it. You're the only one who could help yourself, and as long as you're on suspension, you're in no position to do that."

"Explain."

"All right, I don't want to sound too pessimistic, but it seems to me that with all the pressure on you from the mayor — and I'll concede that it looks like that's where it's coming from — the only way you're going to relieve that pressure is by putting greater pressure on the mayor."

At that, Conroy and LeMoyne Tolliver exchanged looks that could only be described as conspiratorial.

"LeMoyne and I were thinking along those same lines. We're putting something together

265

that we want to run past you."

"Go ahead, by all means."

"Okay, but more background first. After Duckett walked out of court a free man and retired to the Bahamas, it was clear that if we were to make any real impact on drugs and through that on crime in general, we would have to find some way to get at the mayor. He was the disease. The rest, all the rest, were just symptoms."

"Maybe you're right, and maybe not. But go on."

"It seemed that the best way to get at him was through the Mayor's Squad. These guys are at least supposed to be cops, after all. Maybe we could find one who was a little digusted by what was going on at Manoogian. We looked them over, romanced a couple, and finally one found us. That seemed a little questionable at first, but he was from a cop family, all the way back to his grandfather in the days of the Purple Gang. And he had a great record before he went on the Mayor's Squad, so we were at least interested when he approached us and said he'd had it up to here with the mayor and his scams and skims. And then he began feeding us information that proved out — led to arrests. Nothing huge, nothing that even approached the Duckett bust, but good stuff. We were finally satisfied — we had a man on the inside.

"But what I didn't realize was that we were

feeding him information, too, about our intentions and our plans. The Mouse and I were the only ones who dealt with him — and more and more, it was the Mouse who kept contact. In the process, I guess, he got turned around. Who knows what he was offered? So what I'm saying is that our man on the inside turned out to be a double agent, working both sides to his own advantage but mostly for the mayor, and on the mayor's orders."

"Who're we talking about here? Timmerman?"

I surprised Conroy with that, maybe even astonished him. His mouth didn't fly open. His eyes didn't widen. But I knew from his silence that I'd gotten to him.

"How did you work that one out?" he asked at last.

"Give me a little credit," I said. "When I told you that Mary Margaret Tucker had dropped that name, I could tell, even on the telephone, that it hit you pretty hard."

"It did."

"And besides, I heard that Timmerman was on the Mayor's Squad — Sergeant Timmerman, right?"

"You knew he was on the Mayor's Squad? How did you find out? Did she tell you?"

"No, all I heard from her was the name. I got his connection from what we shall call an independent source. Just because I'm up here in Pickeral Point doesn't mean I don't have a few contacts back in Detroit." He didn't say anything to that, and so I continued: "So Timmerman served as a double agent. Maybe he planned the whole thing, too. And if he didn't, he certainly must have put it into operation. How long has he had your ear? How long has he been working with the Mouse?"

"A year, maybe a little more. He'd been feeding me information right up to the end. It was Timmerman who told me that they had the Mouse stashed at the Whitehall."

"Knowing that it would do us no good to talk to him, anyway," I put in. "They must have felt they had him in their pocket after his testimony at the preliminary hearing."

"Okay, look," said Conroy, "maybe I'm on suspension, and I'm limited in what I can do, but it doesn't put me out of the picture entirely. Where they've got the Mouse now, he *is* out of the picture. What I'm getting at is this. The task force is still operating independently, or at least some of it is. LeMoyne here brought me something big, very big, that the Mouse doesn't know about and neither does Timmerman. It's clean, uncompromised, and I think it's what we need to put the squeeze on the mayor."

"Let's hear it."

"Not with that van down there. Come on, Sloan, let's take a walk, just the three of us."

He stood up and Tolliver followed. More than a little confused, I rose from the table and went into the living room after them. There Conroy pulled me close and whispered in my ear: "I'll need a rag, something soft."

I nodded, returned to the kitchen, and pulled a torn T-shirt out of the box in the utility closet.

He beckoned and we went quietly out the door and into the hall. We backtracked to the elevator and took it down to the first floor. He took the T-shirt and began ripping it into strips on the trip down, saying nothing. I looked at Tolliver; there was a knowing smile on his face; I was glad that at least somebody seemed to know what was going on.

Out of the elevator, I turned toward the exit to the parking lot in back, more or less out of habit, I suppose. Conroy jerked me back and pointed in the other direction, toward the front door of the building. He led us out through the lobby outside, toward the trees on one side of the building.

About half a grove of trees, elms and spruces, had been leveled to provide space for the building and the parking lot behind it. That left half of the trees surrounding the lot in a kind of rectangular crescent. And so it was into the trees we went, moving quietly along one side of the building, the depth of the parking lot, and halfway across it to the van, which stood exactly as it had before. All the while we moved through the cover of the trees. They were thick enough and old enough so that we remained fairly well hidden, even though the elms were bare; the leaves were wet from the successive snowfalls, so we made little noise as we came up behind the van.

It had been backed into its parking space. We approached it from the rear. There were great fluffy clouds of smoke pouring out at us from the exhaust pipe. Conroy knelt down, selected a strip of T-shirt from those he had torn up, wet it in a patch of unmelted snow, and wadded it up. Motioning to me and Tolliver to remain where we were, he hopped forward and jammed the wet rag into the exhaust pipe.

He motioned Tolliver to the passenger side of the van and ran to a place just behind the driver's door. I followed Conroy.

"This shouldn't take long," he said with a wink.

It didn't.

It couldn't have been more than a minute before the motor of the van began sputtering and missing, and only seconds after that when it shut off altogether. The driver's door flew open, and a figure tumbled out, coughing. Conroy jerked him to his feet and slammed him against the side of the van, face first. He gave the driver a fast frisk and came up empty-handed.

From the commotion on the other side of the van, I assumed something similar was happening there.

"You got your guy?" Conroy called out to Tolliver.

"I got him."

"He give you any trouble?"

"You gotta be kiddin'."

"Then bring him over here." Conroy turned to me. "Sloan," he said, "stick your head inside and see if there's anybody still in there."

There wasn't. There was, however, enough exhaust smoke inside, even with both doors open, to start me coughing. I got it under control quickly enough and told Conroy the van was empty. By that time Tolliver had hustled his man over and had him up against the van beside his partner. Neither he nor Conroy was waving a gun around — though I was fairly certain that Tolliver, at least, had tucked one away. What they had done they had managed to do by pure physical mastery, helped out of course by the element of surprise.

Not that the two from the van were likely to offer much resistance. Both men were on the small side, about five-eight or five-nine, thin, young, and sort of nerdy. That's what my daughter, Lisa, would call them. I didn't recognize either of them from the team of phony Michigan Bell repairmen who had invaded my office — though the driver could have been the guy down on the ground, working from the truck. Each looked about equal parts scared and indignant at the moment. Tolliver was patting down his man.

"We don't got guns," the driver said. "We're tekkies."

"We're working on contract," said the other one.

I decided it was time for me to speak up. "What you did on contract is against the law. I'm an officer of the court, and I speak with some authority on this matter." That ought to impress them.

"It can't be against the law. It was the cops who hired us."

"The Detroit cops," I said. "Maybe you haven't noticed, but you're in Kerry County."

Neither of them had anything to say to that.

"The time has come," said Conroy, "for you to leave. Only first I'd like to see you take down that directional receiver on top of your van."

One turned to the other. Both shrugged. There were clamps on either side of the van roof holding the dish antenna in place, as well as wires that had to be detached. The two tekkies, working under close supervision, managed it all in a minute or two. That was all the time I needed to go back inside the van, this time covering my nose with a handkerchief, and pull off the reel of audiotape that was still revolving slowly on the oversized professional recording deck. I got a nod of approval from Conroy when he saw it.

"You don't need that," said the guy with Tolliver. "I wasn't getting anything on tape anyway, just radio and water running."

"We'll keep it as a souvenir," Conroy said. "That, too." He nodded at the dish antenna that Tolliver held cradled in his arms.

"Hey, man, you can't do that," said the driver. "We need it for work. That baby's worth ten long ones."

I pulled out my wallet. "I'll tell you what," I said, whipping my business card from it. "Wait a while and check with me, and you might get it back. I'll let you know."

"But . . ."

The other one flashed him a warning look that shut him up. Then he said to me, almost apologetically, "We're kind of new at this. Can we go now?"

"Sounds like a good idea to me."

They piled back into the van. Conroy removed the rag plug from the exhaust pipe, and the three of us aided with a push as the motor coughed unwillingly back to life. They were out of the parking lot in no time at all.

"Whatta you want me to do with this?" LeMoyne Tolliver pointed down where he had put aside the dish antenna as he set his solid right shoulder to the van.

"I don't know, in my car, I guess. Is it heavy?"

"Heavy enough."

It was too big for the trunk, but Tolliver managed to wedge it into the backseat. From there we adjourned to Conroy's Cadillac to keep warm as we continued our talk. Tolliver picked up where we had left off, turning in the front seat to address me in the back as Conroy stared out the windshield.

"I got a pigeon," he said. "Now, he ain't no ordinary pigeon 'cause he's been a trusted man in one of the big organizations in Detroit for about five years."

"What kind of organization?"

"Well, I ain't talkin' about no Big Three automaker." He giggled at that. That sounded a little silly coming from such a big man.

"Narcotics, Sloan," said Conroy. "One of the big dealers in town. Go on, LeMoyne, tell the man."

"I *know* he's trusted because he's a bagman. He not only did the collections; he did the payoffs, too. So this man's *very* trusted, if you get my meaning. He made deliveries first day every month to Manoogian Mansion, and he stood right there in that big red dining room while they did a count on the cash. Now, he was a good bagman, no sticky fingers on my pigeon, didn't do no skim. But still, they made him stand right there while they counted it out, goodly sums, too — went up and up as the organization prospered, so it was in the nature of a percentage instead of a flat sum, see?

"There was two there, one to count and one to check. From way back he remembers Benjamin Timothy, but not after he went into the prosecutor's office. But a few times, at least three but no more than five, he remembers the mayor himself was present. He just sort of watched over it all, made some remarks, joked with my pigeon about how his boss could surely afford a great contribution to his campaign fund, shit like that.

"He's still doin' it. Come first of December he'll make another visit. But he's suddenly been seized by a fit of conscience, wants to be a good citizen, and he's made a generous offer to assist us. Maybe even wear a wire, 'cause they so used to him after five years, they don't even pat him down. Oh, he's a good pigeon. He's an *outstanding* pigeon, wouldn't you say?"

Then LeMoyne Tolliver giggled again.

"He's better than that," said Conroy. "He even knows the mayor's bank and his special account number."

"Well, I'm impressed, all right," I said, "but since the safe has been emptied, how're you going to compensate him for his good citizenship? It seems to me he'd need all you had to get as far away from Detroit as he'd need to."

"Not a problem," said Tolliver. "I got something on my pigeon. I got it on so tight, he *knows* he's goin' to Jackson for the term of his natural life if he don't come across for us. Besides, he get put in that Federal witness program, and he got a good chance. He knows that."

"We figure to wrap up the package and

present it to the Feds unless the mayor calls off the prosecution," Conroy said. "We give him the option."

"Supposing the mayor takes the deal, how's he going to call off the case? It's in the court now. We've gone through preliminary examination. The trial's on the docket."

"He'll find a way."

"And what happens to your pigeon?"

"That's his lookout, right?" Tolliver seemed fairly indifferent; he probably hadn't given the matter much thought.

"We'll make leaving-town money for him part of the deal with the mayor." Conroy seemed to be improvising. "But don't worry about him, Sloan. The guy's no angel, believe me. You want to know what LeMoyne's got on him?"

"Not really."

A silence of some duration followed. All this time Conroy had been sitting behind the wheel of the Cadillac with his back to me. He seemed almost to be ignoring me physically even while he spoke, although once or twice I caught his eyes in the rearview mirror. But at last he turned around and gave me a hard stare.

"LeMoyne set up a meeting with this guy tomorrow night. We want you to come along."

"Why? You seem to have it all worked out on your own."

"We want you to take his statement. It has to be perfect for the Feds."

"I don't like it. It's messy."

"What's the matter with you, Sloan? You said yourself that the only way out of this was to apply some sort of counterpressure. This is the only kind that the mayor will understand. Of course it's messy!"

"You worried about my pigeon," said Tolliver, "he'll feel better if you along. He'll see we're serious about the Feds and the witness protection, all that. We'll take care of him, don't you worry."

"Look," I said, "what you're asking is out of line for an attorney. For a defendant awaiting trial, it's way over the line. I advise you against it."

"Sloan, do you call tapping your office telephone and sending those two after us to listen in with a directional receiver playing fair? Forget your tennis rules for once, why don't you?"

I sighed. "If you want an answer now, it would have to be no. The best I can do is say that I'll think it over. Maybe I'll consult my book of tennis rules and see what it has to say."

He wasn't amused. "I'll come back tomorrow, and we'll talk about it again. I think there are good reasons for you to be along on this. But it's going to happen with you or without you."

I could tell he meant it.

I was exhausted. It wasn't just all that running around, but what I'd heard from Tolliver and Conroy at the end had left me feeling so utterly wasted. Now, as I sat at my desk, I was trying to go over it, bit by bit, fact by fact, to see how something might be worked out that wouldn't be quite so risky. I'd brought up the possibility of counterpressure. What could I offer as an alternative?

How far could Tolliver's talking pigeon be trusted? After all, if he was as desperate as they said, he would tell them whatever he thought they wanted to hear, wouldn't he? Evidently he was out on the street with something, probably murder, hanging over him. What was to prevent him from leaving town, permanently? Just disappearing completely? I had my doubts.

And as for the fabled corruption of the mayor's administration, I still had my doubts about that, too. There were three views on the matter. What Mark Conroy said was true: There was a lot of money out there on the street, most of it from the huge Detroit drug market. Money corrupts; absolute money corrupts absolutely. But *who* was it corrupting? The popular view was that all that dirty money went right into the mayor's pocket. He was the big boss. A more sophisticated view, the one held by Conroy until he found himself in his present, desperate situation, was that the mayor accepted tribute from the local barons and allowed them to run things in their respective territories just about as they wanted. Finally, the one held by only a few was that others in his administration or under his protection might be making money, but that he himself was clean, satisfied with wielding the power that came with the office. I'm not quite sure why, but that last was the one that I had tended to support. Maybe it was because for years I was a student of Richard M. Daley, the late mayor of Chicago. Bad as his reputation was, and after the Democratic Convention of 1968 no politician in America had a worse one, nobody ever came even close to proving that Daley, himself, was corrupt; the man just loved the power he had. I'd also heard somewhere that the mayor was a fan of Dickie Daley's.

And after all, how badly had John Henry Harland performed as mayor? He had promoted and stimulated considerable reconstruction in the riverfront area of downtown Detroit — new hotels and office buildings, new stores and restaurants — so that tourists might be impressed, and never see the hotels shuttered and the abandoned office buildings, stores, and restaurants just a few blocks beyond that. Except for the annual Devil's Night Madness, he'd kept a tight lid on a city simmering with rage. And if you believed in the democratic system — one man, one vote — you had to admit that the mayor had satisfied the overwhelming majority of the people of Detroit.

The worst that could verifiably be said of him was that he dealt harshly with his enemies. It was clear that he considered Mark Conroy an enemy, and just as clear from my aborted lunch with Jack Rivers that the mayor meant to take this opportunity to deal harshly with Conroy.

But maybe there was an opening here, if I could just see it. Did I know anyone close to the mayor besides Jack Rivers? Was there any way I could send him a message? If I could, what message would I send?

The telephone rang. It was Sue.

"Hey, Charley. Sorry I wasn't awake when you left. You must have made your eight o'clock with time to spare."

"No trouble at all."

"You know, I'm still on this unrequested leave. How about lunch?"

I glanced at my watch. It was almost twelve. No breakfast. I was starving.

"Sounds good," I said. "You want to meet at Benny's, or were you thinking of something a little nicer?"

"Mmm, a *little* nicer."

"Then how about the Pickeral Inn?"

"You read my mind. I have to confess that's where I am right now."

"I'll be right over."

On the way, I circled the block looking for the brown van, or one from Michigan Bell, or anything even remotely like them. Nothing. At least theoretically, everything that was said in my office or on the telephone could now be taken down on tape. I was going to have to do something about that, though I wasn't quite sure what it would be.

Sue was waiting at a good table with a view. I settled in across from her and thanked her for the Diet Coke that was waiting for me.

"Did you sleep in?" I asked. "Mother Nature's own cure for everything that ails you."

"No, I'd slept enough," she said. "Actually, I've been pretty busy today. I had breakfast with Bud Billings."

"Uh-oh. Doesn't sound to me like you're maintaining proper distance."

"I'm not maintaining distance from the case — after all, I'm going back to it tomorrow — but what I'm working on is the 'proper' part."

"Which means?"

"I'm working on my attitude."

The waitress appeared. Whatever Sue had, she'd picked out while she was waiting for me. I ordered pickerel, the obvious specialty of the house.

Once the waitress was gone, Sue leaned forward and said quietly, "Bud likes old man Evans for these awful murders, all of them."

"I gathered as much from a little talk I had with him yesterday morning."

"There're a lot of things that tie up with his daughter's death."

"I know. I was interested enough in the case

that I looked up the newspaper accounts. It all happened before I hit town, you know."

She nodded. "Bud worked the case."

"Yeah, I know."

"Look, I know you're thinking we've both got the Evanses on our mind — if it's not Sam, it's got to be Delbert. But there are some troubling coincidences."

"Such as the dates?"

"So, you noticed, too. These murders began just about *four years to the day* from the time that Evans's daughter died and was buried."

"That might be an absolutely bona fide, one hundred percent coincidence, kiddo."

"All right," she said, "it could be a coincidence, but listen to this. Bud was present when the little Evans girl's body was exhumed. He said at each one of these 'snow burials,' he's flashed back to it. First of all, there was snow on the ground at the time."

"Not unusual for Michigan in November."

"All right, but get this, Charley. Bud says that she hadn't been under ground long, and the cold helped preserve the body. She was in her best dress, freshly washed, and the little girl was wrapped in clear plastic, the kind that your clothes come in from the cleaners, just like —"

"Listen, Sue, all I can say is that yes, there do seem to be a lot of coincidences, but I think maybe you're getting into dangerous waters here, and a lot of what you're saying is pretty circumstantial.

"It would be natural for Mrs. Evans to prepare her daughter for burial and dress her in her finest, wouldn't it? But can you really see her doing that for the little bodies that were found out there in the snow?

"And can you imagine old man Evans taking that kind of care with those same bodies? I think you'd agree that he's not the kind of guy who's too concerned with appearances. As for the coincidence of the clear plastic, it's an intriguing detail, but what else would you bury a body in if you weren't going to use a coffin?"

As I was winding down my spiel, it occurred to me that maybe I was protesting too much. After all, when I'd first read the account of Annie Louise Evans's strange death and even stranger burial, didn't I have my own suspicions? No one ever said that they were Christian Scientists who refused to call a doctor for their little girl, so religion evidently didn't play a part in her death. And Mrs. Fenton had said that somehow the Evans family always seemed to find money when they needed it, so it wasn't that they couldn't afford a casket.

Maybe they were the kind of sickos who hate their kids and kill them. Look at Susan Smith, drowning her two children in that lake. Sam was still alive, sure, but you could see that old man Evans despised him. Maybe Mr. and Mrs. Evans were depraved and thought the world would be a better place without children. Sure, the past and present events could be seen as mere coincidence, but they might also point to a killer. All I knew at the moment was that I didn't like the way this conversation was going.

"Look, Sue, let's just drop this, shall we? I'm sounding more like a defense lawyer every minute, and you're sounding more like a cop. Just remember what you said last night about having a lot to protect."

I watched her go through the same process: about to respond sharply, then checking herself, thinking about it, and nodding in assent.

"Okay, Charley."

Just then our salads arrived, along with a plateful of rolls. The waitress served us and fled back to the kitchen. She may not have shown much style, but it was a welcome interruption. It gave us time to regroup.

"Anyway, that's not all I did this morning," she said brightly.

"Oh? What else?"

"I drove out to Hub City."

"So you could nose around a little on your own? Really, Sue, don't you think —"

"Hush, Charley, shush, shush, please. Remember? I told you I was working on my attitude?"

I nodded.

"Well, that's what this was all about. I needed to talk to someone, and I drove out to

Hub City and had a session with Father Chuck. Remember him?"

"Sure, I represented him in that phony lawsuit the Evanses were threatening — Father Charles Albertus."

"You said you liked him."

"And you said if he weren't a priest, you could really go for him."

"Come on, Charley, give me a break."

I offered an apology in the form of a wink. Just kidding. "How did it go?" I asked.

"It went just great. I'll tell you, if there'd been more like him, I might never have left the Church."

"He probably told you that you never did."

"Something like that. But there is that somewhat pivotal divorce I went through about ten years ago."

"Not to mention the three I've had over the last twenty. Did he tell you he'd like to have you back in the Church?"

"Something like that."

"He made a pitch to get me back in, too — mild, restrained, but a pitch."

"But that wasn't what it was about, really. No, he was trying to be helpful. He said he'd just come back from a retreat with some other priests, and they got to talking about how adults never come to them with their problems. Oh, there's confession, of course, but that's often desperation for the one who's doing the confessing, and for the priest, it's, well, it's a formula — garbage in, garbage out. Priests just never get a chance to talk things through with people anymore. He says it's like they've been left out of the equation."

"So I suppose he was quite receptive."

"He helped me a lot. First of all, he listened. Total attention. Not that you don't, but I don't know, in a way you're too close to help. I guess what I needed was somebody objective who'd listen and tell me that I might have a problem. I told him about how the stress was built right into the job, that I handled sex crimes, and I gave him as a more or less typical example of my cases that kid who raped his grandmother. He was properly horrified and said that mine was probably the toughest job of all because I saw humanity at its worst."

"It's true, of course. I've wondered myself sometimes how you put up with it."

"But if you'd only *say* that, Charley, it'd really help a lot. Okay, okay, I didn't want to get together just to dump on you, so forget I said that. What I told Father Chuck is that what really troubled me was working on these serial murders of children. He was interested in that, wanted to know how the investigation was going. No, I didn't mention anything about the Evans family, but I did tell him we had some definite leads."

"You've got a witness. Sam Evans. He saw something, but he doesn't seem to know who or what he saw, though."

"Let's not go into that again. Father Chuck seemed surprised I was working on the case."

"How come?"

"He said he didn't know that they were being classified as sex crimes. He hadn't seen anything about that in the newspapers. He wanted to know if there was some reason to think they were. I explained that until we knew otherwise, we were assuming there was a sexual element involved, and besides, they had all available personnel working on it. I was just part of the team.

"But then I told him about my own response to the murders," she continued, "how I'd lost it out there on Beulah Road, gotten hysterical and everything. I'll tell you, Charley, when I saw little Billy Bartkowski in his jeans and plaid shirt, half-covered with snow, he looked like he was asleep, not dead. His eyes were shut. His mouth was just slightly open, like he was just taking a nap."

She almost lost it again. Tears formed in the corners of her eyes. She turned away from me and wiped at them with one hand. I reached across the table, grasped the other hand, and gave it a squeeze.

"Was that the boy's name?" I asked. "Billy Bartkowski?"

She cleared her throat. "That's right. Didn't you see the papers? The ones in Detroit are really giving it a big play — 'the third dead

287

and no end in sight,' " she quoted.

"I hope they're wrong about that."

"You're not the only one. But I must say Father Chuck had a very interesting take on all this. He reminded me of the three murders, two of the children were from his parish. He said it's not easy to face parents in such a situation, but that he would tell me just what he had told the Quigleys and the Bartkowskis. He said that the world is a sad and terrible place, that life can be hurtful to children as well as adults. Who knows what terrible trials awaited them as adults, what evils they might have met in their lives? Catherine and Billy had been spared all that. Every one of us has to die, so isn't it at least in some sense better to die when you're without sin and assured of a place at God's right hand?"

"I take it you're quoting him pretty directly?"

"Almost word for word."

"Did he say how the parents took that?"

She thought about that a moment. "No."

"What did you think about it? I have to say, Sue, it's talk like that that drove me out of the Church."

"And not your divorces?"

"They came afterward."

"I don't know, Charley," she said. "I have to say that I was moved. He *is* right, after all, the world *is* a terrible place. Maybe it's a case of you had to be there. If you'd seen him, heard him, you might have understood."

It wasn't often that I'd seen Sue so intense. Of course, she was badly tossed by these murders. Who wasn't? The death of a child is unthinkable, and now there were three children dead and not much to go on as to who killed them or why.

And it was clear that Father Chuck was in his compassionate way trying to help her through this nightmare. He was a priest, after all, a good one at that, and his offer of comfort was much appreciated. I was glad that he was there for her, in a way that apparently I was not, because I was thinking that she had begun to unravel.

As much as I liked and admired Father Chuck, I couldn't shake my innate ambivalence about the Church and its theology. Which was basically what he was spouting to her. Yes, I had been brought up to believe that God is good and that when a good person dies, it's God's will. And that the person will be assured a place in heaven at His side. But time and life had pretty much turned me into a skeptic, and now what I believe is that when you're dead, you're dead, and who knows if there's a heaven or a hell?

As good-hearted as Father Chuck was trying to be with Sue, I couldn't help but think that he was full of it. Someone had killed those poor kids for no good reason other than madness. They were little people who deserved to lead a full life. They were dead and they shouldn't be.

As I drove back to my office, I did another trip around the block, searching for potential eavesdroppers. Again, I was relieved to find no suspicious vans or trucks, no dish antennas pointing in the direction of the office. About halfway around the circuit, I stopped at a red light and was hailed from the left. I looked over there and found Dominic Benda waving and grinning. It seemed like he was back on the job — in uniform, except for the insignia, driving a patrol car without the domelight and the official county markings — just painted over.

"Hey, Charley!" he yelled. "How's the girl-friend? She recover from the party yet?"

I forced a smile and nodded as I waved back at him.

Then he leaned back behind the steering wheel, waved again as the light changed to green, and pulled away. Would you call that impersonating an officer of the law, or just refusing to accept retirement? Either way, it seemed sort of sick. He couldn't be much over sixty, maybe sixty-two, having spent his whole working life behind the wheel of a Kerry County Police patrol car. He'd probably been back at the station, hanging out with his former fellow officers, or maybe at lunch with them. They'd get tired of having him around soon, and he might wind up as a security guard someplace in Port Huron. If I'd asked him how he liked retirement, he would have told me it was terrific. They ought to have mandatory psychiatric care as part of the retirement package.

I pulled into the office parking lot and found it right there waiting for me — a Ford van, blue but otherwise like the brown one that had made life miserable for me that morning. Who knows? Maybe they'd just given it a quick paint job. I jumped out of my car and walked over to it, determined to have it out with them, no matter who they were — tekkies, Mayor's Squad, it didn't matter to me at that moment.

It was empty. Nobody in the cab, and although there was equipment of some kind in the back, nobody was concealed there. Confused, still annoyed, I trudged up the stairs and walked into my office.

Mrs. Fenton pointed behind me to the couch. "This gentleman has been waiting for you for about fifteen minutes." Something in her manner said that she approved of him.

He advanced toward me, a small man in his fifties, neatly dressed, what you might even call dapper.

Offering me his card with a modest smile, he said, "A mutual friend told me you might have need of my services." He smiled again, looking like a gerbil with a secret.

The card read ALONZO BRAGG, COMMU-

NICATIONS SECURITY SPECIALIST. Beneath that was a Detroit phone number but no address.

I frowned, unable to think for a moment what a communications security specialist might be.

"I understand you had a surprise visit from Michigan Bell yesterday afternoon. They may have left some equipment behind. Perhaps you might like me to look? They can be quite forgetful sometimes."

It had to be Mark Conroy who had sent him over. "This mutual friend," I said, "have you looked around his place?"

"Oh yes, this morning. It was very messy, bits and pieces left all over. He was sure you would have a similar problem."

"Certainly, Mr. Bragg, do what you can."

He brought up his equipment case, laid it on the coffee table, and unpacked it. When he finished, he had outfitted himself with a kind of electronic stethoscope that ended in a wand that could be pointed anywhere he liked. The entire contraption was powered by a battery pack he strapped around his waist. He smiled at me and nodded.

"Ready," he said.

"Then go right ahead."

He did, moving quite professionally and thoroughly through the room, covering it with the wand as he waved it this way and that.

Mrs. Fenton watched, fascinated by the entire operation. As he approached her desk, she stood up and moved away, taking a place beside me.

"He's the most fascinating man," she whispered. "We were having a conversation about astronomy before you came in, actually about the planets, the possibility of life on them. All very well informed. None of this UFO nonsense," she added firmly. If I didn't know better, I'd think she was smitten.

He pulled her phone apart and took out a little half-inch dot of a receiver and transmitter, all in one. He found one just like it in my phone, too, but made sure that my entire office was otherwise clean. When he'd finished, he held them out in the palm of his hand for my inspection. They seemed impossibly small to do all that they were supposed to do.

"These are *very* nice," said Mr. Bragg, "much better than that Brazilian junk I usually find. Would you mind if I kept them?" He was almost giddy with anticipation.

"I have no use for them."

"What about that item in the corner?" He pointed to the dish antenna.

"I'm holding that for the owners."

"You never know." He gave me an amused little smile then, as if he'd made quite a joke. "Now, I was told there's also some question about your place of abode."

"I suppose there is."

He followed me over to my apartment building in his blue van, did a sweep of my three rooms and kitchen, and pronounced them clean. We walked together back down to the parking lot, and he explained that he really hadn't expected to find anything in my apartment.

"How much do I owe you, Mr. Bragg?"

"Oh, don't worry about that. Our mutual friend has already taken care of it."

11

The next day took me by surprise. It was Saturday. What with running from the tekkies, trying to free that lamebrained Evans kid from the fell clutches of the county cops, and all of the attendant difficulties with Sue Gillis, I had lost track of time — or the day of the week, anyway.

I got to the office a little after nine and was surprised to find the door locked. That meant Mrs. Fenton hadn't arrived yet. Well, that seemed kind of funny. I let myself in and checked the answering machine for messages. There weren't any. If Mrs. Fenton was sick, she would have phoned in by now. She may not have been very likable — her constant air of fussy disapproval sometimes annoyed me — but she was dependable.

So I made the coffee and settled down to read the newspapers. I hadn't been at that very long when the telephone rang. Expecting it to be Mrs. Fenton, I was a little surprised when I recognized Stash Olesky's voice at the other end of the line. Hadn't we finished our business? Or was this something else?

"I tried you at home, Charley. Didn't expect to find you at the office today. I hope it's nothing too pressing."

"Oh? Why not?"

"You were coming over to our place today — remember? The Michigan–Michigan State game?"

I glanced up to the top of the page of the *Free Press*. My God, it was Saturday, wasn't it? No wonder Mrs. Fenton wasn't around. "To tell you the truth, Stash, what with all that's going on, I'd forgotten about it completely."

"Listen," he said, suddenly serious, "I hope you're not holding that business with the Evans kid against me. No hard feelings?"

"No, no, no, certainly not. I've pulled too many fast ones myself to be put out by that. And I must say that was a pretty speedy little maneuver. Your timing was impeccable."

"Oh, you mean the Annual Conference of Southeastern Michigan County Judges? That was just something I'd be more aware of than you would be." He paused. "But how about it, Charley? Should be a nice little TV party. Not a mob of people, just a few. Some of them you know, and some of them you don't. Come on by. You'll have a good time. Lorraine's cooking up a big spread for halftime."

"Yeah, well, Stash, the only thing is that when we made that date, I thought Sue would be available, and she's not."

"The Evans thing, huh?"

"No, we got past that. But they've got her

back on those gruesome child murders."

"I thought they took her off. Sent her home."

"Yeah, but they brought her back. It's a pretty small force, as you well know."

"Okay, then, Sue can't make it. I might have to run out anytime, myself. And I hope that's how it works out. It'll mean there's a break in the case. But what do women know about football, right? Come without her."

"I've got a conference with a client at eleven."

"Just so you're here by one. That's kickoff time. One o'clock, Charley. See you then. You know the address."

And before I could offer any more excuses, he hung up.

The client I was meeting was Mark Conroy, and experience told me that when somebody really begins to open up, they soon find they have a lot more to tell. And if he didn't, then I had a few questions that might stimulate his memory. But what we really had to talk about was his proposed course of action, what could be done and what couldn't. He would be trying to persuade me to come along and take part in this plan he'd worked out with Tolliver. I'd be trying to persuade him to drop it completely.

Conroy would be driving out to Pickeral Point, alone, and coming to my office. Whether we'd talk here or not, I wasn't sure.

Once bitten, twice shy. After all, I'd been out of the office more than eighteen hours. Somebody could have paid another visit during the night and rewired the place.

I closed up the *Free Press* and put it aside, then I hauled out a clean pad from the drawer and began making notes for my meeting with Conroy. About halfway through, my mind drifted off to more subjective matters. It bothered me a little that I had lost track of the day of the week. Was I such a workaholic that I just trudged off automatically to the office like some sort of programmed automaton? I hoped not. But then, this Conroy thing was big. Big politically, big news, and big in the sense that it was going to be damned tough to beat. It was going to take all I could give it, and that meant seven days a week.

That wasn't the question, though. For the better part of a year, my life had revolved around Sue Gillis and the office. The man said that what you needed for happiness was love and work. I had both, so why wasn't I happier? I'd never really thought much about it before. Since I'd moved up here to Pickeral Point, I'd been so busy putting my life back in order that I hadn't really noticed how much it had shrunk in the process. In the old days the booze had fueled a manic cycle that had lasted just about two decades. A long time. Take away the booze, and there was sure to have been a downturn. I didn't regret that. I made up for it by hard work, trying to build up this small-town practice so that it would support me, pay Mrs. Fenton's salary, and the office rent.

And, perhaps against all odds, I had succeeded in coming back from the abyss. After I'd won the Angel Harwell murder case, the clients came waddling in like a string of ducks on the shores of Lake Michigan. The Dr. Death trial had brought me a fair share of acclaim, too, and then there was the personal injury case I managed to finesse. I didn't have the gold Rolex and the red Rolls anymore, but I had recovered a large part of my self-esteem, something no one can put a price on. And I was off the booze, one day at a time.

But now, with my confidence mostly restored and with an ongoing involvement with a woman who was first-class all the way, I seemed to want something more. Maybe it was the confinement of small-town life. Maybe I missed the glamor and the glitz of my glory days in Detroit. Or maybe it was something far deeper, something I couldn't even define. Maybe inside me, somewhere hidden and unknown, there was a time bomb ticking, waiting to explode.

I decided to talk about it to Bob Williams. He was a friend. He was also my professional listener, my sponsor. It might be worth dinner to him. And I'd make it a point to look in on Stash Olesky's TV football party. My circle of friends and acquaintances was really pretty limited — clients, people in the justice system, and whoever might show up at an AA meeting. There had to be more to life.

My sit-down with Mark Conroy turned out to be a walkabout. Even after Mr. Bragg's thorough cleanup, Conroy was inclined, just as I was, to be distrustful of my four walls. I wondered how long it would take me to feel completely comfortable in my office again.

"What do you say we take a walk?" I suggested.

He nodded. "Sounds good to me."

I took him down River Road, and for the first block he seemed moderately interested in a couple of the old mansions on the left. He also kept an eye open for any suspicious vehicles along the way. But gradually he warmed to the subject at hand, and in no time at all he was talking as freely as he had in his Cadillac the morning before. He had some interesting things to say, though, and for the first time he revealed himself in ways I never would have guessed.

He began by saying he had the feeling that they had failed to convince me on the matter of the mayor's complicity in the drug trade. I confessed I still had a few doubts on that count.

"What would it take, Sloan?"

"More than an informant you've got so tight by the balls he'd be willing to tell you anything you want to hear. How do you know he's not just buying time to organize his departure? How do you know he hasn't left town already?"

"Because LeMoyne's got somebody sitting on him, somebody undercover, somebody we trust."

"Every minute of the day?"

"Every minute of the day."

"That must look a little strange. How can you be so sure you can trust him?"

"It isn't a him, it's a her, and that's why it doesn't look so strange. I trust her because LeMoyne trusts her. Any cop who would put herself in that sort of situation commands trust."

"For that matter, how do you know Tolliver is on the level?"

I could tell I was getting to him. That was my intention. I wanted him to see the holes in this plan of his. (Plan? The more I thought about it, the more it seemed like so much wishful thinking.)

"Sloan, look, I don't know how it is for you, but in my business there are certain people you trust all the way, and certain people you don't."

"You seemed to trust Timmerman up to a point. You trusted the Mouse all the way. Your record isn't exactly infallible, you know."

He looked at me darkly and said nothing. Staring ahead then, he just kept plodding along. While Conroy was not, as far as I could tell, one of those arrogant individuals who thought himself above criticism, he obviously didn't like to be reminded of his lapses in judgment. None of us do. It occurred to me at that point that this might turn out to be a very short meeting. I didn't want that, and so I spoke up.

"Okay, look," I said, "maybe that wasn't exactly generous of me. We probably ought to start this discussion all over again."

"Oh no." He shook his head emphatically. "You didn't say anything I haven't told myself over and over again in these past few weeks."

"We all make mistakes. Looking back, I have to say that the first twenty-five years of my adult life were one big mistake."

He responded with a thin smile, walked on a bit, and then: "You look at me, my color — not black and not quite white — and you can see the source of my problem. Or maybe I should say the source of my confusion. My mother was white. She was tough, and strong, and capable, and she gave me a real sense of my own worth. She never told me who my father was, but she never allowed any doubt in my mind that I was welcome in her life. We got through all of that illegitimate shit better than any mother and child ever did. I really believe that. I grew up right up the river in Port Huron, but I knew she was from Detroit, had family there she never knew. It was just the two of us, but that was all the family I ever needed. She made a good living for us keeping books for one of the shipping companies up there, and she sent me to college, Michigan State, and died while I was in my senior year — cancer — and she never even let me know that she was sick.

"But out of college and with her dead," he continued, "I headed straight for Detroit and the police academy. I had some idea I was going to investigate those relatives, find them, confront them, and give them holy hell for what I supposed they'd done to her. I found them, all right, her mother and father in Southfield and two brothers in Royal Oak, but by that time I was getting on with my own life, and they just weren't worth bothering with, the hell with them."

"Good decision," I put in at that point.

"They were just ordinary people," he said, "and she was probably as dissatisfied with them as they were with her. But I have to say, Sloan, that the way she brought me up, good as it was for me as a boy, it didn't really prepare me for life in Detroit."

"Why? How do you mean?"

"I mean that she brought me up thinking that color didn't matter and I found out in Detroit that it did."

"That's kind of an understatement."

"So I guess I chose to be black, while before that I chose to be white, or maybe not consider

303

it at all. I married black — a woman even more ambitious than I was, if that's possible. My partners were black. And if the overwhelming majority of those we pursued and arrested were black, well, that sort of rounded out the equation.

"But then a funny thing happened. While I was on a TAC Squad operation, one night ten years ago, Ralph Smerka saved my life."

"The Mouse."

"Yeah. He didn't just pull me back or push my head down, he stepped in front of me and took one in the gut, one that would have hit me, or anyone else of normal size, right in the chest. So I was his for life, which made us more or less best friends. And he was white. So I had to sort that out. Timmerman came along and volunteered his services. And then Mary Margaret turned me inside out, and . . . Well, you know what happened, or you must have a pretty good idea."

Conroy was as close to sounding human as I had ever heard him. His honesty was almost unsettling.

"We'll work out the details later," I said.

"Betrayal is what happened," he said, his voice firm.

"And it looks to you like a conspiracy."

"Something like that. Call it an unorganized conspiracy."

"Timmerman's white?"

"That's right. So now I'm thinking black

304

again, and LeMoyne is my man. I do trust him, Sloan. He's a crude, tough, mean, old-fashioned cop, just the kind I'm not — or so I've told myself ever since I entered the academy. But he's on my side, and he's come up with a way to help me out of this mess I'm in. Listen, you think I'm blind to all the difficulties with this scheme of his? Certainly it's got holes in it. But right now it's the best shot I've got, so I owe it to LeMoyne and to that cop who's baby-sitting the pigeon to give it a try. They've stuck their necks out for me. I owe them."

"And you feel I owe them, too?"

"That's for you to say. Your presence tonight would be appreciated."

It was my turn to remain silent for a while, quite a while, as we continued our amble down River Road. Traffic seemed to have picked up, cars whizzing back and forth in both directions, people rushing to get through their Saturday errands before the big game began. Fully half the houses in town would be shut down tight through the afternoon, their occupants settled before television sets, participating global village–style in a fall ritual, Michigan versus Michigan State.

There was a little park at the next corner. I led Conroy off the sidewalk and down a path to a bench on one side of it. This had been the only vacant lot there on River Road. A few years before, the town of Pickeral Point had

305

acquired the property and done a little to improve it — put in grass, some playground equipment — and christened it the George Romney Memorial Park. On this raw November morning, it was empty except for two kids, about eight and nine, playing on the swings. They were bundled up against the cold, but from what I could see, they looked like brothers. Neither of them paid us any attention.

Conroy gave me one of his thin smiles as we sat down on the park bench. From there we had a close view of the river. We watched a freighter northward bound. There was something almost majestic about it — an object that big, so close, moving along so slowly. He seemed to sense it, too. We both kept quiet until it had passed out of sight. Only then did he speak up.

"Let me tell you a story, Sloan," he said. "It's one that you've heard before, read in the newspapers, but I've got a few comments on it you ought to hear."

"Okay, go ahead."

"You remember some years ago, you were still in Detroit at the time, there was a van found downtown on a riverside parking lot? Well, it wasn't exactly 'found.' Nine-one-one got an anonymous call telling us it was there and that we should take a look inside. I was working late that night — I worked late a lot of nights back then — and so I went out on it with the Mouse. We weren't the first on the scene. A patrol car in the area had been dispatched right away. But when we pulled up, the two uniform cops were still arguing about opening up the back doors of the van to take a look inside. They'd taken their time because one of them thought that what was inside might be a bomb. Not a wild idea at all. He wanted to call out the bomb squad. Well, I took responsibility. I had a hunch, and I was acting on that hunch, and since I was still playing supercop, I sent everyone back behind the patrol car and opened up the van myself. You know what I found, don't you? You remember?"

These rhetorical halts were getting on my nerves. I signaled for him to get on with his story. But yes, he was right. I remembered what was in that van. There was no one in Detroit who didn't.

"The doors weren't locked." He seemed a little obsessed, as if he had to get this out, no matter what it cost him. Cops have these stories, and they have to tell them. "All I did was give the doors a quick pull and jump back, like maybe I was afraid of a bomb, too. But there was no bomb, just a bad smell. The light was bad. I called for a light, and one of the patrol cops shined his flashlight inside. At first, I thought it was a joke. I thought maybe somebody had stolen a butcher's van and phoned it in as sort of a prank. It was a pile of raw meat, cut and stacked loose on the floor of the

307

van. But then we saw the heads. Just tossed off to one side, two men and a woman. The raw meat, it was body parts — legs, arms, torsos, a pelvis separated from a torso, hands, feet.

"The cop holding the light let out a yell and dropped it. His partner threw up all over the Mouse, and me, I just picked up the flashlight and looked again. I thought I'd seen everything, but I'd never seen anything like that. And of course it got better afterward. You remember, don't you, Sloan?"

It was a rhetorical question.

"It turned out that it had all been done with a chain saw. The woman, at least, had been shot dead first. That was the coroner's report. We got IDs on them and knew what it was about — drugs, crack in this case. And knowing the victims, we had a pretty good idea who was responsible. It looked to be territorial — kids trying to bust Minto the big-time; the oldest of them was just twenty-two. But where had it taken place? Where was the butcher shop? The van was clean, stolen the night before from out in Birmingham someplace. So we had to find the crime scene. And what happened? The janitor up at the Democratic Party Club called us up and said somebody sure made a mess in the basement. That was what they'd used for their slaughterhouse.

"The Democratic Party Club." Conroy's voice was getting tighter. "Now, you tell me,

Sloan, who is the head of the Democratic Party in Wayne County?"

"Are you going to say that the mayor was present, that he witnessed it, that he ordered it?" I asked. "That's a very big jump. Too big. The way I remember it, the building was closed that night. Anybody with a key could have gotten in and used the basement, and just about every registered Democrat in the county had a key. I exaggerate, of course, but there were a lot of them floating around. And who knows how many unauthorized copies there were?"

He stared at me. Then he said slowly, as if trying to reason with a child, "I'm saying that they couldn't have used the basement of the Democratic Party Club without the mayor's say-so. I'm convinced, I've always been convinced, of his complicity in this."

"It would seem a lot more reasonable," I said, "that they did it there to embarrass him, to make people think exactly what you're thinking. It looks to me like it was a clear shot at the mayor, Conroy."

"Oh, a Republican plot — is that it?"

"Don't be absurd." He *was* being absurd, of course, ridiculing my effort to be rational about something about which he had become blindly emotional. I looked at him — no more than a couple of feet separated us on the park bench — and I wondered what had happened to that supremely confident man who had walked into my office at the beginning of the month. Though not exactly wild eyed, there was something altogether too intense about him. He had the squirrely look of a true believer that made you want to back away fast. It revealed what he'd kept hidden before: Conroy was a man with a monkey on his back.

"You hate him," I said, "don't you?"

He took that, gave it a moment's consideration, and said, "Yes, I guess I do." It was as if it had come clear to him for the first time. He leaned back on the bench and thought about it some more. "If I could bring the mayor down, send him to prison for the rest of his life, then I wouldn't mind doing time myself."

"Then you won't deal with him? You just want to make a case against him and hand it over to the Feds?"

"I don't know. I haven't thought it through yet." At that moment, Mark Conroy, who once carried himself like a cock of the walk, looked like a small boy who couldn't find his mother at the shopping mall.

Getting up from the bench, he walked slowly off toward the river. I watched him go, feeling pity for him for the first time. There was a walkway above the riverbank with a protective guardrail that ran the length of the park. He didn't stop until he reached it. He stood with his back to me, leaning against the guardrail, gazing off across the river to Canada. Time passes slowly when you're sitting alone like that, so I don't really know how long I left Conroy to himself. Not long, probably a couple of minutes. The boys had left the swings for the slides; they were climbing up the slippery descent, falling back, laughing, climbing up again. At last I rose and went to join Conroy.

By the time I reached him, another freighter was moving up the river. We watched it together. It wouldn't be long before the big boats disappeared until spring.

Conroy spoke up. "You know, when I was a kid in Port Huron I used to go down to the riverfront and just watch those big things go by. When I was eleven or twelve, I spent a lot of Saturdays like that. I used to think it'd be great to work on one of those boats. I'd go around the world and see it all."

"A kid could have worse ambitions," I said.

"I told my mother about it. You know what she said? 'Not good enough. You were meant to be somebody.' "

"And so she was right. You are somebody."

"Yeah, I'm a cop."

He didn't look bitter. He looked thoughtful.

"I've got a question for you."

"What is it?"

"Did Mary Margaret Tucker know the combination to the safe in your office?"

He took a deep breath. "I know I told you," he said, "that the Mouse was in charge of the safe. He kept the records, and he went into it for the payouts, though I okayed each one. So on the books, there were only two of us who knew the combination, but in practice only one of us used it. The Mouse. I don't think I had occasion to open it up more than three or four times in as many years. Because of that, I had a hard time remembering the combination to the safe. I guess I don't have a very good memory for figures."

"I'm not sure anybody could keep a safe combination in his head under those circumstances. I know I couldn't."

"Once or twice I had to ask the Mouse to open it for me, which was annoying, so I decided to write the combination down someplace. What I did was put it on a card in my Rolodex. I didn't want to make it too obvious, so I put down the name Henry Mosler and entered the combination, made it look more or less like a telephone number."

"Seems like a good idea."

"As my secretary, Mary Margaret had access to my Rolodex, used it all the time. She must have noticed the card and figured it out because once she made some sort of reference, I forget exactly what it was. I think she said someone was as rich as Henry Mosler, something like that, and gave me a wink and a big laugh."

"What was your reaction?"

"None. I didn't say anything and didn't

even wink back."

"It sounds like she knew the combination, all right, or could have written it down herself."

"Yeah, I guess so." He nodded. "She must have known it." Then he dug into the pocket of his jacket and produced an index card. "But here," he said, offering it to me, "I brought a little present for you. You can ask her about it yourself."

I took the card. On it were Mary Margaret Tucker's name, address, and telephone number. I was surprised. I wondered how long he'd had them.

"You were right," he said. "She wasn't that hard to find. I didn't go out looking myself. I thought for a couple of reasons it'd be better if I kept my distance. A friend of mine from my old TAC Squad days looked her up for me."

"Thanks," I said, "I'll ask her. But tell me something. Why did you two break up?"

He sighed audibly. "Oh, the usual reason in situations like that. She wanted me to leave my wife, wanted us to get married, and I didn't know if I wanted to do that, so I stalled. I guess I stalled too long because we had a big blowup. Not the first, but it turned out to be the last. I sure as hell hated to lose her, though."

"And when did the final break come?"

"In the fall — not too long after her classes

at Wayne State began."

"And the money was in the safe?"

"Look, if you're thinking she might have taken it, it was a good week after she left before the money turned up missing."

It took only a moment to consider that. "But you said yourself that the Mouse was in charge of the safe," I said. "He was the one who found the safe empty, wasn't he?"

"Yes, he was."

There was a silence that went on for too long.

"Ladies and gentlemen of the jury, I rest my case."

Either one of them could have taken the money. They could have been in collusion, or could have worked independently. At this point it didn't matter. What did matter was that I had extended the possibilities by one. That might prove to be the most important thing to come out of this morning's meeting.

I looked at my watch. "Let's go back," I said.

On the return trip we didn't have much to say for a while. The light wind we'd had at our backs seemed much sharper as we walked into it, sharp enough to discourage conversation. And besides, I had temporarily exhausted my store of questions pertaining to the disappearance of the W-91 Fund. And Conroy had evidently run out of arguments intended to bring me out with him and Tolliver that night.

You didn't engage in small talk with a guy like Conroy. But when, about halfway back to my office, he started to talk, he wasn't talking small.

"You've got some nasty homicides out here," he said.

"We sure do. Children. Bodies wrapped in soft plastic. Left in the snow. Three so far. No solid leads, as far as I can tell."

"Yeah, I read about it in the papers." He held back, as if he were deciding whether or not to go on. But then, after five or six paces, he began talking: "You know, when I was homicide detective — this was about ten or twelve years ago — we had a case sort of similar to this one up here. You were in Detroit then. Maybe you remember it."

There was something back there in my memory, but it was vague. "Maybe," I said. "Tell me about it."

"There were two homicides — both victims were kids, eight and nine, both black, both in the same part of town — east side, off Jefferson. The bodies were found about three weeks apart. Similar circumstances, sexual element in both instances. It looked like we had a serial killer on our hands. I'll spare you the details of the investigation. But you know who it turned out to be?"

I matched Conroy stride-for-stride, waiting for him to continue. He looked straight ahead, his face in that same tight mask.

"It was a cop," he said, "a uniform cop. I knew the guy myself. I'd done a little time in a patrol car with him not long after I was out of the academy. He was black, too. See, the operative principle in our investigation was that it had to be somebody children would trust. He asked the kids if they wanted to take a ride in a police car. That's all it took. It turned out he'd operated without a partner on both occasions. The department was short-handed then, and on the day-watch, if a partner slicked out, they'd do one man in a car. So that was it. The days his partner was out were the days the murders happened — on his beat."

"I remember the case. The guy was convicted."

"He got two consecutive life terms. Didn't last a year in Jackson."

"Quite a story."

"You know any of the detectives up here who're working the case?"

"I know a couple of them, one very well." I hesitated to mention Sue Gillis, but knowing Conroy, he probably already knew about her.

"Tell them to check out their own. Maybe also the town cops up in that little town — what's the name of the place?"

"Hub City?"

"That's it," said Conroy. "Yeah, tell them to check out the cops."

That took us to the office parking lot. I went

with him to his Cadillac. There we stood regarding each other silently for a moment.

Then, with a stretch of his mouth that was more grimace than smile, he said, "Well, what about it, Sloan? You with us tonight?"

"I'm going to surprise you."

"Okay, surprise me."

"I'll come along, but I'll be with you mainly as an observer. You need protection, Conroy. Protection from your enemies, your friends, and protection from yourself."

"Just along for the ride, then?"

"Coming along to keep you out of trouble."

Although he'd gone to Wayne State Law, Stash Olesky had done his four undergraduate years at Michigan State. I'm not sure I knew that until the afternoon I spent at his house watching the Spartans do battle with the Wolverines. It only took a minute or two in front of the TV set with him to make it clear whom he was rooting for. He was partisan. He was passionate. He was loud. When Michigan State took the opening kickoff, he jumped up from his chair and began shouting encouragement to the receiver, who, with Stash's vocal help, managed to run the ball back to the 25. That, of course, was just the beginning. He was up and cheering on every offensive play, no matter how small the gain. Dropped passes drew agonized groans from him. Then, after a couple of measured first downs, the Spartans

317

were forced to punt from the 50, and Stash proved nearly as noisy when his team went on defense. Funny, I thought, he'd always seemed like a pretty normal guy up until now.

Anybody who had spent as much time on barstools as I had has watched a lot of football. But in my condition I had never been quite attentive enough to pick up the fine points of the game. Most of the time I was lucky if I knew which side had scored the touchdown or even who had won the game. Up here in Pickeral Point, I just never seemed to turn on the television set on Saturday or Sunday afternoons or even Monday nights. It occurred to me that this Michigan–Michigan State game was probably the first football since I was a teenager that I'd watched absolutely stone-cold sober.

Somebody had shoved a beer at me the moment I walked in the door. I declined and asked for a Diet Coke. It was just something to hold in my hand. I sipped at it as I listened to Stash going crazy beside me and took stock of the others assembled in the big living room. There were about a dozen of us, counting the two Olesky kids, Tommy and Stan, who were about eleven or twelve. Stash, it turned out, had played football in high school and had red-shirted at State for two years — "the toughest and greatest time of my life," he later claimed. John Dibble, who had a storefront practice across from the courthouse, was seated on the other side of Stash, quietly but emphatically rooting for Michigan. Mrs. D was there, too, looking a little embarrassed by the frequent outbursts of our host. The others were neighbors and friends, I guess. I'd been introduced to them hastily, male and female, when I made my appearance just before kick-off. I'm not much good at names, especially in situations like this, but they seemed a lively, affable bunch — or maybe they'd been jacked up to a pitch by the host's high spirits.

At any rate, nearly everybody seemed to be having more fun than I was, and I felt a little guilty about that. The beer flowed freely, though most of the women sipped white wine, and there I was, pulling away at my can of soda, trying to keep my mind on the game. It wasn't so easy, considering the talk I'd had with Mark Conroy. He'd given me a lot of information I'd have to process later. And I felt obliged to pass on to Sue that bit of advice he'd offered: "Tell the cops to check out their own." How she would take that I had no idea.

That was how the first quarter went. At the end of it, I took advantage of the commercial break and headed back to the kitchen for another Diet Coke.

Mrs. Olesky — Lorraine — was there, bustling around, pulling things from the oven, putting together the halftime feast that Stash had promised.

"How's the game going?" she asked.

"Nothing to nothing, about as even as it can be."

"That's good." Then, probably thinking that sounded disloyal, she said, "Or is it? I mean, Michigan's favored, right? Don't tell Stash I said that."

"My lips are sealed, Lorraine."

Laughing, I knelt down and began feeling around in the ice-filled tub for a can of Diet Coke or its near-equivalent.

"There's a little of everything in there, Charley."

I found what I was looking for, and Lorraine tossed me a dish towel for drying my wet hands.

"Where's Sue Gillis?" she asked. "Couldn't make it?"

"Sue is probably out in the county someplace chasing down a lead on these hideous child murders. If there are any leads."

"Working Saturdays on it?"

"She'll work every day of the week if that's what it takes."

"According to Stash, she might be a bit too involved."

"They grounded her for a couple of days because of it," I said. "And now she's back on the case, more determined than ever, or maybe more obsessed. We're having dinner tonight. I'll try to lighten her load a little."

Lorraine Olesky listened, nodding sympathetically. Then a great roar went up from the living room. That had to be a Michigan State touchdown.

I heard Stash yelling, "Charley! Charley! You gotta see this on replay."

"I've been summoned," I said to her. "See you at lunchtime."

I arrived in time to see a Spartan running back thread his way through half the Michigan team and do a silly little dance of triumph in the end zone. Football players just don't have much dignity anymore. But Stash seemed to enjoy the performance just as much the second time around.

The rest of the second quarter belonged to Michigan State. They went charging up the field but seemed to lose the ball — a fumble, an intercepted pass — just when it looked like they might push it over. They did, however, come away with a field goal, so that when the half ended the score stood at 10 to 0, Michigan State.

"Well," said Stash, rising, "I can live with that. Should be a good second half." He went over to the TV set and turned down the sound, then gave his belly a healthy slap. "How about something to eat, you guys?"

Lorraine had laid on quite a spread. There was chicken, baked beans, and salad, and for the more ethnic among us, kielbasa and kraut. Not to mention a mighty array of condiments, a chocolate cake, and a plateful of cookies. It was a little after two, and I was hungry. I grabbed up a plate and some silverware and joined the line that had formed around the table.

John Dibble was just ahead of me. He turned in my direction and looked at me suspiciously.

"Did you send Delbert Evans over to me?" he asked.

"No, but I tried. That was when his son got taken in for questioning on the Catherine Quigley homicide. I got trapped into taking care of it myself. He's not a very likable man, is he?"

"No, he's not. He came over to my office trying to promote a false arrest suit. When I turned him down, said I didn't think he had a case, he accused me of cozying with the cops."

"I suppose he figured it'd worked with me, why shouldn't it work with you."

Mrs. Dibble stuck her head out from behind her husband. "He's a terrible man, Mr. Sloan."

"Charley."

"All right, Charley then. But he *is* terrible. Before you came up here, he was involved in a child-neglect case that was — oh, I don't even like to talk about it, it was so awful. They ought to just lock him up and throw away the key."

"Come now, Sarah, everybody deserves due process. Where would Charley and I be without it, right, Charley?"

"Our bread and butter. Speaking of which . . ."

I nodded at the table, and the Dibbles realized their turn had come. They excused themselves and began piling their plates high, perhaps with the intention of adding an inch or two to their already considerable waists.

As for myself, I went ethnic. The kielbasa and kraut looked too good to pass up.

I had dinner with Sue that night. I wasn't quite sure what her mood would be. All too soon these murders would tie her up in knots again. Why not? They had us all tied up. The whole county seemed to be talking about nothing else. I had heard at Benny's Diner that Hub City had virtually shut down. A pall of fear had settled over the place. Parents refused to let their kids out to play after school. Mothers were probably going nuts keeping their kids in. This was a tough one for a town that had already had its share of hard knocks. I wondered what Sue would have to say over dinner.

I picked her up at her place about seven-thirty. I suspected she hadn't been home long, not long enough to change clothes, anyway. She managed a wan smile and a greeting, grabbed her purse, and we were off. I'd made a reservation at a steakhouse in St. Clair, so it took a bit of a drive to get us there. She was quiet on the way, though not sullen.

"How's the investigation going?" I asked. "Are you still working for the Evans family?" "Forget I asked."

So maybe she was a little bit sullen.

But she apologized later and unburdened herself during dinner. Bud Billings still liked Delbert Evans for the homicide, and she respected his intuitions. After all, there was that matter of the time of year the murders had begun and the way the daughter had been buried. It seemed to me we were having the same conversation we'd had at lunch one day before. But since, as they had heard, old man Evans was going around the county trying to peddle a false arrest suit for his son, the two of them had been told to steer clear of Delbert until they might actually get something on him.

"But how are we going to do that," she asked, "unless we bring him in for questioning and then check out his story?"

"Evans may get a buyer on that false arrest suit," I said.

"Yeah," she said, "that's what Bud's afraid of." She sighed. "So we've just been rechecking details at the crime scenes, trying to get anything that we might have overlooked. We've got a tire print now, but it matches Ford, Mercury, Chevrolet, Pontiac, Dodge, and Plymouth. Any idea how many of those there are in the county?"

I was about to mention to her what Mark

Conroy had told me when she changed the subject.

"I told my parents to set an extra plate at Thanksgiving," she said.

"And how did they react?"

"Very positively. They can't wait to see you."

I couldn't say I was that eager. Although I'd said yes to the occasion, I still felt uneasy about it. To me it seemed to imply a commitment that I hadn't yet fully made.

"How many will be there?" I asked.

"Oh, just family."

"Out in Southfield?"

"Yes, that's the house where I grew up."

"But bigger now, I suppose. Empty nest and all that."

"I suppose so, but their part of Southfield's been changing."

"That's changing, as in ethnic composition?"

"Yes, the usual."

"I see."

"Don't judge them, Charley. They're a different generation."

"I'm not so sure of that," I said. "How old's your father?"

She hesitated, then: "He's sixty-two."

"Not all that much older than I am."

"Now, don't start up, okay? Just let me handle it."

"With pleasure, my dear."

There was a break then, during which I polished off the remainder of the lake perch on my plate, and Sue chewed away dutifully at two bites of sirloin from the slab of meat on her plate. She swallowed them, first one and after great effort, the other. Then, with a sense of firm resolution, she pushed it away from her.

"That's it," she said. "I can't finish this."

"You don't have to," I said. "Want them to wrap it up for you?"

"No, I'll just look at it in the refrigerator in a week and decide it's not fit for human consumption."

I signaled for the waiter to bring me the check.

"Sue," I said, "there's something I wanted to pass on to you."

"What's that?"

I told her what Mark Conroy had told me. Although I didn't mention him by name, I'm sure she knew who he was when I described him as a client of mine who used to be a cop.

She looked at me skeptically and said, "I'm not sure just how seriously I ought to take that. 'Check out your own'? Our own look pretty good to me."

"Yes, but both the county and the Hub City cops operate in their patrol cars without partners."

"You know the reason for that, Charley. Both the county and Hub City are short-handed, undermanned. Underwomanned, too."

"That's not the point, Sue. The point is, they're out there completely on their own. And kids of that age are crazy for policemen."

"The point is, Charley, the guy who gave that to you may have been a pretty good cop, but he's in so much trouble now that any advice he hands out is subject to question."

"I'm not going to argue that with you, Sue. Not now."

"Oh, Charley, I'm sorry." She shook her head unhappily. "All this has me so confused, so frustrated, so miserable that I just don't want to talk about it. Is that okay?"

She was right. There was no point in continuing the discussion. The waiter came with the bill. I laid down enough to cover it plus a reasonable tip.

On the way home I was wondering just what sort of apology I should offer when I ran out on her later. She seemed so frayed and unhappy that I was afraid she might take it terribly personally if I left her at her door. Still, I'd promised Conroy I'd go with him. I was due in Detroit in a little over an hour.

But as I pulled up to the entrance of her apartment building, she laid a hand on my shoulder. "Charley, if you don't mind, I'll leave you here," she said. "I'm afraid I wouldn't be very good company tonight."

I nodded. "Of course. I understand. See you

later, kiddo." She gave me a quick kiss and waved from the doorway, disappearing inside. As I pulled away, I was making plans to gas up before hitting the Interstate. It wouldn't be such a great idea to run out of gas on some dark street in Detroit.

Most of the streets are dark in Detroit. There is a sort of primeval quality to great stretches of the city — whole neighborhoods of boarded-up houses, blocks razed during the 1967 riots and never again reconstructed — so that the place has about it the look, the atmosphere, and the smell of an urban jungle. And it was at a corner in this grim terrain, one I hadn't had any trouble finding in the daylight, that I was to meet my two guides.

Conroy's instructions were to meet him in front of the building he owned at Parker and Lafayette. This, of course, was the place where he had kept the apartment with Mary Margaret Tucker that I had visited not so very long before. Because I had come down Jefferson on that earlier occasion, I'd had no difficulty at all finding it. This time, however, since I was in a hurry, I stayed on Interstate 94 a little too long, got off at the wrong exit, and wandered around the dark streets until at last I got on Van Dyke heading in the right direction and managed to pull up some minutes late at the designated corner.

I thought perhaps they had left without me

until down the line of cars parked on the street a set of big headlights flashed at me — one, two, three times. I managed to find a place nearby and pulled my car right into it. I hurried over to Conroy's Cadillac Seville. The driver's-side window slid open automatically.

"You're late, Sloan," said Conroy. "Get in the back. We've got an appointment to keep."

"Will my car be safe here?"

"Who'd steal that car of yours? It's only a Chrysler." I heard a cackle of laughter at that from Tolliver. "Get in."

Still a bit reluctant, I complied. The truth was, at that late moment I was having second thoughts about going with the two of them on this expedition. All the good arguments against seemed twice as good just then. But I'd promised, and here I was, and so there was no backing out now. Or was there?

With just a twist of the steering wheel, Conroy rocketed out of the parking space. I hadn't even noticed that the motor was running.

We took Lafayette toward downtown Detroit. The high-rise office buildings surrounding Cadillac Square rose up in the middle-distance ahead. I'd had an office on the tenth floor of one of them for more than a decade. That was before my life fell apart. From where we were, I couldn't tell which had been my building. Somehow they all looked alike to me.

"Sorry I was late," I muttered to Conroy. "I guess I got lost."

"You got what? I thought you lived your whole life here."

"I did, except for the last three and a half years up in Pickeral Point. It's just that Detroit has changed a lot. It doesn't look the same to me anymore, especially at night."

"I know what you mean, man," said LeMoyne Tolliver. "I get turned around once in a while myself. At night."

"Sometimes it seems to me I'm not absolutely sure where anything is anymore — except for the Frank Murphy Hall of Justice. I could find my way there in my sleep. In fact," I added, "I've been told that I've done just that on a number of occasions."

That got a chuckle from Tolliver. Conroy ignored us both as he concentrated on his driving and the route he had chosen. Somewhere east of the Chrysler Freeway, he turned right, then left again and onto the freeway.

"Where are we going?" I asked him.

"You'll know when we get there."

"Are you sure about this, Conroy? All of a sudden, I've got a bad feeling about it. Call it a premonition or something. I don't know."

I caught his eyes on me in the rearview mirror. "Look," he said, "I don't know about your premonitions. To tell you the truth, it doesn't feel quite right to me, either. But you heard all the reasons why we have to make this meet, and you agreed to come along. Am I right?"

"Yes, you're right."

"You can wait in the car if you want to."

"No, I'm with you."

"That's it, then."

Not another word passed between the three of us for a few minutes. Conroy left the freeway and found his way smoothly to John R, where he turned north. He slowed the car, and Tolliver leaned forward and began studying the blighted cityscape ahead.

John R (named after an early inhabitant of these parts who ran a fur trading post and general store before there ever really was a Detroit) is one of those boulevards that was hit hard during the riots; perhaps of them all, it was hit hardest. Once lined with museums, brownstone professional societies, and august residences from the turn of the century, John R must have seemed like one of the power centers to the rioters, for they burned a lot of it, broke windows and doors, and threw a lot of furniture out into the street. What's left today is a wide street lined, for the most part, with burned-out brick shells and deserted stone structures.

"That's the place," said Tolliver, pointing ahead, "right there at the end of the block."

Conroy slowed the car to a crawl. There was nobody behind us to honk a protest. We were virtually alone there on the boulevard. He pulled over to the curb, bumped over a loose brick or two, and came to a halt. If I understood correctly, the building that Tolliver had pointed to was a three-story structure of blackened stone. As nearly as I could tell, it hadn't suffered much, if any, fire damage, but doors and windows were boarded up and spray-painted with gang graffiti. The place looked completely deserted.

"There's a driveway," said Tolliver. "You could leave the car there if you wanted to. It'd be in the shadows."

"Be pretty obvious where we'd come to call," Conroy pointed out. "Look, there's a driveway in front of that building across the street. I'll leave it there."

It took less than a minute to reposition the Cadillac. It was half hidden by a wall and the trunk of a big tree.

"You got your tape recorder?"

"Right in my pocket," said Tolliver.

"And I've got mine." Conroy turned to me in the backseat. "Two taped copies of the interrogation. That gives us backup and confirmation. We're going to do this by the book. Ready? Then let's go."

The two of them left the car in a rush. I bounded out, hoping to keep up with them. But it was no use. Conroy barely paused to point the gadget that locked the car electronically. Then they were out in the street, scurrying for the other side. The best I could manage was a determined jog in pursuit. Even LeMoyne Tolliver, who was probably about ten years my senior, seemed to move faster than me. The idea was to get across before we were caught in the headlights of an oncoming car. But the nearest, a good two blocks away, didn't seem to me to pose much of a threat. Maybe they were just trying to show me up.

"Around in back?" Conroy asked the question just as I made it to the curb.

"That's right, Chief. Better let me lead the way."

Tolliver took over, hustling us up the driveway and out of sight from the street. The passage between buildings narrowed, and as we moved ahead I seemed to be struck night-blind in the deep shadows, unable to make out shapes ahead, or even detect movement. About all I could rely on to guide me was my hearing. And when Conroy suddenly went silent and slowed down, I plowed into him from behind, nearly knocking us both down.

"Hey, watch it, Sloan," he said in a hoarse whisper.

"Sorry. Hasn't he got a flashlight?"

"It's up to him when to use it. Shhhh!"

My sense of smell wasn't much help. It wasn't that it had failed me. No, it was working all too well, overwhelming me with odors of an open latrine. Whatever this building once had been, it seemed that it wasn't much more than a three-story outhouse today.

When at last we came to the rear of the

building, there was a bit of open space and some welcome light — dim, but enough to make out Tolliver and Conroy. They were some paces ahead of me by now, just starting down steps that led, I assumed, to a rear, basement entrance.

I was right. They disappeared. I followed. By the time I joined them in front of the battered, spray-painted door, Tolliver was shining his flashlight around. Although this one appeared to be as tightly sealed as the rest, close inspection revealed that an opening had been jigsawed in the plywood around a lock. All that was needed was the right key to open it.

Tolliver got a nod from Conroy and proceeded to give a knock in code (three-two-one) on the door. They waited. Conroy nodded again, and Tolliver repeated the knock. Again, no response.

"What do you think?"

"We're not that late," Conroy whispered. He held his wristwatch into the flashlight's beam. "Just nine, maybe ten minutes is all. Better open it up. You've got the key?"

Tolliver nodded, dug into a pocket, and produced it.

"Go ahead, then. Only open it fast and step back."

As Tolliver inserted the key, Conroy reached back into his jacket, and from somewhere around the small of his back, he pulled a semi-automatic pistol. It was big, and it looked deadly. The last thing in the world I wanted was to see guns waved around. How did I get in this mess, anyway? I was at that moment in a situation no lawyer should ever be. Conroy waved me back behind him. Only too happily I took shelter.

Tolliver waited for a long moment. Maybe they counted to sixty or something, I don't know. Whatever the drill was, after a certain delay, Tolliver, who now had his flashlight in one hand and his revolver in the other, jumped out from our side of the door frame, and Conroy followed him in. I did the sensible thing and hung back.

Maybe I counted to sixty, or maybe it was a hundred and twenty. Who knows? But I waited until it seemed safe — no gunshots, no cries of a alarm — and only then did I step through the door. There was a bad smell in the place.

I found them looking up at something.

I couldn't quite recognize it as much of anything — a dummy? What? It was elevated a bit from the floor. Tolliver's flashlight played up and down, flicking this way and that.

"Is there a light?" Conroy asked.

"Yeah, here someplace."

The beam played around the rest of the room and settled on a single bulb hanging down from the ceiling just behind me.

"Get that, will you, Sloan? Turn it on."

335

Tolliver held his light on it until I pulled the chain. The sudden explosion of light from what must have been a hundred-watt bulb dazzled me. I suppose I was blinded for a moment. When I regained full vision, I found the two of them staring at the thing that was tied to an insulated pipe up near the low ceiling. I was shocked to see that it was the body of a man, or what was left of one. Naked to the waist, he had had his stomach slit vertically and horizontally, opened, and his intestines pulled out. There were small cuts all over his torso. He wasn't hanging from his neck but from his wrists, which were bound and stretched above him. His head was hung low, and his face was invisible to us.

"They really did a job on him, didn't they? Cut him down, LeMoyne."

Tolliver produced a spring knife and popped it open. He sawed away at the ropes that held up the corpse. They went all at once, and the body of the nameless informant collapsed onto the floor, hiding the foul mess of his insides beneath him, and revealing his face for the first time. His eyes were closed, but his mouth was open.

Conroy knelt down and studied the face on the floor. He seemed especially interested in his mouth. He looked up at me then, almost accusingly.

"They cut out his tongue," he said.

There is no suitable response to such a message.

"That means they were on to us. That means they did it for the mayor. Hell, he probably ordered it."

12

I woke up early Sunday morning, surprised and gratified that I had been able to sleep at all. I hardly bothered to check the newspapers; their late-Sunday editions were all wrapped up early Saturday night. There was no local news on television until late that same afternoon. So I went to the only possible source for information on the grim escapade of the night before.

From Detroit's All-News Radio, I learned that the victim's name was Willie Albright, described as "a small-time criminal with connections to Detroit's drug world." He was found in the basement of a deserted building on John R, "evidently the victim of a torture murder. In a related development, the body of Policewoman Madge Turnaby was found in Albright's Highland Park apartment, the victim of an execution-style slaying." It certainly wasn't the top story of the hour. Less than sixty seconds in the clichéd vocabulary of broadcast news was all that they were given on the seven o'clock report. Maybe later there would be more details. After all, it wasn't every day that a policewoman was murdered, was it? No, not even in Detroit.

I recalled there'd been a discussion between Conroy and Tolliver regarding the fate of Madge Turnaby. It had been brief and to the point.

"Well," Conroy had said, "if she's alive, then she gave him over."

"And if she's dead, she didn't."

There was something so cold-blooded about the way they speculated that it occurred to me as I stood listening to them that I was awfully glad I had never met Ms. Madge Turnaby. If I had, I might think that she deserved somewhat more than what she got from them.

All this was just before Conroy and I left the scene. Tolliver had called it in on the police radio in the chief's Cadillac. It wouldn't be long until we saw domelights flashing at one end of John R or the other. We had to get out of there. Conroy climbed in behind the wheel of his car, and I followed him inside. Conroy had little, or nothing, to say on the drive back to Parker. He was tight lipped and frowning all the way there.

Although for my part, I certainly regretted the terrible death of the informant and was fearful for the policewoman who had been assigned to watch over him, I was not really sorry that Conroy's plan had failed. It seemed to me like a piece of pure kamikaze. He had let his hatred of the mayor rule him. His primary objective, his only objective, had to be saving himself. He should know that, but it wasn't the time for me to lecture him.

It was that night that I decided to visit Mary Margaret Tucker. It was the only possibility I had for pushing things forward, the only thing left to be done. And Sunday morning seemed the best time to catch her.

Coming in down I-94, I got off at Vernier and followed it around onto 8 Mile Road. Somewhere around Gratiot I turned off and followed the route I'd worked out on the Detroit city map. Mary Margaret Tucker's address wasn't hard to locate on the grid. It was an address on Eastburn, one of a row of Midwest bungalows, no different from the rest. It was early, not too much after eight, and that was how I'd planned it. Wake her up, catch her off guard, get her to talk. That was the plan, anyway. The way it worked out was something different.

So I went up and rang her bell and waited. Nothing. I rang it again. I rang it so loud and long that I was sure my auditory assault would have awakened the neighbors. Mary Margaret Tucker just wasn't home. Discouraged but not despairing, I returned to my car, got in behind the wheel, and waited. I was parked across the street, so I wasn't likely to be noticed.

I must have waited about twenty minutes when at last she appeared. I spotted her in the rearview mirror. There she was, chugging along on the sidewalk at a steady grind, dressed in a no-frills sweatsuit, eschewing the final sprint with which so many joggers ended their workout. She looked tired, physically exhausted, not many endorphins left working in her bloodstream at that moment. I wondered how far she'd run, and how long. I fought the impulse to confront her right there on the sidewalk in front of her house. No, let her go inside and then hit her with the doorbell. As tired as she looked, the effect might be comparable to rousing her from a sound sleep. But timing was all. Wait too long, and she'd probably be in the shower.

Gulping in great drafts of air, she turned down the walk toward the house. On the porch she fumbled out a small set of keys from an invisible pocket in her sweatpants, fitted one of them into the door, swung the door open, and stepped inside. I jumped out of my car. Seconds later, I was laying on the bell, refusing to be ignored.

It didn't take long. The door swung wide, and there she was, still panting, sweat running down her pretty face. It took her a moment to recognize me. When she did, she looked about as angry as her condition allowed, her green eyes blazing.

Still sucking wind, she gasped, *"You!"* She panted a couple of times more and said, "You've fucked everything up!"

Then she shut the door in my face.

I'd come prepared for that. Dressing for

battle that morning, I had put on the thickest, heaviest, toughest boots I owned, old wafflestompers from the sixties, the kind made to withstand a direct assault by the right front foot of an elephant. Either one could easily repel a door flung by an exhausted woman. The left one did the job. The door bounced back, yawning wide. It revealed Mary Margaret Tucker, stalking away, her back turned to me. Since the door was open, I took that as an invitation to enter.

When I caught up with her in the kitchen, she looked at me, not so much angrily as in sudden confusion.

"You still here?" she said. "I told you to leave."

"No you didn't."

"Well, I shut the door on you."

"It came open again."

"Okay then, I'm telling you now — get out!"

I took a deep breath and a step back and put a careful smile upon my face. I decided this would probably be the best time to push the button.

"Mary Margaret," I said, "I'm here to save you some trouble."

"Bullshit," she growled, "you've caused me plenty already."

"No, I mean it," I said. "Why don't you just sit down and answer some questions for me like the intelligent human being you are. That way maybe I can save you the trouble of going downtown, missing classes and all that, to talk to me with some prosecutor present. Maybe. I can't promise that."

"I don't have to talk to you."

"You were on the list of witnesses at the arraignment."

"I didn't testify, though."

"The fact that you were on the list gives me the right to talk to you. In fact, it makes it necessary for me to talk to you. Now, why can't we do it in a sensible way?"

Her cheeks puffed. She blew out some air and looked at me skeptically.

"If I do, you'll leave me alone for a while?"

"For a while. I promise."

She sighed. "All right, but let me drink some orange juice first. I need some sugar after that run."

She took a tall glass from the cupboard and went to the refrigerator.

"How far did you go?" I asked her.

"Three miles. First time I've gone that far. I only started jogging in September after Mark and I . . ." She trailed off. "Would you like one, too?" she asked brightly, raising her glass.

Although she was in her twenties, she was still a lot like a kid. I could understand her appeal to someone like Conroy, and his to her.

"Sure," I said, "why not?"

"Get a glass."

I got one down from the cupboard. She gave

me a tentative smile as she poured the orange juice from a nearly full carton. Then she put it back on the shelf and kicked the door shut with her knee.

"All right if we talk in the kitchen?" She seemed pretty sure of herself.

"Of course."

We settled in chairs across the kitchen table. She slugged down half the glass of juice in three big gulps.

"I'll be okay now. Go ahead, ask me some questions."

Was there a dare in that? An implication that, Hey, I got past the cops, I can get around you, Charley Sloan? We'd have to see about that. I took a sip of the orange juice and hit her with the kind of question I hoped might shake her.

"Just a moment ago, you had a little difficulty saying exactly what you and Mark Conroy had done. In fact, you broke up. Tell me about that. Who broke up with who?"

"Is that important?" she asked, unruffled. "The cops didn't ask me about that. They just wanted to know if Mark had given me money, and how much."

"I'm aware what the cops asked you. I'm asking you now to tell me about it. Who instigated the breakup?"

She hesitated, perhaps looking for the right word, the right phrase. "Mutual consent," she said at last.

"And how did this come about, this mutual consent?"

"All right, you want to know what it was about? It was about how Mark wouldn't accept me as an independent woman. He just wanted me to be his little playmate in his little love nest. He wanted me to be *available*, you know? It wasn't like I had a life of my own or my own needs. It was just what *he* wanted when *he* wanted it."

The mistress's lot is generally not a happy one, but I was betting that Mary Margaret Tucker did not, probably did not ever, think of herself as Mark Conroy's mistress. Maybe that was part of the trouble. If she had, and had accepted the rules of the game, the two of them might still be together. Then I thought of Althea Conroy and how she'd badgered her husband to cop a plea, and I wondered at his choice of women.

"Could you give me a time frame for this?"

"Oh, it had been building through the summer. By the end of September, it was all over. At the end of the third week in September, we had a big fight, and that ended it."

"Did you move out of the apartment on Parker right away?"

"No."

"How long did you stay?"

"Just after classes started, until about the end of October."

"Did Mark Conroy ask you to move out then?"

"No. He said he owned the building, I could stay as long as I wanted."

"Then why did you move out?"

She frowned at me, letting me know she wasn't enjoying this. "I moved out," she said, speaking slowly, emphasizing her words, "because I wanted to let him know it was really all over. He tried to start up again. Let's say, he tried to start up again in a very physical way."

"Are you suggesting rape?"

She started to say yes, but then caught herself.

"Attempted rape?"

"Let's just say old Mark knew how to push my buttons, he really did. He's kind of a control freak, you know? It's, like, he has to have power over everyone and everything. I just knew I had to get away from him, completely away, or I'd never, like, be in charge of my life again."

"And so you left?"

"Yeah."

"Did you move in here right away?"

"No, I didn't. I moved in with a friend." Then she added, anticipating my question, "*Female* friend. I needed some time to get my feet on the ground and look around for a place of my own."

"And this is what you found. A house. You

share it with anyone?"

"No. It's just me here, me alone. I like it that way."

"I remember from having read your police interrogation that you said you'd been given money on a regular basis by Mark Conroy. For how long?"

"Over a year, or just about a year. It wasn't huge amounts of money. Just a thousand a month, sometimes a little more. It probably didn't amount to more than ten thousand dollars."

"Not an inconsiderable sum," I said. "So tell me, what did you spend it on?"

"On food, mostly. A few clothes, nothing expensive. Mark bought me a few things. Incidental expenses."

"So in effect, with these regular payments, and the rent-free accommodations he offered you, you were able to save the entire salary you were paid as his secretary at 1300 Beaubien. Is that correct?"

She glowered at me. "Yes."

"And you told the police that Mark Conroy paid your tuition and expenses for this fall semester at Wayne State. Is that correct?"

She glowered at me even more darkly. "Yes."

"Tell me, then, what are your feelings toward Mark Conroy today?"

"I don't want to see him. I hope I never see him again."

"But why? He seems to have been generous to you, paid for your college this semester, made it possible for you to live in this house. And the furniture?"

"Salvation Army."

"Okay, but the question remains, why?"

She was fuming now, and holding back a lot, most of it emotional.

"You wouldn't understand," she said as coldly as she was able, "it's a woman thing." She really meant to flatten me with that one.

"Do you want to see him go to jail?"

"That's out of my hands."

Was this just a case of the woman scorned, or was it something deeper? I wasn't sure. I leaned back in my chair, took a drink of the orange juice she'd provided, and studied her for a minute or more.

"There was a period of about three weeks between your break with him in the third week of September, and the second week of October, that you continued to work for Conroy as his secretary. Right?"

She nodded.

"What was your relationship with Mark Conroy during this period?"

"Armed truce."

"Did other people in the office know about your relationship with Mark Conroy?"

"Some did," she said, "a few women, most of whom disapproved. And the Mouse, the Mouse knew about us."

"And what was his attitude?"

"Nonjudgmental, but he was sympathetic. During this time you're talking about, the 'armed truce' period, the Mouse and I had a couple of talks. Big as he is, ugly as he is, he's a pretty tenderhearted dude."

Not quite my impression of him, but then, who was I to say?

"This money given to you by Conroy," I began, still pecking away at her, "you said it amounted to about ten thousand dollars?"

"That's about it," she said, "no more than that."

"Did you report it to the IRS?"

"Most of it was this year."

"But not all of it."

"No, not all of it. So okay, here's what I did. I filed an addendum to last year's report. Cool. There's a penalty, but I can handle it. This year I'm listing everything he gave me."

"Sounds like you got good advice. When did you do that?"

"A little over a month ago." She seemed to realize the significance of this. "You want my accountant's name and number?"

"Not now. Just have it handy in the future. And how did you list these payments from Mark Conroy? As income?"

The fiercest look yet. "No, as gifts."

"And how did these payments come to you?"

"What do you mean?" She really didn't

seem to understand the question.

"I mean, were they in cash or were they by check? Personal check or some other account? Were they delivered in person, or did they come by mail?"

She sighed. "Different ways, right? I mean, it was just money to me, you know? But it was important for Mark to give it. Money is power, right? So it was important to him that I take it. The first couple of times he had the Mouse pass it on to me in cash."

"Did it come from the W-91 Fund?"

"You mean the safe in Mark's office? Well, obviously it did. That's where they kept the money. Besides, the Mouse told me it did."

"You said that only the first couple of payments came that way. How did the rest come?"

"By check. He said he didn't like dipping like that. It was too hard getting the money back in from his personal account."

"He said that, did he? So I take it the checks weren't on his personal account?"

"No, he set up a special account, called it Ad Astra, Inc. He said that meant 'to the stars.' " She frowned. "He was sort of romantic that way."

"And he paid you out of that account from then on?"

"Yeah, from about the first of this year on."

"A thousand a month?"

"That's right."

"Plus gifts of what? Clothes?"

"Mostly clothes, yeah. I mean, no mink coats or anything. A couple of nice dresses, a coat last December — Christmas, cloth coat that cost a few hundred." Then she added almost plaintively, "And flowers. He brought me flowers all the time, even in the winter. Like I said, he was sort of romantic."

"Jewelry?"

"No, he wasn't the type, neither am I."

"Did you take vacations together?"

"We got away for a couple of weekends, once to Chicago, that was nice, and once to Port Huron, the Hermitage up there, but that wasn't so nice."

"Why not?"

"He got recognized with me."

"By whom?"

"He didn't say, wouldn't say. Someone who had to do with police stuff. We did take one vacation, though. But that was a real disaster."

"Where was that? And how was it a disaster?"

"He took me with him to a law enforcement convention in Las Vegas. That's pretty funny, isn't it? A cop convention in Las Vegas. Anyway, he was, like, *so* afraid he'd get spotted with me there that I was all alone most of the time. He was busy during the days, so I was off by myself in and out of all the hotels on the Strip, listening to the lounge bands. I walked around downtown, and believe me, downtown Las

351

Vegas is the pits!" She thought, remembered, seemed for a moment positively nostalgic. "I don't know, though, in a way it wasn't so bad. We had some nice dinners together, went to some shows. I probably wasn't any worse off than some of the wives who were there."

"Did you gamble?"

"Why else would anyone go to Vegas?"

"Did you win? Lose? Did he give you money to gamble with?"

"He gave me, oh, about two hundred. I had three hundred of my own. I came home with about a hundred, so I guess you could say I won. All my walking-around money came out of that. You know, you win a little, you lose a little. I played the slots. I'm no gambler."

"What about Conroy? Did he gamble? Did he lose?"

"You're kidding, right? Mark Conroy is so far from being a gambler that . . . Well, he's basically pretty conservative. He was always saying, 'The ducks have to be in a row.' He drove me crazy with that." She shook her head emphatically. "No, Mark did not gamble."

"And you weren't recognized on that trip to Las Vegas?"

"Obviously we were together — went to dinner, shows, and so on. But Mark is not the kind who is what you'd call demonstrative in public. We didn't hold hands. He didn't put his arm around me. He never did that out in public. That's one of the things that made things hard. A couple of times we met people from the convention, they even sat down with us. He introduced me as Sergeant Tucker, 'our top computer programmer.' Everything was cool. Nobody cared. Frankly, I don't think they would have cared if we'd been sleeping together. They must have suspected, some of them anyway. For them, I mean, basically it was, like, who cared? Mark got too nervous about shit like that."

Then I asked in an easy, conversational tone, "Did Timmerman contact you first, or did you contact him?"

"Timmerman," she answered. "He's a neat guy on the phone. He —"

She stopped. Full stop. She pulled herself up in her chair and looked at me, at first puzzled, then hostile.

"I'm not supposed to talk about that," she said.

"Why not?" Friendly, easygoing. "You'll have to talk about it eventually. I thought we could discuss it sort of informally right now when you're not under oath. Just some details. For instance, have you met Timmerman yet, or has it all been over the telephone?"

She got to her feet.

"You ought to know all about that. That same afternoon you followed me at school I'll bet you were trying to track him down, weren't you?"

I didn't move.

"What did he promise you, Mary Margaret? A job with the city when you finished law school?"

"Out!"

"You really want me to go? I think it's in your interest to talk to me."

"We're through talking right now. Just get out."

Reluctantly, I rose to my feet, still arguing in the voice of sweet reason. It did no good whatever.

"Out!" she screamed.

There was no point in trying to hold out against that. I turned and started out of the kitchen, heading for the front door. But I did have one parting shot left to fire.

"Mary Margaret," I said, turning at the door, "I hope you remembered to get a receipt from those guys in the Mayor's Squad for all that money. Otherwise, you know, you could wind up taking the rap for all this. I hope you realize that."

The look of sudden consternation on her face told me that my educated guess had hit the mark, as I'd intended.

"Any time you want to resume this conversation," I said, "just let me know. You have my card. Just give me a call. See you, Mary Margaret. Thanks for your time."

Although I made it to my car without looking back, I had the distinct feeling she was standing there in the doorway, watching me go. Still, I resisted the impulse even to glance over my shoulder as I started the car, slipped it into drive, and pulled away from the bungalow on Eastburn.

It was only then, a block away and completely out of sight, that I dared to take the thing out of my inside coat pocket, detach a tiny microphone from by buttonhole, and put the entire apparatus down on the seat beside me.

I'd asked Mark Conroy if I might borrow his tape recorder when I parted company with him the night before. He had shown me how it worked, even rummaged around in the glove compartment of his Cadillac and found a new cassette and the right sort of microphone to do the job I had in mind. He checked me a few times until I was pretty sure I could turn it on simply by touch. Then he wished me luck. I hoped that would be enough to get the interview with Mary Margaret Tucker down on tape. As it turned out, there was no difficulty at all.

I stopped at a convenience store in her neighborhood to make a telephone call. This one, like so many others in Detroit, had a protective wall of inch-thick, bulletproof plastic to shield the clerk in the very likely event of a visit by an armed robber.

I glanced around but saw no telephone.

"Got a pay phone?" I asked the clerk.

He pushed up close to the three holes that had been drilled in the plastic wall to ease communication. A young guy, in his twenties, he was dark complected and dark haired. He looked at me sharply and must have decided I was okay.

"It's in the back," he said, "against the wall."

I know Bob Williams's number by heart. He picked up on the first ring.

"It's Charley," I said. "You got a meeting tonight?"

"Sure we do," he said. "But it's a matinee. Three P.M., St. Jude's basement. We'll get you home in time for dinner."

"I was thinking we might have dinner afterward, that is, if you don't have anything planned."

"Sounds good to me. Are you in special need?"

"Let's just say I've got a few things I'd like to discuss."

"I'm all ears. See you at three."

I walked back to the glass booth where the clerk, still regarding me with some slight suspicion, sat on a high stool. I took him to be Chaldean, a Christian Arab. There were a lot of Chaldeans in Detroit, most from Lebanon, some from Syria and Iraq. I'd defended one of them on a murder charge five or six years ago. He'd shot a robber dead in his small grocery store in Dearborn; he probably wouldn't have been charged, except that it turned out the robber had a replica gun, very realistic but made from plastic and inoperable, and the *Free Press* expressed editorial outrage. I got him off without much trouble. He might not have had the problem at all if he'd been encased in bulletproof plastic the way this guy was.

I lingered at the booth and noticed a box of unfamiliar cigars among the cigarettes on display on his side of the wall. They were on the small side, a handy size for an occasional smoker like me.

"Are those pretty good?" I asked, pointing at the cigars.

"Very good," he said. "From Lebanon. I smoke them myself."

"Give me three of them, would you?"

They turned out to be a dollar apiece, pricey little devils, but they looked good. I shoved a five through the bankteller slot and got back my change.

"The telephone used to be there." He pointed to the wall behind me. "One night, late, one of them came in, just this one and me, and he tore the phone apart right in front of me."

"Why did he do that?"

"He thought he'd get me to come out of here so he could rob me. He had a gun. I could tell. I just sat here and called the cops."

"Did they catch him?" Stupid question.

"No, they came an hour later. I stayed open and waited for them. They said I did the right thing just to sit and watch him do this. 'Better luck next time,' they said. What does that mean?" He shook his head angrily. "That's crazy — 'next time.' How could something so stupid happen two times?"

"I hope you're right, friend. I hope you're right."

I gave him a wave and stepped outside. It was hard to live in a city with so much frustration and anger simmering away day after day — just simmering, though. Things hadn't come to a boil since the '67 riots. And for that, whether it pleased all the citizens of Detroit or not, they had the mayor to thank.

Then, as I took a moment to light one of the cigars, I happened to remember something — or rather, someone. It struck me that I knew an associate of the mayor's from a long time back, one who knew him when old Ismail Carter chain-smoked short, slender stogies just like these. In the old days, he'd emptied many a City Council meeting with them, blowing smoke at the opposition. Representing the old Black Bottom, just east of downtown, he was an old-fashioned power broker, a fixer, the kind of pol who loved to wheel and deal almost as much as he loved dispensing largesse to his constituents. Everybody owed him. He liked it that way.

Though not one of his constituents, the

mayor owed him, too. Ismail had taken the mayor-to-be under his wing from the moment he took his seat on the Council in 1968. He taught him how to operate, how to turn Detroit's distress to his personal advantage. He saw in him one who just might grab what he never could — the crown and scepter, the kingship of Detroit. I wonder what Shakespeare could have done with these dramas of big-city politics, these tales of rebellious succession. They were not all that different from the material he had to work with in his own day. I tried to imagine John Henry and old Ismail blathering on in blank verse, but it was hard, damned difficult. Yet it was true that the two did communicate in a kind of gutter poetry. Ismail had taught it to his young protégé, persuaded him that if you wanted the people to vote for you, you had to talk to them in the kind of language they understood and spoke among themselves. You gotta walk the walk and talk the talk. That was how the term *motherfucker* became more or less common in serious political discussion, at least within the limits of the city of Detroit. And that was how, to simplify shamelessly, the mayor first got himself elected.

For a couple of years Ismail Carter was there at his right hand, the mayor's trusted advisor. Yet poor old Ismail had been urban-renewed right out of the business. Black Bottom, most of it, was no more. Where once the frame houses and brick tenements stood, there were now rows of bright and shining high-rise apartment buildings, alternating with whole blocks of steel-and-glass boxes dubbed "townhomes" by the developer. They were occupied by Yuppies and Buppies who felt they owed nothing to any man, least of all to some aging reminder of the city's past. He became a politician without a constituency, as much an anachronism in his own way as were my old pals in the Irish mafia who had formerly ruled Detroit. Ismail lost his seat on the City Council. It wasn't long before he dropped out of sight completely.

But before he did, he and I met under rather strange circumstances. At least at first they seemed strange to me. He'd been hit with a civil rights suit by one Carol Johnson and that dated back a couple of years to when he still held his seat and kept an office in the city building. He showed me the papers he'd been served with, and maybe because I'd had my usual three or four martinis at lunch, I just didn't get it. Why should Ismail Carter be the target of a discrimination suit? Why should he want me to defend him when every black lawyer in town was in his debt for favors and incidentals?

But then Ismail made it all clear to me in just a couple of words: "She's white."

Carol Johnson, a recent graduate of the University of Michigan in political science, who also took shorthand and typed ninety words per minute, applied for a job at his Council office. After displaying her credentials and skills, and following a brief, personal interview with Councilman Carter himself, she was told that others were applying for the job, and she would hear later if her application had been successful. She never did. Later she learned that the position had gone to a Melody Martin, a black woman, who had no college degree, took no shorthand, and could barely type. "Sweet little girl," said Ismail of Ms. Martin. "She was my barber's niece." Although Ms. Johnson had no difficulty finding another job, she brooded upon this injustice, and as a second-year law student at George Washington University in Washington, D.C., she prepared and filed the complaint expertly with the Civil Rights Commission. Because this was back in the Seventies and was one of the first reverse discrimination suits ever brought, it got a lot of attention in newspapers all over the country, even a sound bite or two on national television. I think I tried it pretty well.

Ismail Carter himself gave me the handle I needed when, at our second meeting, he started to tell me what I didn't want to hear, never wanted to hear from a client.

"Now, Charley Sloan," he said to me, "I'm not one of these public servants who gets in a jam and has a sudden attack of amnesia. I'll tell you right off I remember this girl, Johnson, very well, and if you want to know the God's honest truth, I did discriminate against her."

I tried to interrupt him. He poked that ever-present cigar at me and told me to shut up. He would have his say.

"Now, like I say, I did discriminate against her, but not for the reason that's there in the complaint. It had nothin' to do with color, or race, or any of that shit my people been puttin' up with for more years than either of us can count. Fact is, I had a white woman work for me back in the Forties, during the war. She was a Communist and a real good liaison with the unions. She got married after three years, had a baby right away, and quit. Then, well, there was another white woman worked for me, but she just recently died.

"But nossir, it had nothing to do with race, me not hiring that girl. What it had to do with was that she was so damn ugly I didn't want her there every day, lookin' her in the face. Now, Charley Sloan, I don't know how it is with you, though I did notice those young ladies out front in your office are awful easy on the eyes, but I'll tell you how it is with me. See, when I go into the office every morning, it cheers me up to look at those pretty female faces, specially now I'm older. And just say I venture out for a bit of information has to be looked up in the files. 'Oh, Mr. Carter, I'll get that for you right away,' and then she sashays off and hunkers down because what I need is down in the bottom drawer, and I take all this in, and that gives me a serious cheer-up, makes my old pecker tingle. But this young lady, Carol Johnson, she just never would make my pecker tingle. I swear, she got up in the morning and took ugly pills every day of her life."

I remember asking him then if he had taken advantage of any of the young ladies who worked for him. That might indeed prove a problem. But he set me straight on that.

"I have never in my life taken advantage of any woman, never made an unwelcome advance in my life — though I admit, some women have taken advantage of me."

With that to go on, I planned my strategy. I was never able to find the white woman who Ismail had employed during the war. She'd moved to Burbank, California, in 1951 with her husband and two children, and there I lost the trail. But old city records from that era confirmed that yes, she had been employed in the councilman's office, and yes, she was Caucasian. Exhibit A.

But I got as many men as I could on the jury — white or black, it didn't matter — because when I called Ismail Carter's present and former employees to the stand, one after the other, to attest to his sterling character and indifference to color, it was a regular beauty parade there in the courtroom. The gentlemen of the jury not only enjoyed the show, they also got the point, especially when Carol

Johnson came on the stand.

Perhaps Ismail had been unnecessarily cruel in his description of her. She wasn't what I would have called ugly, but she was homely, rather, so gawky and plain that she would have passed any man unnoticed on the street. Or perhaps there was something ugly about her that came from inside. Her small blue eyes, sharp and vengeful, darted about the court-room ceaselessly so that she seemed to be lying even when I knew she was telling the truth. The corners of her mouth turned down in an expression of disapproval whenever she happened not to be speaking in her shrill, grating voice. I had to admit to myself I wouldn't have wanted her working in my office. The gentle-men of the jury must have admitted the same, and the ladies, too, for her suit was denied.

Of course, it helped that I got her to admit, reminding her she was under oath, that when she applied for the job in June, she had not informed Ismail Carter that she would be leaving to attend law school in Washington the following September. That more or less wrapped things up for Carol Johnson.

Ismail was delighted, of course, and paid my stiff fee cheerfully. Few do. Once out of trouble, they forget all too quickly who rescued them. And his last words to me were, "I owe you."

Remembering all this on my drive back home puffing on one of my newly acquired cigars, I wondered why it had not come to mind earlier. All I can say is that booze does funny things to your brain. I was hitting it pretty hard in those days. There are some big blank spots in my past, territories that may be opened up to me suddenly, unexpectedly by some relevant reminder, like how the little cigars looked like the ones Ismail Carter used to smoke.

But now that I had remembered, now that I had my man, I wondered what he could do for me. He owed me. He could carry a message to the mayor. But just what would that message be?

13

There was the rest of the morning and the better part of an afternoon to kill before the AA meeting at St. Jude's was to begin. I tried Sue on the telephone and all I got was her answering machine. Remembering the shape she was in the night before, I left a sympathetic message and asked her to give me a call when she came in. More than likely, she was down at Kerry County Police Headquarters going through the files on the three children who had been killed already. I hoped I was wrong about that. But if that's where she was, there was no telling how long she'd be gone. Poor Sue.

I knew I had no intention of going into the office and looking once more at the Conroy file, or listening to the Mary Margaret Tucker tape, or doing anything more that day even remotely connected with the case. It had taken a while, but the horror of the night before had finally caught up with me. I kept flashing back to the gruesome images right out of some disgusting grade-B slasher movie. I kept seeing that ghastly wound in his middle, the intestines, that face clouded and sorrowful in death. I was exhausted, but I knew that sleep in such circumstances would be impossible.

And so I did the only thing anyone could do in that situation. I put on a pot of coffee.

Defense lawyers are sheltered from the realities of death. I must have tried nearly a hundred cases of first-degree murder in the course of my career. Yet I'd never been right there at the scene of the crime, viewing the remains, looking over the cop's shoulder, not until recently. Oh, I'd looked at forensic photographs often enough, tossed them aside, and then gone on to argue what I assured the judge and jury were the important issues in the case. Whatever I had said those issues were, I was wrong, lying, perhaps, if only to myself. What was important was the victim, the fact that a life had been taken, the even more fundamental face of death.

I'd first discovered that out on Clarion Road when I'd gotten a glimpse of little Catherine Quigley, wrapped in plastic, lying in the snow. And the lesson had been rammed home to me the night before in that filthy basement on John R.

It occurred to me then to wonder how and why it was that I had reacted so much more violently to my first murder victim than to my second. There could be no doubt, after all, that what had been done to Tolliver's "pigeon" was far more hideous to look at and contemplate, yet it hadn't made me vomit nor had it put me immediately into some sort of spiritual crisis.

But why? Why had Catherine Quigley's death hit me immediately harder? Was I just getting used to it? If you saw violent death frequently enough, as a cop did, did it eventually stop affecting you? That wasn't the way it was with Sue Gillis. Or, for that matter, with Bud Billings, or even Stash Olesky.

Maybe my friend and counselor, Bob Williams, had been right. Maybe it was Catherine Quigley's innocence that made the difference. That poor butchered bastard whose guts had been spilled over the floor, whose tongue had been cut from his mouth — he was certainly no innocent — a bagman for one of the big drug dealers, probably a murderer himself, or Tolliver wouldn't have had the hold over him that he did. But how do you measure these things? Certainly a seven-year-old girl was the more innocent of the two, but they were both still dead. And death, not innocence or guilt, was the problem, wasn't it? Death was the great problem of life.

Did they know that up at St. Jude's chapter of Alcoholics Anonymous? Maybe I ought to tell them. For whether violently, or in our sleep in a warm, comfortable bed, death would come to us all. If that was the case, why even bother to stay sober?

That was the nasty question that wormed its way into my brain at some point along the way. Or maybe it was there all the time. The day before, I'd wondered why I wasn't happier. In a way, I'd always been happy during those drinking years. I laughed more, talked more, saw more people, lived a full life, until it all came crashing down on me, nearly burying me in the wreckage. But Ismail Carter was right. I'd done a pretty good job of it, making a comeback in Pickeral Point. I seemed to have things pretty well under control. Maybe I could ease off and enjoy myself a little. Who knows? Maybe I could even have a drink every now and then, like any other normal human being. What could it hurt?

Just about that time, of course, an alarm sounded in my head. Every alcoholic knows that line of reasoning. Every member of Alcoholics Anonymous knows from a painful process of conditioning what it could hurt: everything you've achieved, all the resistance and resolution you've built up, all the self-knowledge you've gained.

All this I knew more or less instinctively by now. But all I could come up with in response to all those "why bothers" and permissive "maybes" were a few of the old AA slogans and buzzwords that had been so deeply ingrained.

"Easy does it." Sure, I knew everything I'd accomplished had been done by increments. I know that I'd discovered a lot about myself in the process and managed to discard a lot of superfluous material baggage along the way.

"One day at a time." That's how I'd done

it. That's how I'd been winning my cases, too, by preparation and planning, rather than trying to think on my feet and depending on oratory, as I had when I tried cases half crocked.

"Broken shoelaces." That's what Bob Williams would call my ruminations on happiness, or, really, my wish for it. He'd say there was no guarantee that sobriety would make anyone happier, just that it was the only way for people like us to live. And after all, happiness wasn't guaranteed as anyone's inalienable right, only its pursuit. I think I'd heard him say that once.

Who knows how long all this thinking took? But before I knew it, the time had come to get ready for the Sunday matinee meeting.

I might have stayed away if I'd known in advance an open meeting had been planned. Just about every AA chapter throws open its doors from time to time to outsiders. The question is, of course, who is an outsider? Predictably, visitors fell into two categories — "heavy drinkers" who said they were "curious" about the program; and the relatives or close friends of such "heavy drinkers," whose presence was necessary to get them there. The general rule seemed to be that if they came under their own steam, it was a pretty good bet they'd come back again and join the program. If they had to be escorted, it was anybody's guess.

And then there were the unpredictable visitors. In a way, you never knew quite who might show up. In the years since I'd been coming to the meetings in St. Jude's basement, there had been a few journalists, a couple of Ph.D. candidates, one in social anthropology and the other in social psychology, both of whom left disappointed when they learned that they would not be allowed free access to regular meetings, simply as observers. Father Phil LeClerc, the pastor of St. Jude's, sat in from time to time at the open meetings just to make sure things were running smoothly. But when he showed up that Sunday night with Father Chuck in tow, I felt a little funny about sticking around. But I couldn't leave. I'd made a postsession dinner date with Bob Williams.

There was a pretty good-sized assembly there in the basement, well over twenty. Most were regulars, but there were four or five who were obviously first-timers. You could tell by their uneasiness, the way they kept looking around without making eye contact. One of them had an escort, and probably a good thing, because he was drunk. You don't have to be sober at an AA meeting, you just have to have the desire to stop drinking. The woman with him, wife or girlfriend, could barely keep him awake.

Bob Williams, who had been buzzing

around and getting things ready, was involved in a brief conversation with the two priests. When he left them, he walked my way.

"Hey, Charley. I wonder if you'd do me a favor."

"Always glad to oblige."

"That priest with Father Phil is from Our Lady of Sorrows in Hub City. He's been asked to start a chapter at his church and wants to see how things work. I wonder if you'd get up and share when the time comes, just so he can get the feel of it."

I must have responded with a pained look because Bob read it immediately.

"What's the problem?" he asked.

"I know Father Charles Albertus."

"Professionally?"

"You could say that."

"I can see that might be kind of awkward. Okay, I'll ask somebody else."

No offense taken, he left with a nod of his head and went right over to someone I knew only as Steve. He evidently put the same request to him and got a positive response, for Bob left him with a handshake and went up to the front to start the meeting.

Was I being difficult? Squeamish? But the second A in AA stood for "Anonymous," after all. Just being here I'd blown my cover. I didn't feel up to blurting out my story to a priest.

Bob convened the meeting in the informal way he always did.

"Hi," he said. "My name is Bob, and I'm an alcoholic. We've got a little formula we start the meetings with here. Since this is an open meeting, and there are newcomers and observers present, I'd like you to listen closely.

"The primary purpose of this organization is to stay sober and help other alcoholics achieve sobriety," he said. He went on to explain that AA was for, by, and of alcoholics; that in practice we had discovered that alcoholics could help other alcoholics far better than priests, ministers, psychiatrists, or therapists could and that we call each other only by our first names.

He went through the 12-step program and concluded: "Is any one of these more important than the others? Maybe. Maybe one is. And that's the belief in a Higher Power. Call It God, Allah, Hashim, whatever you want, but without the help of that Higher Power, an alcoholic just can't make it. You've got to believe in Him to get His help, and there are times when you will only be able to make it with His help."

Was it my imagination, or did Bob's eyes come to rest on me as he spoke those last two sentences? No, it wasn't my imagination. He was addressing me directly.

After some comments from the floor, there was a ceremony for Steve, whose anniversary cake this was. The cake's single candle represented his first 365 consecutive days of sobriety. Since I'd seen him at meetings for a good two years, I knew the effort of will that cake and candle represented.

As I turned away, I came head on with Father Chuck, who looked eager to talk but didn't seem to know quite what to say.

"Imagine meeting me here," I said with a nervous laugh. I felt like an altar boy who'd just stolen a buck from the collection plate. Once a Catholic, always a Catholic, I guess. "You'd be surprised how many of us they let out on the streets," I went on awkwardly, "doctors, lawyers, electricians, cops. A regular secret army." I didn't mention bishops.

"Charley, please, I'm not that naive. I've counseled a lot of people with this" — he hesitated — "problem. I'm aware of the statistics."

"Sorry, Father, I don't really make a secret of my problem. It's just that every once in a while it makes me feel a little like a freak. Maybe today is just one of those days."

"I understand," he said, and I actually think he did. "I remembered when we got together at the rectory and I offered you a drink, you turned it down."

"I turn down drinks on a regular basis, Father. Actually, it's one of the things I do best," I said.

"But I went ahead and had one myself. That was at the very least rude of me, if not unfeeling."

"Think nothing of it, Father. I'm a big boy. We go to parties, some of us even go to bars. We live in the world, and it's a drinking world out there. We're not trying to change that; all we're doing is trying to stay sober."

He clapped me on the back and gave me the high-intensity smile. "Thanks, Charley. That was very well put. I take it you're very much in favor of the program."

"I'm here, aren't I? And all I can say is, it works for me."

He nodded in the direction of Steve and the anniversary cake. "How many candles on your cake?" he asked.

"I don't keep count that way," I said, which was an out-and-out lie; I knew the day, the month, and the year, practically to the minute. "I do it one day at a time. That way I don't get discouraged."

"Right. Got it." He gave me a wink and a nod. "Like I said before, you're a good guy, Charley."

As he went off to find Bob Williams, I figured it hadn't gone so badly. Hell, he was a good guy, too. Like most priests, he was a bit flat-footed socially. Living up there, all alone in the rectory in that decaying town, how could it be otherwise? But he was earnest and well meaning, and there was no doubt Hub City could use another AA chapter.

And then we were called back to our seats by Bob. After the shuffling and shifting had stopped, he addressed the visitors in particular. "Even though I've talked a lot about the program," he said, "I'm afraid I haven't given you a very good idea of how the meetings work. The meetings belong to the members. They get up and have their say, give inspiration to one another, and manage pretty well without me." When he called on Steve to speak, the result was less than inspiring.

Touching as Steve's story was, his was the kind of performance that seemed to discourage others from making comment, or telling collateral stories. That was ordinarily how it worked. Facing a stony silence, Bob looked around hopefully, asked out loud if anyone else had something to share. Not a peep. Then he focused an unspoken appeal on me.

With a sigh, I rose to my feet. "My name is Charley," I said, "and I'm an alcoholic. Those of us, like Steve, who have celebrated that first anniversary remember what an occasion it was in our lives. Those of us who haven't yet achieved three hundred and sixty-five consecutive days of sobriety know how hard he worked to put them together and can imagine his sense of accomplishment.

"But as one who got his cake and candle a couple of years ago, I've got some good news and some bad news for you. The good news is that it really does get a little easier as you go on past that first anniversary. Day by day, and as we all know, that's the only way to measure progress, I keep busy in my line of work, and as long as I'm busy, I don't miss the stuff like I used to. And I've drunk enough coffee and Diet Coke to float an aircraft carrier."

Laughter and applause at this. I was glad to get it. In order to continue, I needed some encouragement.

"But now for the bad news," I said. "I've had a couple of experiences recently that have shaken me pretty badly. Each of them had to do with death, violent death, as it happens, but maybe for purposes of this discussion, that's irrelevant. Maybe it shouldn't matter how death comes, whether it's expected or unexpected, because the point is, it's going to come, no matter what. Death doesn't go away. Early or late, death awaits us all. And drunk or sober, too.

"Just because all of us in AA are in the program to build new lives for ourselves, in the end we'll all lose the game, just as everyone does. So I did a bit of arguing with myself. I said, on the one hand, if we're all going to die, what does it matter whether I die drunk or sober? Maybe I liked my life better the way it was. But I had to admit I liked living sober better than I liked living drunk."

At that point I paused, waited, because what I had to say next was going to be more difficult. I wanted to word it right.

"There's a rabbi out in the East," I began,

"who's written a book called *When Bad Things Happen to Good People*. I want to know what he has to say because I need an explanation. Bad things? I'm talking about the kind of stuff you read about in the paper every day — the grandmother who's raped and robbed, the five-year-old who's hit by a stray bullet in a drive-by shooting, the young woman who loses her life to cancer.

"One of those experiences of violent death I mentioned in the beginning really shook me up. It was the death of a seven-year-old child. She'd been murdered. I saw the body, and it made me sick, literally. I vomited. I came away wanting a drink the way I never had before in my life, because that's the way I'd always dealt with horrors in the past. I didn't deal with it in the old way, didn't go out and get drunk, didn't even have one drink and then catch myself after that. But the truth is, I haven't dealt with it at all.

"My point is that even though we meet together to help each other solve a problem we all have in common, we shouldn't think we can isolate ourselves from the kinds of problems that face us every day: old age, death, the murder of innocents. We can't escape them. We shouldn't even try. We have to face them. But for people like us, the only way to face them is sober."

Exhausted, I sat down. It was a pretty lively meeting from that point on. It seemed as though everyone had something to say — a comment, a story, an opinion. It was all Bob Williams could do to bring things to a close, but he handled it well — passed the collection plate, led the Serenity Prayer, and sent them on their way. Then he beckoned me over. "There's a slight change of plans on dinner tonight," he informed me.

This was disappointing. "What's the matter? Can't you make it?"

"No, nothing like that. I can make it, all right. It's just that priest you know from Hub City."

"What about him?"

"He wants to come, too. Says he's got a lot of questions that didn't seem appropriate during the meeting. When I told him I'd made a date with you for dinner, he was eager to come along."

I really couldn't back out of it now, could I?

At first it seemed as if all those questions he wanted to ask were janitorial in nature. Who prepares the room? Who cleans up afterward? How often would it be necessary to make a room available for AA meetings? How large a room? Was tonight's turnout at St. Jude's about average for this chapter? Was it necessary to provide ashtrays and allow smoking?

While Bob and I together would probably have settled for the back booth at Benny's

Diner, out of deference to our guest, we had proposed the Pickeral Inn; our proposal had been accepted quite without argument. To make things easier, though, each of us went over in separate cars.

It was still early when the three of us convened at the table in the main dining room, and the place was quite empty. There were diners at three or four other tables, but in a room so big you felt kind of lonely unless it was at least half-filled. The first thing Father Chuck did was order a Red Label on the rocks.

Since most of the questions were directed at Bob, and some of them only he could answer, I picked away quietly at my lake trout and studied the interrogator. Father Chuck showed no ill effects from his two Scotches, not talking louder or slurring his words. I wouldn't have either in my drinking days. I supposed that what I'd said during our coffee-break conversation had more or less extended him permission to drink when he sat down with us here. If so, he had certainly —

". . . wouldn't you say so, Charley?" It was Bob. I hadn't been listening.

I looked questioningly from one to the other. "I'm sorry," I said, "I didn't catch that."

Father Chuck beamed indulgently. "I asked Bob here why you people were so shy about using God's name. This 'Higher Power' business seems so vague and, oh, I don't know, New Age or something."

Bob leaned across the table toward me. "And I said it was because we wanted to bring people in, rather than keep them out. Wouldn't you say so, Charley?"

"Of course I would. I'd also say that religion has become a more divisive factor in society than it used to be."

"You mean we used to be a Christian nation," Father Chuck said.

"Something like that. But alcoholics are people who share one problem. We want to concentrate on that. If we introduce other elements — maybe just naming the Deity — aren't you potentially introducing other problems?" I shrugged. "But that's just another way of saying what Bob said a moment ago."

"Look," said the priest, brandishing his fork, "one thing we've got at Our Lady of Sorrows is a good Holy Name Society, a fine bunch of men. Frank McBride, he's the head of it, came to me and said that some of them felt it would be a good idea if we had a chapter of AA at Our Lady of Sorrows. I said, 'Frank, is it a big problem?' He said, 'It is with some.' It saddened me to hear that, but it didn't surprise me completely. As I mentioned to you, Charley, I've done a bit of counseling along that line over the years, enough to know things weren't quite right with some. So that's why I came here tonight on a kind of fact-finding mission.

"Now, don't you think," he continued,

"that these men would be much more comfortable — the ones who need what AA can provide — if it was known that what we had at Our Lady of Sorrows was a specifically Catholic chapter? Wouldn't they be more comfortable with 'God' instead of 'a Higher Power'? And at the end of the meeting maybe saying a decade of the Rosary instead of that nondenominational prayer you said at the end, Bob? Now, don't get me wrong. There's a good philosophy in that prayer, one that I'm basically in agreement with myself, but it's not the kind of prayer, the kind of philosophy, to appeal to Catholic men."

I thought Dr. Bob did a remarkable job of controlling himself. He looked away, then up at the ceiling, as if he was giving careful consideration to what the priest had just said. But I knew he was annoyed, and I knew he was counting to ten.

I jumped in to help. "So you see this proposed chapter as sort of an adjunct of the Holy Name Society?"

Father Chuck thought about that a moment. "I suppose so. Yes, I suppose I do." He stopped for a moment to think. "Now, as I understand it, what I attended tonight was an open meeting?"

"That's right."

"Meaning visitors could attend?"

"Yes. Those are the only meetings they can attend."

"Well, that just doesn't make any sense," said Father Chuck. "I have no intention of joining. This" — he raised his Scotch glass — "just isn't a problem with me. But when we start a chapter at Our Lady, I want to be on board. It would be a crime to deprive those men of the experience in counseling I've had. I think my role would be as a sort of spiritual advisor. They need me. Besides, that way, I could keep an eye on them, at least in the beginning."

"Have you ever stopped to think, Father Albertus," said Bob in a quiet voice, "that to these people, you, as a priest, are a figure of authority?"

"Indeed I have. I think that's as it should be."

"Think about this, then. For a lot of them, their problems with alcohol addiction are traceable directly to their problems with authority. That's why we insist that alcoholics who want to quit are best helped by other alcoholics who want to quit."

Father Chuck seemed to contemplate this as he finished the last of his steak.

At last he spoke up. "If you'll pardon me for saying so, I think this talk of 'problems with authority' is so much modern psychology, and I don't buy any of it."

Bob waved to the waitress for the check. "I hope we've been of some help, Father Albertus."

"You've given me a lot to think about, both of you."

As Bob settled up with the waitress, I passed him thirty bucks, all I had in my pocket, to split the bill; Father Chuck reached over and grasped my arm.

"I want you to know, Charley, that I was really moved by what you said in front of the group tonight." He said it in a quiet voice, not much above a whisper. "It took a lot of courage. I think I can help you. I honestly do." Now he was whispering. "You know, these ancient curses — aging, death, suffering — these are the sort of problems that are best dealt with between a man and his priest. You blurt it out in public like you did, and you're not going to get any help at all."

"That wasn't why I talked about them. I wasn't expecting help from anyone. I was just pointing out that these human problems are there, and will always be there, whether we face them sober or not."

He nodded vigorously. "I understood that," he said, "and you were right to remind them. But you need help. And I can give it to you, I'm sure of it."

At just that moment, Bob rose from the table. A reprieve. "Shall we?"

Father Chuck released my arm at last, and we stood up. Bob led the way from the dining room, now filling completely. I hopped forward to catch up with him. But too late: Father

Chuck was there beside me.

"I mean it, Charley, particularly about death and suffering. I've got something to say about that I think you should hear. I had a loss myself."

I wrenched loose, stopped, and looked him full in the face.

"Father Chuck, I've heard your ideas on these murders, and I want you to know that I'm strongly in disagreement with them."

"Oh? Who told you?" He seemed guarded, almost suspicious.

"Sue Gillis. She's a friend of mine."

"She's a friend of mine, too, now. Terrific girl. I helped her, Charley. I can help you, too. Why not just drop by the rectory sometime soon and —"

"No, I don't think you could help me, Father Chuck. But I'd be willing to debate it with you any time you like."

"Opposing arguments, eh? Well, I'll tell you, I was known as a pretty hot debater back in the seminary, so I'll just take you on, sir. I accept your challenge. You may be a trial lawyer, and a darned good one from what I hear, but I've got the best arguments. You'll see."

"We'll both see."

Then I turned and walked away from him. Bob Williams stepped out and stopped me at the door.

"What was that all about?" he asked.

"I'll tell you later."

Father Chuck caught up with us, smiled his winning smile, and we all walked out together to the parking lot. Bob and I accompanied him to his car, a Ford station wagon, not too many years old and apparently in good condition. We did our handshakes, and Father Chuck thanked us for, as he put it, "a memorably good steak."

Then, to me, he said, "Any time you want to get together, Charley, we'll thrash this out."

"I'll give you a call," I said.

"Do that."

With a wave, he jumped inside the car, started it, and pulled out of the parking space.

"So what do you think of him?" I asked Bob.

"This is the guy who's going to lecture them on sobriety? Well, pardon me, but I think they'll laugh him out of the room. Maybe he'll manage to get the chapter credentialed from the central office, but I don't believe so, not after I tell them what I think. I'm going to sit down with Father Phil and tell him, too."

"I hope you're right."

"I hope I am, too."

By then we'd reached my Chrysler. We stood there, hands in our pockets, looking at each other and saying nothing. If I read Bob right, he was as eager to call it a night as I was.

"What was it you wanted to talk to me about tonight?" he asked.

"I guess I covered that when I got up and talked in front of the group."

"At least you got it off your chest."

"It helped."

"It usually does. And what about that business between you and the priest on the way out? You were really getting into it with him."

"I don't know, Bob, it's too complicated to go into now. Some other time, okay? I've had a pretty rough twenty-four hours."

"Suits me fine," he answered in his usual diplomatic manner.

I don't think I realized how complicated it really was. This Father Chuck was getting to me in ways I hadn't anticipated.

14

I spent a good part of Monday morning with the door to my office closed, playing and replaying the interview I'd recorded the day before with Mary Margaret Tucker. I compared it to the statement she had made as a witness in the police investigation of the theft of the W-91 Fund. There were few discrepancies because there was practically no overlap at all.

When I'd read through her statement before, it seemed to me that it was rather thin. About all that had been established was that as Mark Conroy's secretary, she knew the contents of the safe, that on occasions she had seen the pile of money inside, and was aware of the purpose of the W-91 Fund. Yes, she had accepted small amounts of cash from Mark Conroy, which she referred to as "loans," but she did not know they came from the safe. She confessed that she had been intimate with Conroy on "several" occasions, but that their affair was now over and had ended more than a month before she left her job to begin classes at Wayne State. Quoting the date of her departure and the time she had started back to school, she had thus established her absence at the time the theft had been discovered. She had given her address as a place on Van Dyke and her occupation as "college student."

What her statement to the investigators lacked were any details of her affair with Mark Conroy — its length, the amounts of the "loans" she had received in cash, the fact that they had continued as regular payments from the Ad Astra account, and that she had lived rent-free in a building owned by him. There was nothing about the weekends in Chicago and Port Huron, much less a mention of her Las Vegas trip. They had treated her with kid gloves. She had been groomed as a witness for the prosecution right from the start.

The purpose of this exercise of mine was to put together questions for her cross-examination, when the time came. At the top of the sheet on the yellow pad I had in front of me, I jotted down the matter of the combination to the safe. Did she know it? Conroy had said she almost certainly did. That remark she'd made about Henry Mosler.

Mrs. Fenton buzzed me from the outer office. I picked up the phone.

"A county policeman named Bud Billings on the line," she said.

"Put him through, Mrs. Fenton."

The usual click-click, and there he was. "Charley? I got trouble."

"Is it what you were afraid of? The Evans kid?"

"Yeah, his old man got some young lawyer in Mt. Clemens to take the case. They called me from the courthouse to tell me a false arrest suit against me and the county has just been filed." He paused. I sensed what was coming next. "I was wondering, Charley, could you . . . ?" He left it hanging in the air.

"Could I take you on as a client?"

"Yeah."

"Bud, I don't see how I can. If it comes to a trial, I'll probably be called as a witness."

"Against me?"

"No, well, maybe technically, but not really. There's nothing they'll get from me that's going to hurt you."

"You sure of that?"

"Reasonably sure. Just remember that Judge Brown denied the *Habeas Corpus* I presented about the time the kid was released."

"That's important, huh?"

"You bet it is."

There was a prolonged silence at the other end of the line. "He's getting back at me — old man Evans, I mean. There was this case about four years ago —"

"Yeah," I cut him off, "I read about it in the newspapers at the library."

"Who tipped you?"

"Actually, it was Mrs. Fenton, my secretary here at the office. She is not one of Delbert Evans's big fans."

"Neither am I. Listen, Charley, they're taking me off the case."

"Off the case? Does that mean Sue's handling it alone?"

"Not exactly. They're going to move Larry Antonovich from nights starting tomorrow. By the way, she's working on some new angle, something she says you gave her."

"I gave her?"

"That's what she says."

I tried to think what that might be. All I could come up with was the advice from Mark Conroy I'd passed on to her the night before last at dinner. She certainly hadn't seemed very receptive to it then.

"I'll have to ask her about that," I said. "But Bud, about your immediate problem, I've got a suggestion to make. Give John Dibble a call. Walk over and see him. I think he's the right guy to handle your case."

"Why do you say that? He's the country club lawyer."

"The reason I say that is because he told me that Delbert Evans had come to him and tried to get him to take this false arrest suit. John sent him away, told him he didn't have a case. So, in effect, he's already declared for your side. And as far as him being a country club lawyer, he won't charge any more than I would."

"Should I tell him you sent me?" Bud asked.

"Suit yourself, but I think you'd both be

better off if he thought he was your first choice."

"Yeah, I see what you mean. Okay, then, Charley, I'll try it your way. Thanks for your trouble."

"Think nothing of it, Bud. If there's any other way I can be of help, just let me know. I mean it."

Poor Bud Billings. He had just begun living every cop's nightmare. It was only by an accident of years of service that he was down as the arresting officer on Sam Evans's sheet. The senior investigating officer was the one who signed off on it. Sam had actually been Sue's project. Or what about Stash Olesky? He'd feel properly guilt ridden, I'm sure. But when you came right down to it, Mark Evola was the one who bore the brunt of the blame. If he hadn't called that press conference on the steps of the Kerry County Police Headquarters and announced that an arrest was imminent, there would have been no pressure on the cops to hold Sam Evans overnight.

But parceling blame was useless in a situation like this. Bud Billings was the fall guy. And while I'd presented things to him in a positive light, it wasn't really so certain that he'd win in a walk. If the case went to trial before a jury, then all bets were off. You could never really tell how twelve citizens might vote. I decided to get the name of this young lawyer in Mt. Clemens and find out a little more about him. I'm sure John Dibble wouldn't mind a little sidelines coaching — if it was offered in the right spirit.

I went back to Mary Margaret Tucker. I was getting tired of listening to her. There was something in her voice I found annoying. She seemed self-regarding and self-indulgent, yet at the same time she assumed an attitude of moral superiority, especially about Vegas. And she carried all that, somehow, in her tone of voice. Surprising. Conroy evidently got a lot from her, and she certainly got a lot from him, materially. Maybe the two of them deserved each other.

I'd made a few more notes on the yellow pad when Mrs. Fenton rang me again from the outer office. It was Stash Olesky this time. He sounded glum.

"You heard about Bud Billings." It was a statement, not a question.

"I heard."

"I feel shitty about this," he said.

"Well . . ."

"Meaning, maybe that's just how I should feel, huh?"

"No, come on, Stash. If anyone's to blame, it's Mark Evola."

"Don't remind me. Was it you who recommended John Dibble to Bud?"

"Yes, but I told him to keep it to himself. Obviously I couldn't take the case. No need for John to think he was second choice."

"Agreed. How about we have lunch and knock this around a little?"

"Where and when?"

"Oh, I don't know. I always go to Jimmy Doyle's on Courthouse Square." He hesitated. "Would that be okay with you?"

Jimmy Doyle's was basically a bar that served food, good food, but it was still a bar. Stash knew about the booze and me. He was being considerate.

"Jimmy Doyle's is fine," I said. "Best corned beef and cabbage in the world."

"Sue Gillis may be along a little later. You won't mind that, will you?"

"Certainly not. As long as it's not your boss. You know how I feel about him."

"Get real, Charley. Have I ever inflicted Mark Evola on you in the past? No, something's come up, and I asked Sue to come by and meet me there at one."

After we agreed to meet at twelve-thirty, I couldn't help wondering just what this lunch was really about.

Jimmy Doyle's was one of those old-fashioned Irish places, long and narrow in front along the length of the bar, then expanding to a good-sized dining area in the back. I marched dutifully past the bar, ignoring the array of bottles lined up there, but sneaking a peek at myself behind the jolly red faces in the long mirror. I looked the way I usually did —

a bit settled and serious, older than I felt, and maybe sort of melancholy, I guess that was the word. I was the very picture of sobriety.

Stash was in the far corner of the dining room. He half stood and waved, so that I could hardly miss him in spite of the considerable crowd between us.

"I hope you've recovered from that loss on Saturday," I said to him as I sat down.

"Loss?" He had his mind on other things.

"Michigan State — the football game."

"That, oh yeah. Just wait till next year."

The waitress came. Stash ordered a cheeseburger and fries. He already had a stein of draft in front of him.

"Shouldn't we wait for Sue?" I asked.

"Well, I've got to eat," he said. "And I've got to be back as near to one o'clock as I can make it. I just asked her to meet me here so I could tell her a few things. Go ahead and order."

I asked for a Reuben sandwich and told the waitress to bring me a Diet Coke.

As she turned away to the next table, I leaned closer to Stash and asked, "How's the investigation going?"

"Don't you know? I would imagine you'd be better informed than me. By Sue, I mean."

"She doesn't like to talk about it, at least not to me."

"Consorting with the enemy?"

"That's part of it, I suppose. I told her when

395

we had that fight over Sam Evans —"

"You got that straightened out, didn't you?" Stash interrupted. "The way I handled it was all wrong. We wouldn't be here to talk about Bud's problem if I . . ."

"No, we got it straightened out, more or less. But when I was trying to talk her down, I told her that given the size of Kerry County and the number of attorneys in it, that it was only a matter of time until we found ourselves on opposing sides."

"Well, that's certainly true."

"She later admitted it was, but she still seems to treat me with suspicion. I think there are probably some areas of the investigation she shouldn't discuss with me, but I don't get anything at all from her. I learn more from the newspapers than I do from her. So back to my question: How's the investigation going?"

Stash looked at me like I'd just grown a second nose. "That seems strange."

"What does? What're you talking about?"

"You ask how the investigation's going. The last thing I heard I got direct from Sue this morning. I ran into her outside Mark Evola's office, and she told me she had a new tack. She was taking a direction you'd given her. She seemed quite upbeat about it, and was asking for my help on an interrogation relating to it. That's why she'll be here later. But you don't know what this new tack might be?"

I thought a moment. The only thing it could

be was that bit of advice from Mark Conroy that I'd passed on to her. Yet she certainly hadn't been very receptive when I'd told her. She seemed to wish I'd stop bothering her.

"Yeah, I've got an idea," I said. "But it wasn't something she showed much interest in."

"Maybe she thought it over and changed her mind."

"Maybe she did."

As our harried waitress brought us our food, Stash suddenly blurted out what was on his mind. "I practically framed Bud for this false arrest suit," he said.

"Okay, repeat after me, Stash — *mea culpa, mea culpa, mea maxima culpa*. Get it out of your system."

"No, it's true. If I hadn't been so goddamn tricky —"

"Let's be practical and see what we can put together to help him. What do you know about this lawyer old man Evans got in Mt. Clemens?"

"Not much. I know his name — Dietrick Dornberger — and I know he's young, in his twenties. He went to law school out of state."

"Yeah? Where?"

"I think I heard someplace it was De Paul in Chicago."

"A lot of good guys come out of there, I hear. Has he won any cases?"

"He's won a few, mostly personal injury, all

of them right in Macomb County. A couple more were settled just before the jury went out, but I hear he's pretty good in front of a jury, too."

"Has he ever tried a false arrest suit?" I asked.

"Not that anyone knows about." Stash scarfed down a couple of french fries and took a big bite out of his burger.

"We ought to get hold of the transcript of one of his trials. Could you do that?"

All I got was a nod from Stash.

"We could go over it together, and then you could pass on your suggestions. John Dibble would accept them from you, but maybe not from me."

Another nod.

"What's Dornberger's situation, by the way? Is he a junior partner in a firm? A full partner?"

Stash swallowed the mouthful and washed it down with a man-sized gulp of beer.

"No," he said, "he's on his own."

"Really? As young as he is?" That showed some courage.

"Yeah, his father set him up. His old man's the biggest builder in Macomb County, and he's also his number-one client. Most of the son's business, you won't be surprised to learn, is real-estate law."

Stash looked beyond me then and shot his arm up, just like he might have done at school.

"Here she comes," he said.

Whatever else she was — and she was many things to me — Sue had precisely the looks that would attract me even in a roomful of Miss Americas. There was the deep strength of her eyes, a seriousness in them now as she acknowledged me at the table that should have warned me something big was under way.

"Sit down, Sue," said Stash with a glance at his watch. "I'm going to have to make this fast. I've got to be in court in about a minute and a half."

He crammed another bite into his mouth as he reached over to the empty chair beside him and came up with a large manila envelope, about a half inch thick.

"Now," he began at last, "what you've got in here is Xeroxes from his personnel folder — not the whole file, mind you, just what I thought might be of interest."

"Is this all I've got to go on?"

"Well, it's something. Just work up what you need, the questions you want asked. Don't try to write the script. The psychologist has his own way of phrasing the questions and working them in with others. That's his province. He insists on it. Clear enough."

"I won't know until I start, will I?"

"Probably not. I'll be back in my office sometime in midafternoon, anywhere between two-thirty and four. But I'll need your list of questions before five. Okay?"

Sue nodded vigorously. "Okay, Stash. Really, okay."

"We'll talk if you need to." He stood up and turned to me. "Charley, I'm going to stick you with the check. I got to run. Sorry."

I waved him off, smiling. We watched him go, exchanged looks, and burst out laughing. Poor Stash! He carried the weight of the whole office on his generous shoulders. Mark Evola, the elected Kerry County prosecutor, couldn't do much but get in the way. A couple months before, they'd hired a young assistant prosecutor — very young, right out of my old law school, the University of Detroit. Stash said he was a bright kid and would make a terrific lawyer once he had some experience, but now he was being used strictly on appeal work and can't-lose cases. As of that moment, with one slot still open in the county prosecutor's office, every active case in the county fell to Stanislaus Olesky. I hoped they paid him enough to make it worth his while.

Our laughter subsided quickly enough. It seemed not only unkind, but also misdirected, for the man worked hard, too hard; we both knew that.

"What're these questions you're preparing?" I asked her.

"Charley, I'd really rather not —"

I held up my hand and managed to silence her. "Okay, okay. Not another word. I withdraw the question."

"Thanks," she said. "We may work this out yet."

"Listen, I called a little before midday yesterday and left a message. I hope you weren't putting in another day on this case."

"Of course you called, Charley, and left a lovely message. But no, I wasn't in the office, or out on Clarion Road, or Beulah Road, or in Hub City, or anyplace connected with the murders. I did what every sensible girl does when things just get to be too much."

"What's that?"

"I ran home to Mommy and Daddy."

The look in her eyes told me that it was all right to laugh, so I laughed. "Well, that's all right then," I said, "as long as it did some good. Did it?"

"I think it did me a world of good," she said earnestly. "As a matter of fact, it felt so good that I stayed until after ten, didn't get home until after eleven, and decided it was too late to call you. You'll forgive me, won't you, Charley?"

Just as I was preparing a suitably eloquent speech, the waitress bustled up to the table. "What can I do for you, honey?" she asked Sue. She had her pad and pencil poised.

"Oh, gosh, I don't know." Sue said "gosh" like a kid. "I *am* hungry," she declared. "That cheeseburger Stash had looked awfully good. Give me one of those." And she pointed at the remains of the thing on his plate; it didn't look that tempting to me.

"Okay, so where was I? Oh yes, you were about to forgive me for not returning your call when I came in. I suppose you sat up staring at the telephone until one or two o'clock in the morning?"

"I was asleep before eleven."

"How disappointing."

"I had a pretty rough one the night before."

I don't know why I said that. I had no intention of elaborating on it and I certainly didn't want to arouse her curiosity. Maybe I had some overwhelming secret desire to confide all the bloody details of the Conroy case to somebody so I could get it off my chest. Those were dangerous feelings for a lawyer under any circumstances, and in this instance they could prove positively fatal. Luckily, she wasn't in the least interested in my night out on the town.

"One thing Mom and Dad and I settled, and that's Thanksgiving dinner. It's definitely on. You're definitely expected. It's going to be a real family occasion."

"I'm sure I'll love it," I said, lying, with a smile on my face.

"I'm sure you will, too." There was such obvious sincerity in what she said that I confess I felt a bit guilty.

"They really are nice people, Charley. They just want the best for me."

"As you said before."

"That's right." She leaned close across the table, and without shouting over the crowd in Jimmy Doyle's back room, she managed to make herself understood by some trick of tone, or perhaps by pure force of will.

"I want you to know," she said, "that I'm feeling very good about us. You handled me just right Saturday night. I was a mess, total burnout. You have no idea, Charley, how this case has taken over my life. It's not good for me, I know, and I'm trying to fight it, but it's not easy. Anyway, you didn't try to push me when we went out for dinner to be more communicative. And you didn't try to draw me out to talk about it. I appreciated that. But most of all I was grateful that when I cut the evening short, you didn't take it personally. You were just an absolute gentleman. And for that, dear Charley, I thank you."

This was embarrassing. Though I don't believe I would have behaved any differently, it was also certainly true that I had my own agenda on Saturday night. If she had begged me to stay with her, I would have taken my leave from her regretfully but firmly. And so, for good reason, I felt even more guilty than I had moments before.

"And then," she continued, "to come home last night and hear that wonderful message — 'I hope you're fully recovered and ready to meet the week head-on. Lean on me, kiddo.'" She quoted me word for word.

"I mean, really, Charley Sloan, you're just terrific."

I didn't get back to my office until a little after two. For me, the way I'd operated in Pickeral Point during the last couple of years, it was an exceptionally long lunch. Yet I didn't feel that it was time wasted — good company, good conversation, just exactly what I'd been missing.

Nevertheless, Mrs. Fenton gave me a frown of disapproval when I came in, and she nodded to the couch. I had a visitor. It was Dominic Benda, of all people, dressed in his twill tans and pile jacket, looking quite official, except that the Kerry County Police insignias had been neatly removed; you could hardly tell they'd been there at all. He rose uncertainly from the couch and nodded. No smile.

"What're you doing here, Dominic?"

"Uh, well, I think I might need a lawyer, Charley."

"Please, come on into my office and tell me about it."

I shut the door behind him. We both sat down, and I listened to his story. Although what he told me was unexpected, there had been signs, and I should have read them.

He'd been asked to come into police headquarters early this morning, no reason given. When he got there, he was hustled into Interrogation Room Three. There he was questioned with mounting aggressiveness by Sue Gillis. It soon became obvious that he was a suspect, or at least suspected of being a suspect, in the child murders. Why? Because he had been the officer in the vicinity during the day shift when the first two of the three murders took place.

"But Charley, course I was out there," he declared. "That's been my territory for years. I live out in that direction. I know it real well."

"When did you finish your shift and turn in your patrol car on those days, Dominic?" I asked him.

"Usual time, around five-thirty, maybe a little after."

"And what about the morning out on Beulah Road? When did you start your shift?"

"Usual time, eight o'clock."

Sue admitted to him at the end that there were some difficulties on the matter of time. But that was when the ever-popular Mark Evola made his appearance. He'd evidently been watching the interrogation through the two-way mirror. He told Dominic that he wanted him to take a lie-detector test, just to eliminate him as a suspect. When Dominic said he had some difficulty with that, Evola said that in that case there might be some difficulty continuing his pension.

"He said that? Aren't you protected by Civil Service or something?"

"No, nothing like that. It's all strictly county."

I was incensed. First of all, no trial lawyer, defense or prosecution, puts any faith in the polygraph. There are so many glitches and hitches in their operation and interpretation that no court in the country accepts their results as evidence. Psychopaths and sociopaths have no difficulty beating the polygraph because they lack any ordinary human sense of guilt. And to threaten to take away a man's pension if he refused to take such a faulty test seemed like coercion. It was probably even illegal.

"So what did you tell him?" I asked Dominic.

"I told him I'd take it. I had no choice. But I think I need a lawyer, right?"

"I think you do, yes."

"Well, would you, you know, be my lawyer?"

"Sure, Dominic."

"It's gonna cost me, though, right?"

"There'll be a retainer, yes, but don't worry. We'll work it out."

"Mark Evola said I didn't need a lawyer. That's why I figured I did."

"Good thinking, Dominic."

"But Charley, I gotta tell you I'm really scared of taking that lie-detector test. I didn't kill those children. I could never do that. I raised four kids of my own. I was a good father, or I tried to be." Tears welled in his eyes. "But I'm so scared of that damned machine, I'm afraid I'll set it off, no matter what they ask me."

This wasn't the time to give him a lecture on the fallibility of the polygraph. That was just what he was afraid of. And I couldn't tell him his fears were completely unfounded. Instead, I thought about it for a moment, made my decision, and then gave him a bit of advice.

Later in the afternoon, after Dominic had left, I started thinking again about Ismail Carter, not in a nostalgic way, but rather in strictly utilitarian terms: How could I use him on the Conroy case? And, more important, how could I find him?

He had acknowledged a debt to me, and I knew that the one-time city councilman, a man of many faults, had one outstanding virtue. He honored his debts. I just had no idea where he might be, or if he was even still alive.

But I had an idea just who might be able to help me find Ismail Carter. I picked up the telephone and dialed a number in Detroit I knew by heart, police headquarters, and asked for Detective LeMoyne Tolliver.

I got lucky. He answered on the second ring.

"Tolliver here." His voice sounded even bigger and deeper on the telephone.

"Do you recognize my voice?"

He held off. "I think so."

"From Friday morning and Saturday night."

"Now I do."

"Good, I was just wondering if you could give me some help finding somebody — a local politician who's dropped out of sight. He must be pretty old by now, might be dead for all I know."

"Who you got in mind?"

"Ismail Carter. Remember him?"

"I remember him, all right. Matter of fact, it was him who got me on the force, back when there was a definite quota, if you get my meaning."

"Sure, but do you know how I might reach him?"

"No, I don't, but I'll see what I can do for you. One thing's certain, though."

"What's that?"

"He ain't dead. When he dies, you'll know it. Gonna be one of the biggest funerals this town has ever seen." He paused as if giving preliminary thought to the matter. "I'll be in touch," he said.

"But just one thing more."

"What's that?"

"Don't tell our friend about this. He might not approve."

"You're right. He might not. But I think you're doin' the right thing, anyway."

15

I had agreed to meet Dominic Benda in the parking lot outside my office at eight o'clock in the morning. I began pacing about five minutes after, looking anxiously up the road in the direction I expected him to appear. He didn't appear. My watch said eight-ten the next time I looked. I stopped and scanned River Road in both directions, worried, afraid I'd asked too much of him. He was more than sixty years of age, overweight, and big in the butt from years of pushing that patrol car over the highways and backroads of Kerry County, not really in good physical shape at all. By eight-fifteen I had about decided that it was time for me to jump in my car and backtrack along the route into town. I might find him with his thumb out, or worse, collapsed along the side of the road. But before I climbed into my Chrysler, I went to the curb and took one last look for Dominic, and then I saw him, just about a city block away.

He was limping and staggering along, apparently exhausted totally from his long hike. As he drew closer, he appeared to me for the first time since I'd known him to be dressed in civilian clothes. His Sunday best. He must have started out in a suit and tie, and a top-coat, too. Coats were now thrown over his shoulder, his shirt collar was open, and his tie was askew. I saw that he was red-faced and sweating. I went out to meet him.

"Are you okay, Dominic?" I asked. "Here, let me take your topcoat."

He handed it over without a word.

"Better put your jacket on. It's too cold to go around in your shirt like that."

He nodded, stopped, and pulled on the suit-coat. He wasn't out of breath, just exhausted.

"Come on over and sit in the car. Take a rest. Then we'll drive over." Again, he nodded. He limped over to the Chrysler. I opened the door for him, and he collapsed into the passenger seat. I walked around, tossed his coat in the backseat, and got in behind the wheel. He let out a groan.

"I don't know, Charley," he spoke up at last. "This was more than I expected. I ain't done anything like this since I was in the army, and that was forty years ago."

"Did you stay up the way I told you to?"

"Yeah, I was up all night. I stayed on my feet the last three or four hours. If I even sat down, I would've fallen asleep, I'm sure of that."

"Maybe that was the hardest part," I suggested.

"No, it wasn't. Peggy fixed me breakfast, and that helped. Coffee — man, I needed that

410

— eggs and bacon, so I felt pretty good when I started out, but when I'd walked just a couple of miles, my legs started hurting. And each mile after that they hurt something fierce."

"How far did you come? It was about five miles, wasn't it?"

"No, closer to seven. That last mile or so, I really wasn't sure I'd make it." He shook his head in dismay. "I thought I was in better shape than this."

"If it's any consolation, Dominic, I probably wouldn't have done any better myself."

I slipped the key into the ignition and started the car. "We'd better get over there," I told him. "The test is scheduled for eight-thirty. It wouldn't do to be too late."

On our way to the station, Dominic was pretty quiet. I looked over at him. No, he wasn't tense, he was just plain tired. When we pulled into the parking lot, though, he did seek a little reassurance.

"All this I went through — does this, you know, guarantee I'll pass?"

"I never said that, Dominic, but it sure gives you an edge."

He thought about that a moment. "I'll pass," he said. "I don't give a fuck what they ask me now. I just want to get through this, so I can get home and get some sleep. Besides which, I didn't do any of that horrible shit they more or less accused me of."

"I like your attitude."

I pulled into a visitor's space. Dominic opened the car door and squeezed out. He was too big for my little car. But he got his feet on the ground and struggled to an upright stance. Somehow he took hold of himself then, and in spite of the pain in his legs, he marched beside me to the building and up the steps at a good, soldierly pace. As I held open the door for him, I looked him over. He was a mess, sweat streaked, hair matted; the ordeal he'd been put through was written on his face. His wife was waiting for him inside. They said their hellos; her concern was written on her face.

"Dominic," I said, "I want you to go into the washroom and clean up. Wipe your hair dry and comb it, button your shirt, and pull that tie all the way up. When you come out, I want you to look like you're ready for them."

He nodded and set off once again like a good soldier. Tony Makarides, the desk sergeant, watched him go. A couple of the girls in the front exchanged looks.

"Is he okay?" Peg Benda asked.

"He'll be all right. It was good of you to come here to give him moral support. He needs all he can get."

"Well, yeah," she said, "but that wasn't the only reason. I had to drive the car in — the old patrol car he bought off them. I told him he was crazy when he did that."

"Wait a minute. What do you mean, you 'had to'?"

"That was part of the deal he made with them so he could keep his pension. Take the lie-detector test and let them go over the old patrol car for, you know, evidence."

"He didn't tell me about that."

"He was probably ashamed. No kidding, Mr. Sloan, this really isn't fair. I mean, all the years he put in for this lousy county, and this is what they give him. I'm telling you, his heart's broke over this."

"Do you know if he signed something giving them permission to go through the car?"

"Oh, sure, just like he did for this damn old lie test."

It was probably too late to stop them, and maybe it was best I didn't. If they went ahead, anything they tried to use as evidence should be relatively easy to keep out of court on the grounds that Dominic had been coerced. If it ever came to trial. Let well enough alone, Charley.

"I passed him out on the road when I was drivin' in," said Peg. "He was really draggin'. I pulled over and asked him, did he want to ride the rest of the way. But he said no. He's really got a lotta faith in you, Mr. Sloan."

I gave her a little lecture on the subject of the polygraph, stressing that it was notoriously unreliable and that its results couldn't be used against him. She'd have to wait here, I told her, and the test would probably take about forty-five minutes to an hour. Peg took it all in without complaint or comment.

When Dominic reappeared, he looked a lot better, though he may have felt just as bad. Peg sent him on his way with a kiss on the cheek. Sergeant Makarides buzzed us in, and the two of us started on our way to Interrogation Room Three.

"How you holding up?" I asked Dominic.

"Not bad. Better."

"Good man."

I knocked on the door. It was opened by a man named Brunner, whom I'd met on a couple of occasions. He was the forensic psychologist usually employed by the Kerry County prosecutor's office. A short, squat man in a badly rumpled suit, he seemed okay.

"Hello, Mr. Sloan. Is this Dominic Benda?"

"It is."

"Come on in. I'll acquaint both of you with the procedure."

Leading the way, I looked around the room and took in the setup. It was about what I expected. There was an old reel-to-reel tape recorder and microphone on the table. The polygraph operator had tucked himself away behind his equipment in the far corner; he barely looked up at us, so intent was he on testing the movement of the stylus on the roll of graph paper in the machine. There were only three chairs in the room. I was about to call Brunner's attention to that when Mark Evola burst into the room, followed by Sue Gillis. Pausing just long enough to throw me a dirty look, he went up to Dominic Benda and, fists on his hips, confronted him. He was one angry county prosecutor.

"I thought I told you that you wouldn't need a lawyer for this."

Dominic didn't know quite what to say. I didn't want him upset. I gave him a touch on the arm and a wink I meant to be reassuring.

"He's entitled to have counsel present during every step of an investigation. Surely you know that, Mark."

"But this is a test — it's scientific! It's not an interrogation. You can't tell him what to answer, or not to answer. No Fifth Amendment."

"I'm aware of that," I said, "and I —"

"Gentlemen," Brunner interrupted, "maybe I can help settle this. The truth is, I'd prefer to have Mr. Sloan present during the test as an observer. After the test has been administered, he will be free to register any and all objections he has to the test, either procedural or material. They will be duly noted in my report. Does that satisfy you both?"

"My objections" — up on my high horse — "are not to the polygraph test per se but to the method in which permission to administer it was obtained from my client. He was coerced into this by the threat of —"

"Mr. Sloan," said Brunner severely, "do you agree to remain as an observer?"

Taking a deep breath, I said I agreed.

"Are you satisfied, Mr. Evola?"

"I suppose so."

Evola turned and stalked out of Interrogation Room Three, leaving Sue alone to glare at me. But it wasn't to me she spoke.

"It might interest you to know, Dominic," she said, "that Charley Sloan —"

"*Please*, Detective Gillis," Brunner interrupted for the third time, "if this test is to be administered fairly, then Mr. Benda must feel at ease. Unless what you wish to tell him is intended to promote that, I urge you to say nothing at all."

She pursed her lips, looked from Brunner to me and back to Dominic, then she walked out the door, slamming it behind her. Clearly, for the time it took to administer the polygraph test, Interrogation Room Three was Brunner's turf, and he was going to make damned sure we all knew that. Good style — you had to admire him for it.

"Now, Mr. Sloan, since you were not expected, we don't have a chair for you. Would you mind getting one?"

"Gladly."

In the empty office where I'd talked to Sam Evans the week before, I found just what I was looking for, a swivel chair, padded and upholstered sufficiently to fit my own soft frame. I wheeled it out of the office and across the hall. Once back in the room, I saw that the polygraph operator was busy pasting electrodes on Dominic's skin. Shirt open, tie off, sleeves rolled up — this after all Dominic's efforts to make himself presentable.

"Sit anywhere, just so long as you're out of Mr. Benda's line of vision."

I chose a place behind them all that offered me a good view of the polygraph. The angle was perfect for me to watch the action of the stylus on the graph paper as the questions were asked.

The operator had finished with Dominic. Brunner introduced me to him — Gulbranssen was his name — and I got up and shook hands with him, then retired to my swivel chair. Once the operator had signaled to Brunner that he was ready, he made a brief speech to Dominic about what lay ahead. His manner was reassuring. His tone was sympathetic. The tape was rolling.

"Now, Mr. Benda, what happens is very simple," he said. "I will simply ask you a number of questions. They are not trick questions, but they are questions that can and should be answered with a simple yes or no. Please answer them truthfully. The polygraph will measure your physical response to each one. It will not tell us whether or not you are lying. No machine can do that. All that it can do is note an increase in physical tension in your response to a question, should you have some difficulty with it. Is this understood?"

Dominic nodded.

"If you could give an oral response, please, for the tape."

"I understand, yeah."

"Now, Mr. Sloan, since you are here as Mr. Benda's attorney, you must understand that, as agreed, you are here strictly as an observer. This is a test, not an interrogation. Maintaining the flow of questions is very important. If you interrupt, you will be obliged to leave, and we shall have to resume the questioning from the beginning. If you will come forward and speak your agreement for the tape?"

I did as he said. He signaled when I was close enough to the microphone, and I spoke up loud and clear.

"I understand, and I agree."

"Now," he said, "I think we may begin."

After all that, the polygraph test that followed was rather anticlimatic. I soon understood that whatever art there was to the process was all in the preparation of the questions. What could a trial lawyer do if he was restricted to asking questions of a witness that could only be answered yes or no? Not much. By and large, Dominic kept to the rules, except for a few understandable slipups.

For instance, after Dominic's identity and his service with the Kerry County Police Department had been established, there was this exchange:

BRUNNER: "Are you married?"
DOMINIC: "Yes."
BRUNNER: "Have you ever abused your wife?"
DOMINIC: "No."
BRUNNER: "You have four children?"
DOMINIC: "Yes."
BRUNNER: "Have you ever abused them?"
DOMINIC: "No."
BRUNNER: "Have you ever struck them?"
DOMINIC: "Well, sure, ever'body does, but I only spanked them, and —"
BRUNNER: "Please restrict your answers to yes or no, Mr. Benda."

During that little tiff at the end, the stylus did move minimally beyond the narrow limits that proved Dominic was awake and breathing.

Gulbranssen, the operator, dutifully noted the number of each question as it was asked on the graph paper that crawled slowly across the machine. Each time he consulted his copy of the list of questions. He was methodical and, I'm sure, quite accurate.

Even later in the interview, when the questions were more direct and specific, Dominic's line hummed along in the same, steady up-and-down movement. When he was asked if he had known Lee Higgins, and then Catherine Quigley, his negative responses showed no tremor on the graph. When he was asked if he knew Billy Bartkowski and answered with a yes, again there was no discernible variation in the line. Brunner deviated from his prepared script very calmly and asked if Billy Bartkowski had ever ridden in Dominic's patrol car. Dominic replied with a no, but then amended that: "Oh yeah, a couple of times." No change on the graph. Then Brunner asked if either of these two occasions was at or near the time of Billy Bartkowski's death, and Dominic gave an emphatic no. Again, there was no change in the pattern of the line. Gulbranssen marked these two follow-up questions, 23A and 23B. Then very directly:

> BRUNNER: "Have you ever taken human life?"
> DOMINIC: "Yes."
> BRUNNER: "In your line of duty as a policeman?"
> DOMINIC: "Yes."
> BRUNNER: "Only in the line of duty?"
> DOMINIC: "Yes."

No change, the stylus hummed on.

And that was about it, except for one embarrassing moment at the end. Brunner asked if Dominic had ever represented himself as an active-duty police officer since his retirement.

This must have been inserted by Stash or Sue to get him to account for his curious habit of wearing his uniform and driving around the county in his old patrol car. But Dominic said nothing. What was the problem? Maybe he had been up to no good, doing — what? Then I glanced over at the polygraph and saw that the up-and-down movement of the line had fallen even below Dominic's normal low. The problem was, he had dozed off for a moment.

BRUNNER: "Mr. Benda, did you hear the question?"

DOMINIC: "What? Oh . . . no, I guess I didn't. Could you repeat it?"

BRUNNER: "Have you ever represented yourself as an active-duty policeman since your retirement?"

DOMINIC: "No."

And that was the last question. Brunner turned to me.

"Mr. Sloan, now is the time for you to register your objections to this test. Please come forward and speak into the microphone."

I got up and walked over to them. As I leaned forward to the microphone, I gave Dominic a reassuring pat on the back.

"I have no objections to the content or the conduct of this examination."

"Thank you, Mr. Sloan."

Brunner switched off the tape recorder and

tossed his list of questions onto the table. Then he winked at me.

He knew.

I was feeling pretty good by the time I got to the office. I knew that Dominic Benda had passed his polygraph test with flying colors. The fact that neither Mark Evola nor Sue Gillis was around afterward to complain or demand told me as much about that as my observation of the polygraph during Brunner's questioning. Dominic was feeling good, too. Maybe that little catnap he'd taken at the end had refreshed him. Anyway, he was moving at a quick-march step after we left Interrogation Room Three, and he gave Peg a happy face and a big embrace when they met.

And we all had a nice surprise waiting for us in a note from Stash Olesky that was passed to me by Sergeant Makarides. I opened the envelope, not knowing quite what to expect.

"Charley," it said, "I managed to intercede on the matter of the patrol car. I convinced the power-that-is that whatever was pulled from it in the way of evidence would be tainted and not useable in a trial. So you will find Dominic's famous go-car exactly where it was parked, wherever that may be. It has not — I repeat *not* — been touched by forensic hands. The Bendas, Mr. and Mrs., may drive it home. This is not to say, however, that the said go-car will not in the future be given a thorough going-over at a time more advantageous to the prosecution. Understood? Burn this after reading. Stash."

So the Bendas headed home in Dominic's beloved car. I walked them into the parking lot, gave Dominic another slap on the back and Peg a hug as I whispered in her ear, "You do the driving." They went to the car, and I was glad to see her slip in behind the steering wheel. I gave them a wave as they drove away, and then I discovered I had Dominic's topcoat in the backseat of my car.

Mrs. Fenton handed me a pile of messages, a lot more than I would ordinarily have expected at ten-twenty in the morning.

"And don't forget," she said, "you've got a real-estate closing at eleven."

I had forgotten. I was lucky to have Mrs. Fenton around to remind me. I went into my office and got busy on the callbacks.

The first one had to do with the real-estate deal. I wouldn't have been in it at all, except that there was a title search involved, just a matter of research in the county courthouse that I handled in an afternoon. I called the salesman, assured him everything was in order, and that I would be expecting him and all concerned parties in my office at the appointed hour.

There were a couple of dud calls, telephone solicitations for life insurance and for a subscription to the *Wall Street Journal*.

There was one I wish I'd been around for — LeMoyne Tolliver. Briefly I weighed the possibility of putting in another call to 1300 Beaubien, then decided against it. I'd let him do it his way and just hope I was around when he called back.

And Father Chuck had called. I came close to filing that one in the wastebasket. I even wadded it up. But in the end I smoothed it out and put it up in one corner of my desk blotter, tucked halfway under the leatherette border. Maybe later. Who knows?

The last one in the pile was the last received. The time: 10:05. The caller: Sue Gillis. The message: "Let's have lunch. Call me." This was a pleasant surprise. When last seen, she was staring daggers at me, trying to inform Dominic Benda that it was me, his lawyer, who had fingered him, more or less, with a tip from a Detroit cop who was now under indictment. Had it come from anyone else, I might even call it mean-spirited. Maybe she'd called to apologize. I dialed her number.

She answered in her usual terse, professional manner: "Gillis."

"Sloan, here, Gillis. I'm returning your call."

"Ah, Charley, I'm surprised you're back so soon. I figured you and Dominic would be out celebrating the rest of the morning. But maybe not, considering your client was practically comatose through the entire test."

"Oh, come on, Sue."

"Don't think it went unnoticed. Mark Evola was watching with me through the two-way mirror, and he said he'd never seen anything so outrageous in his life. What did you do, give Dominic sleeping pills? Valium?"

I waited. Let her vent. When at last her sarcasm seemed to have subsided, I said, "I believe you mentioned lunch in your phone message."

"Yes, I did."

"Well?"

"Let's forget about it."

Was I supposed to beg her? "All right, it's forgotten."

"Charley," she said, her tone was less strident, "is it really necessary for you to take on every suspect I bring in as a client? I was even acting on your advice with Dominic. I'm trying to do my job, working overtime to break this terrible, terrible case. Some nights I hardly get any sleep at all, thinking about it, worrying about it. That was how it happened with Dominic. After we had dinner Saturday night, I got to thinking about what you said, or rather what your client in Detroit said and you passed on to me. I thought maybe it's worth checking out, so I went in Sunday before I went to see Mom and Dad and began checking out duty rosters, and I came up with Dominic. He was out in that same territory on the days of the first two murders, and as for the Bartkowski homicide, he drives around in uniform in that patrol car, and —"

"Yeah," I interrupted, "he said he'd had the kid in the patrol car a couple of times. He must have known them, known the family."

"Didn't he tell you? The Bartkowskis were neighbors, just three or four houses down on the same street. Dominic was at the funeral. I can see there's a lot you don't know about this case, Charley. Frankly, I'm surprised at you."

"My chief interest in Dominic Benda, Sue, was that he had been coerced into taking an unreliable test with the threat of depriving him of his pension."

"Oh, that didn't matter," she said dismissively. "The important thing was to scare him. But how could he be scared, drugged to the gills, and with that shrink feeding him those soft pitches?"

"First of all, Dominic was not drugged. I give you my word on that. Secondly, what fault could you possibly find with the way Brunner conducted the test?"

"He should have been more aggressive."

"Sue, a polygraph examination is not an interrogation."

"Not the way he handled it."

"Let me tell you, I've sat through two or three others in my day, and I've never seen one handled as competently, as professionally, as he handled this one. I may not have any faith in the damned tests, but if you're going to give them, that's the way to do it. Now, admit it — that was your first polygraph, wasn't it?"

She ignored my question. "What I'd like from you, Charley, is a little support. This isn't easy, what I'm going through. But when I see you show up whenever we bring in a suspect, I just don't feel you're on my side. Now, I think I have to tell you that the reason I'm backing out on lunch is because I certainly haven't given up on Dominic. I'm sending out for a sandwich, and I'm really going to dig into this. The radio logs are next. And we will get a look at that patrol car of his. If he washes it, vacuums it, or gets it painted, we'll consider that as good as an admission of guilt."

"Does this mean there'll be further interrogation?"

"I'll bring him in when I'm good and ready."

"When you do, Sue, I'll be there at his side."

"I'll remember that." She said it as if it was a threat.

Having heard about as much of this as I wanted to, I was about to say good-bye when she came back at me suddenly with something that threw me into total confusion.

"And, Charley?"

"Yes?"

"Don't forget about a week from Thursday."

"Thursday?"

"Thanksgiving, you dummy. Dinner's at four, and I think we ought to be there about an hour beforehand. It's probably going to take another hour to get there — Southfield, you know. So, what do you say? Two o'clock?"

For a moment I was struck dumb. She'd switched gears on me so fast that I was left eating dust at the side of the road. All I could do was respond in my most docile manner. "Two o'clock sounds fine, Sue."

"See you then, if not before."

She hung up. I hung up. I sat there, trying to figure out who was on first.

After saying the things she had, after practically accusing me of using underhanded tactics, after threatening my client, she would turn around and blandly remind me of this Thanksgiving date she'd inveigled me into. Was this her idea of separating our professional lives from our private ones?

The trouble with her, the trouble with most cops — including Mark Conroy — was that they had absolutely no idea of the law. If it worked against them, if it got in the way, then they'd just sweep it aside, or find some way around it. A suspect was guilty unless he could prove otherwise, and even then he was subject to doubt. If hard evidence was lacking, they'd fake it, plant it, or try to scare the suspect into making some statement that could be used against him, the way they'd tried to do with

Dominic. What lawyers were for was to see that the game was played according to the rules. And thank God there were rules.

Were my tactics with Dominic and the polygraph test underhanded? No, but they were questionable, and I'd be happy to argue the ethics of that question with anyone on the basis of the polygraph's inherent inaccuracy and the manner in which Mark Evola had twisted Dominic's arm to get him to agree to take the test in the first place. I felt I was justified. But Evola had no better idea of the law than most cops. He didn't care what he did as long as he got a conviction.

Something occurred to me, a memory from a couple of weeks ago. It was Sue at Dominic's retirement party at the Glisten Inn. She had ranted at him, furious that a stripper had appeared, personally insulted and offended on behalf of Peg Benda and all the other women there. Then the next morning, she was embarrassed that she'd passed out in front of the guys. Could she have remembered this, too? Could she have set out, unconsciously, to pay him back? I had to admit there was a possibility. With her, everything seemed to be personal.

But then again, maybe it was getting personal with me, too. I was so furious about that smart-ass Evola's threat to take away Dominic's pension if he didn't submit to the polygraph test, I hadn't even really thought of

Dominic Benda as a real suspect.

If I went by Mark Conroy's theory, Dominic could very well be under suspicion. Conroy had said to look at people children trust. Like cops. Dominic knew everyone and everyone knew him, including all the kids. He'd been on the force so long, he was almost like a fixture. People loved Dominic, which was why it was hard to think of him as a possible murderer. But you never know, do you? Maybe Dominic was getting freaked out about having to retire after thirty-five years. Maybe he was unstable.

But I remembered how upset he was and how he cried at the Glisten Inn over the death of little Catherine Quigley. He was very drunk, but his tears seemed genuine. Maybe he'd been drinking too much in general and was suffering from blackouts. There've been thousands of killers who say they don't remember doing it.

Hell, maybe I was unraveling myself. These murders, and the fact that they continued to be unsolved, were driving people nuts.

One thing was clear, though. I'd better call Peg Benda and tell her I'd be out to talk with Dominic around three o'clock in the afternoon. That would give him a nap of four or five hours. If they were still treating him as a suspect, then I'd better hear his story, if he even had one. Besides, I had his topcoat in the back of my car.

I left Dominic's tract house after about an hour with him, not having learned all that much, yet feeling a lot better about what, if anything, lay ahead. We had talked over coffee at his kitchen table as Peg moved quietly about attending to things there. She poured the coffee. We did the talking. Dominic was sleepy but coherent.

I had to tell him they were still treating him as a suspect. Sue had said she'd be digging into the radio logs next. Did he have anything to fear there? Dominic wanted to know what I meant by that. Was he in regular contact with the dispatcher? On the other hand, maybe there was something that might help him. Maybe he'd been sent out on some special call on those late afternoons when Lee Higgins and Catherine Quigley had been killed, something that would have established him at a specific place for a considerable period of time.

Dominic gave that a moment's thought and shrugged. "They were just days like any other days," he said. "Nothing special about them."

Then I brought up the subject of his patrol car, and he interrupted me.

"Wait a minute. Maybe there *was* something the day the little girl was killed. That was the day before my retirement, the day before the party. I was rolling someplace, and I got a call on a rowdy drunk at the Dew Drop Inn on Beulah Road. That's outside Hub City, so it's county jurisdiction. I got the call around four, and it took me five, maybe ten minutes to get there. I remember it was starting to get dark.

"Anyways, I was all alone. We'd been singles in patrol cars since 1981 when they had the first big cutback. And I remember thinkin', I sure hope this doesn't give me any trouble — you know, the day before retirement — because if they called for a cop, it meant the bartender couldn't handle the guy alone. You never know what you're in for in a situation like that, see. The guy's drunk, he's out of control, maybe he's armed, got a gun or a knife, you don't know. I just remember I didn't like it, going into that place."

"So what happened?"

"Nothing much. The bartender pointed him out when I come in. He was a little bigger than they was used to. He'd taken a poke at some guy sitting next to him because he didn't like what he said, but I just walked over and talked to him, talked him into coming to the station with me. But believe me, I had my hand on the butt of my pistol the whole time. Mostly I just talk to them, see, and they come along. He came. I patted him down, put the cuffs on him, and put him in the backseat of the patrol car. I remember driving through the snow back to Pickeral Point and him tellin' me his whole sad story about how his girlfriend walked out on him and went to Texas. They booked him for D and D. You could look it up. I think he spent the night in jail. But I do remember it was a short day for me. When I finished the paperwork on him, it was almost five. Makarides said just turn in the car, no point in going out again. See, my usual route back to town was down Clarion Road. Who knows? Maybe I'd've seen the guy planting the little girl's body if I'd come in at my regular time."

"Do you remember the name of the guy you brought in?"

He thought about it. "No, but Makarides can look it up for you."

Then back to the matter of the patrol car. I told Dominic what Sue had said, that it wasn't to be cleaned, washed, or painted until they'd had a chance to go over it. Otherwise, she'd consider it an admission of guilt.

Dominic looked across the kitchen at Peg.

"Too late," she said.

"What do you mean?"

"I washed out the inside. I had to. It smelled of vomit."

"The guy I took for D and D, the one I told you about," Dominic said, "he barfed in the back. I wiped it up, but there was still lots of stink."

"When he brought the car home, it still stank," said Peg. "I told him, 'Dominic, I ain't ridin' in that thing until it smells right.' So I really went after it. Did a good job."

Sue and Mark Evola would have to live with

that. "That should be easy to verify," I said.

Dominic laughed. "You bet! Phil Kizer had to drive it on the next watch, and he was really pissed off about it."

Finally, I asked about Billy Bartkowski. How long had they known the family? How well did Dominic know Billy?

He shook his head and looked away. "I don't even like to talk about it," he said. "The Bartkowskis moved in . . . how long ago, Peg?"

"Seven, eight years ago. Joanie was pregnant with Billy. Remember?"

"Yeah, so we knew the kid his whole life long. Pretty short life. He was like our first grandkid. We got three of our own now, but he was just like one of ours. Peg baby-sat Billy and the other Bartkowski kids. Billy was always around."

"You said you gave him a ride in the patrol car a couple of times."

"Yeah, that was last summer. See, sometimes I sneak home and have lunch here. Billy was always after me to get inside the patrol car, so a couple of times I took him into town and bought him an ice cream, and I brought him right back."

I was satisfied. "Anything else you want to add, Dominic? Peg?"

There was nothing. So I got up from the kitchen table, thanked them both, and headed for the front door.

"Now, Dominic," I cautioned him there,

"you let me know the minute you hear from Sue Gillis, or Evola, or Olesky, or anyone. If they come by to bring you in for questioning, call me before you leave here, and I'll be there at the station waiting for you. Got it?"

I backed out of the driveway and drove slowly by the Bartkowski home, checking the address, noting how empty and deserted it looked. But not nearly as empty as it must seem inside. Once past, I sped up and headed on my way. I took the turn into Hub City.

Maybe it was because of that telephone conversation I'd had with Sue, or perhaps I had been brooding subconsciously on the matter ever since Sunday evening. Whatever it was that had impelled me, I had given Father Charles Albertus a call before I left to talk to Dominic. I told him I would be in the neighborhood late in the afternoon and might drop by. He seemed eager to see me. He told me I'd better be wearing my debater's cap.

In any case, I was ready for him, contentious and argumentative, looking for a fight. I drove past Our Lady of Sorrows, then turned the corner and parked in front of the rectory, behind his station wagon. Walking briskly to the door, I gave the bell three hard, impatient rings.

Only moments later Father Chuck appeared. He was dressed in a cassock and wore his Roman collar. Maybe he thought he looked more priestly in that outfit, and actually, he did.

"Ah, Charley," he said, "I'm so happy to see you, glad you accepted my invitation. Or was it I who accepted yours? Not that it matters."

He let forth a jovial laugh and stuck out his hand to me. But as he gave mine a shake, his eyes shifted to some point behind me, and an expression of concern touched his face.

"Excuse me a moment," he said and brushed past me, leaving the door to the rectory open.

I turned and looked after him. A boy was running as fast as he could for the rectory and Father Chuck. He seemed to have come from the woods behind the church and the parking lot. You could tell the kid was upset. He wasn't crying, but his face was all puckered from the effort to keep from it. The priest went out to meet him. Curious, after a moment's hesitation, I followed. I got there as the boy was blurting out his story to Father Chuck, who had gone down on one knee to listen.

". . . and he looked real mean, Father. I was a-scared of him, I really was."

"Did he try to grab you, Tommy? Try to get you to stay or anything?"

"N— No, it was just the way he jumped out of that ol' shack and yelled at me to get outa there — real mean."

"What were you doing there?"

"Just cutting through on my way home from school. You said it was okay, remember?"

The priest nodded. "So I did. But I'll tell you what. You go on home, and you can tell Mommy and Daddy about it, and say that Father Chuck's going to take care of things. But you better check with me before you cut through the woods again. Is that understood?"

"Yes, Father."

With a quick hug, the priest sent the boy on his way. He rose and said apologetically, "Look, Charley, I think I'd better take care of this. Would you mind waiting around for a bit? It shouldn't take long."

"I'll go with you," I said, thinking he could use some backup.

He thought about that a moment and nodded. "All right. I'll just duck back into the rectory for a moment."

When he reemerged he had a shotgun tucked under his arm. I must have looked a bit surprised at that.

"It's hard to get people to take a man in skirts seriously," he said as he touched the cassock at about thigh level. "But don't worry, it isn't loaded."

Together we set off down the path that led to the trees and through the woods. As we went along he explained again that the property belonged to the church. There were a couple of acres of undeveloped woodland, quite empty except for a caretaker's cabin that had fallen deep into disrepair.

"Nobody lives there now," he said.

"At least not the last time you looked."

He gave me a rather solemn smile and nodded at that.

The boy, Tommy, had called the place a "shack." That about said it. It leaned a little to the left, and there was a hole or two in the roof, but the windows, remarkably, remained unbroken. The door of the place stood open. We approached it quietly and carefully. There was someone inside moving about.

Father Chuck put a finger to his lips and stepped in front of me, and then to one side of the door of the shack. There at last he stopped, listened, and waited. I kept back.

"All right," said the priest, his voice ringing with authority, "I think you'd better come out of there now."

"Gimme a minute," someone answered. "I'm almost packed up. I'll be out of here before you know it."

We gave him a minute, or two or three. But in decidedly less than five he was finished inside and through the door. A small, wiry man, he looked at us right and left and pulled down his wool cap to cover his ears. He was dressed in wafflestompers, jeans, and a good warm winter jacket that covered his hips. He hauled after him a big pack, complete with sleeping bag. Once he was outside the shack, he took a firm position against the shack, put a pipe in his mouth, and took the time to light it up.

"Give me a minute with this," he said.

He had a tough little face, bearded and shaggy. His eyes were blue and a bit fierce.

"I s'pose it was that kid I yelled at told you I was out here," he said. He pulled deep on the pipe and let go a great cloud of smoke.

"You frightened him," said Father Chuck.

"He shouldn't of come nosin' around. I had the door open, but he had no right comin' in on me the way he did. Even somebody in my situation's got rights, you know."

"You're homeless, I take it."

"No, I ain't homeless. You mean, sort of a victim, right? I ain't beggin'. I'm a tramp, a vagabond. I live this way because I like to live rough."

"Even in the winter?" I asked.

"In the winter it's harder, but I get by. I coulda made a nice little home of this place, take me through to spring, if that kid hadn't . . ."

"Well, you can't, and that's that," said Father Chuck.

"I ain't arguin'. You don't need that shotgun. I'll be on my way now."

Father Chuck eyed him uneasily, and said with a frown, "Where will you go? There's snow on the ground. You can't just curl up under a tree."

Then he hiked up the skirt of his cassock and dug into his pants pocket. He pulled out a few bills, peeled off a five, and offered it to the man.

"I usually do work for pay."

"I feel like I owe you something," said Father Chuck, "since I'm turning you out of your cabin."

The man who called himself a tramp took the five and the ten I offered him with a nod and reluctant thanks. "I'll be on my way," he said. He left us, marching down the path in the direction opposite the way we had come, toward the highway.

Father Chuck stuck his head inside the door to the cabin, looked around, and shut it tightly behind him. "I ought to get a padlock for that," he said. Then we started back toward the rectory.

"How was it in there?" I asked.

"Neat as a pin. He'd swept the place out and straightened up."

"Did you notice his clothes were clean, too?"

"I did, yes."

We walked along in silence until at last we emerged from the woods.

"Independent cuss, wasn't he?" remarked Father Chuck as we were crossing the church parking lot.

"He certainly was."

"You know, I kind of envy him."

By the time we got back to the rectory, I'd lost my fighting edge and would gladly have put off the great debate until another day or let it go completely. Yet Father Chuck clearly expected us to proceed according to plan. He unlocked the front door and gestured me inside. I remembered the way as he led me down the long hall, past the rooms that smelled of furniture wax. The place seemed even emptier than it had when I first visited him. I wondered why.

"You really are all alone here, aren't you?"

"Oh yes, as I think I told you before, a housekeeper comes in a couple of times a week. A good thing she does, too, because I'm by nature a pretty messy guy."

"Do your own cooking, laundry, everything?"

"That's right. Why do you ask?"

"Not much fun, is it?"

He laughed that laugh of his again. "I get your point, Charley. We're both a couple of old bachelors, aren't we? Yes, well, I've been at it longer than you, though. How many times have you been married, Charley?"

We'd entered "his" room, an amazing place — a kind of combination den, trophy room, and office with deer heads, shotguns, and rifles on the wall; a huge, wild-eyed muskie seemed to snarl at me from the far side next to a window. Father Chuck leaned the shotgun in one corner near the desk. Then he unloaded his pockets, tossing out four shotgun shells on the desktop.

"What was that you asked?" I said. "How many times? Too many, Father, take it from me."

"Let's just take it from that point, Charley. Sit down, please."

He pointed to an old-fashioned, three-cushioned couch in the middle of the room and took a place opposite me in an overstuffed easy chair, pulling it closer to the sofa.

"What do you mean by that?" I asked.

"I mean, look at your own life," he said. "Your answer indicates that you've been married a number of times. Unhappily. Your appearance at that fascinating meeting of Alcoholics Anonymous tells me that you've had a lot of tension in your life. Misery, too. Wouldn't you have preferred to have done without all that?"

"I don't quite follow you, Father. Do you mean what I think you mean?"

"Charley, your soul, every soul, yearns for God, yearns to go to heaven. Why stop it? Why impede it on its way?"

"I can think of one objection to that," I said, "one that could be made within your own frame of reference. Not all of us may be ready for that journey that you've described. Father, I'm not sure I believe in good but I know I believe in evil. And so it follows that I'm not sure I believe in heaven, but I know I believe in hell. Our souls may yearn for heaven, but they fear hell."

He raised his arms above him and cupped his hands. These were preaching gestures. They reminded me of my youth.

"Charley, we cannot fear God. Think of His infinite mercy. Think of Jesus."

"That's probably easier for you to do than for me. Look, Father Chuck, for most of us, at least for a lot of us, the second half of our lives is nothing more or less than an opportunity to undo the damage we did in the first half, or to try to make up for it in some way. Surely you're not advocating suicide."

"Oh, Charley, Charley, you don't understand."

"No, I probably don't," I answered, wanting this whole discussion to be over and done with. I wasn't even sure he knew what he was saying.

Suddenly he smiled and leaned forward. Maybe he was winding down, maybe he was going to lighten up a little bit.

"By the way, I know I can't offer you anything alcoholic, but I'm sure I've got some ginger ale somewhere. Would you like some?"

"Sure," I said, relieved that he was sensitive enough this time not to drink in front me. Generally, I don't mind at all. It's no problem when Sue has wine when we're together, but for whatever reason, it did make me nervous when Father Chuck started knocking the stuff back in front of me.

He found some soda and ice in his liquor cabinet, poured two glasses, and brought mine over. Was it my imagination or did I detect a whiff of Scotch on his breath? I wondered if he'd been drinking before I arrived.

"You know, you and Sue have a lot in common," he resumed, as though he and I had been talking about her all along.

"How's that?"

"You both get awfully close to sin in your separate lines of work, all kinds of sin — theft, violence of all kinds, rape, the whole ugly list you can pull from the docket of any police station in the country. They're not just crimes, Charley; they're sins. Sue, it seems to me, has kept herself remarkably free of contamination by all of the ugliness she deals with day to day. I say it's remarkable because what she handles regularly are sex crimes, the worst of all. She told me about one of her cases involving a grandmother and her grandson that was just beyond belief. Yet it happened, right here in Kerry County. But she keeps her feet on the ground, Sue does, keeps the Catholic values she was brought up with. She's quite a gal.

"But you, Charley, in your line of work, you get even closer to sin. You have to defend these people, or you've chosen to. I keep up with things. I read the newspapers. I know that you've defended murderers, thieves of all kinds. Why, right now you've got a case in

Detroit involving the theft of something over a million dollars — by a policeman!"

"I never discuss my cases," I said firmly.

"There's not much to discuss, is there? How you can bring yourself to associate with these people, much less defend them, I don't understand. But, in the words of Our Lord, 'Judge not, that we be not judged.' Fair enough. I withhold judgment. But since you are even closer to sin than Sue, you run an even greater danger of being tainted by it. Whether you have or haven't been tainted is a question only you can answer. I must say, however, that your problem with alcohol indicates some difficulty of that kind."

What about *your* problem with alcohol? I thought, remembering how his breath smelled. "Father Albertus, I think you've gotten a long way from the subject at hand."

"And what is that?"

"I believe that you were about to tell me that I'm so close to sin, I'm becoming sullied by it. Or maybe you were about to say that I'm beyond redemption."

"Oh, Charley, really? Do you think I would say that?"

I didn't know the answer to that one, and frankly, I was feeling as though I didn't know the answer to anything at all. It wasn't even clear to me why I was here. He had invited me to meet with him for what he thought was going to be an intellectual debate, but this was turning into a kind of diatribe. While I respected him and certainly did not doubt his intelligence, I was getting confused.

Maybe by being in this rectory with him I was remembering how it was when I was a boy, my mother and father taking me to church during a time when I looked at the world through innocent eyes. Maybe the chaos was finally getting to me, the violence, the corruption, the deaths, my own search for a solid center.

And then suddenly the picture came into my mind: Catherine Quigley in the snow, her sweet, sleeping face visible through the clear plastic. She looked just like an angel. I kept trying to shut the picture down, but it was like a videotape playing over and over again and I couldn't stop it.

Finally, I completely lost it right on that couch with all those silent deer faces staring down at me. I began crying, unable to help myself, unable to push Father Chuck away from me when he tried to offer comfort. Maybe he was right: I'd been too close for too long to all of the ugliness.

"It's okay, Charley," he said, his voice quietly soothing. "Some things aren't easily understood, are they?"

He went on, muttering phrases that were meant to be consoling. I didn't have the strength to ask him to stop. All I could do was cry for that poor little girl in the snow.

16

So I lost the debate, such as it was, by default. Failure to perform. I stumbled out of the rectory, eyes puffy, nose running, my voice diminished to little more than a hoarse whisper. Yet I wasn't ashamed. As I drove through the dark back to Pickeral Point, it occurred to me that my response to that little girl's death, and the deaths of the other two children, was more genuine than anything Father Chuck had to say.

His reaction to my sudden breakdown was interesting. Once I had calmed down a bit and begun to get myself under control, he gave me a fatherly pat on the back, went to his L-shaped desk and typewriter stand, and returned with a tissue.

"I'll tell you, Charley," he said then. "It wasn't much more than a couple of weeks ago that I sat right here and did just what you're doing now. My nephew died in terrible circumstances. My sister's boy. He was the closest I ever had to a son. So I understand better than you think."

I got up from the couch. It took some effort. Suddenly I felt exhausted.

"I'd better go now," I said.

447

"Sure, I understand. And don't worry about this, Charley. No one should be ashamed to cry."

"I'll remember that."

"I'll pray for you," he said. "You might try it yourself."

Maybe he was right.

I was still thinking about this when I turned from River Road into the office parking lot. It was empty. The building was dark. As I got out of the car, I took a look at my wristwatch and saw that it was about five-thirty. I'd spent more time at the rectory than I'd have guessed. Taking a moment to lock my car — yes, even here in sleepy old Pickeral Point — I realized how cold my hands were. I wiggled my fingers and rubbed my palms to warm them. During this late-fall, not-quite-winter period, the days were tolerably warm, but nights hit pretty close to freezing and sometimes dropped below. I needed gloves. It so happens that I'm one of these guys who can't hold on to a pair from one winter to the next. I don't know what happens to them; they just disappear. I spent a good part of one morning the week before, going through coats, jackets, drawers, and looking on all the closet shelves, trying to find this year's gloves. All to no avail. I'd have to buy a new pair. Tomorrow, if I could find the time.

Mrs. Fenton would have left at five, or

shortly thereafter. I hadn't returned to do any specific piece of work. No, I'd come back to check my messages. I let myself in and switched on the lights. There was nothing on Mrs. Fenton's desk, and the red light on the message machine wasn't blinking, so I went into my office to have a look. Yes, there was a small pile of slips on my desk. I sat down and shuffled through them. And yes, here was one from Tolliver. Dammit! I wish I'd been here when it had come in.

I was consoling myself when Mrs. Fenton's phone rang in the outer office. I picked up immediately at my desk and found my own voice reeling off a message to the caller, urging him (or her) to leave a communication at the sound of the tone, and promising that it would be answered at the earliest possible opportunity. Mrs. Fenton had the machine set to pick up on the first ring.

All I could do was shout encouragement into the receiver: "Hang on, hang on. There's somebody here. I'm here."

At last my recorded voice fell silent. "This is Charles Sloan," I said, doing all I could to recover my dignity following my desperate pleas with the party at the other end of the line not to hang up. But as it turned out, the call was worth all my pleading.

"Oh, now I don't know. I wasn' callin' for no *Charles* Sloan. I was hopin' to talk to Charley. You got him around there someplace?"

449

It was a small voice, and it was weaker by far than the one I remembered from years before, but it was unmistakably that of Ismail Carter.

"Ismail! Is that you? This is Charley, all right. How you doing?"

"I'm doin' fine, but I had the idea you might be tryin' to get hold of me."

"That's right," I said. "Yes, I have."

"Well, that's a coincidence, ain't it? 'Cause I been tryin' to get you. Called a couple of times, but I got discouraged talkin' to that secretary of yours. She got a constipation problem, or something?"

"Something like that," I said.

"It took me some time to find out exactly where you are. Pickeral Point? Way up in the Thumb someplace, isn't it?"

"Just near the bottom, almost to Port Huron."

"I thought you were true-blue to old Detroit. Last man I'd ever tag for a white flight."

"It's a long, sad story, Ismail, but it's got a fairly happy ending to it."

"Hmmm," he said, just like that, then paused. I couldn't tell whether he was giving thought to what he might say next, or gathering strength to say it. "Well, I'll tell you, Charley, I think we better get together pretty soon to talk things over."

"What kind of things?"

"Oh, don't get cute now. I think you figured

out we have a mutual interest in a certain case you are handlin' now."

"I don't know what your interest is in it, but I'd be more than happy to find out."

"Maybe you will and maybe you won't, but I think we better talk." He gave me the address of a convalescent hospital on Jefferson, not far from where I'd rendezvoused with Conroy and Tolliver only a few nights before. I'd passed the place three or four times in the past couple of weeks.

"What time do you want me to come by tomorrow, Ismail?"

"No time. I'm due for an examination to-morrow, and it generally takes me a couple of days to recover from their exams. Make it Saturday, in the afternoon. Saturday's my best visiting day."

And with that — no good-bye or see-you-later — he hung up on me. This was better than I'd hoped for, or so it seemed. Ismail Carter was apparently more than willing to talk with me on the Conroy matter: He was eager. He must have called just as soon as he heard from Tolliver that I was trying to contact him. And while I'd rather see him earlier than Saturday, I had to respect the limits he put on his strength. I realized that he must be a pretty sick man.

By the time the next morning came, my attitude on the Conroy matter had improved considerably. I'd allowed myself to sink into pessimism, which is surely the unpardonable sin for any defense attorney. To carry him through a trial, a lawyer needed inexhaustible reservoirs of optimism. A client's innocence was beside the point; it was such an elusive ideal that it could only be considered in the abstract. No, what a lawyer had to believe in was the cause of his client — that justice could best be served only by finding in his favor. Perhaps most of all, a lawyer had to believe in himself and his ability to sway the jury in the direction he desired. For all that, he needed the kind of optimism that would fuel him right through his final argument.

I'd lost that. Or perhaps better put, I'd been unable to generate it. Things just seemed to have gone from bad to worse. The more I came to back Conroy's cause, the less I felt I could do to make it prevail. I had, in short, become pessimistic about his chances in front of any judge or jury. That, I think, was why I allowed him to go out on that fool's errand with Tolliver. I must have been desperate myself, or I would never have accompanied him.

But now I suddenly felt different about it all. Was it simply because of the contact I'd made with Ismail Carter? Surely not. I didn't know how he could help me, and perhaps he didn't either, nor could I be certain that between us, we would think of something. Why, I couldn't even be certain that he would want to help Conroy, though he had given some indication that he did when we talked on the telephone. Still, I felt strangely lifted by the encounter. For no good reason I felt a sudden rush of optimism.

That enabled me to do a bit of constructive work on the case. I had listened a number of times to the interview I had tape-recorded with Mary Margaret Tucker. Well, I listened to it a couple of times more. Then I thought about what I heard from Conroy about the safe and its positioning in his office, and then I thought about the Mouse, as well. And in no time at all, I had postulated a theory of the crime.

In a criminal case, the lawyer for each side, prosecution and defense, has a theory of the crime that he must try to sell to the jury. What have you got? A murder? A theft? The fact of a corpse or missing money is undeniable. But how the corpse got dead or the money went missing is, to some extent, a matter of theory and sometimes even conjecture. The prosecution's theory of the crime has been, for the most part, determined by the police investigation that preceded it. The prosecution must try the case on what they've been given, but the defense, in offering its theory of the crime, has far more latitude — and that's where conjecture often comes in. I have taken juries on some pretty wild journeys into what-if land. Yet they must have liked what I showed them, for more often than not, they accepted my theory and rejected that put forward by the prosecution.

In the case at hand, however, no great leaps were necessary, nor suspension of disbelief. It was simply a basic knowledge of office customs and folkways that was required, and almost any member of any jury had that, certainly.

This is how I had it figured:

Mark Conroy had made it clear that even though Mary Margaret Tucker was not officially in possession of the combination to the safe that contained the W-91 Fund, it was certain from her remarks that she had easy access to the combination and may well have had it memorized. She had the requisite knowledge.

She broke with Conroy in the third week of September, and left her employment as his secretary at 1300 Beaubien during the first week in October, so that she might begin classes at Wayne State.

On her last day of employment, she would almost certainly have been taken to lunch by her office mates and presented with a gift, probably one in a good-sized box. I would check on this.

Winding up office matters with Conroy in absentia would have meant writing notes, pulling files, and leaving them on his desk. All this and other matters as well would have meant making frequent trips in and out of his office.

No one would have expected otherwise.

On one of these trips to Conroy's office, Ms. Tucker took with her the gift box, or perhaps just another large box with which she would have been expected to take home with her anything of a personal nature — pictures, letters, notes, everything that would have carried her imprint. She would then have opened the safe and emptied it, putting its contents in either the gift box, providing it was large enough, or the one intended for her personal effects.

Either box would have served just as well in getting the money out past the guard in the lobby. He would have been as uninterested in the contents of one box as the other. Giving her a wave, he would have wished her good luck and urged her to come back and visit them sometime soon.

What she would have done with the money after leaving the building, I couldn't say. I don't think she kept it. Although she was probably following Timmerman's orders, she couldn't have handed the prize over to him, for as late as my meeting with her at Wayne State, she still did not know what he looked like. That, I decided, was a loose end. I would have to work on that, as well as the extent and nature of the Mouse's participation in the master plan. It was he, over a week later, who discovered the theft.

You may not believe it, since all this may

seem fairly obvious to you, but working my way through this bit by supportable bit took me the better part of the day. Yet what I had by the time I finished was considerable. I knew that even though there were holes to be filled and details to discover, my theory of the theft was reasonable and sound. I stood a good chance of selling it to a jury, almost any jury, and I could shape my whole defense to it.

I called up Mark Conroy and asked him to come out the next day. I told him I had something to talk about that couldn't be discussed on the phone.

"Be at my office tomorrow morning by ten o'clock at the latest," I said. "Be prepared to stay through lunch and afterward, if need be. We've got a lot to talk about and some decisions to make."

Then, without waiting for him to agree, object, or otherwise extend the conversation, I hung up on him. That made me feel good. He hadn't, after all, been the most cooperative of clients. Let him feel a little of the frustration I had felt in dealing with him.

It didn't take me long to decide that I was probably being a little too tough on him. After all, if I'd been infected by the virus of pessimism myself and only a day ago had managed to shake it off, Mark Conroy must be suffering a severe attack right now. And why not? He knew as well as I that as far as I was concerned, if I lost the case, I simply lost the case — he, on the other hand, would go to jail.

Then, near the end of the day, I got a telephone call that in a way surprised me even more profoundly than my talk with Conroy.

"It's that man, Tolliver," Mrs. Fenton called in to me. "He's been trying to reach you."

"Put him through, Mrs. Fenton."

I picked up the phone on my desk, and there he was.

"Ah, Mr. Sloan!"

"Charley, please!"

"Okay then, Mr. Charley. I just called to tell you that I'm still workin' real hard to find out where Ismail Carter might be."

I didn't know quite what to say to that. Hadn't it been through LeMoyne Tolliver that Ismail had reached me yesterday? I started to tell him that all that had been taken care of: Ismail and I were in contact, and a meeting had been arranged.

But for some reason, I withheld that. I said simply that I appreciated his efforts on my behalf, more than appreciated them, for though I hoped to talk to him soon, I could wait for a while because the important thing was to come at Carter from the right direction.

"Oh, I agree," said Tolliver. "I agree, totally."

"Yeah, I thought you would. Didn't you say

that Ismail Carter got you your job as a policeman?"

"He did, he sure did."

"Then you're the one to approach him."

"Right. I'll do what I can."

He said his good-bye then and left me wondering at these circumstances and my reaction to them. Why had I held back? Mark Conroy said he trusted LeMoyne Tolliver and had certainly shown his trust. Shouldn't I trust him, too? But what was his point in calling me if he had nothing to report?

One thing was plain. Ismail Carter was far more interested in talking to me than I had realized. He had sought me out just as I was seeking him. That meant he was willing to do more than listen. He really must have something to say.

It was well before ten when Mark Conroy arrived at my office the next morning. I hadn't been there long myself. The phone rang.

"This is Sloan," I growled into the receiver. "Are you just leaving?"

"No, I've arrived. I'm downstairs in the car right now. Why don't you come down?"

"You still don't trust my office — even after you had it swept clean?"

Well, why not? I wasn't entirely comfortable myself talking to Conroy there in the office. And it was too damned cold that morning to take another walk.

"I'll be down in a few minutes," I said to him. "I have to do some organizing first."

It took me no more than five minutes — a phone call or two, a hurried conference with Mrs. Fenton — and I was downstairs, climbing into the passenger's seat beside Conroy. He simply nodded and twisted the key in the starter. I assume the engine started, for a moment later we were in motion — yet I heard nothing.

We were out on I-94 before he said a word. He surprised me by turning in the direction of Port Huron, instead of Detroit. Our last, long conversation had taken rather a philosophical turn. He had revealed a good deal more of his personal history than I had ever expected him to do. Perhaps he had it in mind to take me on a nostalgic tour of the town where he'd grown up. Well, if that was what I expected, I got a bit of a start when at last he did speak up.

"I'm going to miss this car," he said. "You can drive all day in it and never notice."

At first I didn't grasp what he was getting at. "Are you going to sell it? Better wait until you get my bill."

"No reason to keep it. By the time I get out of Jackson, it'll be an antique. They probably won't even let gas-burning cars on the road in twenty-five years."

It was his relaxed manner that had confused me, a cop's stoicism. It disguised more of that defeatist talk I'd heard from him yesterday.

"You really seem to have made up your mind to lose this one," I said to him.

"It's not up to me, is it?"

"I told you I have no intention of losing, but I can't win it if you don't want me to. Look, Conroy, I've never had a client just quit on me. I've lost some, I admit it, but it wasn't because I didn't try, and it wasn't because the client was indifferent."

"I'm not indifferent."

"Glad to hear it."

"I just think they've got us — I mean, you and me — in a bind, a place that's just too damned hard to get out of. You saw what happened Saturday night. I've run out of options."

"Well, I haven't," I said a bit immodestly. "Now listen to me."

And so he listened as I narrated the scenario I had devised the day before. I was mildly surprised when, at the interchange, he took Interstate 69 toward Flint; we went cruising at about seventy, voyaging. It had been some time since I had been out in this direction, and I found myself looking once again at the passing, snow-dusted countryside as I talked to Conroy. Just look at it out there — fields plowed under, and stands, clumps, clusters, and whole orchards of trees, trees of all kinds. Even as I talked, it occurred to me that in spite of Henry Ford and Lee Iacocca, and all the rest of those giants of industry, this state of Michigan was, in its great expanses, long acres, and country miles, dedicated to agriculture, or to just plain wild growth. The assembly plants and parts warehouses would never win, not completely.

It was a good day to go for a long drive like this one. The sun still slanted at the morning angle. The flocks of geese flew high above, south from Canada. I found myself pausing a few times in the course of the story I told to look up at the sky and out at the flat landscape of late fall.

Mark Conroy did his part. He listened. It's funny but sometimes, out there on the highway with your eyes fixed on the road ahead, you can put forth a keener sense of concentration than in a more conventional setting. I don't think he looked at me once as I told this tale, which was about equal wild hypothesis and educated supposition. Yet he took it all in, examined its implications, and tested it with his developed instincts for discerning a story that sounds right and real.

When I finished, he said nothing for a mile or so — not much time by the clock at the rate we were traveling — and seemed to be savoring the story, tasting it, trying it.

"I think it works," he said, still staring at the road ahead.

"There may be some holes in it, but —"

"Fewer than you think," he put in.

"Well, for instance, were you out of the office, or off the floor for any extended period on her last day there? Would she have had time enough to manage the sort of transfer we're talking about?"

"Would she?" He chuckled. "Sloan, I made it a point to be away the whole day she left. I didn't want any contact at all with her. It seemed best for both of us that way. I was naive enough to think she might be throwing me soulful looks." Then he turned to me. "I'll tell you something else. Mary Margaret had a key to my office. She used it. People were used to seeing her go in and out. She had a daylong opportunity."

"What about a farewell party — a lunch?"

"There was one for her. They took her to Greektown. I heard all about it from the Mouse the next day."

"Did she get going-away presents? One big one?"

"Well, I contributed twenty bucks to something. But I don't know the physical size, whatever it was. I'll have to check on that."

"Do you think the Mouse was in on it?"

"Sure."

"Could she have delivered the take to the Mouse once she got out the door?"

"Sure."

"If it happened the way I'm suggesting it did, then it would have taken a lot of nerve on her part. Is she cool enough to pull off something like this?"

"She has the reserves of cool you and I could only envy, Sloan."

"But why would she have agreed to it? Why would she have done it?"

"Two reasons. Career insurance — she's even more obsessed by her future, by getting ahead, than I was at her age."

"Okay, what's the other reason?"

"To get back at me."

I let that go for the time being. I'd met her twice, talked at length with her once. I couldn't understand the reason for the animosity she seemed to feel toward Conroy, but there was no denying that it was there. For what, though? What had he done to her to inspire such desire for revenge?

"Where are we headed, anyway?" I asked him.

"We're going to hang a left at Flint and take Twenty-three down to Ann Arbor. I know a good place for lunch right outside of town. We're going to box the compass today, Sloan."

I was saddened to find Ismail Carter in a convalescent home. Maybe it was temporary, a period of recovery from who knew what sort of surgery or illness. But remembering his political history, which must have begun some time in the Thirties, I realized he now had to be in his middle to late seventies, at least. I supposed that I expected him to look just as he did then. But I knew he would not.

The nursing home in question, the Parkview, lay out beyond Parker and UAW Headquarters and turned out to be, quite reasonably, at the corner of Parkview and Jefferson. Saturday traffic was light. Parking was easy. I left my car right on Jefferson no more than a half block beyond the nursing home and walked back to the entrance. It was a good-sized building in good repair and looked like it might have begun life many decades past as a hotel, or an apartment hotel. In any case, it looked a lot better than newer buildings around it.

I started up the steps in a purposeful march, entered the building, and continued up another short flight of stairs to the reception office. It, too, was protected by a wall of bulletproof plastic like the one in that convenience store near Mary Margaret Tucker's place, though a nursing home did seem an unlikely target for armed robbery. I walked right up to the transparent wall and spoke through the three holes that had been drilled through it.

"I'd like to see one of your patients."

The young black girl on the other side of the wall smiled prettily and said, "We call them guests."

"Well, all right then, one of your guests — Mr. Ismail Carter."

"Just a moment, please. If you'll wait at the

door, I'll summon the superintendent of his floor."

I did as directed, but the promised moment was more like a full five minutes. When she came, the floor superintendent was apologetic in a no-nonsense professional way. She buzzed me in and started off rapidly down the hall. I assumed I was to follow.

"What sort of shape is he in?" I called out to her back.

"Not bad, considering."

Considering what?

"Can he talk? Can he see visitors?"

"Oh, he likes visitors. You'll see."

I had just about caught up with her when she stopped suddenly and gestured to an open doorway from which football sounds emanated.

"Stay as long as you like," she said. "Dinner isn't until five-thirty."

I muttered a thank-you and went into the room. He'd been there a while, I could tell. Mementos and framed photos seemed to cover every surface of the stark, institutional furniture. There were a few books piled on the night table by the bed. Ismail was sitting in the Eames chair that was somewhat out of harmony with the rest of the room but seemed right for him. He sat in it comfortably, dressed in silk pajamas and a handsome terry-cloth robe, his slippered feet propped on the Eames ottoman. I knew it had to be Ismail Carter,

465

but age had changed him, whitened his hair completely, shrunk him, thinned him, lined his face. I had a moment to look, for as I entered, he was facing away, concentrating on the football game. It was then that I also noticed the oxygen cylinder on the far side of the chair. I wasn't quite sure what that meant.

"Ismail?"

He looked up alertly, frowned for a moment, and then broke into a smile.

"Maybe I ought to come a little later," I said. "You look pretty comfortable."

Age had changed his voice — or maybe it was something more than age. He spoke weakly, not much above a whisper. Ismail held out the remote tuner and zapped off the football game, then reached out to shake my hand.

"Pull over that chair and sit down," he said.

I did as directed and took a place next to him.

"It's been a while," I said.

"Yes it has, but my, wasn't that an occasion! The way you ran them up there to the witness box, it was just like the Miss Bronze America Pageant right in the courtroom, wasn't it? Now, wasn't it?"

"No doubt about it."

"Man, I could pick 'em, couldn't I?"

"No doubt about that, either."

He began laughing. His laugh ended in a cough, and he reached over to the oxygen tank, took the mask off the top, and put it over his face. After taking a couple of deep hits, he returned the mask to the cylinder and switched off the valve. The way he went about it, I could tell it was all strictly routine for him. It helped, though. He sat up a little straighter, seemed perceptibly stronger.

"Great stuff, oxygen, good for what ails you." His voice was stronger, too.

"What's the problem, Ismail?"

"Old age is the problem, Charley. I'm eighty. They never thought I'd make it to eighty with this emphysema I got. See, it was those damned little cigars I used to smoke put me in this condition. I used to inhale 'em just like cigarettes. Truth is, if they were cigarettes, I'd a been dead a long time ago. But I loved them, no doubt about that. You pays your money, and you takes your chances. That's what life's all about, isn't it?"

"I guess when it comes right down to it, that's what we all do. How long have you been in here?"

"Five years — ever since they put me on oxygen. They bring people around to see me like I was the eighth wonder of the world or somethin'. Doctor says it's a marvel I've survived this long with these lungs of mine. My secret is, I keep eating. Whatever they put in front of me, man, I put it down." He grinned. Then the grin faded quickly. "Yessir, I been here in Parkview five years, but I keep in touch — read the papers, keep my ear to the ground,

467

got my own private communications network. I heard a lot about you lately, Charley Sloan."

"Not much of it good, I'm afraid."

"Oh, now, I wouldn't say that."

"I messed up pretty good, Ismail. Since we last met, I drank my way through two — no, three marriages, lost some cases I shouldn't have, lost a big income, and a perfectly good Rolls-Royce — all to the bottle."

"Well, some of us have problems like that. I never did."

"I hit bottom — lost it all."

"No, Charley, the way I heard it, you almost hit bottom. You got a year's suspension from the Bar Association, then you went up to that little town by Port Huron, kicked the booze, and you been working your way back."

I nodded. "Well, I've been trying. I'm what they call a recovering alcoholic."

"They got all kinds of fancy names for things these days. Main thing is, you're off the stuff now, and I hear you won a couple of pretty big cases. I know you did. I read it in the papers. I just couldn't find which one of those little towns was yours. Charley, anybody can take a dive. One way or another, I did it myself a couple of times. It takes a man to come back up. You've done all right for yourself."

I didn't know quite what to say. Hearing this from an eighty-four-year-old man with an oxygen cylinder beside him lent considerable weight to his words. What he was saying was

468

that I had his respect. That meant more to me than he would ever suppose.

"Well," I managed at last, "thanks, Ismail."

He looked at me, nodded, and said, "Now let's talk about this new case of yours — Mark Conroy. I'll be honest with you, Charley Sloan, there's not many men I owe a damn thing to — not anymore, since most of them are dead. And I do believe you are the only white man still around I owe anything to. So tell me your situation on the case, and let's see what we can do."

"It's not good, Ismail," I said. "But I'm going all the way for him."

"That doesn't quite surprise me. I know the trouble he's in. I knew you were his lawyer. The boy must be pretty desperate."

"He is, but he hasn't shown it to anyone but me."

"Tough cop. I know the type." He had something more to say, but he thought a long moment and decided to keep quiet.

"He didn't take the money." I said it firmly. I felt I ought to convince him.

"Well, that's good to know. But I want to hear the story."

"You mind if I close the door?"

"I'd be obliged if you did."

I got up and did that. Then I sat down beside him and started to talk.

There were parts of it I left out, had to leave out, for different reasons. Telling Ismail Carter anything at all might well have been construed as a breach of client confidentiality. I knew if I'd consulted with Conroy beforehand, he would never have allowed it. But I felt he was in the sort of situation that called for extreme measures. So I tiptoed a fine line and did a little dance around the more sensitive areas — not a word about our adventure on John R last Saturday night.

Even so, Ismail was impressed. "That's a lot," he said with a grin. Then he reached over to the oxygen cylinder beside him and took another hit through the mask, three deep ones this time. When he finished the operation, he nodded. "Go on, Charley."

I did, but just as carefully as before. I made the point that two other people knew the combination to the safe in Conroy's office. The Mouse had it officially — he kept the books and handled the payouts through the ledger, now missing. I told Ismail, too, that Mary Margaret Tucker had it unofficially. As Conroy's secretary, she had access to it. I made clear her relation to Mark Conroy, before and after their breakup. I told him I thought she had managed the actual theft — though not necessarily as her own little get-rich-quick scheme.

All this and more I told Ismail Carter. He took everything in, for the most part without interruption. When I'd finished, I leaned back and realized I was sweating. I took out my handkerchief and mopped my face and neck.

"That's it, huh?"

"More or less."

"Probably less than more. But I realize you've got responsibilities to your client. I trust what you gave me, and what you gave me is a lot."

"It's more than anybody else knows about it except for me and Conroy."

He frowned. "What do you want me to do with all this shit, Charley? I have some ideas myself."

"That's up to you, Ismail. I thought, hoped, you might still have a channel open to the mayor, and you could get him to read a letter I might send, something like that, I don't know."

"What would you say in it?"

"That's just it. I'm not sure. Conroy is convinced that he's been made the object of this frame because he's been after the mayor in a series of investigations. He's certain that the mayor's out to get him. I'm less certain of that than he is — although I am sure one of the cops on the Mayor's Squad is involved."

"Guilt by association?"

"Maybe more than that, and maybe not. What do you think? You surprised me with that phone call the other night. You said you'd been trying to get hold of me. I hoped you'd have some ideas about getting him out."

"Well, I think maybe I do," he said.

Ismail fell silent, lost in thought for a while. With his eyes shut and his face at rest, I thought for a moment that he'd fallen asleep. But no, his eyes opened and he fixed them on me.

"You know, a lot of people make fun of us old-time politicians. Some do worse than that: revile us and curse us, call us Uncle Toms, and all. They say what we did was just horse-tradin', makin' deals, and so on. And it's true, I made a lot of deals in my time, but I never begged. I always had something to offer in return. That's what politics is — something for something — and if you don't keep your word, then you ain't long for politics, my friend.

"My deals benefited my people — meaning black folks and specifically those in Black Bottom — but some benefited white folks, too. And some, I admit, benefited me as well. Just a few. I am not a rich man, and I wasn't when I left office. Main thing is, I didn't have my hand out, like so many did and do.

"Yessir, Charley, I am an unreconstructed, old-time pol. Only time I ever did anything to get modern, go with the flow and that shit, was when I changed my name."

"What? I never heard about that."

"Oh, I didn't change it, really — just how I spelled it. I was born Ishmael, just the way it's spelled in the Bible. My mama's name was Hagar, and she thought Ishmael, therefore, the most fittin' name for me. You do know your Bible, I hope, Charley."

He looked at me severely, and in response I waggled a flat hand at him, as if to say so-so.

"Well, you should. It ain't just a comfort. There's a lot of wisdom in it, too. But anyhow, that's what I was named, Ish-ma-el — means 'God hears.' But in the Sixties, when the Black Muslims was gettin' so powerful, I decided it wouldn't hurt nothin' if I spelled my name their way, show I was with them, see? I ain't sure it got me even one vote. Back then, mostly they didn't vote at all."

A knock interrupted him. A shy smile spread over his deeply lined face. "That'll be my regular Saturday visitors," he said. "I wonder, would you mind opening the door for them?"

As I got up to do that, Ismail reached over for the oxygen mask once again. I didn't know quite what to expect, but in no way did I expect what was just beyond the closed door.

Women — there were three of them. They bustled by, paying me no attention at all. They were well dressed, wonderfully coiffed, and beautifully perfumed. They livened the room with giggles and brightened it with their greetings to Ismail, who they addressed most respectfully. They fussed over him, patted his shoulders, his hands, whispered in his ear, while all the while he beamed back at them, like the happy boy he seemed just then. He assured them he was feeling fine, just fine, and urged them all to find places and seat themselves.

As they moved chairs and settled on the bed, I went unnoticed by the ladies and said a quick good-bye.

"I can see you'll be busy for a while," I said to Ismail.

"Oh, I will indeed. These ladies will keep me entertained the rest of the day, just like they do every Saturday. But I have some special interest in that young man Conroy. I want to help. I'll give some thought to how I can do that. I'll respect your confidence, and get back to you on this matter."

I thanked him, and we shook hands. Then, as I turned to leave, one of the visiting harem caught my eye, winked, and waved. I recognized her from all those years ago — Melody Martin, the barber's niece, her face a bit rounder, her figure amplified, but with the same sweet smile she had shown the jury when she testified to Ismail Carter's fine character and fair nature.

I waved back to her on my way out the door.

17

I hadn't gotten as much from Ismail Carter as I had hoped. During the next few days, I scolded myself often for relying upon him as I had. What help, after all, could a sick old man in a nursing home be likely to give? I might as well have applied for aid from the tooth fairy. Or so I was telling myself by Tuesday.

In the meantime, I worked, filling a couple of yellow legal pads with speculations, arguments with myself, questions, and details, details, details. My theory of the crime was supported by a couple of facts dug up by Mark Conroy and sent by messenger to me late on Monday. The first was a confirmation that, as I had supposed, Mary Margaret Tucker had indeed left 1300 Beaubien bearing a cardboard box nearly half her size; in it were the gifts that had been showered upon her and the contents of her desktop and middle drawer, which would have left plenty of room for a million or so in cash. When one of the detectives on the Untouchable squad had tried to take it from her to help her with it down to her car, she resisted his efforts almost to the point of physical violence.

The second bit of information sent to me by Conroy was unexpected — in fact, I could not have anticipated it. But it may certainly have had greater significance: It seemed that the house on Westburn, where Mary Margaret Tucker resided and where I had spoken to her, was the property of the City of Detroit, taken over earlier that same year for nonpayment of taxes.

By Tuesday, as I said, I had lost all faith in Ismail Carter's ability to influence the situation. It seemed unlikely that he would have the clout to do Conroy any real good; he might not even have the inclination.

Yet Tuesday morning, of course, was when Ismail called.

"Charley, I got good news for you."

"What's that, Ismail?"

"I got an audience with the pope."

"The pope?"

"Okay, have it your way. The mayor?"

"You're serious?"

"Very serious indeed. I dropped so many nickels, dimes, and quarters down this little project, I might as well have been droppin' them down a well. You think it's hard gettin' through to you with that constipated secretary? It's about ten times harder to get His Royal Highness on the phone. And I got what's supposed to be his private number!"

"But you did talk to him?"

"Oh, yeah, and a meeting's all arranged.

Manoogian Mansion, four o'clock tomorrow afternoon."

"But I don't have any idea what I'll say to him." I moaned a bit. I sounded pretty ineffectual even to myself.

"I can tell you what you'll say to him — not a damn thing! You better understand right from the start that I do all the talking."

"You mean you're coming along with me?"

"No, you're coming along with me. I'm *lettin'* you come along, Charley, because I *might* need a little help gettin' in and out of the car. Now, you tell me, what kind you got?"

"What kind of what? Car?"

"Yeah. I mean what are you driving?"

"A Chrysler. It gets me where I want to go."

"Well, it won't do to drive up to the mayor's front door in one of those. Order up a limo, Charley. Take your pick, Lincoln Town car or Cadillac, but make it big and make it black. Have it in front of Parkview about three-thirty. That'll give me plenty of time to get in and out, maybe take a little drive around town. Just be there. Understood?"

He didn't even wait for me to say yes. His receiver clicked in my ear.

I sat for a moment, weighing what I had just heard. He had surprised me by coming through for me, as requested. Yet doubts lingered. He would do the talking? How did I know what he had to say? How did I know he had anything to say? And this business of the

477

limousine, that seemed downright stupid to me. Were we being asked to finance an old man's last hurrah? Well, maybe we were. I shuffled back through the pages I had written on the legal pad in front of me. There were some good ideas there. I had some degree of confidence in the case as it was shaping up. I wasn't desperate. But I knew Conroy needed all the help he could get, all that I could get for him. If a direct appeal to the mayor would help, and Ismail Carter seemed to believe it would, then it should be tried. I only wished that I knew what sort of approach Ismail intended to use.

During the morning Dominic Benda called. No, he hadn't been asked to come in. Yes, he was feeling a lot better now, recovering from his long walk into Pickeral Point. I talked to him for a while just to keep his spirits up, and by the time he hung up, he seemed good. The whole family was getting together for Thanksgiving dinner day after tomorrow, he told me, and that was just what he needed.

I walked over to Benny's around noon. It was damned cold and getting colder. I had a bowl of chili, eating at the counter and reading my copy of the *Free Press* without interruption. That suited me just fine.

The bank's time and temperature clock read thirty-five degrees as I left Benny's. I tucked the paper under my arm and headed for the men's store in the mall just down the street from my office. I'd bought a suit there last winter. It fit as well as any of mine did, but it seemed kind of pricey for Pickeral Point — who did they sell to in this town, anyway? I'd more or less promised myself I'd do my buying elsewhere. But being without gloves on a day like this constituted an emergency.

Just as I expected, the clerk brought out a pair from under the counter that looked like they'd go for a good hundred bucks.

"We just got these in," he said. "They're really something special."

They looked like kidskin, light in color, and so slender that I doubted they would fit my stubby hands. But they did — perfectly, snug and tight as if they'd been made of rubber.

"They're unlined, aren't they? They won't keep my hands very warm."

"No, look here." He slipped it off my hand. It certainly didn't feel like rubber coming off. Then he folded it back and showed me that it had a micro-thin plastic lining with a pattern of holes throughout. "That's so your hand can breathe," he said. "You'll never pull it out sweaty. And look at the workmanship. You can barely see the stitching."

It turned out that they were from Argentina, calfskin, boiled and rubbed down to the consistency of kid.

"They're trying to break into the luxury leather market, show what they can do," the clerk explained. "The price is the best part —

fifty bucks. They can also use the hard currency."

I was sold. I whipped out my checkbook and wrote one out on the spot. They felt like a second skin as I wore them out of the shop. Flexing my hands into fists, wiggling my fingers, it didn't take me long to decide I'd never had a pair of gloves I liked as well as these. If I couldn't hold on to this pair into next winter, I'd never forgive myself.

It's odd how much these little blessings can cheer you up. I jogged across the street, feeling the way I used to when I'd just won a tough one in Recorder's Court. Hopping up to the curb on my side of River Road, I almost bumped into Sue. Literally. She didn't seem shocked or annoyed, but she did give me a puzzled frown.

"My," she said, "you're certainly acting chipper."

"New gloves," I said.

I held up my hands and wiggled my fingers at her.

"Aren't they pretty?" She sounded singularly unenthusiastic.

"How've you been, Sue?"

Although we hadn't seen each other since Dominic Benda's polygraph examination, and our last direct communication had been the telephone conversation that followed it, the decision to cool it had been hers. She had left a message for me on my answering machine, asking me if we might not "give our relation-ship a rest while we still had one." She'd gone on and on, talked nearly the length of the tape and pointed out along the way that I seemed to show up "on the wrong side" every time a suspect was brought in. She had ended quiz-zically, "What is it about you, Charley?"

But here she was, only about a block from my office. I wondered if she had popped in to see me. I wasn't sure whether she'd want to be asked that or not. Oh well, what the hell.

"Were you looking for me?"

"Not exactly," she said. "But I was just up at your office."

"I don't quite follow."

"I brought you your copy of the report on Dominic Benda's polygraph test. I left it with that cute little secretary of yours, Charley. If you want to give a copy to Dominic, you'll have to Xerox it off the one I gave Mrs. Fen-ton. You only get one copy. Mark Evola be-grudged you even that."

"Well, thanks for sticking up for me."

"Oh no, Charley, it wasn't me. It was Stash."

"Well, thank Stash for me, then."

She nodded but made no move to go. She seemed to want to talk but evidently had little or nothing to say.

"How's the investigation going?" I asked. "In general, I mean."

"In general? Well, I suppose it's — what's

the phrase? — proceeding apace. I think that's what Mark tells the reporters. Between you and me, I still think Bud Billings may be right about old Delbert Evans."

"And Dominic?"

"Charley, let's not talk about Dominic."

"Why not? Look, Sue, you said you were going to check the radio logs. You must have discovered that the night Catherine Quigley was murdered, Dominic brought in a prisoner and turned in his patrol car early. He wasn't around. He's eliminated."

"Why do you always have to act like a lawyer?"

"Because I *am* a lawyer, dammit!"

"I can see this isn't getting us anyplace. Let's get together when this is all over. We'll look back on it and talk it over."

"A little damage control?"

"Damage assessment comes first."

It is always remarkable to me how long people — intelligent, sophisticated people — will submit to police interrogation before calling in a lawyer. Often it has to do with feelings of blamelessness and innocence. If you feel that you have nothing to hide, of course you will be happy to answer questions, any questions that the police might have. Often one question leads to another and another and another, and soon the individual who had nothing to hide finds himself chased up a dead-end street, his way out blocked by the cops. That's when he wants a lawyer.

That wasn't how it went with Doris Dieberman, Lee Higgins's teacher. She made it clear from the start that she would answer no questions whatever unless a lawyer was present to give counsel. And not just any lawyer would do; it could be none other than Charles Sloan. They tried to intimidate her into responding. They asked provocative questions that any lesser person would have answered readily enough in his or her own defense. They made implications. They made accusations. Yet she remained silent, except to repeat again that she wished Charles Sloan there as her lawyer.

Why? Was she a friend of mine? A former client?

No, I'd never met the woman before in my life.

But as she explained to me on Wednesday morning in that empty office opposite Interrogation Room Three, Doris Dieberman is a serious and faithful newspaper reader. She is well informed and remembers what she reads. She recalled me from the Harwell murder trial and the Becky Harris case. And more recently, she had been following the story of the child murders, and noticed my name come up twice as counsel for two who had been brought in for questioning on the matter. Since she had been taken in for questioning on the same investigation, it seemed reasonable to her to ask for help.

"After all," she said to me, "you must be pretty familiar with the facts of this terrible case by now."

Ms. Dieberman taught second grade at the Hub City Primary School. Catherine Quigley and Billy Bartkowski both had been in her class. Lee Higgins, a little older, had been Ms. Dieberman's student the previous year. She was the teacher whom Bud Billings had denounced so bitterly for the callous way she had informed her class of Catherine Quigley's death. As I talked with her, she didn't seem particularly callous to me, just kind of withdrawn and impersonal. It made me wonder if the woman really could hold her own before a bunch of lusty, wild second-graders. It also made me wonder if she was hiding anything.

"I really don't understand what they want from me, Mr. Sloan. They were never really very specific about that. I tried to get her to tell me that before they brought me here."

The "her" was Sue Gillis, of course. She and Larry Antonovich had reported early to the office of the principal of Hub City Primary School and asked to talk to Doris Dieberman.

The principal, a man who was certainly used to having his own way at the primary school, began to dictate to Sue just where and how long she and Larry might talk to the teacher. Sue objected. It became a contest of wills, and in order to enforce hers, put the principal in his place, and win the day, Sue ordered Ms. Dieberman to get her coat and climb into the car, for she was going down to Kerry County Police Headquarters. More shouting, but Sue prevailed. And so here we were again: same situation, a few of the roles changed, new lines improvised.

This was getting to be like déjà vu all over again. In her growing desperation, Sue had decided that a small child would certainly trust his or her teacher, so naturally Ms. Dieberman seemed to her to be a natural suspect.

To date, it had not been established if the serial killer was a man or a woman; in fact, so little had been established that frustration levels were running at an all-time high. This was, after all, a small community where practically everyone was on a first-name basis with one another. Now three children had been murdered, and the killer was unaccounted for. Doris Dieberman was next up at bat.

"You said they kept asking you questions, Ms. Dieberman, even though you'd made it clear you wanted me here. What were the questions?"

"I don't know. I tuned them out."

"Tuned them out?" That was a strange response.

"Yes, I do that all the time with my kids in school. I don't think I could survive all that noise if I didn't tune them out. I just put my mind on something else and don't listen."

"That's a fascinating technique," I said. "Nevertheless, I'm sure you want to get back to your kids, noise and all, and get away from here, so let's assume they'll want to know about the three children who were murdered. They'll want to know if they knew each other and which adults they may have known that might have driven them home."

"I'll have to think about that."

Another peculiar response.

"They'll probably also want to know if you can account for your time on the evenings that the children were murdered."

"You mean, do I have an alibi? Three alibis?"

"I don't think it's come to that, at least not yet. Just tell them what you remember. Are you married?"

"No, but I live with someone."

"Then," I said, "you can give his name, and I'm sure he'll vouch for you."

"Her name. We share a house." She seemed embarrassed.

"Okay, hers."

"I remember we went to the movies in Port Huron the night that Catherine Quigley died. The other nights I have no idea."

"Tell that to them; all the details you can come up with will help. But it would be better if you could recall where you were when Lee and Billy were found."

A serious expression fixed upon her face and

she gave a nod of agreement.

"And I'll be sitting beside you all the while. If they ask something I think is improper, I'll say so to them, and I'll advise you not to answer it."

"Right in front of them?"

"Right in front of them," I declared. "One thing I would caution you about, however. Just answer the question. Don't give them more than they ask for. Ready?"

"I suppose so."

We got up and went across the hall to Interrogation Room Three, settling into two chairs behind the table. I gave her a critical look before questioning began. She had a strong profile, a long, prominent nose, and a firm chin. I hadn't noticed that, talking with her in the other room. She didn't seem intimidated by Sue or Larry Antonovich. It was the situation that caused her some distress.

There was something about the way that she responded to their questions that kept them at a safe distance. There was a rising inflection in her answers, which gave them a positive tone. And I noticed she would hold her chin a bit higher when she spoke. She was addressing the two detectives with the same authority she would have displayed before her class of second-graders.

There was only one incident during more than an hour of interrogation that would have counted against her. It turned, as it happened, on a point of honor. Doris Dieberman had finally accounted for her time during those evenings when the three children were murdered, but she had done so without mentioning that she lived with another woman. Sue seemed suspicious; I guessed she knew something about this coming in.

"You say you went to the movies in Port Huron?"

"That's right."

"Were you alone?"

"No."

"Who were you with?"

There was a long silence from Ms. Dieberman. I glanced over and saw that she was literally biting her lip.

"I'd like to be cooperative," she said, "but I'm afraid I can't tell you that."

"What?" Sue was overacting. She jumped from her chair, rolling her eyes in irritation. "You can't do that. You can't simply refuse to answer."

"I'll tell you anything you want to know about me, but I won't talk about other people, or even give you their names."

"All right, tell me this, then. Do you live alone at the address you gave?"

Again Ms. Dieberman chewed lightly on her lower lip, then gave a sharp, negative shake of her head. "No, I do not, but I won't give you the name of the person I live with. I'm sorry, but it's a matter of principle."

I cleared my throat to announce myself. "May I intercede here?"

"What is it, Mr. Sloan?" Cold irony fairly dripped from Sue's polite inquiry.

"I just wanted to say at this point that since you have my client's address, you have it in your power to secure the name of the party with whom she shares her residence. Why demand it from her? If you care to pursue the matter, you may also find confirmation on this matter of the trip to the movies, without her help. If we respect your right to interrogate her where you choose, why not also respect her right to withhold names?" I ended that with a smile; sweet reason always speaks with a smile.

Sue pursed her lips and said nothing. Then, after a considerable pause, she seemed to back off. "Perhaps she can tell us something about the children in her class who've been murdered."

As it turned out, she had a couple of interesting bits of information to impart. First of all, she mentioned that from time to time Father Albertus collected some of the children from his parish after school for events at the Catholic church in Hub City. That was always arranged beforehand. Then she pointed out that all three victims were on the same bus route, that much she had noticed. Sue asked her the name of the bus driver, and Ms. Dieberman said she did not know and would not tell her if she did.

That seemed unnecessarily provocative, especially since it was clear that the bus driver would be brought in for questioning next, and so I signaled her to hold it down. She did. All proceeded quietly between Sue and Doris Dieberman from that point on. The interrogation ended shortly thereafter, not with a bang or a whimper, but rather with a curt "That'll be all" from Sue Gillis.

Following that, there was some discussion between us as to whose responsibility it was to return Ms. Dieberman to Hub City Primary School. Sue pointed out that I was, after all, the woman's attorney, which was certainly true. Then I countered that it was they who had brought her there in the first place, and besides, I had business in Detroit. Larry Antonovich, who had been little more than a witness to the entire proceeding, seemed not a bit surprised when he was asked to play chauffeur to the teacher.

"Don't forget tomorrow, Charley."

I must have blinked two or three times. "Tomorrow?"

"Thanksgiving."

With her reminding me about it every other minute, how could I?

It was raining by the time I hit I-94. Even in good weather it was best to allow an hour for the trip to Detroit. Since they had predicted rain that would turn to snow in the evening, I gave myself an extra fifteen or twenty minutes to get there. By the time I reached Harper Woods, traffic began to pack together and slow down. It looked like I should have allowed myself even more time than I had.

I'd agreed to meet the limousine in front of Parkview Convalescent Hospital at the hour Ismail Carter had stipulated. I didn't want the driver to decide I wouldn't show up and head back to the garage. Ismail had demanded a limo. And while the demand may have seemed a bit excessive at the time, he was right to insist that we arrive in something grander than my Chrysler. They didn't know that its predecessor was a lowly, beat-up Ford Escort, a reminder of how low my fortunes had plummeted. Detroit, even on its uppers as it had been for years, was a place where putting up a front really mattered. I'd played by their rules all through that long chapter in my life as a big-time trial attorney in Motor City. I'd driven Cadillacs and finally a red Rolls-Royce, which I lost to creditors when I was suspended from the Michigan Bar.

Although traffic remained tight, speed picked up as the rain slacked off. Having driven the route once before, I knew just where to leave the Interstate and made good time on the surface streets to Parkview and Jefferson. I glimpsed the limo as I shot across Jefferson and made my way for a parking spot on the side street. As I hurried along on the rain-puddled sidewalk, coat collar turned up, wishing I'd worn some sort of hat, I glanced at my watch and saw that I'd actually made it five minutes early. It was three-twenty-five.

I tapped on the limo driver's window. "You don't need to yell," he said. People tend to talk loud in the rain; I guess I'm no exception. "You want to get in the back?"

"No, we're picking up somebody here," I said. "I'll see if he's ready."

"Give me your credit card, and I'll write up the order."

Frustration, annoyance, as I pulled out my wallet, clumsily dropped it to the sidewalk, retrieved it, and managed to extract the card he'd asked for. Handing it over, I turned and jogged up the stairs and into the building. There I was stopped by a pair of frowning faces, neither of them Ismail's.

The receptionist and the floor superintendent glowered down at me through the bulletproof plastic window. I approached it and leaned forward, about to explain my mission when the buzzer sounded, unlocking the door and admitting me.

Inside, I looked around and spotted Ismail, sitting quietly on a cushioned bench, bundled in a coat, wearing an impressive homburg hat, and holding an aluminum cane in his hand. He looked up at me and smiled tentatively. I started over to him but found my way blocked by the floor superintendent.

"Surely," she said, "you're not taking him out on a day like this."

I have to confess at this point that I hadn't given much thought to the weather and how it might affect someone in Ismail's weakened condition. The truth is, I hadn't given any thought to it at all.

"Don't pay no attention to them, Charley," he said. "They been talkin' like this ever since I sat down here. I can come and go from here anytime I've a mind. They know that. Now, if the limo is down there waitin' . . ."

With no small effort, he rose, pushing up with his weight on the cane until he stood to his full, shrunken dimension. I saw then that the cashmere coat hung loosely on him, as if it belonged to a man two or three sizes larger.

"I see you don't have an umbrella," said the superintendent, pulling one from the stand behind her and shoving it at me. "You will return this when you bring our Mr. Carter back safe, sound, and uninfected. Is that clear?"

"Yes, ma'am. Very clear."

"Charley?" Ismail nodded at the metal cylinder left on the bench. It was about a foot long and three inches in diameter and looked remarkably like a bomb. "I wonder, could you stick that in your pocket? It's my portable oxygen."

I managed to get it inside my coat. It was much heavier than I had expected.

"Take him out by the ambulance entrance," said the floor superintendent. "There's a ramp. It'll be easier for him."

"To hell with the ambulance entrance," he said. Then to me: "All right, Charley, let's give it a try."

We moved forward slowly at first, then a little faster as the receptionist pushed open the door for us. Ismail was leaning hard upon my arm and picking his way with the cane. He was moving along pretty well.

But then we came to the stairs, and these presented a considerable difficulty to him. Descending, he teetered on each one, carefully regaining his balance before attempting the next. It was very slow going.

Just as I was beginning to wonder if it might not be wise to turn around and return him to his room, the door at the bottom of the stairs opened and the limo driver popped his head inside.

"You look like you could use some help," he said.

"We sure could."

He held open the door and steadied Ismail as he hobbled forward and through it. By this time he was panting from his exertions. I opened the umbrella, glad to see that for now at least the rain had slowed to a cold, steady drizzle.

"Hey, I got an idea," the driver said to me. "What do you say we carry him down? Grab my two hands, and we'll make a chair for him."

I handed the umbrella to Ismail and did as the driver directed. Ismail sank back, putting his faith in us. Our shoulders gave support to his back, and he nodded his approval. We gingerly took him down the few steps to the sidewalk and across the short space to the waiting limo. He was light as a child in our arms.

He let out one of his surprising cackles. "This is what you call traveling in style. It's the cat's ass."

We set him down carefully at the car door. Once on his feet again, he took a moment to steady himself, then gave us his okay. I preceded him into the Cadillac and was there to settle him into the backseat. He let forth a great sigh.

"Well done, well done, you two! I might just keep you on the payroll to move me around like that."

I signed the order that the driver handed across to me along with my credit card.

"Where to?" he asked.

"Manoogian Mansion," I said.

"I believe we have some time," said Ismail, his voice rising slightly. "I wonder, driver, if you would take us on a bit of a drive through downtown. I've been cooped up in that place so damn long I practically forgot what this city looked like."

"Be glad to, sir," said the driver. "I'll take you on my special twenty-five-minute tour. You want the front-seat window up or down?"

"Down, by all means. I have no secrets." He laughed again. "And if you believe that, I've got a nice bridge I'd like to sell you real cheap."

We drove off into the rain, the windshield wipers moving silently, revealing our round-about route back on Jefferson toward the Renaissance Center, still visible in spite of the wall of clouds and mist that had descended. The neon lights along the way seemed to vibrate and shimmer, as they do in wet weather. It seemed much later than it was. A kind of twilight had fallen over the city.

"This is not the day I would have chosen to make this visit," said Ismail. "But come to think of it, it wasn't me who chose it but His Royal Highness."

Then he lapsed into a long silence, his face turned toward the window, taking in all that the rain streaks permitted, looking out from time to time through the windshield for a better view. Once, as he looked forward, I saw a tear on his cheek. He wiped it away.

"This was a great city, Charley. You remember it during the war?"

"Yeah, but I was just a kid."

"There wasn't anything couldn't be done here. I've heard it said the whole war was won right here on those assembly lines. But then they took the assembly lines away, and the city's tax base went with them. The Big Three made this town, and now they got it just about unmade."

"I agree," the limo driver called back, tossing in his two cents like a New York cab driver. "You said it in a nutshell, my friend."

Ismail turned to me with a grin. "There. You see?"

But then we fell back into silence, an even longer silence this time. Downtown — Cadillac Square, Grand Circus with its empty buildings and deserted hotels. They made Ismail's point so well he had no need to comment, no need at all.

He was angry, and he was sad. It occurred to me that this might indeed be his last look at the city he had served long and conscientiously in his left-handed way.

"We better head for Manoogian now," he said to the driver. "Can't keep the man waiting."

Then to me he whispered, "Could you give me that can of oxygen, Charley? I'm in need of a hit."

I dug it out of my coat pocket and handed it over to him. He did the rest, fixing the mouthpiece, rationing two generous doses to himself, nodding afterward in satisfaction. "Good stuff, take it from me."

He didn't say another word until we were

back on Jefferson headed for Dwight and the mayor's residence. As it turned out, he'd put the bad news off to the end.

"You aren't going to like this, Charley, but I'm going in there to talk to him all by myself, solo. You got that?"

"I don't think I understand that at all, Ismail. I've got a client. I'm here to represent his interests."

He waved me to silence.

"There's things going to be discussed in there you probably shouldn't hear. I want to keep it so those things can be discussed, and I've decided that the presence of a third party, any third party, might just make it impossible to get down and dirty. I'm for your boy. It's for him I'll be talkin', but I can't do it with you listenin' in. Now, is that clear?"

There really wasn't much I could say.

"My way or no way," said Ismail.

The driver turned off Jefferson and onto Dwight. There was no mistaking our destination; two police cars were parked in front.

"Your way, of course."

"Thank you, Charley. I knew you were a gentleman."

The limo pulled up at the entrance. A uniformed policeman opened the car door. "Councilman Carter? The mayor thought you might need some assistance. We have a wheelchair for you."

"How very thoughtful of him," said Ismail.

18

After stopping at the office, I headed back to my apartment, satisfied that nothing had come in that couldn't be handled the next day. The next day? No, Friday would have to do. Tomorrow was Thanksgiving, and I had that burdensome dinner with Sue and her parents in Southfield. She'd made it an obligation and was going to make sure I honored it, despite the uneasy terms we'd been on for the past few weeks. At this point I saw little future for us. Even though we'd had a good run of it for a while, I wondered why I had ever speculated, even briefly, that a policewoman and a defense lawyer just might manage something permanent together. Our interests were opposite. Our minds worked differently. We were natural adversaries. The sooner Sue admitted that, the sooner we'd be on our separate ways. All this made me question what had kept us together for so long. Loneliness, I suppose. There was so much of it in places like Pickeral Point.

For the second time in recent memory, I contemplated leaving town. Living someplace farther out in Oakland County might be possible. There was a good, active court in Pontiac, and I'd tried a couple of minor cases there. But the difficulties involved in opening up an office and establishing a new practice seemed, at this point, just insurmountable. I was still known in Detroit, of course. I tried a case in Recorder's Court nearly every month. Yet returning there seemed out of the question. Had I any friends there? No, just colleagues, other lawyers — and most of them lived out in the suburbs someplace and commuted to offices in town. I couldn't quite picture myself as a suburban resident. No, professionally, Pickeral Point was just right for me. But like a lot of men my age, I'd lost the knack of making friends. Bob Williams was about the only one I had, a "best friend," as the phrase goes. He knew all my secrets and liked me anyway.

On an impulse, I went to the phone and gave Bob a call. As usual, I got his answering machine. At the beep I told him I was just checking in and he could call me if he wanted, nothing urgent. Bob was so often involved in AA business, even on those nights he didn't have a meeting to lead, and probably was on this night. Or maybe he'd gone to the movies. It was a thought, getting together with him, a reason to get out of the house.

I didn't have to dig too deep to discover what had put me in this frame of mind. It was the time I had spent with Ismail Carter. He hadn't been far out of my thoughts since I'd left him back at the Parkview Convalescent Hospital in the care of that fierce floor superintendent, now my enemy for life. Ismail had seemed satisfied and none the worse for his excursion in the rain. All he had said about his hour-long meeting with the mayor came on the drive back to the Parkview. "We had a lot to talk about," he told me. "I told him some things he hadn't heard before. He's thinking it over."

I didn't ask him to be more specific, didn't ply him with questions. "You'll let me know?" I said.

"Sure, Charley. Course I will."

And that was that.

Whatever he had had to say to the mayor, he judged it to be of considerable importance. First of all, he had sought me out. Interestingly enough, I hadn't heard from LeMoyne Tolliver since I'd first seen Ismail. He had wanted to know the details of the case against Mark Conroy and would not have allowed me to withhold anything from him. And finally, he had not only sought the appointment with the mayor, he had also ventured out to keep it on a day that would have kept any other man in his condition safe and warm inside his room. The floor superintendent was absolutely right to object as she had. He was frail and might indeed be near death.

It was that — his own knowledge of his approaching death — that had given dignity

501

and tragedy to the day's whole adventure. Whatever happened in the matter of the *State of Michigan v. Mark Conroy*, it was certain that one old-time politician named Ismail Carter had done all he could to help the defendant.

I'd given a lot of thought to that on the drive back to Pickeral Point. It was only out there someplace in Macomb County when the rain changed to snow that I began to think on matters even darker.

Snow brought with it the threat of death, the death of a child. Murder. Whoever the killer was, he hadn't missed an opportunity yet. There had been three snowfalls so far in this season, and each had left a dead child. They had a psychologist or two trying to explain the symbolism of snow and death, but so far no one had come up with anything helpful.

The Kerry County administration had been roundly criticized by the media not only for its failure to capture the killer, but also for failing to adopt any sort of preventive measures. It was true that up to now they had done nothing but send policemen and policewomen around to the schools in Kerry County to warn children against accepting rides from anyone, even people they knew. Bud Billings, who had been removed from direct participation in the case because of the false arrest suit, was put in charge of this program. But sometime during Stash Olesky's big football party, he took me aside and told me that at the next threat of snow, there was a plan to put every patrol car available out on the roads in and around Hub City. Domelights flashing. "Any kids they see they'll send home," he told me. "And we'll just keep them out there all night long, if we have to, so we can be sure nothing will happen." He sounded bold and determined. I remember thinking at the time that it might not be foolproof, but at least it was a plan. I sure hoped it would be effective.

That night's supper came out of the freezer, which was well stocked with TV dinners for occasions like this. I had no desire to take a table for one at one of the three or four restaurants around town, and I'd already made one visit that day to Benny's Diner.

Frozen dinners are getting better, I guess. I followed the simple directions, and the lasagna tasted pretty good right out of the microwave. It was about as good as what they give you on the airlines. I sat there in the kitchen, eating it slowly and making it last, and listened to the all-news station on the radio. After I'd finished and was sipping my second cup of coffee, they did a brief feature on the murders, making it sound like all Kerry County would be awake tonight on a vigil, "hoping against hope" that their children would be spared by the killer on this snowy night. There were a couple of interviews done in advance from Hub City, ordinary citizens mumbling inarticulately about what a shame it was, asking why the police couldn't do something. The usual, wrapped up in two minutes' time, followed by a supermarket commercial.

All that seemed a little too much, so I switched off the radio and rinsed the few dishes I'd dirtied and put them away in the big, noisy dishwasher. It would take at least three days to make even a light load for washing.

Did the people of Kerry County "wait in terror," as the interviewer had suggested in her sign-off? For most, it was business as usual; they might not even be aware of the threat brought by the snow. But for some, anxiety, fright, terror — all that was real enough. Parents in Hub City and surrounding areas were certainly in that minority; and if there were any whose kids weren't safely in or accounted for, they must be going through hell right now. Doris Dieberman, Dominic Benda, and perhaps even the crazy Evans family felt a chill that night that had little to do with the temperature outside.

I felt it, too. Having seen those people through their separate ordeals with the police, and having watched as these terrible killings tore apart Sue, I felt tied to the case, bound to it in ways that surprised me. I had viewed one of the victims, that was the beginning of it for me. As it happened, I knew more about the killings than a lot of the cops did, those

504

who were not directly concerned with the investigation. I had my own vague suspicions and theories that seemed invariably to run counter to those of Bud Billings, Sue, and the office of the county prosecutor. That night, I felt so emotionally involved in all of that, I was tempted to jump into my car and head out to Hub City and help the cops patrol the roads. But I knew they wouldn't welcome my help.

I hadn't been asleep long when the telephone rang. I'd listened one last time to the all-news station at the top of the hour just to reassure myself that nothing had happened, no plastic-wrapped package had been found by the side of the road; they didn't even rerun the feature on Kerry County's vigil. I'd say the call must have come about ten-thirty, certainly not much later. The funny thing was, I never looked at my watch, just reacted sort of zombielike, sleep fogged.

"Charley, it's Sue. There's . . ."

I waited for her to finish the sentence, fearing, knowing just how it would end.

"There's been another murder. This one was closer to us here in town, at our end of Copper Creek Road."

"Everything else the same?"

"That's what I'm going to find out." She hesitated. "Charley, I was wondering . . . Look, I know I woke you up."

"That's all right."

"I know we've been sort of on the outs because of this investigation, but Charley, could you go out to the crime scene with me? I know it's a lot to ask. I remember how you reacted before, but I'm scared to death I'm going to lose it again. What I need badly is some support out there, the kind you could give."

She sounded desperate, already near tears.

"Where are you now?"

"I'm downstairs in my car."

"Okay," I said. "I just have to get dressed. I'll be there in a couple of minutes."

I hung up and stood there for a moment, blinking in the dark. What else could I say to her? What else could I do? Whatever else she was, she was a friend in that peculiarly complicated way in which love and sex get mixed into the equation and confuse things so. But a friend nevertheless. I couldn't have said no to her, but later, knowing the price I would pay, I wished to God that I had.

All right, it may have taken me three minutes, although I'm sure it was less than five from the time I hung up the telephone to the time I slid in beside her in the front seat of the Chevy Caprice. I gave her a hug. She seemed to need that.

"Thanks, Charley. I knew I could count on you."

She started the car, put the emergency light on the dashboard and activated it.

"This stuff is terrible to drive in," she said. "We've already lost one car tonight."

"How was that?"

"We almost got him. We came so close. This time we had a plan. Every patrol car we had was out on the road, the Hub City cars, too."

"I know. I heard about it beforehand."

"Oh?" Suddenly cautious. "Who from?"

"Stash Olesky."

"Well," she said uncertainly, "it was his idea, so I guess he can talk about it if he wanted to. The point is, it almost worked."

She went on to tell how Steve Majeski had been patrolling Copper Creek Road out as far as Beulah, with his domelights flashing. Back and forth, for about four hours, he drove, there in the snow. It had slowed after-work traffic on the road considerably in the beginning, but three hours later there was really very little traffic anyway. Once home, people were kept in by the snow. And after all, Copper Creek Road went as far as the edge of the county, and not many lived out that way. It wasn't a direct route to anyplace.

That was probably why they'd assigned it to Majeski, in his mid-twenties and the youngest man on the Kerry County police force. More important, he'd had a little less than a year in a patrol car, so they tucked him off in a corner of the grid they'd drawn around Hub City. One thing about Copper Creek Road, however: It's damned tricky to drive it even in good weather. There aren't many straight stretches on it. Winding along the creek bed, it runs from Pickeral Point, meets Beulah Road out in the country someplace, then gets lost way up in the northwestern reaches of the county.

This was the road, in any case, that Officer Steve Majeski was patrolling that night. He'd been fighting the snow for four hours and was bored and close to exhaustion. He rounded a bend, and just beyond his high beams, he saw a car's lights come on. A second later those lights began to move, swing out, disappear; Majeski had the presence of mind to punch his odometer to mark the location, then went after the vehicle, whatever it was, with his siren going full blast. In decent road conditions, he would have caught up with it without difficulty, but in the snow, it was an unequal pursuit. The Caprice, with its big engine, was just too much car for the road. In his eagerness to overtake the car ahead, he kept his foot heavy on the gas, too heavy, and the Chevy slewed back and forth in the snow at every curve, while the one ahead went around each bend like it was on rails. Majeski realized he was chasing some sort of four-wheel-drive vehicle. Still, he managed to keep it in sight. As he would emerge perilously from one curve, whipping the steering wheel left and right, he would see his quarry disappearing around the next. So it went until he hit the straightaway leading to the junction with Beulah Road. Majeski picked up speed and saw that the general shape of the car ahead conformed to that of a so-called off-road vehicle, but he couldn't get close enough to read the license plate. He tried a little too hard to do that and still had his foot on the accelerator as the junction loomed up ahead. The off-roader made the turn onto Beulah Road, but Majeski's patrol car did not.

The Caprice made two complete revolutions in the middle of the intersection, then ended up in a ditch by the side of the road. It was in deep, snow up to his hubcaps. Majeski hadn't a chance in the world of getting it out. Because he'd had his hands full during the chase, he hadn't radioed in. He did that at last, giving his position and asking for help, telling what had happened, and describing how the off-roader somehow slipped through. Taking the reading from the odometer in his own patrol car, he was able to guide his rescuer back to the approximate place where the pursuit began. After a bit of searching, they found the body of a young boy, sheathed in plastic, half covered in snow.

By the time Sue finished telling the story, we were on Copper Creek Road and close to the crime scene. She had had it only in fragments she'd heard from the radio dispatcher, then direct from Officer Majeski before she headed out to my place. But it seemed to do her good to tell it to me. She was less distraught and more professional in manner, apparently ready to meet what lay ahead. I only hoped that I was, too.

There was a cop stationed in the road to direct traffic around the line of patrol cars on the right. He stopped us with his flashlight, then walked up when he recognized the county plate on our car.

When he stuck his head in the window, I recognized him, more or less, but couldn't come up with his name.

"Yeah, hi, Sue. Just pull in behind my car there."

She nodded and mumbled a few words I didn't catch.

"We kept a clean scene for you this time," he said. "I guess we're learning the hard way."

A swirl of snow swept into the car before she could get the window up. She guided her car into the spot to which she'd been directed, then cut the motor and killed the lights.

"Stay close to me, Charley, unless I tell you different," she said, now the complete professional.

"Fair enough," I agreed.

I followed in her footsteps, shuffling through the soft snow. There was a wet hard pack beneath it. All told, I thought about three inches had fallen. The temperature had dropped steadily, and it had to be well down in the twenties. I was glad I'd worn my snow boots and remembered my new gloves.

Emergency lights running off the generators of two of the patrol cars were pointed at a mound in the snow beyond the yellow tape. There was a slight glint on the plastic and an indication of flesh color beneath it where the face would be. If they left the corpse undisturbed, it would be only a matter of minutes until it would be invisible beneath the snow. There was just one set of footprints leading up to the mound.

"All right," said Sue, "who was it just had to take a look? Who tracked up there to the body?"

"It was me." The cop's name was Bert Bossey. I knew him from a trial a year ago, a tough, no-nonsense police officer. He stepped forward to face her. "We were the first on the scene. Steve Majeski found the body; because I was senior officer, I took charge."

"Did that mean you had to mess things up like that?"

"For Christ's sake, Sue, I had to see if the kid was dead."

"You satisfied that he is?"

"Yeah, I cut into the plastic, felt for a pulse and didn't get any, then I tried for a heartbeat. Nothing."

All the cops were edgy because they were tired. They'd been out a long time, and the effort they'd put in patrolling the roads had gone for nothing. And the proof of that was before them right there under the lights.

"Larry?" she called out. "Are you here?"

Larry Antonovich came forward, a camera in hand. Sue took him over to one side. The two detectives held a hurried conference in whispers. One or two of the cops, those who recognized me, looked at me curiously, all but asking out loud what I was doing there.

As they talked on, flashing lights down the road caught my eye. The cops saw it, too, but barely glanced up. It was all part of the routine. It was moving along from the direction we had come at a speed so deliberate that the flashing lights in the rack on the roof seemed altogether unnecessary. It looked like an ambulance, but it turned out to be the county coroner's van from Pickeral Point. Identification was emblazoned in big letters on the side.

They pulled up on the highway just opposite the yellow tape, and there they waited, motor running. The window came down on the passenger's side.

"How long?" came the call from inside.

"Not long," Sue called back.

The window rolled back up. The snow had slacked off, nearly stopped. Sue took a deep breath, led Antonovich to the tape, and ducked under, approaching the body from one side. Did she intend that I should accompany her? She must have remembered me at the last moment, for she looked back and made a quick gesture that told me to stay where I was.

Antonovich ducked under. I noticed that in addition to the camera, he had something that looked like a screen under his arm, about a foot-and-a-half square.

He began taking pictures, circling the mound, getting it from every angle. Sue produced a carpenter's tape from her coat pocket and called over one of the cops, telling him to measure from the edge of the road. She took it to the mound and noted the figure in a notebook, all business but not a glance at the small window left uncovered by the snow. When Antonovich had finished that round of picture taking, she carefully scooped the snow from the plastic wrap and placed it on the screen, yet doing it in such a way that her eyes never seemed to leave her hands. She stepped away and sifted the snow through the screen. Nothing stuck; it was all snow and nothing more. Antonovich took more pictures. Then Sue beckoned in the direction of the county coroner's van, and the two inside got out, opened up the back, and pulled out a stretcher.

They weren't so careful once they'd stepped inside the perimeter. Sue warned them away from the direct route and made them take the circular way that she and Larry Antonovich had taken. In any case, the body was shifted onto the stretcher and moved in less than a minute. Somehow she managed to be looking the other way through it all. More pictures of the spot where the body had lain, then they both went to work sifting through the snow beneath the resting place and all around it — again, nothing, nothing but snow. Finished, they left a marker, and returned the long way around.

"Steve Majeski?" Sue called. "I need to get a statement from you."

She produced a small hand-held tape recorder from that voluminous coat pocket and talked him through the chase from this point to Beulah Road, a good three miles, and she wanted all the details.

Sue was doing pretty well through this ordeal she had dreaded. She recovered well after a bad start by admitting her error to the cops assembled at the scene. Whatever help she supposed I might provide was unneeded.

How was I doing? Not quite so well.

Standing by myself, off to one side, I had looked on, not so much with interest but with fascination. Every time Sue turned away from that mound nearly covered by snow, I found myself staring at it. I wasn't even sure of the contents of that plastic-wrapped package. I hadn't heard whether it was a boy or a girl inside, only that it was a child. Another child, the fourth in this monstrous chain of killings. It had to be a kind of monster responsible, didn't it? There was such a confusion of purpose evident: the care taken with the bodies, clothes washed, the plastic shroud to protect each one from the snow. Yes, the snow. What did that mean? Clearly, it meant a great deal to the murderer. What was the snow symbolizing? Purity? Theirs, not his? How could you get into such a mind to even begin to guess what went on there?

I thought I'd distanced myself pretty well from the county coroner's team as they returned with the small body on the stretcher. Yet as they came, the cops seemed to drift away, leaving me alone, the only one within calling distance when they cleared the yellow tape.

Me? I was staring in spite of myself.

"Hey buddy, want to give us a hand here? Come on over and open the door to the van."

I couldn't say no. I couldn't say, "Get one of those cops to help you — they've seen more death than I have, more than I ever want to." No, I couldn't say that, so I nodded and went to help.

It was a boy. Dark haired and darker skinned than was usual in this county of Slavs, Scandinavians, and Celtics. His features suggested he might have a bit of Indian blood. Though his eyes were shut, his mouth was stern. He looked angry. I'll bet he'd put up a fight.

I walked away. My vision was blurred. Hell, who am I kidding? I was half blind from the tears that wouldn't stop. I wiped at them, then more sobs came and more tears. So I just kept walking, trying to get away. I heard the county coroner's van turn around in the road and start on its trip back. Finally, I was surprised when I heard Sue's voice calling me back, not so much that she called but that her voice was so distant. I turned around and saw that I was a good city block away.

"Charley," she called. "Where are you? Charley!"

She must have lost me in the darkness. I cleared my throat and yelled back as loudly as I was able, "I'm here. I'm coming, I'm coming."

On the drive back to Pickeral Point, neither Sue nor Larry Antonovich said a word about my disappearance. Not much was said at all. But I had a question.

"Who was the boy?"

"We don't know yet," said Sue.

"No missing child reported? What did Hub City have to say?"

"Nothing there. We just don't know."

"Strange."

Yes, it was strange. Could the boy have been picked off the streets of Detroit? Port Huron? Mt. Clemens? Wherever he had come from, he had parents who missed him, lost him, who were frantic to find him. The dead boy in plastic wrap on the stretcher looked like he was about the same age as the first three victims. He couldn't have been a runaway, not likely at that age.

When we came to Pickeral Point, Sue headed for Kerry County Police Headquarters. Larry Antonovich was to be dropped off there. He had been driving up and down Beulah Road with one of the two cars assigned to that stretch. The idea was to have one detective rolling and Sue back at headquarters to coordinate things. He was young, from Detroit, and had gone to Wayne State.

"Wouldn't it be nice," he said to Sue, "if we had a crime-scene squad like a big grownup police department."

"Not likely," said Sue, "with all the budget cuts."

"I hope these pictures I took come out. You think there was enough light out there?"

"You'd know that better than I would, Larry. I'm no photographer."

He was quiet for a moment. "They'll be okay, I guess."

She pulled up in the lot, which was nearly empty by now, well after midnight. Antonovich got out, taking his camera equipment with him.

"I'll leave the film with a note before I go. If George Bester gets right on it, the roll should be printed by midmorning."

"Do that. I'll be back by eleven. We'll go to the location on Copper Creek Road then."

"I don't envy you."

Sue drove out of the parking lot and turned

517

in the direction of my place. She turned to me.

"Charley, I was wondering . . ."

I knew that approach, and I thought I knew what her request would be.

"Sure, Sue, you can stay with me tonight."

"You really know me inside and out, don't you?"

"Let's just say I know you pretty well by now."

We drove in silence for a block or two.

"I got off on the wrong foot with the cops, didn't I? Of course Bossey was right. He had to make sure the kid was dead."

"But you handled it right from then on."

"There's a few things different about this one, you know."

"Well, for one thing," I said, "no report of a missing child. You don't know who the kid is."

"Right, but finding him on Copper Creek Road is sort of odd — miles from Hub City. The location was a lot closer to town, this town, than any of the others. And there was something else, too."

"What's that?"

"Larry said it looked like the kid's clothes were dirty — not filthy or anything, just like he'd been out in the snow — his hands, too, the way kids get dirty playing anyplace. I didn't see it myself. I made it a point not to look at the body."

"Yeah, I noticed."

She sighed. "Well, I got through it."

"Whatever works, Sue. You did fine."

"At least we know now what kind of car the killer has."

"Four-wheel drive."

"Dark color, black or maybe brown. I wonder how many of those there are in the county."

"Not an infinite number. It's a place to start."

"Oh, yes."

My apartment building loomed ahead. Emotionally, rather than physically, I was exhausted. Perhaps, in a way, I felt even worse than I had that night on Clarion Road when little Catherine Quigley was found. But I felt different. I had no wish to talk with Bob Williams about what it all meant, nor certainly with Sue Gillis. My problems with the Higher Power remained unsolved.

Something struck me just then. "Larry said something when you dropped him off. He said he didn't envy you. What did he mean?"

"I have to go to the autopsy tomorrow morning," she said, turning into my driveway. "It's customary for an officer to be present. Since I'm heading the investigation now, it's up to me."

It wasn't until later, when we were in bed and I was close to sleep, that she asked me to go with her to the autopsy.

"I don't believe I was much help to you out there tonight," I responded.

"Yes you were. Just having you there meant everything to me."

Because she had to go to headquarters first, Sue left my apartment early the next morning. I was to meet her a little before nine at the entrance to the Kerry County Community Hospital. I was early, pacing before the doors of the place, and nervous, nervous, nervous. It wasn't that I was afraid she'd be late or might not come — I would have been delighted if she hadn't shown up. No, it was dissatisfaction with myself, annoyance that she had managed to persuade me to do something I certainly did not want to do, and fear of what lay ahead. If someone had come along and asked me what I felt right then and there, the only honest answer I could have given would have been anger.

God knows I'm no wimp. In front of a judge and jury, I can breathe fire with the best of them. Yet when Sue began to plead over coffee, I found I simply couldn't turn her down. I know now what the problem was. I couldn't refuse her because I had made up my mind that we had to break up, that our romance had ended or that it would end when I sat down with her and explained why it was impossible. I felt certain she would be hurt by that, and so I had unconsciously decided to give her what she wanted until then. As I look back, it seems that this all came about because I was determined to let her down easy.

I had even agreed to keep that Thanksgiving dinner date with her parents that afternoon following all this. She had obtusely and stubbornly insisted that nothing was changed, that the date still stood, that following the autopsy and her return visit to the crime scene with Larry Antonovich, we would set off for Southfield. It was over the meadow and through the woods, and let's be sure to get there on time. The woman had a Thanksgiving obsession.

And so I paced angrily back and forth in front of the entrance to the hospital. It was chilly, rather than cold. Even at this early hour the temperature had risen above freezing, and the bright sun had begun melting last night's snowfall. By afternoon the streets and sidewalks would be a mess. By evening the snow would probably be gone entirely.

Sue appeared, walking swiftly from the hospital parking lot. I hadn't noticed the big Caprice make its entrance. Maybe it was in some special corner reserved for the police. She clipped up the two steps and gave me a nod and a faint smile.

I opened the door for her.

As she passed through, she said, "We've got an ID on the boy now."

"Who is it? Where's he from?"

I caught up with her, and we hurried along

521

to the reception desk. She stopped there just long enough to inquire where the autopsy was to be held.

"In the operating theater on the third floor," said the receptionist. "But that's not open to the public."

"I'm not the public," said Sue, flashing her police ID.

"What about him?" Meaning me.

"He's with me," she called back. Already we were on our way to the elevator.

As we waited, it took her about a minute to tell me that the victim's name was Richard Fauret. He was the youngest in a French-Canadian farming family from Copper Creek, an unincorporated area up in that empty northwest corner of the county. She said they were old-fashioned backwoods people who believed in taking care of their own problems, so they had searched for their Dickey, as they called him, for about three hours, maybe more, before they gave in and called the local police. The local police force in Clayville, population just under a thousand, was comprised of three. There was some difficulty in communication because the father's English was far from perfect. Finally, the night-duty man decided that this just might have something to do with all those murders around Hub City, and he passed it on to the county police around midnight.

"But the Faurets have seen their son?" I

asked. "Made a positive identification?"

"Yes, they were here about seven o'clock. I heard it was a pretty bad scene."

"I'm not surprised."

Sue rushed me off the elevator. She seemed to know her way around the hospital pretty well, far better than I did, anyway. We turned to the right and scurried to a door about half-way down the hall. She opened it and pushed me inside.

I was surprised to find it really was an operating theater. I expected something more on the order of what I had seen in my few brief visits to the morgue in Detroit — cold-box storage drawers, a slab, running water, scales, little more than that.

This was something much grander.

The door through which we entered was raised above the operating room by a number of feet to accommodate two rows of benches that ran around the floor in three sides of a rectangle. It wasn't until we descended a few steps and took our places on the nearest bench that I saw we were separated from the operating room by a glass panel, which ran all the way around the room.

Sue must have noticed my surprise at this elaborate setup, for she leaned toward me and whispered, "This hospital was built in the early Sixties by a surgeon who thought he was pretty hot stuff. He thought if he built a space like this, all southeastern Michigan would come and watch him perform."

"And is that how it worked out?"

"No, he died."

"So they use this for autopsies, too?"

"There aren't that many needed in the county, Charley."

"I suppose not."

We didn't have long to wait. The body of the boy was wheeled in on a gurney by an attendant. The medical examiner followed them in, wearing surgical pajamas, gloved but unmasked. He looked up and waved at Sue as the attendant pulled the sheet from the boy's naked body and transferred him to the operating table. There was a tape recorder and a microphone on a smaller wheeled table next to the big one. The microphone was raised and bent in such a way that the medical examiner could speak into it easily while going about his business.

"All ready up there?" he asked. His voice came through speakers on both sides of us. Stereophonic sound.

Sue nodded.

"Now, when I switch on the tape recorder, everything I say will go on the tape, but you'll be able to hear it, too. There's no way for you to speak to me from where you are, so all you can do is watch. If you have any questions, take notes, and see me afterward. Is all that understood?"

Sue nodded again. She fished out a notebook and a ballpoint pen from her purse.

"All right, here we go."

He switched on the tape recorder and began speaking in a less casual, more authoritative manner, giving the date, the time, and the place. He identified himself.

"The subject," he began, "is Richard Fauret. He is a Caucasian male, about seven years old. His height is" — here he used a tape measure — "forty and one half inches. He has been weighed at forty-two pounds. He appears to have been in good health. He has good muscular development and is of stocky physique. There are no exterior wounds or scars. Previous to being washed for this autopsy procedure, the subject's hands showed traces of dried mud and dirt."

He paused at this point and looked across the operating table at the attendant.

"I will now make a butterfly incision around his thorax area."

He picked up a scalpel and proceeded to do just that. The famous butterfly incision. I'd heard of it, of course, but had never seen it done. There was very little blood, just a red line that followed the path of the knife. Yet I hadn't expected what came next. The instrument he chose then had a small hand-sized grip and at the end of it a circular saw blade about two inches in diameter. He switched it on, and the blade glinted in the light as it whirled.

I looked at Sue in panic. I found her leaning forward, quite absorbed in the action before us.

My hands began to tremble.

He dug the saw in the hollow at the bottom of the boy's throat and proceeded downward, cutting through the sternum, attaching the two wings of the butterfly.

I looked on, not quite believing, as the medical examiner put aside the saw, and with the help of the attendant, pulled open the boy's chest. Except for the glass between us, I was sure I would have heard the rip of flesh, the tearing of bones.

And there was little Richard Fauret, more than naked, exposed. It was almost as if his killer had planned this as the final insult. I'd seen the bagman for Detroit's biggest dealer similarly violated, his intestines exposed, drooping down from his slit belly. I'd managed somehow to handle that, but this was different because Richard Fauret was innocent. Just as innocent as Catherine Quigley, or Lee Higgins, or Billy Bartkowski. What Bob Williams had said to me that night after my experience out on Clarion Road was true: It's the destruction of the innocents that hurts the most, that calls our most deeply held beliefs to question.

What did I do? What could I do? I left there in full flight, actually running to get away. I knew I couldn't stay to see the boy's organs lifted out, examined, and weighed. I had to get out of there.

I went toward the elevator, then saw the sign that led me to the stairway. I must have gone down the stairs, because I remember getting out of the hospital without passing the reception desk, or going through the lobby. Finding myself out in the hospital parking lot, I looked around, feeling disoriented, lost, and needing a drink.

Oh, yes, needing a drink very badly.

After some difficulty, I found my car and drove straight to Jimmy Doyle's. It was the only bar I knew of that was open at that hour of the morning.

19

About what happened during the next three days, I don't have much to say. That's partly because I feel a certain guilt, even shame, about it all. After all, I'd gone years without a drink, and though I never lost sight of the fact that I was a recovering alcoholic, I had built up confidence that I could go years more without a drink. I thought I had the problem under control.

I didn't.

At Jimmy Doyle's I had three straight shots of bar Scotch, but they weren't enough to erase those images from the autopsy from my mind. The two old geezers at the end of the bar watched me rather carefully; they seemed to know something was seriously wrong. When I called for a fourth shot, the bartender refused to serve me. I didn't make a fuss; I couldn't; he was right to cut me off. I paid up, remembering to tip him just to show there were no hard feelings, went out to my car, and vomited in the gutter. What a pretty picture.

That didn't stop me, didn't even slow me down. I got into the car and drove in that slow, extra-careful way that drunks do. Not directly home, but to a liquor store on the way. If I was going to do this, then I was going to do it right. I bought a half-gallon bottle of Johnnie Walker Red, my old brand of preference, assuring myself that the reason I'd thrown up was that I'd drunk bad Scotch. That never happened when I drank Johnnie Walker. Then, as an afterthought, since I was obliged to keep office hours the next day, I bought a bottle of vodka. At some unspecified time later today, I would switch to vodka, and no one would know tomorrow that I'd been drinking. Sure.

Returning to my apartment, I made a vow not to answer the telephone — it was sure to be Sue, and I had no wish to speak to her — and settled down for some serious drinking. I can't say that I didn't enjoy it. The rich, golden liquid hit my tongue like so much nectar, yet there was enough bite to it to let me know that this was the real stuff, the right stuff. Oh yes, I remembered it well.

I started out drinking it on ice, more civilized that way, and settled in a living room chair with the television set switched on. I can't say that I was watching it. But the changing flow of images on the screen gave me something on which to concentrate my vision, and the voices occupied some part of my mind. I heard, I saw, though I didn't really listen or watch. I was in my old drinking mode, running on automatic pilot. The idea was not to think and not to remember. And for a while it was working pretty well. I eventually decided it wasn't really necessary to put ice in the glass. No ice, more Scotch. Then I passed out, unconscious, a dreamless sleep.

The telephone woke me. Sue, of course, and the thought of her annoyed me — no, more than that, it made me angry. Or perhaps it was simply the persistent ringing that made me angry. In any case, I decided to do something about it. I slipped off the chair and crawled over to the telephone. Reaching up, I pulled the receiver off its cradle. Then I went into the next room and collapsed on the bed.

Some time later, Sue was at my door, banging, kicking, and yelling about Thanksgiving. She said she knew I was there because my car was in the parking lot. There were some other things, too, that I didn't quite understand or don't remember. I do recall, though, that I wished she wouldn't make such a racket because it was a holiday — that much I knew, at least — and all the neighbors, such as they were, would be around to hear her. I couldn't call the cops because she was the cops.

How long did she continue? Not long, probably, but she had succeeded in bringing me to some degree of wakefulness. I got up, relieved myself in the bathroom, and sat down in the living room again and finished off the half-full glass of Scotch I'd left. There was a football game on television, Dallas and some other team. Dazed, I tried to give some attention to the progress of the game. Failing that, I could at least find out the score, or what team Dallas was playing. But no, even that proved too much. After another drink, a short one this time, I stumbled back to the bedroom.

Bad dreams. Maybe it was the violence of the football game, or maybe I failed to drink enough to obliterate those images I'd tried to escape earlier. Whatever the cause, along with sleep came something like a movie montage of all the worst I had known and seen in these past weeks. There were monster football players pulling apart children. There was a hanging man, eviscerated, trying to talk without a tongue. There were angels in the snow — Catherine Quigley and Richard Fauret — rising, trailing their plastic shrouds. There were other horrors, too, which were, I guess, just the product of my alcoholic state, fantasies unconnected to memories.

They seemed to last a long time, but how could I tell? It was enough to wake me in a sweat about half sober. It was dark out. I threw off my clothes and took a shower and realized I was hungry, a good sign. Wrapped in my bathrobe, I had a cheese sandwich and a glass of orange juice, a strange combination, but the orange juice tasted good. And so, when I'd finished, I kept on drinking orange juice with vodka. There went the rest of the evening and a good deal of the next day.

I'm not going to prolong this account because the truth is, I don't remember much of the rest of it. I do know that sometime during the day on Saturday I drank the last of the Johnnie Walker Red and, having also finished up the vodka, went out and bought some more. I managed to eat something each day and kept drinking orange juice with the new bottle of vodka, because I'd made up my mind that no matter what condition I was in, I had to get into the office on Monday. During the weekend I must also have replaced the telephone receiver, because later on the calls started again, though I didn't answer them. I was doing a pretty good imitation of Ray Milland in *The Lost Weekend*.

Late Sunday afternoon or early evening, I was dozing in the living room chair in front of the television. Another football game, this one from the West Coast, was rocketing to a finish. There was a knock on the door, followed by another one, followed by another and another. This couldn't be Sue. Whoever this was at the door wasn't interested in making a fuss; he intended to break it down. He beat it. He kicked it. But he didn't say a word.

I struggled out of the chair and made it to the door.

"Who is it?" I yelled, trying to sound gruff. "Who's there?" Actually, I was kind of frightened, knowing how incapable I was at that moment.

"Bob Williams. And you'd better open this

door while it's still in one piece."

He was the last guy in the world I wanted to see. My best friend? My AA sponsor? Forget it. When he saw me in the condition I was in, he'd be my worst enemy. I couldn't deal with him. I didn't want to try.

"Go away, Bob. I'll see you tomorrow."

He let fly a great kick right around the lock. I saw it give. A couple more like that, and it would fly open. I could put on the chain, but the damage would still be done. And so I surrendered, unlocking the door, opening it, and I saw him poised to deliver the next threatened kick. A couple of doors were open down the hall. My so-called neighbors peeked out at us. They didn't know me, and I didn't know them.

Bob rushed in, perhaps fearing I might change my mind and close the door again. He pulled it shut behind him, and then he looked me up and down.

"Just what I suspected," he said, his face filled with concern.

I didn't answer. At various times in the last few days I knew I'd been in worse condition than I was then. There was no point in telling him that.

He swept past me, picked up the glass of vodka with its faint orange coloration, and headed for the kitchen. Without a pause, he dumped its contents down the drain of the kitchen sink.

"Hey," I said, "who gave you permission?"

"You did, when you joined the program. Or have you forgotten? I'm your sponsor. Remember?"

He turned and looked at the table with its array of bottles, then he shook his head in disbelief.

"Did you drink all that?"

"It was a long weekend."

"You ever hear of alcohol poisoning?"

He grabbed the quarter-full bottle of vodka and the supplementary fifth of Johnnie Walker Red, just about half full. "Go on," he said. "Take a shower. You smell bad. Shave, if you can manage it. If you've got an electric razor, it might be safer."

Arms folded, feet planted wide, I stared at him, trying to decide whether to tell him to go to hell and get out of my kitchen. But in the end, I turned around, went into the bathroom, and did as I was told. On my way, I heard the gurgle from the bottles as he emptied them down the drain.

On the drive to St. Jude's Church, Bob surprised me by saying that he blamed himself in large measure for my fall from grace.

"I take responsibility for my own acts," I said, "my own failures, too."

"Okay, tough guy, but the way I see it, you've been heading for this for about a month, maybe longer. I remember the night of that big early snow when you saw that little girl's body out on Clarion Road. You were shattered, had to talk. And what did I do? I gave you a pat on the back and told you to go talk to Father Phil."

"You gave me more than that, Bob."

"Let me finish. Then there was last Sunday. You wanted to have dinner after the meeting. What you really wanted to do was talk about all these things that were bothering you. But then that priest came along, the one from Hub City. We had dinner, and that's all we had. We had to listen to his loony ideas on how Double-A really ought to be run. Then, finally, on Wednesday I got a message from you on my machine, very innocuous — 'just checking in,' you said. No, you weren't. You were asking for help, and I've been too damned busy to give it to you. It's been a fault with me, Charley. I get too involved in details, administrative bullshit. I seem to have forgotten the program is about people. A fine psychiatrist I am."

We drove along saying nothing for a while. Having listened to Bob's mea culpa, I had no wish to add to his indictment. It seemed to me he was being much too hard on himself. I decided to move him away from the question of blame.

"How did you know what I'd done?"

"Sixth sense, I guess. No, actually I'd put some of this together and came up with a

535

guilty conscience. I started calling you and not even getting your answering machine. Somehow that didn't seem right, so I came over and knocked on your door."

I chuckled appreciatively. "That was some knock."

"Your response through the door told me my hunch was dead-on."

"You mean if I'd been a little more polite, you might have gone away?"

"I mean here we are at St. Jude's just in time for the regular Sunday meeting in the basement. Amazing how these things work out, isn't it?"

He turned into the parking lot and pulled in close to the door. It looked like there was a pretty light turnout that night.

"And you may or may not be happy to learn, Charley, that I got on the phone while you were in the shower and made an appointment with Father Phil for right after the meeting."

"I'm not sure how I feel about that." That was an honest response. It was no good feigning enthusiasm I didn't feel.

"He's a good man. He'll talk to you straight. I don't think he'll pretend to have answers he doesn't have." He nodded and opened the car door. "Come on, let's go."

It's true the meeting that night wasn't very well attended, yet it was good for me to go, even in my condition. In spite of the shower and shave, and notwithstanding the reasonable manner I'd conversed with Bob, I was still about half trashed. I'd long ago learned how to fake sobriety. I sat in back and listened as Bob ad-libbed a brief sermon on the duties of a sponsor. Just as he was about to wind things up, he happened to pause, and I took that opportunity to rise. Bob recognized me.

"My name is Charley, and I'm an alcoholic," I said, then I waited, not knowing quite how to continue. "I made quite a speech here last Sunday about how those big problems of life, the ones we share with everybody, have to be faced along with the particular problem we have here. Well, no big speech tonight. I'm just going to say that one of those big life problems caught up with me and gave me a big kick in the behind. I tried to get away from it in the old way, the way all of us here know so well. I just want to tell you that the answer to any problem can't be found in a bottle. So now I start over again, counting the days, one at a time."

I sat down. Bob nodded, looked around to be sure that each had had his say, then ended the meeting with the familiar prayer. A moment later, in the midst of the shuffling of feet and the scraping of chairs, he appeared at my side, eager to rush me out.

"Ready to see Father Phil now?"

I sighed. "Okay, I guess."

I grabbed my coat and was taken by the elbow, up the stairs to the exit. And outside.

It was a chilly night. If there had been a cloud in the sky, there might have been snow in the air. But there were only stars and an enormous three-quarter moon. Somehow the right sky made the walk to the rectory in the cold more tolerable.

We hurried up the stairs to the entrance of the old brick building.

"I'll come by for you," said Bob, "just as soon as I drink some coffee with those guys and clean up the place."

He rang the bell.

Only moments later the door opened, revealing the Reverend Philip LeClerc. He must have been hovering nearby. Father Phil was a slender man of about forty who, except for the fact that his hair was beginning to gray, looked quite youthful. Wearing gold-rimmed glasses, he had an almost ascetic appearance. We shook hands. I'd met him on a number of previous occasions, of course, and we'd had a couple of conversations about nothing in particular. If anyone had asked me what I thought of him, I would have said simply that he seemed like a nice man.

Bob left us alone, promising to be back in about half an hour. I entered the rectory and was shown directly into a small room right off the hall. It was lit by a single desk lamp, but that was enough to reveal the floor-to-ceiling shelves, crowded with hundreds of books.

"So I've got just half an hour to restore your

faith?" he asked with a wry smile. "Sit down. We'd better get to work."

"I'm afraid there wasn't much there to begin with," I said, taking a chair across the desk from him.

"Lapsed Catholic?"

"A long time ago, Father."

"Divorced?"

"More than once. I'm the undisputed king of divorce."

"And of course as a trial lawyer, you've seen your share of rough stuff."

"More than I'd like to have seen."

"Close up?"

"Close up."

He took a moment, folded his hands loosely before him on the desk, and gave me a hard look with his soft eyes. "You are in a state of crisis, though, aren't you? Or at least that's what Bob said. What brought it on, Charley?"

And so I told him. I told him about Catherine Quigley out on Clarion Road, my unsatisfying discussion with Bob Williams afterward, and about the recent episode that sent me into the bottle. I didn't indulge in emotional rhetoric, just laid it out before him: These are the facts of the case. I did take my time, though, and cited Sue Gillis as my direct connection with these two incidents, and I even mentioned my so-called debate with Father Charles Albertus. All in all, I thought I did a pretty fair job, considering the volatile matter I was dealing with. It took a while to tell it, but I made it through without breaking down. My eyes were a bit wet at the end of my recital.

Father Phil knew how to listen — good eye contact, sympathetic nods, but no interruptions. He sat back then, frowning in concentration, as if trying to organize his response. This, as I recall, is how it went:

"Charley, in theological terms, what has put you through the wringer is that you can't reconcile the attributes of God. You know what I mean? God is good. He is just. God is omnipotent. He's also omniscient. You remember that old canard they use on high school kids to demonstrate that man's free will isn't in conflict with God's omnipotence or omniscience? Sure you do. You're on top of a mountain, and there's a narrow, winding road below; you see two cars hurtling along, invisible to each other. You see they're certain to crash. In that sense, you see the future. Yet the driver of each car has chosen to drive at an excessive speed on this dangerous road, and you can't stop either one of them. That's supposed to be God up on that mountain, looking down in dismay at us.

"Yet this supposed analogy doesn't hold water at all, because God, if He's God, is truly omnipotent, and He could cause one of the cars to run out of gas and the other one to get a flat tire. He could do this if He chose to, and what God chooses to do gets us into that very nasty problem of Divine Providence. You remember that one? Nothing happens that God does not will to happen. It's all in God's plan, and it's not for us to understand. Remember? Or maybe, God writes straight with crooked lines. You recall being told that?

"That may work in the classroom, but when you grow up, and you go to war and see what happens in war, or you go out with the police on a country road and see the murdered body of a child lying beside it, then it's time for a reality check. Is God good? Is He just? If He's omnipotent, would He permit such things to happen? Worse yet, does He will them to happen?"

At this point, he stopped, raised his hands, and shook his head in a gesture of bewilderment.

"I'm not much help, am I? You know why? Because I can't give you an answer that either you or I would accept as valid, or consistent with human experience. You think I haven't had these same problems myself? I used to try to work these things out by some complicated equation that made allowance for God's omnipotence, His omniscience, and God's will. I gave up on it, because I was beginning to have doubts. When I have doubts about the existence of God, well, that's unfortunate; you might go back to the bottle, but somehow you soldier on. But when I have doubts, I'm out of a job."

He meant it as a joke, a serious joke, but I thought he made his point pretty well.

"So," I said, "what do you do?"

"I do the only thing that any sensible adult who's thought about these matters would do. I take a chance. Way back in the seventeenth century, Pascal called it the divine wager. You just have to bet there is a God of the sort we believe in, the kind we've accepted all these centuries. Unamuno, the Spanish philosopher, said we had to take a 'death-defying leap.' "

"A what?"

He laughed. "I admit it doesn't translate very well, but it's a good image. If you ever went to the circus as a kid, you saw the acrobats. I guess they call them aerialists. They leap from the trapeze, maybe do a somersault in the air, and all they can do is hope their partner is there, swinging from the other trapeze to make the catch. I guess he was talking specifically about immortality, but what he really meant was the leap of faith. Thomas Aquinas notwithstanding, there is a point at which all rational approaches to God fail, and you have to take that leap into the unknown, the leap of faith."

As far as Father Phil was concerned, that seemed to end it. He'd had his say. He sat back and looked at me, certainly not triumphantly, as if everything that needed to be said had been said, but hopefully, as if he hoped some of this had done some good.

I hoped it had, too, but I wasn't so sure. I gave him high marks for honesty, but I would have to think about what he had said. I didn't say that to him, though. I backed off and changed the subject, more or less.

"Whatever else, Father, this conversation was certainly a lot different from the one I had in Hub City with Father Albertus."

"We're both priests, but it's a big Church, Charley. We have our differences. He'd probably call for a ban of excommunication on me if he'd been witness to some of the things I've said to you just now. But he's a good man and a good priest. Whatever else, you must remember he's under a terrible strain at the present."

"In what way?"

"He lost a nephew about a month ago, a boy very dear to him, as I understand. We were at a retreat together. He missed the first day because he went back to Detroit to say a funeral Mass for his nephew. Then he had to leave a couple of days early because of the death of that first boy — Lee Higgins was his name — the first one in these gruesome murders."

"So there were funeral Masses at the beginning and the end for him?" I prompted.

"Yes, he was only around for a couple of days, if that. He said he'd looked forward to the retreat, too, getting away from his parish duties. Those mission churches out in the boondocks really keep him hopping around. They were all his children, you know."

"Pardon? I don't quite . . ."

He caught himself and grinned in embarrassment. "That was a bit of a non sequitur, wasn't it? No, what I meant was that he saw all his parishioners as his children. It's a terrible thing for a priest, especially since two were actually in his parish."

"Not the last one, though. The French boy from Copper Creek."

"No. He and his family worshipped at another church."

I was about to ask another question when the doorbell rang.

Father Phil rose. "That'd be Bob. Have I restored your faith, Charley?" It was said with that same wry smile.

"Hallelujah!"

"All right, give me a break. But think about what I've said, and if you'd like, I could lend you some books. Unamuno's good, won't insult your intelligence." Then, as we went together to the door, he added, "And prayer, Charley, prayer can help a lot."

It was Bob Williams, all right, standing patiently with a serious look on his face. He seemed relieved when he saw we were wearing smiles. I said my good-bye to the priest, and he said he hoped we'd stay in touch. That was how we left it.

Bob had the good sense, or the tact, not to inquire deeply into my session in the rectory. His only comment came as we walked to the car.

"Good man, isn't he?"

I gave an affirmative grunt, and that seemed to satisfy him. But on the drive back to my place, I gave some thought to the priest and, of course, what he'd had to say to me. Yes, Father Phil was decent. And in spite of his talk about the leap of faith, he was more of an intellectual than I had expected to encounter here in Pickeral Point. I wondered how he had managed to escape the Jesuits. Prayer? About the only praying I'd done in the last thirty years or so was the one we said at the end of every Double-A meeting. But yes, I'd give some thought to our discussion. How could I dismiss things that he said with such humility? He'd talked to me more as a fellow sufferer than as a priest, the sort of priest I was used to, anyway.

It wasn't easy trying to get rid of Bob. He went with me up to my apartment and offered to make a pot of coffee. I think he wanted to be reassured that I didn't have another bottle stashed away someplace. I didn't, but I was damned if I was going to tell him so. In the end, he had a Diet Coke, and I brewed up that same hangover remedy I'd fixed for Sue Gillis. It was pretty fierce. How did she ever manage to get it down? Bob suggested delicately that I might do well to look for professional counseling. I told him I'd think about it. Not long afterward, I kicked him out. I told him I was exhausted, wanted to go to bed and sleep it off. A little reluctantly, he rose and forced a smile.

"Call if you need me, Charley. Don't worry about the hour. I'll come in the middle of the night."

"I'll be okay, Bob. I'm sure I will."

"We'll get together for dinner whenever you want."

"During the week," I said.

"I really do blame myself for this."

"You shouldn't."

"I'll call you tomorrow." He put out his hand, and I shook it.

"If you don't, I'll call you."

He backed away into the hall and turned once to wave, then I eased the door shut.

I was exhausted. I undressed, throwing my clothes indifferently onto a chair, then threw myself just as indifferently into bed. But sleep wouldn't come, not immediately. Something nagged at me. It was that bit of information that had been passed on to me about Father Charles Albertus. He'd been at the retreat only two days, perhaps less. That might have put him in Hub City at the time that both Lee Higgins and Catherine Quigley were murdered. It might, but so what? So were all the rest of the citizens of Kerry County. I'd simply been misinformed by his housekeeper. Still, it was strange that two of the murdered children were from churches ministered to by him. This was an area that was heavily, even preponderantly, Catholic. What did I expect? I ran it through my mind a couple of times, perhaps three, looking at it this way and that, trying to decide what it was that nagged at me. I must have given up then, for sleep came at last, and with it no bad dreams, thank God. That's pretty funny. Me, of all people, thanking God.

Although I hadn't slept badly, with all that alcohol in my system I was hung over, dehydrated, and felt greatly in need of a drink. So I coped with the situation as best I could, drank a lot of water, and had another one of my hangover specials. That took away my desire for a drink, and for that matter took away my desire to eat, as well. Not that I could have kept anything down.

Before I left for the office, I tried my answering machine. Pulling out the phone jack had scrambled it badly, so that when I pushed playback, what I got were messages from a couple of weeks ago, or maybe even further back. So I had to listen to the whole tape. At the end of it, there were the messages from Sue I'd expected to hear, demanding my presence at her parents' Thanksgiving feast, and angrily repeating it on successive calls. Then there was one I couldn't figure out.

"Charley, this is Dominic," I heard Dominic say. "I been calling you at your office, which was probably a mistake. But I need you, Charley. They got me here at the station house, and I need you here now. You said you'd be available any time. Charley? Charley?"

When was that? It had to be a call that came in on Thanksgiving. As it happened, it was the last message on the tape. I must have pulled the jack right after it was recorded. Then, when I plugged the phone back in, whenever that was, the answering machine had rewound and gone on strike. I'd have to reprogram it or something. But that could wait. I grabbed the county phone book and searched for Dominic Benda's phone number.

Peg answered. She seemed reluctant to talk when I identified myself.

"Oh, Mr. Sloan, I don't know. He's here, all right, but I don't think he wants to talk to you. He's still mad at you, but he's even madder at Larry Antonovich and that Sue Gillis. Larry came for him right when we were sitting down to dinner with the whole family. 'Questioning,' he called it."

"I'm sorry, Peg," I said. "I had no idea."

"I mean the kids were there and everything, seeing their grandpa getting taken in like that. It just wasn't right. He didn't put cuffs on him or anything, but it just wasn't right."

"No, it wasn't. I'll talk to Dominic about it

later. Just tell him I'm deeply sorry he had to go through that alone, sorry he had to go through it at all. Give him my apologies."

"I will, Mr. Sloan. I'll tell him when he cools down."

With that behind me, I set off for the office, thinking grim thoughts about Sue and her ideas of what might be fair in love and war. Mrs. Fenton's ancient but well-preserved Plymouth sat in its usual corner of the small office parking lot. She awaited me upstairs. I'd have to get past her to start the day.

As it happened, like so many things in life, this was less of an ordeal than I anticipated. She greeted me with an expression even more strained and disapproving than usual. Without a word, she handed me a stack of messages. I thanked her and started for my private office.

"When you weren't back by lunchtime," she said, addressing my back, "I began telling them you wouldn't be coming in."

"And right you were, Mrs. Fenton."

"I tried to reach you at home several times. I think you switched off your phone."

"Things happen," I said and shut the door.

There were seven messages. Sue Gillis and Mark Conroy had each called me once. Dominic Benda had called me twice, and Ismail Carter had put in three calls, the last in the afternoon. I wadded the message from Sue Gillis and tossed it in the wastebasket, decided to allow the talk I'd had earlier with Peg stand as a response to Dominic's two calls, and picked up the phone and punched in Mark Conroy's number. He picked up. I hoped that didn't mean that his wife had moved out.

"Yeah, I was just checking in," he said. "I guess you took the day off. You want me to find another phone and call you back?"

"No need," I said. "But stick around. I may be calling you again."

"I have no place to go."

"Later, then."

After I'd hung up, I gave some thought to Mark Conroy. He sounded glum, discouraged, and for good reason. If Ismail Carter had tried three times to reach me, then he must have something important to say. While I had reason to hope, Conroy had none. No wonder he was down. Since Ismail had no telephone in his room, I thought it best simply to wait.

Yet, knowing I could not bet all my money on the results of that mysterious trip in the rain to Manoogian Mansion, I hauled out the file on the Conroy case and began going through it carefully for the umpteenth time, checking my notes, rereading, and stopping frequently to speculate. Powered by a new surge of energy that seemed to come from nowhere at all, I began to see things I hadn't seen before.

What I saw was that the prosecution's star

witness was actually its weak point. The Mouse had access to the money. He had motive. He had opportunity. Put him before a jury, and I'd make him the villain of the piece. Hell, with that gangster face and huge body, he looked like the villain, and that alone should be enough to persuade most jurors. And if the prosecution dared put Mary Margaret Tucker on the stand, I'd prove she had access, motive, and opportunity, too — my theory of the crime. I began to see that I had a chance, maybe even a good chance, with or without Ismail's help. What I had to do to win was attack, attack, and attack. Benjamin Timothy wouldn't know what hit him.

Feeling empowered, I buzzed Mrs. Fenton and told her to get the Parkview Convalescent Hospital on the line. The call came through, and I found myself talking to the cute little receptionist. I could handle her.

"Switch me," I said, with a threat in my voice, "to the phone nearest Ismail Carter. This is Charles Sloan. I'm an attorney and I need to speak to him."

Just like that I had the floor supervisor.

"Are you speaking to me on a cordless phone?"

I knew damned well she was. I'd seen her using it.

"Yes, I am," she said, clearly taken aback.

"Then bring it with you to Mr. Carter's room and hand it to him. This is Charles

Sloan. Mr. Carter and I have business to discuss."

"He tried all day Friday to reach you, and you weren't there."

"I know that. And that's precisely why I'm calling now."

That did it. There was a pause of about half a minute.

"He just woke up. He's been napping. Here he is."

"Charley?"

"Tell her to take a walk, Ismail."

He cackled at that and repeated the suggestion to the nurse. There was a pause, and then he said she was gone.

"How come you've got everything else in that room of yours but a phone?"

"Aw, they say it'll disturb my daytime sleeping. All I do is sleep, seems to me."

"What have you got for me?"

"Instructions, Charley. What day of the week is this, anyway? It's easy to lose count where I am."

"It's Monday. Sorry I missed your calls on Friday."

"Never mind that. But okay, it's Monday. Now, day after tomorrow, Wednesday, you go to 1300 Beaubien at nine o'clock in the morning for an examination of Mark Conroy's office. You have already petitioned for this. I'm told the visit's all part of the discovery process, or something like that. I'm not a lawyer, so I really don't know what that means. But like I say, it's all been fixed up. You just go there."

"I understand."

"And when you get there, Charley, you're to give special attention to the safe. You got that?"

"Got it."

"Now, this is the important part. Number one, you got to get Mark Conroy out of the way for the next couple of days, just as far as he can legally go while he's under indictment, someplace it's pretty well established he's out of the city, way out. Number two — if all this goes right, he's got to agree to resign from the police department. If he won't agree to that, then the deal's off. You understand that?"

"I understand."

"Then see that he understands, too. Call me if he refuses. Otherwise, just be there on Wednesday. Good luck to you both."

Ismail Carter found the right button and switched off.

This was it, what I'd waited for, all that I'd hoped for. As I dialed Conroy's number, I thought perhaps we should meet on this. He might need some heavy-duty persuading.

20

I hid out most of the time until Wednesday. I read a book cover to cover on Monday night. Then I played hooky from the office again on Tuesday and did something I'd been wanting to do for quite some time. I went out and bought a videocassette recorder, otherwise known through the civilized world as a VCR. It came with a booklet of instructions that seemed to have been translated quite literally from Japanese into English. Yet somehow I managed to get the thing hooked up to the television set.

I stepped into a video shop for the first time in my life, signed up, and began browsing. Talk about a kid in a candy store. I came away with four movies, the store's limit, all but one of them from the "Classics" rack: *The African Queen*, *Witness for the Prosecution*, and *On the Waterfront*; I even liked the one I hadn't seen before, a weird western with Willie Nelson called *Barbarosa*. So I spent that day and night at the movies.

Who was I hiding from? From Sue, mainly. In the course of three calls — messages left on my machine that weekend — she went from jeering to apologetic. I listened to each one, tempted each time to call her back, yet each time resisting. I was still furious at her for what she pulled on Thanksgiving — having Dominic Benda pulled in when she knew I wouldn't be around to accompany him. I did my part, too, but she set me up. One thing I was sure of: I didn't want to be married to a woman who didn't play by the rules. I'd been married to three of those before. Maybe two would be more accurate; the first one played fair. At any rate, that was my judgment, and I didn't want to deliver it until I'd settled down a bit.

I did talk to Dominic, though. I called him on Saturday and found him in better spirits. He'd gotten his patrol car back late Friday afternoon, and had been told informally by one of the forensic team that it was clean.

"You wouldn't have gotten it back otherwise," I told him. "They would have impounded it."

"Yeah, I guess."

I tried to explain how it happened I had been unavailable. He listened without comment, then said that he understood.

"Peggy told me what you told her. I know you been through a lot lately. We all have. None of us is perfect, Charley. I'm willing to forget if you are. But you know, the strange thing about it was that Larry Antonovich just gave me a routine questioning. He took me through it a couple of times. I got in about

555

the Drunk and Disorderly at the Dew Drop Inn the night the little girl was killed. I got that in. I think he was pissed off having to be there himself, putting his own Thanksgiving off, like."

"It wasn't his idea, then?"

"Oh, no, it was you-know-who."

"Sue Gillis?"

"Yeah, but she had some backing. You know what, Charley?"

"What's that, Dominic?"

"I think bringing me in like that, spoiling my Thanksgiving, was more about you than it was about me."

"You're probably partly right. But I think it was mostly about the polygraph test. She and Evola were pretty pissed afterward. They knew something was up when you came in so tired."

"And I fell asleep?"

"Yeah, well, that was my fault, though. I put you up to it."

"Let me tell you something, Charley. I didn't answer one question untrue in that whole test. All that walking in those seven miles did was put me in the mood I didn't give a shit. And that's the way you should take those tests. I was so damned scared when they told me I had to take it, I probably would have told a lie by the machine if I said my name was Dominic Benda. No, Charley, I ain't a bit sorry what we done."

"You did. You had to do all the work."

"Okay. You know . . ." He paused. It was as if he had something to say but couldn't quite figure the right words to say it. "You know, what I've been doing, hanging around the station, keeping contact with all those guys, I don't think I'll do that anymore. That was my life for a long time. But I gotta get a new life now. That's what Peg says, anyway. I think she's right."

"I think she's right, too, Dominic."

"No hard feelings, Charley."

"None whatsoever, Dominic."

It was late Tuesday morning when I put the call into the Hermitage. I wondered how Conroy and his wife were doing up there, or if they were still up there at all.

I called information and got the number of the hotel in Port Huron. When I got through to the switchboard, I asked if there was a Mr. and Mrs. Conroy registered there. She said she'd connect me. Mrs. Conroy answered.

"Hi, this is Charley Sloan. I just called to find out how you're doing."

"Mr. Sloan," she cooed. "We are doing just great. We dressed warm so we could take walks along the river. And the food is just out of this world! How'd you hear about this place?"

"I've had some good meals there, and it always seemed to me like it would be a good place to spend a little time away from it all."

"You sure got that right."

557

"I met the owner and his wife, a guy named Lydecker, not long ago. His family owns the hotel and he runs it. His wife runs the kitchen. If you happen to see them, say hello for me."

"Sure I will. But I suppose you'd like to talk to Mark."

"Yes, if he's around."

I heard her identify me as she passed the phone to him.

"Hey, Sloan." He sounded relatively relaxed. I could almost see a smile on his face.

"Hello, Conroy, I was just calling to find out how you two were doing there."

"We're doing fine. Allie loves it."

"What about you?"

"Well, yeah, I like it, too." He lowered his voice. "Allie's in the bathroom now, so I guess I can talk. I was scared to death they'd welcome me back when we registered at the desk. I guess they didn't remember me."

"Or they were being discreet."

"Something like that."

"Okay, listen, it's all set up for tomorrow morning. I go into your office at 1300 Beaubien with Benjamin Timothy, and that's when things are supposed to start going our way."

"After this is all over, you're going to have to take me aside and explain to me how all this worked."

"That's okay, but at this point, I don't have the answers myself." I hesitated. "You understand the terms?"

"I know the terms. It's not going to be as hard to quit the department as you think. Quitting won't be hard. It's just what comes afterward. I haven't got the slightest idea what I can do, or where I can go. I've spent my whole adult life as a cop, Sloan."

"We'll talk about that later," I said. "Right now we've just got to hope everything comes off without a hitch tomorrow."

"There's some danger it won't, then?"

"There'll have to be some tricky maneuvering to pull it off, but it can be done."

"Okay, I understand."

"But it's important that you're nowhere near Detroit. Just stay close to the hotel. If you haven't checked your car out of the garage yet, I'd just leave it there, if I were you. Don't come back until Thursday afternoon. You might even eat lunch there."

"Whatever you say." By now he sounded a little more glum than when he'd picked up.

"Come on," I said encouragingly, "in another few days it may all be over. *Ad astra*, Conroy."

"Jesus, Sloan. I don't have any secrets from you, do I?"

1300 Beaubien, the address of police headquarters in Detroit, is located comfortably close to the Frank Murphy Hall of Justice and the Detention Center, and across Clinton from Wayne County Jail. So you could be

559

arrested, locked up to await trial, be found guilty and sentenced, and then serve out your term, if it was a short one, all within the space of a single city block.

Unfortunately, all this centralization makes parking pretty damned difficult. I put my car in a lot just off Greektown and walked the rest of the way. I crossed St. Antoine, cut over to Clinton, and saw that the hot dog wagon had already opened up for business in front of the Frank Murphy Hall of Justice. Lawyers and friends and families of the accused streamed in and out, up and down the steps.

I'd spent the best and worst years of my life at Recorder's Court in the Murphy Hall of Justice. The two sentences ran concurrently. I still passed through its doors and its tight security checks — Mark Conroy had brought me inside on a couple of recent occasions — yet somehow I thought of that building as a huge relic of my past. I felt I didn't belong there anymore. I could never again be a real Detroit lawyer.

It also occurred to me, as I turned the corner and made for the entrance of police headquarters, that although years and status separated them, Dominic Benda and Mark Conroy were in much the same position. Each had given his life to police work. Now neither one of them had the faintest notion of what to do with the rest of his life.

The cop at the reception desk stopped me

and asked my business there.

"I'm here to meet with Benjamin Timothy to inspect the office of the deputy chief."

He held up a clipboard. "Your name, sir?"

"Charles Sloan. Is Mr. Timothy here yet?"

The cop put a check by my name. "No, sir, he isn't. Now, if you will take the elevator behind me and to your right to the second floor, then go along the hall, through the big room to the far end, you will find one or two officers waiting there for you and Mr. Timothy. You'll see them, I'm sure."

I thanked him for his directions, and followed the route exactly as he had laid it out for me. He was a well-spoken young man, probably on the fast track. I'm sure I must have known the layout of the building better than he did.

On the elevator I brooded a little more about Benda and Conroy. Dominic would find something — security guard, or maybe he'd pump gas close to home. His retirement pay was no longer in jeopardy. He'd get by. But Mark Conroy had a bigger problem. He'd risen so high. Where could he go? All that he knew was police work, and there wasn't much that was like police work at his level. But then I had an idea, something that I thought might work out for him.

The "big room" mentioned by the cop at the door was fairly familiar to me. I'd made visits in the past to the department's public information officer there, and also to Mark Conroy's predecessor, Frank Quilty, the last high-ranking Irishman on the force until he dropped dead one night at the bar in Jacoby's. Theirs were the big offices in each corner. The rest of the room — most of it, anyway — looked just about like what you'd find in any insurance office: a typing pool; secretaries at their desks; and, against one wall, a row of partitioned support offices.

Against the other wall, however, stood a row of desks where the real cops had set up shop. A few of them had gathered near the closed door of the deputy commissioner's office. They leaned against one desk, jackets off, holsters exposed, drinking coffee and talking among themselves. These, unless I missed my guess, were the Mouse's Untouchables, the special antidrug unit handpicked by him and Conroy. Then I saw that the desk around which they'd gathered belonged to none other than Ralph Smerka himself. He sat, holding court, his fingers folded over his belly, still wearing his trenchcoat and hat. He looked like he'd just come in. There was a rumble of talk as I approached, and then the group burst into loud laughter.

They fell silent when I arrived. The Mouse looked up at me without bothering to move his head more than an inch; he did it all with his eyes, a flat, cold stare.

"Why, if it isn't Ralph Smerka," I said, with

all the false joviality I could summon. "The last time I saw you, they had you locked up in the Whitehall. Did you escape, or did they let you out?"

"Don't be a pain in the ass, Sloan. I just got put back on the active list, that's all. I requested it."

"I wonder what they could be thinking of. You're far too valuable as a witness against your old boss to be wasted on ordinary police work."

Three or four of the Mouse's audience had drifted away by this time. Two stuck around to listen.

"Well, maybe they figured it's time ordinary police work got done around here." That was said with a swaggering smile that seemed to say that he, the Mouse, was the only one who could get things done. Not the sort of remark to endear him to the Untouchables.

"I hope you haven't lost the knack. There's a lot of Alzheimer's around the Whitehall, after all. It could be contagious."

"I ain't worried."

I noticed one of the Untouchables looking beyond me. So I turned around and saw Benjamin Timothy coming down the long aisle in the company of a uniformed cop.

He stopped at the desk, looked around, and shook my hand. He said my name, proving he remembered who I was, and I said his. Then he offered his hand to the Mouse, who took it without rising.

"Detective Smerka," said Timothy, "I wonder if you'd mind coming into the deputy chief's office while Mr. Sloan has a look at it. You, better than anyone else, could answer questions on its condition — what's where, if anything's been altered, and so on."

The Mouse pushed his huge body off the chair and rose to his full six-feet-six. He pushed his face into a smile.

"Sure," he said, "I don't mind."

Timothy turned to the cop beside him. "Officer Rylewicz, would you open it up, please?"

The cop was kind of a custodian. In his hand he had a huge ring of keys. He tried one, and then another, and then a third in the door to Conroy's office, without success. Smiling back at us apologetically, he tried another. It was only with the fifth key that the lock turned.

"They all look alike," he said as he swung open the door.

I went in first, followed by the Mouse, with Benjamin Timothy taking up the rear. Officer Rylewicz hung back and watched from the doorway.

"Could we have some light in here?" I asked him.

"Oh, sure, sorry."

Rylewicz flipped the switch, and two big fluorescent fixtures above blinked into life, illuminating the dark wood-paneled office in a sort of warm glow, definitely not hard on the eyes.

I gave the place a once-over from where I stood, careful to keep my gaze from the safe over in the corner. Just taking it all in. I turned to the Mouse.

"This place is pretty big," I said, "but there're only two chairs besides the big one behind the desk. Didn't you sometimes use this for meetings of your squad, your antidrug unit?"

He frowned. "Yeah, sometimes we did. The guys brought their chairs in from the outside. We had to discuss some pretty confidential stuff. We needed a place where we could shut the door."

"Was Deputy Chief Conroy always present?"

"Not always, no."

"So, in effect, you sometimes used the office as your own."

"Well, yeah, but he knew about it. He gave us permission."

I didn't follow up with the obvious question: Did you have a key? I knew he did. I just wanted him to know I knew. A frown passed over Benjamin Timothy's face. Mouse was his star witness, after all.

But then I quickly went over to the desk and surveyed the objects on top of it. I would have taken Mark Conroy for a clean-desk man — but this was ridiculous. About all that remained there was a picture of Althea Conroy (some years younger), a desk blotter, a pen in a holder, an In Box and an Out Box, and a telephone.

"Is this desk as it was when Mark Conroy vacated his office?"

The Mouse shrugged. "Pretty much the same, yeah."

"What does that mean?"

"There were some papers on the desk, current stuff that needed action — I took them."

"The In Box and the Out Box?" Both were bare.

"I emptied them, too. Same reason — they needed action."

"So, in effect, you appointed yourself acting deputy chief? For how long?"

"Until they got the workload redistributed. Until I went into the Whitehall. How do I know? I was doing two fucking jobs, and it was driving me crazy. I should've gotten a fucking medal."

"Put a length of time on it. Was it a month? A day?"

He took a moment to think, his face screwed into an expression of intense annoyance. "A week," he said.

I shook my head. "They don't give medals for a week," I said. "What about mail? He must have received mail here at the office during that week. Did you open it?"

"Yes!" He spat it out like a curse.

I tapped the desktop. "There was a Rolodex here. What happened to it?"

The Mouse sighed a great sigh of exasperation. "I took that, too."

"Why?"

"So I could do Conroy's goddamn work for him."

"Where is it now?"

"At my desk."

"Will you get it, please?"

He turned around and stormed out of the room, almost knocking over Office Rylewicz at the door. I turned to Assistant Prosecutor Benjamin Timothy and raised my eyebrows in mock astonishment. Timothy looked away.

The Mouse returned with a very full Rolodex, banging it down without a word on the polished desktop. I picked it up, noting the gouge he had put in the wood with a "tsk-tsk-tsk," then handed it over to Benjamin Timothy.

"I'd like this held as evidence," I said.

I'd caught him by surprise.

"All right," he said.

He held the thing awkwardly, looking down at it, trying to determine its significance. The Mouse was simply puzzled.

I tried all the drawers in Conroy's desk. They were all locked. I wouldn't have to keep this up forever.

"Were these drawers all locked when Deputy Chief Conroy vacated his office?"

"Sure they were," said the Mouse.

"Do you have the key or keys to open them?"

"Course not. You want them opened, you get the keys from him."

I nodded.

Then I started around the room, tugging at the drawers in the file cabinet, finding them locked, looking into one corner, then crossing over to the other corner, the one where the safe stood. There it was, the cause of all the grief. It was not particularly imposing, about three feet high and not quite as wide, an ordinary Mosler safe. It looked stronger than it was; its walls seemed to be of something between steel and granite. Very impressive. Its door was shut. I pointed at the safe and turned to Timothy.

"Isn't the safe supposed to be open?"

He came over and stared down at it with me.

"Yes, I believe so," he said. "It's probably unlocked. It's just that the door is shut."

He bent down and tried the door handle. He tried it to the right, and then to the left. Nothing happened.

"Detective Smerka," he said. "The safe is supposed to be open, just as it was when the theft was discovered. Clearly" — wiggling the handle to the door — "it is now locked. Do you know anything about this?"

"Me? No, nothing. The safe door was open

when the office was closed up. I know that for sure."

"How do you know that for 'for sure'?" Timothy demanded.

"Because I looked. Because I saw it."

"You know the combination, don't you?"

"Well . . . yeah."

"Open it up."

The Mouse pushed past us and knelt in front of the safe. His big fingers had a surprisingly light touch. He had no difficulty hitting the right numbers on the first try. He smiled up at Benjamin Timothy.

"You want it open?" he asked.

"Of course."

The Mouse swung the door wide. Both Timothy and I had bent down to look inside. There it was. I guess I'd never seen so much money, so much cash, before in my life. Piles of the stuff — but it didn't really take up quite as much space as I expected. There was still room left in the safe for another million or two. My God, I thought, look at it!

Benjamin Timothy jerked upright. "Close it up!" he said.

"Shouldn't we count it?" the Mouse asked.

"No, no, just leave it. Close up the safe. Lock it!"

He was clearly flustered, uncertain how to deal with this development. He was either not in on the scam, or had a great career waiting for him in Hollywood.

Once the Mouse had closed the safe and spun the dial, I rose up and looked Timothy squarely in the eye.

"I'm going to move that charges be dropped," I said.

He was shocked. This seemed more than he could take. "On what basis?"

"That no crime has been committed. Prove that it has."

"All that money was gone. It had been stolen."

"And now it's back."

"Conroy could have returned it."

"How? He gave up his keys to the office when he vacated it. If you check the sheets downstairs, you'll find he hasn't been inside this building since then. That I can guarantee."

"That's all very interesting, but I think we should get out of here right now."

"Surely you're not serious."

"Of course I am. We're going to leave it, lock up the room, get out of here, and consider this matter."

"We'll do nothing of the kind." I sounded adamant. I was.

"What do you mean?"

"At the very least, this safe and its contents have become evidence, very important evidence. Do you intend to leave the safe here so that it can be picked clean by some vulture?"

I cast an accusing glance in the direction of

the Mouse. He responded, showing no class, by giving me the finger. Benjamin Timothy didn't see it.

"So what do you propose?"

"That the safe and its contents be held, just as they are, as evidence."

He looked around the room, as if hoping to find the proper answer in one of its corners.

"The safe is on casters," I said, "it shouldn't be too hard to move. Detective Smerka, you wouldn't mind giving us a hand in getting this thing down to the evidence room, would you? Oh, and Mr. Timothy, don't forget the Rolodex."

It was their move. I retired to my corner — up I-94 to Pickeral Point — feeling, if not exactly jubilant, at least well satisfied with the morning's work. The money was back in the safe. I was fairly certain the Mouse himself had served as courier, and the safe was now locked away. But I'd also demonstrated to the young assistant prosecutor that his star witness could be made to look pretty bad in court before the jury. Once he'd had a chance to sit alone and consider, Timothy would see that the only sensible thing to do was to drop the charges against Mark Conroy. Pressure from the mayor might not even be needed.

Mission accomplished.

So when I breezed into my office, I was in a buoyant mood, much in need of communication. I picked up the phone and dialed the Hermitage. The hotel operator informed me that Mr. and Mrs. Conroy had checked out. I asked her to connect me with the dining room. I asked the headwaiter if Mark Conroy could be paged. Conroy was at the phone in less than a minute.

"Sloan?"

"Yeah, it's me. Listen, everything went just the way we wanted. It was as though I'd written the script myself."

"You practically did, didn't you? The . . ." He hesitated. "The stuff was back where it belonged?"

"That's right, and I got them to put it and the safe in the evidence room."

"You know who put it back?"

"I've got my ideas about that. We'll talk about it later."

"So now what do we do?"

"We wait. Don't say anything. No remarks to the press. Don't get flattered into going on TV. Don't even talk to friends about what may or may not happen next."

"Okay. Agreed."

"Work on your resignation statement. It should be as positive as possible. Maybe I can give you some input. But nothing gets said until charges are dropped."

"I understand. And so that's it?"

"That's it."

"Okay, Sloan, and . . . thanks."

After I had hung up, it occurred to me that, coming from Mark Conroy, that "thanks" I got would be like a tearful speech promising undying gratitude from anybody else. I'd have to be satisfied with what I got.

I started through the pile of call slips Mrs. Fenton had left me, wadding up two from Sue and filing them in the basket. I came across one that made me curious. Bud Billings had called a little before noon from county police headquarters. I dialed the number, and he picked up immediately.

"I guess you've heard by now, Charley."

"Heard what?"

I still had my mind on the Conroy business. Nothing would have been made public on that yet. Besides, Bud wouldn't have called me about Conroy, no matter what the news.

"The Evans kid was shot dead."

"What? Sam Evans? Who did it, his father?" I wouldn't put it past that nut case.

"No, Delbert was confirmed clear over on the other side of the county. It happened right on the Evans place around ten o'clock. The kid's mother was looking out the window at the time and saw him go down like he'd been knocked over with a baseball bat. It wasn't any baseball bat knocked him down."

"What did?"

"It looks like it was a 30-30 fired from quite some distance away. There's a grove of trees about five hundred yards from where the kid was hit. They figure it came from there. I'll tell you, it was a great shot at that distance, and it went right through his heart. Mrs. Evans didn't hear it, but from five hundred yards away, and with her inside the house, she wouldn't have, not necessarily."

"Where'd you get all this information?" I asked. "You weren't there, were you?"

"Oh, no, they've still got me pushing papers here at headquarters because of the false arrest suit."

"So they know where you were at ten o'clock this morning."

"Yeah, thank God," he said. "It was Sue Gillis who called it in. They're tying it to the other murders. They sent her and Antonovich out to the crime scene."

"How does that figure? I don't quite see the connection to the murders."

"I hate to say it, but they're examining the possibility that maybe one of the fathers of the children was so convinced that Sam Evans did it, he decided to play judge and jury. Sue's out talking to Catherine Quigley's father now."

Jesus. Weren't four murders of innocent children in one small county enough for anyone to bear? Now there was the possibility that a vigilante was out there, a father deranged and destroyed by grief seeking revenge. If someone murdered my daughter, Lisa, would I do the same? I had never taken the life of another human being, but under similar circumstances, would I be able to kill?

"I thought I would call you and let you know. Evans was your client, after all. Oh, and by the way, it's working out fine for me with John Dibble. You were right. He's behind me all the way. I don't know how the kid's death is going to change things, though."

Billings and I said our good-byes and hung up. Stunned by what I'd just learned, I sat nearly immobile, staring out into the middle distance. Swinging my chair around to face the river, I knew I needed to do some thinking. Some very serious thinking.

21

I don't know how long I sat there, utterly lost in thought. Looking back, it must have been nearly two hours. Mrs. Fenton came in from lunch, and I told her to hold all my calls. I just kept staring out at the river, mesmerized by its tranquility. How many ore boats went by? I have no idea, and I was feeling anything but serene.

The more I thought, the more often I came back to Father Chuck. And the more I came back to him, the more often I veered away.

How could he? How could a priest, a man of God, do such an ungodly thing? Certainly they were right in thinking Sam Evans's murder was tied to the deaths of the children, but not in the way they thought. They'd find that Mr. Higgins, Mr. Quigley, and Mr. Bartkowski were all at work at ten o'clock. No, not Bartkowski; he wouldn't even be questioned. He couldn't possibly be a suspect; Sam Evans was in the lockup when Billy Bartkowski was murdered and his body laid out beside Beulah Road. None of the fathers would be suspects.

But what about Father Charles Albertus?

I'd learned a lot from Father LeClerc: that Father Chuck's housekeeper was wrong when she told me that he had been away at the retreat that whole week; that he could have easily been in Hub City at the time the first murder took place, and that he was almost certainly back from the retreat that ill-fated night Catherine Quigley was killed. That, as I had persuaded myself, didn't prove that he had committed the unthinkable crimes, only that he could have.

And what about the van that had eluded the cops out on Copper Creed Road? It could have been the one I'd seen parked by the rectory on my two visits to Father Chuck, and the same one in which, according to Doris Dieberman, the priest would pick up the children from school for special activities at Our Lady of Sorrows.

And it was funny that Bud Billings hadn't mentioned it, but he had had the strong feeling during the interrogation of Sam Evans that the kid had recognized the driver of the car out there on Clarion Road, the one who had placed the body of Catherine Quigley by the side of the road. Because of Bud's own feelings about Sam's father, he had suspected that it was Delbert Evans that young Sam had seen out there. Well, clearly it was not. Clearly, it was somebody else.

Just say that it had been Father Chuck who he had seen out there that night; why would Sam Evans have held back? First of all, because of the false accusation he had earlier leveled at Father Chuck. Who would believe him after that if he were to point the finger at him a second time? The boy cried wolf. What else? Could Sam have conceived of blackmail in that little pea brain of his? Perhaps. He'd certainly gotten the idea from his father that people would pay to keep certain matters secret. That would have given him a reason to keep it quiet, to hold it back from everyone, perhaps even from his father. This would be Sam's enterprise and nobody else's.

And who but Father Chuck fit Mark Conroy's tip so well? Conroy had said it had to be someone that the kids could trust, that kids would naturally trust. Then he had told the story of the bent cop. That was what confused things. Sue — and maybe even me, too — had taken it too literally. But later on, the next day in fact, Conroy had reiterated the principle: It had to be someone the children would be drawn to. And who were they going to trust more than good old Father Chuck in his Roman collar? Two of the children who had died were in some way connected to Our Lady of Sorrows.

Motive? I'd gotten that during my so-called debate from Father Chuck himself. He'd stuck by that nutty idea that the children were better off dead because they wouldn't be exposed to all the sin and misery that would have been their lot if they had lived out their lives.

Putting myself back in that trophy room of

his where we had our discussion, I saw the deer heads on the wall, the mounted rifles and shotguns. Did one of the rifles have a telescopic sight? If not, one could have been mounted. Surely one of those rifles was a 30–30. He could probably have dropped Sam Evans easily at five hundred yards. He may not even have needed a telescopic sight.

He had it all: the "motive" to kill the children, twisted and perverse though it was, the skill to kill Sam Evans, and a possible reason. But he would have to be deeply disturbed to do such things. But hadn't he shown that to me? Wasn't his drinking a sign of something? Maybe he downed all that whiskey to keep a lid on it. Or worse, maybe he drank to empower himself, to permit himself, to let himself go.

And it was at this point that I always stopped and sorted through things all over again. Who could believe this of a priest, a man of God, a celibate, a man who hated sin? How could such a man commit such sins? Who would believe it? Certainly not Sue. She had been inspired, uplifted, just talking to Father Chuck. It would do no good to pass any of this on to her. No, I told myself again and again, I'd better rethink this, and I did. But each time I came up with the same conclusion.

Finally, I turned away from my view of the river, got up from my desk, pulled on my trenchcoat and gloves, and walked out to Mrs. Fenton.

"You've certainly been deep in thought in there," she said. "Or have you been taking a little nap?"

"It doesn't matter much, one way or the other. Look, I'm going out for a while. I don't really know how long. If I'm not back by the time you go, just put the messages on my desk with the others. I'll come in later to check them."

"One of your nocturnal visits?"

"Yeah, I seem to be making a lot of those lately, don't I?"

All the way out Clarion Road to Hub City, I asked myself why I was going and what I hoped to accomplish. Did I intend to confront him? With what? My suspicions? Only in Perry Mason do murderers crumble before stern accusation. I should probably have gone to Bud Billings and voiced my thoughts about Father Chuck to him. He'd take me seriously. He'd understand how it all fit together. I could still do that. All I needed to do was find a nice wide spot on the road and make a U-turn.

But I drove on.

What was it that made me continue? In some sense, I think, it was that I saw something of myself in Father Chuck. There was what I perceived as his alcoholism. We shared that, certainly, though I acknowledged it in myself, and he was still in denial. Perhaps subtler and more complex but even more important was the fact that he was a priest, the Catholic Church personified. He represented, if anyone did, the values, the attitudes toward sex and women, the qualified system of rewards and punishments, with which I'd grown up. I'd put all that behind me because I soon learned out in the great world that it was many times more complicated than that. In my profession, that all became very clear. But growing to maturity as I did in the old Church had certainly left its mark on me, probably an indelible one. And each time I was face-to-face with Father Charles Albertus, I saw not so much myself in him, but the representative of all that had held such powerful sway over me when I was young, all that I had eventually rejected.

I was aware, too, that perhaps I had rejected too much. I needed something. I knew that. Slowly, imperceptibly at first, I seemed to be moving through a sort of low-grade spiritual crisis. It first made itself known to me that night nearly a month ago when I'd driven Sue out this very road to the place where Catherine Quigley's body had been placed by her murderer. Looking at that little body in the snow had had a traumatic effect upon me. It had made me physically sick, but that was the least of it. The conversation with Bob Williams that same night at Benny's, which I remembered so vividly, had done nothing to help. All it did was bring to the surface the questions that had been deep in my mind for who-knows-how-long. Was there a Higher Power? Was He all-powerful? If so, how could He allow such monstrous things as the murder of a little child to happen? There was the horror of that experience at the autopsy and the lost weekend that followed, an eruption from deep in the soul, a cry for an answer to these paralyzing questions. My talk with Father LeClerc hadn't helped that much. I felt a reluctance to seek the old remedies for problems that were new to me. Yet Phil LeClerc was a good priest. I recognized that.

One way or another, with all this on my mind, I made it into Hub City. By now I knew the way to Our Lady of Sorrows and the rectory around the corner from it. I made all the correct turns, through what was left of the downtown area of this decaying little metropolis, and then I took Kellogg Street out to the edge of town. There it was, the most imposing building for blocks, Gothic in style and a light stone gray in color. I then turned the corner, drove the length of the church, and parked in front of the rectory.

I went to the door and gave a good long rap with a heavy knocker, which was cased in the shape of a human hand. I hadn't noticed that before.

After what seemed to me a considerable

amount of time, Father Chuck appeared, dressed informally. He wore his dickey, shirt, and collar but beneath them was a pair of old, faded jeans.

"Why, Charley! Come on in!" He threw open the door. "Did you just decide to drop by? Were you in the neighborhood? Maybe you want to continue our great debate."

I stepped inside. He gave me his usual clap on the back and led the way down the long hall.

"Let's say I was in the neighborhood," I called out to him.

"Great!" he said over his shoulder. "I get few enough visitors here. I'm always glad for some company. Come on in," he said, gesturing me through the open door of his office. "Just sit down and tell me what's on your mind."

The room was the way I remembered it, deer heads and an angry fish mounted on the wall, along with a rack of seriously lethal hardware. I took a seat on the sofa again. But he sat behind his desk. That's where his drink was. I must have been agitated, for I made no move to take off my coat or gloves.

"Not going to stay?" he asked. "You seem a bit upset. Anything wrong?"

He took a good, healthy slug of his Scotch.

I hesitated uncertainly. "I don't know quite where to begin."

And that was the truth. I had been wrestling

with the facts, with my speculations, and with myself so energetically during the last couple of hours that I really hadn't given much, if any, thought to what I might say to Father Chuck once we were alone. This wasn't like me at all.

"In that case," he said cheerfully, "I suppose that the thing to do is to begin at the beginning."

That's just what I did.

"You may or may not know that I was along with Sue Gillis the night that Catherine Quigley's body was discovered out on Clarion Road."

"No, Charley, I didn't know that."

"Seeing that child dead in the snow affected me deeply. It threw me into a moral turmoil. I asked myself how, if there is a just God, He can permit such things to take place. Then I —"

"If you'll forgive me for interrupting, I really think I can help you here. We priests see —"

"And if you'll pardon me for interrupting, Father, but please, now that I'm started, I'd like to tell this in my own way."

"Of course. Go ahead."

He seemed upset by that, even slightly intimidated, enough so that he finished off the neat Scotch he'd been drinking. As I resumed talking, he went to the cupboard and replenished his drink from one of the bottles there.

"Also, as you may or may not know, Sam

Evans was out on Clarion Road that night. The pickup truck he was driving broke down, and he was on foot. He saw a car make a U-turn and pull over to the side of the road. The driver got out, took a large bundle from the back, and placed it near the side of the road. Then the car went back in the direction of Hub City. Sam was naturally curious what the driver had left, so he went for a look and discovered what was in the bundle. Another car came along then and caught him in its lights. Sam panicked and ran. Because he had left a footprint at the scene, and because he had been seen and identified earlier by another motorist on the road at that time, he was taken in for questioning by the county police, specifically by Sue Gillis and Bud Billings.

"I served as Sam Evans's attorney during his interrogation by the police, at least during the latter stages. I gave him counsel and was present during the final time he was made to tell his story. The cops treated him as a suspect and kept him overnight on a trumped-up holding charge, but then they had to release him because the very evening he was in their custody, Billy Bartkowski was murdered and laid out by the side of the road, just as the others had been."

I paused then just a little too long, for Father Chuck jumped in with a bit of quick-shot detection.

"But you know, Charley, Sam Evans could

have killed the Quigley girl, and Lee Higgins, too," he said. "Somebody else could have killed Billy Bartkowski. You know how it's done — to make it look like the others?"

"A copy-cat murder?"

"That's what they call them. Exactly! No, I think they were wrong to let Evans go. That kid was bad news. And I don't mean just because of that stupid lie he told about me. It was worse than that. There was something sinister about him."

"Sinister?" I shrugged. "At any rate, Bud Billings, one of the detectives who questioned him, felt strongly that Sam Evans was holding something back."

"See? I told you."

"No, Bud believed the kid's story, by and large, but he thought Sam Evans had recognized the driver of the car, the one who had deposited the child's body at the side of the road. Evans claimed he was too far away, and that the snow was coming down too hard for him to tell who it was. Bud thought he knew, and for whatever reason, didn't want to tell."

"This is all very interesting, Charley, sort of the inside story, isn't it? Fascinating, really, but why are you telling me all this?"

"Because Sam Evans was murdered this morning."

"*Really*? I didn't know."

"Now, why would anyone want to kill a lamebrain kid like him?" I asked rhetorically.

"What motive could they have? That's a big puzzle."

"I take it they don't know who shot him, then?"

"No, they don't. But let's just theorize. Let's say that Bud Billings was right, that Sam Evans had recognized the driver of that car out on Clarion Road. Suppose he had let the driver know he had been recognized and asked for something — money, whatever — to keep quiet about it. This is, of course, commonly known as blackmail, and it is a crime punishable by a prison term. Now, while I don't condone the murder of Sam Evans, I think it might be entirely understandable. Look at it this way. Sam Evans had committed the crime of blackmail. Perhaps he had been incorrect in his identification of the driver of the car that night and the party he went to was altogether innocent. Or perhaps he had willfully gone to a certain party, someone he bore a grudge against in revenge, threatened to bear false witness against him unless he was paid. So you see, Father, there are all sorts of possible extenuating circumstances here. There is, in other words, murder, and murder of a different sort."

I let him chew on this a bit. But he didn't chew, he drank. He was putting down great gulps of the stuff as he sat behind his desk and listened, nodding his interest and understanding but with his face averted. His focus seemed to be on the fire that blazed in the fireplace behind his desk.

"Are we talking about justifiable homicide?" he asked at last.

"I'm sure the man who disposed of that greedy — and yes, perhaps slightly sinister — young moron would have regarded his action as justified."

He nodded. "Yes, I suppose so."

"Father Chuck," I asked quietly, "were you that man?"

There was a lapse of a couple of seconds, then he suddenly came to life, turned and faced me. "What a question, Charley! How could you possibly think that of me? I'm a *priest*."

"Frankly, for a couple of reasons," I said, still quiet and persuasive, "three, actually. First of all, without any prompting from me, when you spoke of Sam Evans as 'bad news' and 'sinister,' you used the past tense, as if to say he's no longer with us."

"Don't be ridiculous. That's nitpicking. I was probably thinking of him in the past tense as a worry that was now out of my life." Then he added, "Thanks to you."

"All right then, what about this? When I told you Sam Evans had been murdered, you said he'd been shot. In fact, he was, but I didn't say so."

"Aren't firearms responsible for most homicides today?"

"And finally," I said, "there's the matter of

the shot that killed Sam Evans. Bud Billings told me that it had probably been fired from a grove of trees some five hundred yards away — all that distance and it was a clean hit right through the heart. He said that only a master marksman could have hit on a shot like that." I gestured to the trophy heads on the wall. "If anybody in Kerry County fits that description, you certainly do."

He had nothing to say to that, so I got up and walked over to the gun rack on the wall. I lifted one down.

"It was probably something like this that took Sam Evans out. Maybe this is the very weapon that did it. Bud Billings said they thought it would probably have been a 30-30 that did the job. Is that what this is?"

"That's what it is." He said it in a slightly removed, thoughtful sort of voice.

"You know when they find the slug that killed him, they can match it perfectly with the gun that fired it. It's just like fingerprints."

I examined the rifle, hefted it. It wasn't nearly as heavy as it looked, well balanced, a beautiful piece of lethal machinery. I noticed flanges along the rear of the barrel. Holding it up to him, I pointed them out.

"What are these?" I asked. "They couldn't be mounts for a telescopic sight, could they?"

"Yes, that's exactly what they are."

"Do you have a telescopic sight for this rifle, Father Chuck?"

"I have one around here somewhere."

"Bud Billings said it would have taken one of those to place the shot that killed Sam Evans. Has this gun been fired recently?"

I turned the rifle around and smelled the barrel.

"Careful, Charley," he cautioned. "Even unloaded guns are dangerous."

"No, it smells like it's just been cleaned."

"All my weapons have just been cleaned."

"Look, Father, wouldn't it be better if you came in with me and talked to Bud? He's a parishioner. He'll understand. Tell him about Sam Evans: how he tried to blackmail you, threatened to bear false witness against you the way he did in that miserable business of the civil suit that they threatened against you. Let me assure you, he'll understand."

"I understand far more than you think I do," he said. He seemed to have collected himself, readied himself for some sort of counterattack. "I understand that you're conning me. You know that if I go in and let them question me about Sam Evans's death, it won't stop there. They'll go on and question me about all kinds of things, things I don't want to talk about, things that should remain hidden. Very few would understand them, and most of them are saints, dead and gone."

"Father Chuck, you're not making good sense."

"Oh, I'm making sense, all right, better

sense than you do with all your modern rationalism, your defense of the real criminals who prey upon us. You and your 'suicide doctor'! I'm surprised you haven't found an abortionist to defend. You know, Charley, you make me sick. You really do. I honestly don't know how you live with yourself, the way you seem to seek out the dregs of society and add them to your list. What do you say? 'I got this drug dealer off, this murderer, this rapist.' Do you keep count?

"I tried to talk to you," he ranted on, his voice louder, rising to his feet. "You called it a debate, but then you began cross-examining me! I didn't break, you did! I'd like to have seen *that* in court, the witness breaking down the lawyer in cross-examination. Let me tell you, Charley, God is with me. He spoke to me and told me to protect the innocents, and He told me that the only way to protect them from this world of drugs and violence was to take action. What could I do? What could anyone do but protect the innocents from such a world? And how do you do that? You send them to God in their pure state, without sin but just at the age of reason. Couldn't you understand that yourself? Why couldn't you? I wanted you to. I wanted you to with all my heart! Oh, but clearly, you have turned your back on me, just as you've turned your back on God. Why, Charley? Why can't you understand?"

"I'm trying, Father Chuck," I said. "I really am. But I'll tell you, though, that in all honesty, I think you need some help, not help in the parish, or with the outlying churches. No, I think you need help for yourself. Do you remember who sent me here in the first place to help you out with the Sam Evans problem? It was Bishop Solar. I think that from what I've heard from you, and from what I've observed from your drinking, I really owe it to him and to you to tell him about your difficulties here. I think he'll recommend psychiatric help for you. I think you need it."

"Oh no, Charley, I don't think I do, and I don't think I can permit another one of those doctors looking inside my head to tell me that I had a serious problem with repression, and that what I was doing was living an abnormal life. I like my abnormal life. I believe in celibacy. I believe in the Church, the way it's been for two thousand years, give or take a decade or two."

He regarded me in exasperation and then shook his head in angry disapproval.

"I really don't like you waving that rifle around the way you're doing. It shows ignorance, for one thing. I told you that even unloaded guns are dangerous. Even though I emptied that one you've got in your hand this morning — yes, and I took the telescopic sight off it, too — I know that it's still dangerous to wave it around like that. It's also useless, if you're trying to threaten me. This, on the other hand, is a loaded gun, and if I threaten you with this, you should indeed feel afraid."

He had brought up a pump shotgun from behind the desk, one of his trap guns, and he leveled it at me.

"Are you threatening me with it?" I asked.

"Yes, I guess I am," he said. "Now, I think the best thing for us to do would be to walk out to the back to settle this."

Stupidly, ignorantly, I had not counted on a development such as this. Defense lawyers deal with violence all the time, but we deal with it at a remove, safely distanced from any threat to ourselves. What did he have in mind?

"Do you want me to raise my hands in the air or something?" I tried to make it sound like a joke, but it seemed flat even to me. What he said then made it seem that much flatter.

"I don't care what you do, just so long as you remember that there's a shotgun pointed at your back. Go down the hall, through the kitchen, and out the door."

I walked on ahead of him, opening the back door as I came to it, going on ahead into that wide expanse behind the rectory and the parking lot that ended in the woods a few hundred yards away. It must have been about four o'clock, not yet dark but getting close to it. It was almost winter, after all, and the cold in the air confirmed it. It was damp, too; there would be a snowfall soon.

"What're you going to do?" Another attempt at humor. "Wrap me up in plastic and set me by the side of the road?"

"Not at all. There's going to be a terrible accident," he said. "I was giving you a lesson in trap shooting, and you handled the gun so awkwardly that you shot yourself, fatally. I'll call the police, the local police, of course. I know all five of them by their first names. There shouldn't be any need to involve your friend Bud Billings in this at all. Why should he be interested in a shooting accident?"

"He might be. I've told him all about you, Father Chuck."

"Charley, you're bluffing. Remember, I'm an old poker player. I'm calling your hand, and I'm not impressed with what you've got to show."

For once I didn't have a ready reply. Yet he had a lot to say, it seemed, and I had no choice but to listen to him ramble on.

"You know, you're very clever, questioning me the way you did about the death of that little moron, Sam Evans. You called him a moron yourself. You were so sympathetic, offering me a way out, suggesting that he might have threatened to bear false witness against me just as he had before. No, not that kid. He saw me out on Clarion Road that night, all right, and he recognized me. And you know what he wanted for his silence? A new pickup truck. That's right, he wanted just enough for

594

a down payment in the beginning and then enough for payments every month. Isn't that disgusting? The greed for things. It's a universal disease these days. But you almost got me with your talk, you really did. I actually wanted to say yes, I killed that worthless little excuse for a human being. He tried to make me sound like a queer, and he deserved it. I did it with one shot, and you were right, it was a damned good shot. I may not hunt anymore, but I keep my shooting eye sharp working on targets. Probably not another man in the county could have placed that shot at such a distance.

"But of course if I had admitted to that, I would have admitted to all the rest. Those four children. And there'll be more, believe me. But you don't understand about that, do you? They die painlessly, and I honor them for their purity. That's why I put them out in the snow. What could be purer than new-fallen snow? Their little bodies washed, their clothes cleaned, lying out there in the snow, the white, white snow. But their souls, their sinless souls, are with God.

"Why do I do it? I even told you, but you weren't listening, you wouldn't listen to me, I suppose because I'm a priest. It was my nephew, Tom. I said he was the closest thing to a son I'd had, would ever have. I told you that he died, but I didn't tell you how. He was still a child, seventeen, just into college at U of D. Yes, Detroit, Charley, that cesspool that vomited you up here to Kerry County. He was a bright boy, a good kid, and I thought the Jesuits could keep him on the straight and narrow. But I'm afraid I underestimated the malice and the snares of the Devil. Poor Tom, while he was still in grade school, he fell in with a bad crowd out around Palmer Park. He died of a heroin overdose at seventeen. I said the funeral Mass for him, and I drove back here to Hub City in the snow. So deep in sadness, I can't express it. And on my way to the rectory, I saw little Lee Higgins and offered him a ride. And I remember thinking how much better it would have been for Tom if he'd died at Lee's age. Think of the pain he would have missed, the sin he would have been saved from.

"Look at yourself. If you had died at just such an age, you would have gone straight to heaven. Ah, but Charley, where you're going now, at best you have long ages of suffering in purgatory before you. But I'll pray for you, I will, really. Perhaps others will, too. You'll need all the prayers you can get. And I think you had better begin praying right now for yourself. Do you think you can summon up an Act of Contrition from the dim recesses of your memory?"

"Yes, I think I can."

"Then you'd better say it now."

About ten feet separated us. Father Chuck had held the pump shotgun pointed at me, but now he elevated it, resting the butt of the stock on his hip, indicating in a sportsmanlike way that he was ready to wait a bit. I blessed myself, dropped down on one knee, and bowed my head.

Yes, I really did pray, but it was not the Act of Contrition that I said. I'm not even sure that I put it into words, but if I did, it would have sounded something like this: "Higher Power, God, whatever You call Yourself, please give me the strength to stop this sick, mad priest before he kills more children. I may not be much, but I'm the only weapon You've got."

Although my head was bowed, my eyes were slitted open. I watched, and I saw my opportunity when his head tilted slightly upward. A passing bird? Perhaps a late flock of Canadian geese flying south, the hunter's instinct. I never knew what caught his attention; I simply saw my chance and took it.

From my crouch I threw myself bodily through the air, a flying tackle. He was taller, heavier, and stronger than I was, but he collapsed under the sudden impact of my body at his knees.

He went down.

As I struggled up to his torso, he began kicking and twisting, trying to throw me off. I hung on. At the same time he was trying to bring the shotgun around to club me. He hit me once on the temple with the barrel. I didn't feel a thing. I grabbed his hair and beat his head against the ground. That did no good, the ground was still soft. He had the shotgun between us now, trying to get it into my face. I pushed it away. Then, with a mighty heave, he threw me over, rolled on top of me. His bearded face was only inches from mine. The shotgun came up. I jerked it down.

His face, so close, suddenly collapsed.

Did I hear the gun go off? I'm not sure that I did, I only know I was deaf for about an hour afterward and hard of hearing for the next couple of days.

It took a great push to get him off me, but I managed it. I rolled his body over onto his back, and I struggled up to my feet. I stood there, panting hard, my breath coming in racking sobs, and looked at what I had done. His finger was still on the trigger. The shotgun charge had entered at his chin below his beard and blown out the back and top of his head.

It was a suicide wound.

When I saw that, a plan began to form in my mind. Alive, he might have been persuaded to confess; evidence would have been found; a full investigation would have proven the case against him. But dead, he was just poor Father Chuck. No one would ever believe that a priest had done the things that he had done.

I went back through the open door into the rectory. Although I was wearing those new gloves and had never taken them off, in fact, I was nevertheless careful about what I touched. I found a mirror in the kitchen, and I saw that there was surprisingly little blood on my coat, but my chin and part of my throat had been darkened by all that powder from the muzzle of the shotgun. I could wash it off, but not here, not now.

I found my way back to the room where we'd held our conversations. It was just as we'd left it, of course. The 30-30 stood against the couch where I'd propped it when he'd marched me out to that vast backyard. I didn't touch it. There was no need to replace it. I'd left no prints on it.

It was only because I was wearing those skintight gloves that I was able to type Father Chuck's suicide note. I was careful. I took my time. I simply enumerated his crimes in the first person, then added, "May God have mercy on my soul," and signed his name. All on the typewriter.

It was nearly dark when I left by the back door. I gave the body one last look as I headed for my car. There was snow in the air. Father Charles Albertus would be covered by it in the morning.

EPILOGUE

In the beginning, the Kerry County Police treated Father Chuck's death as a homicide. There were smudges on the typewriter keys and on the rifle where there might have been fingerprints. That made them suspicious. Besides, the idea of a priest committing suicide, not to mention the hideous crimes to which he'd confessed in that questionable suicide note — well, it was just unthinkable.

But the evidence against him mounted.

First, the bullet that had killed Sam Evans was found, beyond a shadow of a doubt, to have been fired from the rifle I had handled and left propped against the sofa. And that rifle was known by Father Chuck's former hunting companions to belong to him. It was his favorite.

There had been some doubt voiced that anyone would type a suicide note. It seemed impersonal, inappropriate somehow. But then his housekeeper and some parishioners said that Father Chuck's handwriting was so illegible that he typed everything. I hadn't known. The Force was with me on that one.

Finally, tucked away in an upper drawer of the desk, they found items belonging to the murdered children. The county police had withheld word from the press that from each of the young victims something had been taken by the murderer, evidently as a memento. Lee Higgins's pocketknife was there, as were Catherine Quigley's small handkerchief, Billy Bartkowski's favorite marble, and Dicky Fauret's whistle.

The discovery of those grisly souvenirs clinched the case against him. Nobody knew quite how to handle it. The newspapers — even *The New York Times* and the *Washington Post* — editorialized, and the anchorpersons philosophized. He was a sick man, that much was agreed, but in this age when all of us are so much in need of the consolations of religion, we should not allow the insane acts of one man to shake our beliefs. And so on.

Bishop Solar himself said Mass at Our Lady of Sorrows all through that winter in an effort to hold the congregation together. Even so, attendance fell off. In the spring, the bishop brought a young priest in as pastor. I understand he's a man of pleasant disposition and boundless energy.

Sue Gillis and I never got back together. When my anger over the arbitrary Thanksgiving interrogation of Dominic Benda had cooled, we had one last dinner on neutral ground, and I made a little speech to her declaring our break permanent. She took it well enough and had no desire to hear my reasons. That suited me just fine and saved us from a nasty session of mutual recriminations. Not long afterward, I began hearing rumors linking her — how is it they put it? — "romantically" with Mark Evola. That made me sad for her because there is a Mrs. Evola and three little Evolas, and a man with political ambitions as strong as his was not likely to risk a divorce.

By the time Sue and I had our talk, she was just getting over the shock that she had received from the revelations regarding Father Chuck. She said she believed them, but somehow she couldn't accept them.

The Mark Conroy matter ended, just as I hoped it would, without a hitch. Charges were dropped. Conroy resigned. With a little urging from me — it didn't take much — Anthony Mercante asked him out to corporate headquarters and interviewed him for a spot as his number-two man in the security division of that Big Three auto manufacturer. Mercante had believed in Conroy right from the start, after all. He convinced his boss that Conroy's resignation was in no way an admission of guilt, just making the best of a bad situation. Besides, as he pointed out, putting an African American in a high position of trust wouldn't hurt their image in the least. Conroy was hired. At last report, he loved his position in the world of manufacturing and business.

Those two days spent in Port Huron must have helped Mr. and Mrs. Conroy work things out between them because they're still Mr. and Mrs. Conroy. They've moved out to Southfield so Mark can be nearer to corporate headquarters.

As for the spiritual crisis I seemed to be enduring through all this, I guess I'm past that now. I'm not a churchgoer, nor do I offer nightly prayers, but Father Phil LeClerc and I have had a couple of talks since that first one, all pretty casual. But helpful. With Sue no longer in my life and no one else in sight, I have a lot more time for reading these days. I finally took him up on his offer of books and borrowed a couple by his man, Miguel de Unamuno. Good stuff — an emotional intelligence at work and a vigorous style, would have made a good trial lawyer.

I have lots of difficulties still, but I no longer doubt that there's Somebody in charge. I can't pretend to understand what He's up to most of the time, nor how He can permit monsters like Father Charles Albertus to do the things they do, but when you've had a prayer answered as mine was out behind the rectory, it's pretty hard to suppose you're out there flying without a net all the time.

In a way, Ismail Carter did a lot to convince me that there is some sort of moral order at work in the world. He did that partly by just being Ismail, who he is and what he is. They can tell all the stories they want about him and imply he was just another crooked politician, but I don't buy it. In my book, he is and always will be a just man.

I'd always suspected that, but I became firmly convinced once I'd heard the story he told me when I went to visit him that day in December. The note of thanks I wrote right after charges were dropped against Mark Conroy ended with a promise to come and visit sometime soon. That turned out to be nearly three weeks later. Since Christmas was just around the corner, and because he deserved far more than I or Mark Conroy could repay, I brought him a gift. I went shopping in the pricey little boutiques in Grosse Pointe and bought him the classiest pair of silk pajamas I could find. Naturally I had them gift-wrapped — bows, tulle, the works. When I appeared with it tucked under my arm, I found him in bed but awake and alert. In fact, his eyes lit up when he spied the package.

"Is that for me, Charley?"

"Who else?" I thrust it toward him. "Merry Christmas."

"Uh-oh. It's a Christmas present, huh? Does that mean do-not-open-until?"

"Nah, that's just for kids. You're no kid."

He laughed. "I sure ain't!"

Then, very carefully, he removed the ribbon, the bow, the tulle decoration, and un-wrapped it.

"That's the prettiest package I ever got," he said, "and I got some good ones in my time. And you bought whatever it is in Grosse Pointe. You know how to shop with taste, you sure do."

"Well, open it up."

And when he did, I saw that I'd chosen well. He fingered the material, taking pleasure in the pure feel of it.

"You noticed my weakness for silk," he said. "Thank you, Charley, it'll go real well with my robe."

"My pleasure."

"Is this a bribe?"

I laughed in surprise.

He gave me a knowing wink. "The way I figure it, at this moment there is probably nothing in the world you want to know quite so bad as what the mayor and me talked about at that sit-down we had a few weeks back. Am I right?"

"Well, yes you are, but . . ."

"And probably that boy, Conroy, has been after you to tell him what got him off the hook. You ain't told him anything, have you? Never mentioned my name."

"Not a word, I swear."

"I believe you." He looked at me thought-fully. "You're not wired for sound, are you? — no, don't answer that, I know you ain't.

But all right, now, I tell you what. If you promise to go right on sayin' nothing to Conroy or anybody else who asks, and if you'll walk over and shut that door to the hall, I'll just accept your bribe and spill the beans."

I did as he ordered, and on the way back, I said, "You've got my promise, Ismail."

"Good, 'cause this is for your ears only. Pull up a chair. This is gonna take a while to tell."

He sat up a little higher in bed, adjusted his pillows, and got comfortable.

"Maybe you remember and maybe you don't, but back in the Seventies, when I got that discrimination suit thrown at me, you wanted to know, had I ever had any white women workin' for me. I said there'd been two. One was the Communist who moved out to California. Remember?"

"Yeah, I spent time and some of your money on a private detective out there, but she just dropped out of sight completely."

"That's right. And the other one, I said, don't bother to look for her, 'cause she's dead. I knew she was, 'cause we'd kept in touch. I knew she'd got sick, and I went up and visited her in the hospital there at the end. All this happened just about a year before the Federal case.

"She was a remarkable woman in just about every way. She came to work for me early in the Fifties. She'd got herself kicked out of St. Mary's in South Bend just before graduation

606

for some kind of wild insult to Notre Dame, right next door. I never got the straight of it. Anyway, she comes back to Detroit and directly to my office and asks for a job. Well, white women just didn't do that in the Fifties, unless they were Communists, and she wasn't. What I guess you'd say was that she was a Progressive. Hell, Charley, she was a firebrand was what she was! First thing she did, she tried to get me to introduce a resolution in the Council condemning the Korean War, and when I wouldn't do it, she organized a bring-our-boys-home demonstration in Cadillac Square that about ten people showed up at. But she was learning, and there were other causes, petitions, demonstrations — something about County Hospital, some admissions scandal at Wayne State. In those days there was a lot to protest but not much will to do it. She had the will. On top of it all, she was just a demon worker for me in the office, wasn't long before she was running it for me — very smoothly, I might add.

"Now, the thing she was hottest on, and her reason for coming to me in the first place, was what she called racial justice. She moved into a place at the edge of Black Bottom and one way or another began to attract people to her and stir them up. She'd get out the vote like nobody could. She'd organize child care so mothers could work, all kinds of things. But she was always discreet about it, so that what she organized, black people led.

"It was almost certain that in the course of all this, she would meet a certain young black civil rights lawyer, 'cause hell, he was the only one in town in those days, the only one who would take on the system, go against the establishment. He just didn't give a damn. He was a good-lookin' dude, intelligent, kind of haughty, and a real rooster with the ladies. And she, well, I don't think I said how she looked, but she was one of those black-haired, blue-eyed Irish. White? Man, she was like porcelain — not beautiful the way these broads are who spend hours in front of the mirror, makin' up, doin' this and that. She didn't care that much how she looked. But she was a natural beauty, like you see in those old-time paintings.

"Well, anyway, I think the occasion was some appeal for a new trial for some poor nigger who got pretty clearly railroaded first time around. Our young lawyer wanted to turn it into a political thing, so he came to me, and I handed him over to her. So whatever happened, I'm partly responsible for. Well, not for all of it, I guess, because the practical outcome was a big march downtown she organized that politicized it pretty good. The lawyer got his retrial, and his client walked. But what happened between them, the lawyer and my staffer, I do take some responsibility for that.

"Now, there wasn't ever anything between

me and her. Not that I wasn't attracted, God knows. She had a kind of a way that drew people to her. The one or two times I came close to letting her know how I felt with a touch, or a word, I held back. I just didn't want to disappoint her. See, she had a very high opinion of me, and I wanted her to keep it.

"She had a high opinion of her lawyer, too, but that didn't stop him from putting a move on her, and it didn't stop her from falling just crazy in love with him. God, Charley, it was something while it lasted. They were very open about it, didn't try to sneak around at all. He was proud of her — maybe it was just as some kind of trophy, but I don't think so — and she, well, she practically worshipped him. People talked. Blacks gossiped. Whites gossiped. Pretty soon the word got to her folks. They gave her a good talking to, and she talked right back to them.

"The inevitable happened. She got pregnant. I was the first one she told, and I mean, man, she was just delighted, overjoyed is what she was. I asked her if she'd told him, and she said she was just looking for the right moment. Well, she finally did tell him. He goes off and makes a phone call, comes back and gives her the name of an abortionist in Toronto. She was just crushed completely. Without a word, she got up and walked out, and as far as I know that was the last time they ever saw each other.

"What hurt me, though, was that it was damned near the last time I saw her myself. She moved up to Port Huron and had her baby, a boy, and stayed up there. She wanted to cut away from her past, parents and all, so she had her name changed legally from Connery to Conroy. You must have guessed that by now, right, Charley? And she made me swear never to let the boy's father know what had happened to her. We kept in touch. I visited a few times, tried to force money on her, but she never took a nickel. She made her own way up there, did about as well as a woman could in a town like that. The last time I saw her she was in the hospital, and her son, Mark, was in his last year at Michigan State.

"That civil rights lawyer, naturally, rode in on the Sixties, ran for City Council on his own, and got lots of help from me once he was in, and became the mayor of this city. Along the way, he got married to a woman who was about as impossible as any I ever met. They're still married, but they have separate residences. But all this time I kept my word and never told him a thing.

"So now you see what him and I talked about that day last month down there at Manoogian. I told him all this I've told you about her and more. Did he even remember her? Oh, he remembered, all right. He just said her name, Celia, but the way he said it was the way a man does when he remembers something real precious he lost.

"I told him she changed her name to Conroy and named her son, their son, Mark. And then you should have just seen his face. I made it plain, told him he was the same Mark Conroy who was under indictment for grand larceny. And I said I thought he, as mayor, had it in his power to help his son. If it came to it, I was prepared to remind the mayor of all I'd given him in those years he'd spent in the City Council and what I'd done to help him get elected mayor. Hell, I would have shamed him, pleaded with him. But none of that was necessary. All he said was, 'I'll see what I can do for him.'"

"And that's all it took?" I asked.

"It may have taken a lot more," said Ismail. "Maybe he had to lean on some people. Maybe he had to threaten. Or maybe all he had to do was change his mind. In other words, I'm not sure whether or not he engineered all this. I only know what you know."

"Charges dropped."

"That's right, and now, Charley, if you'll pour me a big glass of water, I'll try to get my voice back. Push the oxygen over closer, too. Then I think maybe it's time for you to tiptoe on out of here."

Ismail was wrong. I hadn't suspected the truth. Not for a second. Even having heard from Mark Conroy about his mother, his illegitimate birth, and the fact that he never knew the name of his father, I could never have put together such a tale of coincidence and fate. It would have been well beyond my powers of speculation.

Only God can invent such stories. We want order in the world. We count on Him to make sense of human lives, to give them shape. We want there to be a pattern in the incidents and events that litter all our days. If we could only sort through all that, we might see the beginnings, middles, and the ends of those stories. I'd been given the ending of this one by Ismail Carter. But Mark Conroy would never hear it from me. Somehow he'd have to discover it for himself.